Kate Sawyer worked as an actor short films before turning her han *Stranding*, was shortlisted for the (East Anglian Book Award for Fict 4's *Book at Bedtime* and is being developed for TV by Fremantle and Afua Hirsch's production company Born In Me.

When Kate isn't writing, or talking to other authors about their writing practices for her podcast *Novel Experience*, she is busy producing the annual Bury St Edmunds Literature Festival.

After twenty years living in London, she recently returned to her native East Anglia, where she lives with her young daughter.

Praise for *This Family*

'Kate Sawyer makes the reader feel as though they have a seat at the family table'
Erin Kelly

'A hugely atmospheric, multi-layered family drama that sings with emotion'
Good Housekeeping

'Absorbing and unexpected. It took some turns that I really didn't see coming'
Rebecca Wait

'Guaranteed to keep you on your tiptoes'
Metro

'Friendship, rivalry, infidelity and the love that binds them all together are unpacked in this ambitious, immersive and beautifully written story'
Red

'The vibrant, complex members of *This Family* are still alive and well in my imagination, weeks after I finished reading it'
Jo Browning Wroe

'A bittersweet, deftly woven, captivating portrayal of a mother and daughters'
Jennifer Saint

'A warmly emotional read that's strong on grief, love, family and friendship'
Daily Mail

'A vivid exploration of the complexities of sisterhood'
Daisy Buchanan

'The intimacy of a family with all its complications is a quietly devastating read'
Julie Owen Moylan

'A vivid family saga, rich in character and detail'
Ericka Waller

'Lyrical, literary and luminous . . . buy it and treat yourself to writing at its finest'
Bethany Clift

'Funny and powerful, deeply moving, hugely atmospheric'
Liz Hyder

Kate Sawyer

THIS FAMILY

CORONET

First published in Great Britain in 2023 by Coronet
An imprint of Hodder & Stoughton Limited
An Hachette UK company

This paperback edition published in 2024

1

A CIP catalogue record for this title is available from the British Library

Paperback ISBN 9781529340754
ebook ISBN 9781529340730

Typeset in Adobe Garamond by Hewer Text UK Ltd, Edinburgh
Printed and bound in Great Britain by Clays Ltd, Elcograf S.p.A.

Hodder & Stoughton policy is to use papers that are natural, renewable and recyclable products and made from wood grown in sustainable forests. The logging and manufacturing processes are expected to conform to the environmental regulations of the country of origin.

Hodder & Stoughton Limited
Carmelite House
50 Victoria Embankment
London EC4Y 0DZ

www.hodder.co.uk

For my mother, Valerie Sawyer (née Shaw).

The days are long, but the years are short

Gretchen Rubin

One

Mary steps out of the conservatory down onto the patio. The pips from the radio in the kitchen pierce the heavy air. Midday, five hours until the arrival of the first guest.

On the lawn she glances back over her shoulder, then shifts the heavy bundle of tablecloths in her arms and quickens her pace. Sweat is gathering in the crevices of her body. The new slip beneath her dressing gown is already adhering to her flesh, her thighs catching against one another. There is a dampness, even behind her knees.

She lets the pile of pressed cloths fall with a thud, then closes her eyes and runs her hand over the table as she walks its length.

Almost every flat surface from the house has been tackled outside to create this great, snaking banqueting table. She recognises the textures under her palm, the dips, the changes in height. Even without looking she can identify them. The dining table. Her sewing table. The desk from Rosie's room. The trestle table that Richard bought specifically for Phoebe's Scalextric.

She is beneath the tree now, under its umbrella of shade. The burn of the sun against the back of her neck, the heat of it on her head eases, and there is the brief relief of feeling markedly cooler. She tips her head back, her hand still on the table, and opens her eyes.

* * *

It was the tree, or rather the light through its branches, that was the deciding factor for Mary. She had been in the first flush of discovering gardening when they viewed the house and had become increasingly able to name the plants and trees she came across; it was a new-found passion that had arrived thanks to the evenings she'd sat on the sofa pinned beneath Emma, trying to tune out her mother-in-law, dazedly staring at Geoff Hamilton running compost through his fingers.

During all those months at Irene's, she had dreamed of raised beds, of digging borders, planting bulbs. She remembers the details of a daydream into which she would slip when Irene was ticking her off for one misdemeanour or another: an expanse of lawn, a tree casting its shade upon the sward, a greenhouse with Victorian finials at either end, neat rows of vegetables nestled in home-made compost.

In the years since, as she's sat in her conservatory and taken in the garden, she's considered that, were it not for Irene, she might not have noticed it at all.

'Look at that tree!'

She leaned forward the better to see it through the windscreen of the new Volvo as the drive crunched under its tyres. Richard grunted, tutting that the gravel would chip the paintwork. The house was too big, he said. The garden would be a chore, they'd have to hire someone. And the village didn't even have a pub. How long would it take to get an ambulance out if there was an accident? Or a fire?

She didn't much like the house on first impressions either. It was ridiculously large, bigger than they needed for the three of them, and it was so square, the bricks so grey. She had always wanted a red-brick house or, seeing as she'd fetched up in this part of the world, one that she could paint a Suffolk pink.

But she couldn't take her eyes off the tree. It shimmered. An inconstant light glittering along the side of the house as if a disco ball were turning nearby. It was in full leaf, dancing in the late spring breeze. Slender branches waved like elegant fingers playing through long hair, slicing the light that reflected from the pond beneath it and causing this spectacular light-show on the grey brick facade.

Mary knew she had to have it.

Today, the old willow seems to be as exhausted as the fat ginger cat that is sprawled in its shade.

Looking up into the net of tangled branches overhead, Mary can see little of the perfectly blue sky above her, but still she thinks of Emma. Her eldest daughter, hurtling towards this island like an asteroid. She can imagine her, her head tilted to the window, watching the Atlantic glinting in the sun beneath her, her legs stretched out, crossed at the ankles. She can see the soft leather of her shoes: heels – the sort of shoes that only someone like Emma would wear to fly. She can see her shaking her head, raising her palm against the offer of a complimentary glass of champagne.

Mary looks back towards the house.

The heat is so thick that it has a sort of viscous quality to it, unctuous, like good olive oil. It distorts the house, makes it seem to shift slightly, the bricks undulating. There is barely a whisper of breeze. Above her, even the branches of the willow are motionless. A rare occurrence.

Later, when the guests see the garden, dressed as it will be in hundreds of fairy lights, they might comment on the tree's beauty, but unless the wind picks up before then, it will be witnessed as any other tree: beautiful and still.

The branches hang limp, but the light that reflects up from the water and onto the house still creates that shimmer that she'd fallen in love with all those years ago. And that's despite the low fence that now surrounds the pond.

'Bodies of water and the bodies of small children are rarely compatible, Mary. It's a fence or concrete: your choice!'

The possibility of drowning had been an obsession of his ever since they'd seen *Don't Look Now* on one of their early dates in Cardiff. So it was hardly surprising that Richard had insisted on the fence immediately that he'd got wind that one of the girls had fallen in. All that was lost was a shoe, stuck in the mud or caught beneath the abundant aquatic flora that Mary struggled to keep in check.

It was one of a beautiful shiny pair, fitted by a machine that whirred and vibrated and thrillingly squeezed small feet to gauge their size. The beloved shoe was deeply mourned by the wailing child once she'd been fished from the shallows. Mary had stroked her crying daughter's wet hair, matted with stringy waterweed, and she had known that she'd have to agree on installing some sort of safety measure. Better to fence it off while the only thing for which tears were being shed was a red patent shoe with a shiny metal buckle.

It is the stillness, this blanket of heat that lies so heavily over everything, which renders the radio in the kitchen audible. At the end of the garden, under the willow, if there were even a light breeze, at this distance she wouldn't be able to hear it at all. Now, in the stultifying stillness of midday on this worryingly warm September day, it is just possible to make out the words, to decipher the news stories.

'The hottest September day *since records began.*'

She feels bad for her relief. She knows that it's all wrong, that she should be worrying about climate change. *Climate catastrophe*. Ordinarily she does – they even did a test drive in an electric car a few months ago – but today she can't help but be delighted that it's sunny.

Sunny and warm.

It feels like a blessing.

A wave of nausea washes over her. There is something almost awful about being this excited, it's remarkably similar to terror. Or maybe it *is* terror. For all the reassurances she's had, still lurking beneath the fizz of excitement, there is an unshakeable presentiment that bringing this family together can only end in disaster.

It is my dearest wish—

she'd written, in the same green ink with which she addressed each of the letter-pressed invitations,

—that after so long apart, I am able to bring this family together for my wedding day.

I don't think it's my way to ask much of others, but now I am asking each of you to give me one day where you leave any animosity at the gate and try to remember that you love each other.

When all three of the girls' RSVPs arrived in the affirmative, she was delighted. But she's since wondered if any of them had turned over the card and seen her note.

No. They have their differences, their problems, but she raised these three women. None of them is the sort of person who would ruin her wedding day. Are they?

'Course not!'

Her voice startles the cat, who looks at Mary and seems to roll her eyes before stretching and falling back to sleep. Not for the first time, Mary wonders if it's possible to be pitied by an animal.

Across the garden, the voice of the newsreader on the radio ripples, rich and deep. It is the bass note, the cello to the symphony of birdsong that fills the air: a sound so pervasive that the ear doesn't at first acknowledge it, but treats it as background noise, like the swell of the ocean at the beach. But just as it is when by the sea – once you hear one wave, then *all* you can hear is the never-ending succession lapping at the shore – so it is in the garden: when a single trill of a blackbird is recognised, the swell of the avian orchestra becomes impossible to ignore.

The air is alive with sound. The warble of a song thrush, the coo of the wood pigeons. Blue tits, great tits and goldfinches chirrup with glee as they swoop through the willow's branches, then hover to gorge themselves on the lavender bushes on the wall partitioning the lawn and patio.

Mary takes the top tablecloth from the pile and starts to unfold it, humming to herself, her eyes scanning the scene for what more there is to be done.

There, nestled in the armchair, is Irene, her head lolling back like a broken puppet.

Who brought her out here?

She looks around for her stick, the walking frame, but there is nothing.

Sometimes, if she's feeling particularly uncharitable, Mary wonders if Irene really needs the walker at all. When she finds her like this, moved so quickly from one space to another, she questions if Irene isn't really capable of walking, running, even dancing unaided.

She looks tiny in that armchair. She was always slight, next to Mary, but ever since the fall – the operation – she's looked increasingly shrunken, as if someone is slowly letting out the air.

Holding her own breath, intently she watches Irene's chest for a few seconds, trying to discern movement. It's something she's done multiple times a day, since Irene's been living here. She thought, when the kids left home, that her days of checking people were still breathing whilst they slept were over.

Her stomach pitches. Maybe that's it? The presentiment that's been tormenting her.

Irene emits an almighty snort and Mary draws a breath herself.

She turns away from Irene in the armchair and takes in the long row of tables, steadying herself at the sight of the two regal-looking seats at the end of the table. She places her open palm on her stomach, the way that Rosie showed her last night, and tries to focus on her breathing. What was it that she said she needed to imagine? A triangle?

An instinct to run seizes her. She wants to drop the cloth that she is smoothing over the table and run to the back door, grab her keys off the hook – the rather tasteless one that she bought as a joke in Majorca with Liz – and get in the car and drive.

She won't, of course.

She wants to be here more than anything. She's been waiting for today for nearly two years – forty years, if she's honest with herself.

It's a new beginning.

She should be happy.

And she is. She is.

But where there are beginnings, there are always endings too.

Two

Mary sat on the bench in front of the hotel, looking towards the park. The flint on the perimeter walls glinted in the mid-morning sun and the noise of children playing beyond carried easily on the light breeze.

The walk to the town centre was deceptively taxing, particularly in her condition. The slight incline had taken it out of her in a way she wasn't used to.

She looked up at the sky. Other than a few cotton wool wisps, the wide sky was a perfect baby blue.

'Ah, here we are. Home! Constable Country.' Richard positioned her in front of a painting of some grazing Friesians.

'It says it's Essex.' She pointed to the sign to the right of the ornate frame.

Richard frowned, then shook his head and gestured to the expanse of the gallery.

'Well, it's East Anglia. What I'm saying is that it'll be a nice place to live. Picturesque. Lovely skies.'

He was right about that at least. The skies were beautiful.

Mary looked down at her feet. For weeks she had struggled to recognise them as her own. The sandals were still beautiful, but by the time she'd walked back to the house, she'd be hobbling; her feet had really started to swell in the heat.

The evening ahead prodded at her again. What on earth was she going to wear? Her belly had outgrown most of her good dresses, and she'd discovered this morning that the same was true of her shoes.

She could just imagine Irene's face: the soft perspiration through her pressed powder, the tight smile as Mary waddled down the stairs, chipped nail polish on show for all her guests to see.

Mary had taken her shoes off at the door the first time that Richard took her to meet his parents, thinking it the polite thing to do.

'Oh no!' Mary had watched as Irene quickly gathered herself, forcing herself to smile. 'We're very much a "shoes on" household, Mary.'

She rubbed the top of her foot where the leather was pushing into the flesh. She'd swing by Debenhams, see if she couldn't get a plimsole of some sort. She knew she ought to make an effort for this 'little gathering' of Irene and Bert's, and she'd need something to wear on her feet for the next two months. It wasn't just Irene who was likely to baulk at her wandering around barefoot in this town.

The burn in her oesophagus flared as she swallowed. She rifled in her bag for her Rennies.

That morning she'd been spared the usual Saturday kippers. But she'd still had to see the slime of scrambled eggs coating Irene's tongue as she'd pointed at Mary's plate with raised eyebrows and announced, 'The most important meal of the day.' Mary's stomach had lurched, but she smiled and nodded and forced down as much of the buttered toast as her constant indigestion would allow.

Ordinarily, Mary loved food, particularly the ceremony of sitting down to eat with others, but being presented with a plate piled with hot protein each morning was quickly putting her off. Wearing dirty outdoor shoes on Irene's cream carpets didn't make much sense, but her insistence that everyone join her at 8 a.m., washed and dressed, for a full cooked breakfast, was completely at odds with the Ryvita and cottage cheese that seemed to otherwise make up her diet. But, in the six long weeks that Mary had lived with Richard's parents, she'd learned to brace herself for the unexpected and she'd also become expert at biting her tongue. Not least when the subject of the Prime Minister was raised, which, unfortunately, she was. Often.

Using one hand to lever herself up from the bench, Mary pushed up to standing. She emitted a low grunt – a sound a little too close to those she'd occasionally been known to make in the bedroom. Warm embarrassment spreading across her already flushed cheeks, she looked around her. She was mercifully alone, the pavement unpeopled. Seizing the opportunity, she shifted her knickers from the crease of her buttocks and yanked at her dress to unstick it from her thighs. She knew she was a sight: she'd seen herself in the hall mirror on the way out. She looked as though she'd been pumped full of air, then dressed in a badly stitched together pair of floral curtains.

Mary could pinpoint the exact moment she'd fallen pregnant. She'd never let Richard touch her without a trip to the bathroom to fit her sponge, even on their wedding night. It seemed impossible that that decision, that one fumble on their sofa, could have been so life changing. But there she was: sweating through a floral kaftan in a rural English market town, heavy with a new life.

* * *

The market square had a cadence that Mary had become quickly familiar with. 'Caam and get your narnas!' 'Flaars! Two bunches a paand. Flaars!' 'Laarvly strawbs. Real English strawbs.' The traders' calls echoed through the tightly pulled tarpaulin shells of the stalls. A musky vegetal smell hung in the warm air, a slight undertone of manure from the livestock trading warehouses beyond Woolworth's lingering, and the sharp notes of the fish stall assaulted her nostrils as Mary passed.

She had offered to cook the Sunday lunch the first weekend they'd been at Irene and Bert's. Even though Irene had insisted that they stay with them until they found the right place, she didn't hold back on making it clear that their presence was an inconvenience. The single roast dinner she'd intended had somehow turned into a weekly event. Even though the appeasement had been minimal, she'd persisted. Not least because it was the only meal of the week when she got to eat something she truly wanted. The planning, purchasing and preparation gave her something to do, gave structure to her week. Without work or a home to run, she'd felt lost at first. Lost in a churning sea of weekdays, with only Richard's return on a Friday night and her Saturday morning market trips to look forward to.

If anyone had told her a year ago that by July 1980 the highlight of her week would involve buying potatoes from a man who blew into the paper bag to open it, she'd have laughed in their face. But ever since New Year's Eve it had felt as though she had lost all autonomy. That life was just happening and dragging her along in its wake.

From the courtyard of Richard's new club, they'd been able to hear the roar from Trafalgar Square as Big Ben chimed.

'It's gonna be our decade, Mrs Roberts.'

Richard tucked her recently-permed hair behind her ear. That's when she'd first noticed the dizziness. She'd put it down to the kiss, the champagne, the dancing.

Then the hangover subsided and she'd realised she was late.

On seeing the two stripes, she'd spent several weeks convincing herself that it'd be manageable to live in the city with a baby. She'd grown to love London, their little home, the culture on their doorstep, and she really didn't want to leave it. But as the weeks went on she'd found herself watching women manoeuvring prams on public transport and becoming increasingly aware of the three flights of stairs to their cosy flat. She reflected on the post-baby departures of her colleagues over the past two years, and realised that not all of them were optional. A notion that was confirmed when she confided her condition to Alison from Beauty, and she pointed out that the only parent on the magazine's staff was Ed from Travel. Then in that cold room in St George's Hospital, the sonographer's brow had furrowed, and after several heart-stopping minutes, the monitor had been turned towards them and the ghostly form with its rapidly beating heart had been pointed out to them, she'd felt winded by the reality of it. A baby was coming and she was going to have to look after it and that was going to be almost impossible without more space, and more support than the girls from the office she occasionally enjoyed a glass of wine with might offer.

She decided to float the idea that Sunday on their walk.

'Darling, you read my mind!' Richard grasped her cold hands in his. 'Though obviously, it'll mean a lot of driving for me.'

'I was only thinking of Croydon, like Teresa and Phil, or maybe we could look at Surbiton, then we'd be near Mike and Lou. And the trains are so regular into Waterloo.'

Richard inclined his head, looped her arm through his, and started walking at pace, pulling her through the park in the direction of the river. It made more sense to move further out, he explained. They'd get much more bang for their buck near his parents. With his new salary, in the sticks, they could afford a garden, four bedrooms, and still have spare change for him to rent a room near work.

'And I know Mum'll be very happy to change the odd nappy.'

She'd cried when she handed in her notice and when she packed up the kitchen and the bedlinen. She'd cried, too, for nearly the whole drive to Suffolk. Richard's response had been to click Van Morrison into the cassette player and turn up the volume.

Leaving the newsagent's, Mary pulled the plastic bags up her forearms and into the crook of her elbows. She paused in the glare of the sun, aware of two figures approaching on her left. It took her a second for her eyes to adjust and her brain to compute what she was seeing; their hairstyles made their silhouettes so tall, they seemed a foot or so taller than they were. Punks. Even in this small town there were a few. Not as many as in London, but enough to make their presence known, hanging around, sitting on walls. She wasn't scared of them, as such, but there was something about the clothing, the attitude, that unnerved her. Though she considered herself to be pretty anti-establishment herself, there was something about the movement that she couldn't quite fathom. It wasn't the clothing, after all, her leather jacket from the King's Road was her pride and joy. It was true that she didn't like the music, the Sex Pistols or any of those bands. But that was just timing. At university it had been all disco, and it was only since her Masters that she and Richard had got into some electronic stuff. The Cardiff lot had been a Bob Dylan sort of crowd. She wasn't even really against the ideology; she was certainly no fan of the royals or the government. No, the thing that she didn't like was the attitude. It put her on edge.

As the pair approached, the sun shone through the sculpture of their hair, their luridly coloured Mohicans protruding from their heads like cockerel's combs. Despite the heat they were dressed head to toe in black leather, metal studs liberally decorating their limbs. As they got closer, their faces emerged from shadow and Mary could see them clearly. She knew that she was staring, but she couldn't pull her gaze away: their eyes were lined with kohl, as were their mouths. The careful black lines on the rim of their lips were filled with lurid colours; their eyelids were painted too, a peacock display of green and blue. Blusher sat in fuchsia streaks beneath their cheekbones.

Rationally, she knew they were just young people – barely younger than her – with unusual hairstyles. But she felt a churn of discomfort as they approached.

It annoyed Mary that she found them intimidating. She was Glaswegian. She had lived in London for the last five years, rubbed shoulders with all sorts, and thought nothing of it. But there was something about the audacity of wearing hair raised six inches above a half-shaved scalp that rattled her. It made her feel unworldly, naive. The rings through their ears and noses, the clump of their bovver boots – she didn't understand them at all.

Perhaps she was well suited to living in a small town after all. A depressing thought.

The female punk caught Mary's eye as she neared. Instinctively, Mary stepped back, out of their path. The punk smirked, registering Mary's discomfort, and nudged her companion – a man, just as made-up as her but somewhat broader set, his jaw much squarer, handsome almost. He looked directly at Mary as he approached. A lipstick-edged smile slicing across his face.

Mary stepped back again, her back hitting the glass of the door she'd just exited.

'Oh!'

She watched as they turned their gaze away from her and walked on, continuing their conversation. She was of no interest to them. Of course she wasn't.

Mary was seized by the overwhelming feeling that she might cry.

The stallholder opposite, wrapping patterned paper around a bunch of chrysanthemums, looked at her pityingly.

'All right love?'

'Fine.' She sniffed to hold off the tears. 'Fine, thank you.'

The flower seller nodded.

'Sanths?' He proffered a bunch of lurid flowers. The paper they were wrapped in sopping from where they had been sitting in the bucket of water at his feet. 'Two bunches a paand.'

Laden with bags, Mary held the flowers under her arm as she wove between the stalls, moisture from the wet paper seeping through her dress.

In one hand she gripped the bag containing the rolled pork joint from the butcher's, and two striped carrier bags bulging with brown paper packages of vegetables. On the other side she was weighed down with waxed green apples, for the sauce, and plums – on the cusp of over-ripeness, dampening their bag in blooming spots of juice – bound for a cake, which was one of Richard's favourites.

She paused outside Marks & Spencer, to catch her breath, on the pretence of looking in the window. Then turned to cross through the stalls to Debenhams.

It was then she became aware that the hubbub of the market had changed, there was more noise, raised voices. A woman's scream pierced the air, followed by male voices shouting something other than market calls, and above this, high-pitched squeals punctuated a clamour of boxes and metal poles hitting the ground.

She stepped forward and looked towards the source of the disruption. Between the canopies of striped tarpaulins the crowd shifted, and Mary's eye was drawn to the tarmac of the square. Knee-high to the parting shoppers were two pigs, running. She watched as they careered towards her. People were falling back to get out of their path, but she found herself frozen. The sound around her seemed to stop, the noise of the world muffled.

She could see their skin in detail. It was not pink, as in the children's books she had been buying for the baby, but a colour not dissimilar to the colour of Richard's back in the morning as he sat on the edge of the bed. The pigs were caked in mud around their undercarriages, where a row of tender-looking nipples hung, six in total, as if someone had stuck the teats of baby bottles to their stomachs. The mud had pieces of straw stuck to it, and there was straw on their legs too, some wedged in the cleft of their trotters, pieces flying here and there as they scrabbled towards her.

They were hairy too. So much hairier than she had ever imagined.

She thought of the pork scratchings that her dad used to order by the pint glass when he took her with him to sit on the bench outside the pub. How he'd let her reach her small fingers into the rim of the glass and select a salty treat. She would have to eat it gratefully, under his watchful eye, smiling all the while even if she saw a hair that protruded from the rind of the crackling. She'd concentrated hard not to gag as she chewed it.

The animals running towards her seemed to be looking straight at her then, their black eyes glinting.

Eyelashes, she thought. *I didn't know pigs had eyelashes.*

They were almost upon her, running at speed, heading straight for her.

I wonder if I will fall? she thought, and then she realised she was falling. *My baby*, she thought, *I'll hurt the baby.*

Mary felt something on her elbow then. A hand, then another. Someone taking her weight, holding her, catching her as she fell.

Sound came rushing back. The pigs were hitting her legs and their screams were piercing, the voices of people around her calling to her.

Then, in her ear she heard a soft, calm voice.

'It's okay. I've got you.'

And they had. Mary felt as if she was on a reclined chair. She was so securely held under the arms, the impact of the animals against her shins knocked her back only a few inches. Carefully, the hands tipped her upright and she took her own weight onto her feet again. And then they were gone and she was upright, keenly aware of their absence.

Two men, dressed in the brown coats of the auction house, ran past her, cursing. One gripped a cane to beat the escaped animals, the other a coil of rope to restrain them.

'You all right love?'

Mary nodded, dazed. The men ran on, shouting towards the escaped pigs, their voices blending with the calls of the stall-holders and high-pitched squealing of the animals.

Mary looked down at the ground around her feet. The roll of meat lay on the pavement glistening in its cling-wrap. The plums had burst through their bag and lay strewn across the paving stones. Their pink juice had stained the newsprint of her newspapers, the local news disordered in the kerfuffle, the broadsheets ripped where the pigs charged over the folded sheets.

'Oh dear. Looks like your plums have had it.'

Turning, she was met by kohl-rimmed eyes, creasing slightly at the corner with concern. A raised eyebrow above was pierced by a single silver hoop. He smiled at Mary and then joined the woman with the crimson hair, who was kneeling on the pavement picking up Mary's shopping. The leather of his trousers creaked as he moved, the chains around their necks tinkling as they refilled Mary's bags.

'Thank you.'

Mary didn't recognise her own voice. It sounded small. Croaky.

'Scottish?'

'Ah, yes.'

'Me too! Aberdeen.'

She could hear it, the catch of his accent.

'Pollokshields.'

'How the hell d'we end up down here, eh?'

The woman punched him softly on his upper arm and he laughed.

'You can probably still make a decent jam.' He smiled, holding up the bag dripping with plum juice. 'I'm a fiend for a good jam.'

Mary nodded, swallowed, felt the sting of a blush on her cheeks.

The woman stood and handed the final bag to him. She wiped the juice that covered her hands on her trousers, leaving streaks along the leather, then offered her hand to Mary.

'Lizzie. Liz.'

And then Liz smiled and Mary had to bite down the impulse to tell her how incredibly beautiful she was. Another wave of heat moved across Mary's face and she quickly shifted her gaze away from the violet-blue eyes that were locked on hers and up to Liz's hair. Up close, the hairstyle was even more impressive. It appeared solid, like a shard of bone. *A rhino's horn is actually hair*, Mary thought: a thought so obtuse that it occurred to her that she might have been suffering from shock. Then she noticed that she was swaying slightly and her vision started to lose focus.

'Woah there, you okay?'

The man wrapped his leather-covered arm around Mary's shoulders. Mary nodded, because she was okay, she realised, now that he was supporting her. She wasn't dizzy any more. Just hot, tired, seven months pregnant and, oddly, acutely aware of her blistered toes.

'Can we call someone for you?' Liz pointed to the phone box across the road. 'Help you to the taxi rank?'

'Or walk you home? I'll carry the shopping.'

Mary nodded stupidly.

'Thank you, I'd be really grateful for the help. If you could just get me part of the way.'

Liz smiled again, the fuchsia of her lipstick parting to reveal her teeth. Clean and uniform with just one imperfection, a slight gap between the top two.

'Which way are we headed?'

'Just the other side of the cattle market.' Mary pointed in the general direction of Bert and Irene's house.

'You must be near my parents.'

Carefully, Liz threaded her arm through Mary's, gently supporting her as they started to walk.

A woman pulling a chequered shopping trolley stopped abruptly beside them, staring at the three of them, her mouth hanging open. Indignation sparked in Mary's chest.

'Oh boo – you nosey old coo!'

She stuck her tongue out for good measure. The woman stepped back in horror and Liz exploded into a glorious peal of giggles, dropping her head forward as she laughed.

A flush of pleasure. When was the last time she'd made someone laugh? Mary dared to sneak a glance over the top of Liz's bowed head. A pair of heavily rimmed eyes met hers and she blanched, caught in the act. But then he winked at her and Mary found herself laughing too.

They walked through the market, towards her in-laws'.

It was only later – when Irene was asking her why she'd spent good money on fruit that was in such a state – that she realised that she hadn't thought about her blisters or her rubbing thighs once for the entire walk home.

Three

Rosie pauses, raising her face to the sun, closing her eyes. Beneath her feet, the smooth stones of the patio are so hot that in a moment it will be unbearable. She doesn't move though. She waits, feeling the rays of the sun prickle at her cheeks.

She dreams of it sometimes, the sun. On those nights that she does dream, rather than descend into an exhausted oblivion. She dreams she is in the park, lying in the sun. Rubbing on sun cream. Leafing through the Sunday supplements. Picnicking, crunching on a green apple, the juice tart in her mouth. But then there is a tilt, the words in the newspaper blur, or the apple liquefies, drips through her fingers, and she realises she's asleep. Then that hollow feeling that something, that someone, is missing.

And then she's back in their bed, awake, panic still blocking her throat until she focuses and sees, lit by the digits on the radio alarm, the rise and fall of Danyal's back. And she copies it, measures her breath to his so that soon she falls back into a fitful sleep.

Rosie looks down at the tangled bunting in her arms and for a moment she is blinded. The sun is bouncing off the gold thread in the sunflowers that she spent so long embroidering. She blinks, brings her hands above her eyes against the sun and squints, looking down the garden. She holds the contents of her arms out to Mary; a glittering offering.

'Where'd you want it?'

'Tree, please!'

Mary is spreading out a tablecloth, flattening it with her palm, then, taking the next from the pile, she unfolds and smoothes it. She makes a little noise as she leans across the table and Rosie sees a flash of white from beneath her colourful dressing gown, a glance of lacy trim framing the cleft of her breasts.

Special underwear.

Rosie pulls her arms in closer to her chest, crunches her eyes, tightly.

Please, she thinks, *please let Mary get her day*.

'It's not going to rain, by the way. Checked my phone.'

'Yes.'

Mary smiles briefly.

'Have you done the breathing I showed you? Listened to that meditation?'

'Yes, yes.'

Rosie drops the bunting onto one of the chairs from the conservatory and takes in the transformation of the garden.

All the way from the edge of the patio, beneath the hanging arms of the willow, right to the very end of the garden, a mismatch of tables and chairs stands in an orderly line. The chairs have been scavenged from every corner of the house. The good dining chairs with their cushioned seats alternate with more humble affairs that are out of place at a feast. There are weather-beaten garden chairs – plastic ones, faded from deep emerald to a sun-bleached chartreuse. Wedged between those there are two high-backed chairs, and next to them the old piano stool – the piano itself long gone since the tuner deemed it unsalvageable. None of them had ever progressed much further than Chopsticks, despite Phoebe's intention to become the British Tori Amos. Then there are the hideous cane chairs from the conservatory, even a few of the soft furnishings.

When Mary had told her that there would be forty-four of them, including the babies, Rosie had felt sad that it was going to be so small.

'You can have more now, you know, if you want?'

'It's nothing to do with the bloody government.' Mary's voice was loud, even down the phone. 'It's more about finding everyone somewhere to sit. Anyway, there'll be more for dancing after. Don't you worry! There'll be even more people bopping in that kitchen than there were for Phoebe's twenty-first.'

But hopefully not as many that need to be whisked off to have their stomachs pumped, Rosie had thought.

'Hello Garfield, old friend.' The cat is sprawled on the grass beneath her. 'Poor thing, does she miss Lasagne do you think?'

Mary is still a moment, her face falling serious.

'Sometimes I catch her over there by the damson tree in quiet contemplation.'

'Really?'

'No, Rosie, sweetheart. Not really. That ancient cat doesn't know her tail is attached to her body. Never mind that her late brother is buried in a shoe box under the plum tree.'

Rosie crouches down and runs her fingers along the cat's ginger flanks, then, tentatively, ventures to the soft white tufts of fur across her chest, the soft roundness of her belly. She is fat, this cat, not like the lean city cats that crouch in the gateways of Rosie's road. Nor is she one of the pedigrees that she spots imprisoned behind sash windows as she walks the long car-lined pavements of the residential streets around the hospital. They watch her as she passes, these inmates of privilege, with their too-far-apart eyes, like furry frogs. No, this cat is a country cat, a fat cat who'd break the silver caps on milk bottles to lap the cream, if the milkman still delivered.

Garfield is lying star-shaped, stretched out in the grass, her belly exposed to all the world.

How secure she must feel to lie like that.

The only way Rosie can sleep is with her soft bits tucked away, curled into a ball or, more recently, with the length of her against the warmth of Danyal.

'Did you see how your dad was getting on?'

'Danyal is helping him.' Rosie stands, stretches, pulls the rising bikini top down, tugs at the knot behind her neck, checking it is secure. 'I feel a bit guilty.'

'Dan offered, didn't he?'

'Of course.'

'Then don't feel guilty. Your father needs all the help he can get. Though he'd rather die than admit it, he's bitten off rather more than he can chew.'

Rosie pauses at the armchair. In it, head tipped back, mouth open, is her granny, sleeping soundly. Her face, so animated when she is talking, looks so much older when it is immobile. Her lips are rimmed with a liner, lipstick within. The application is uneven, giving her mouth a slightly drooping appearance on one side. Her eyelashes are grouped together where thick coats of mascara have been applied with her unsteady hand.

Will I wear make-up into my nineties?

She seldom wears any now. She doesn't have the time. She knows Mary and her grandmother both persist with a three-step cleanse, tone and moisturise routine when she barely manages to wash off her mascara using a bit of soap before her head hits the pillow each night.

'Shouldn't we wake her? She doesn't look very comfortable.'

She carefully places her fingers beneath Irene's chin and gently closes her mouth. Immediately, a grating snore is emitted from her granny's nose. A snare drum rattle, accompanying the birdsong.

'I was going to say at least she's keeping quiet, but . . .'

Rosie doesn't join in with Mary's laughter, but reaches out and softly strokes the white, curled hair on her grandmother's head. The curls feel hard under Rosie's fingers, brittle, as if they might snap were she to put any pressure on them. Rosie bends forward and kisses the top of her granny's head, then joins Mary in straightening and smoothing the cloths.

'I like these! They feel expensive.'

'They are expensive. We hired them.'

The mention of money nudges something in Rosie's brain. A falling domino that quickly ripples across her thoughts and explodes in a flash of injustice.

'Why isn't Michael helping Dad?'

'Michael is doing the lights.'

Inside her mouth she places her tongue between her teeth and presses down, hard, until it hurts. Tomorrow. She just needs to keep her thoughts to herself until tomorrow. Then, in the passenger seat next to Danyal, she'll let it all tumble out so anything that threatens to weigh her down will be gone before they see the signs for their junction. Today she just needs to focus on Mary.

Rosie inhales and walks towards the conservatory, grabbing the sun cream from the windowsill. As she walks back over the hot patio, she squirts a thick, mayonnaise-like mound into her palm. Stealthily, she approaches Mary from behind and then shovels little dollops onto the pinkening skin of Mary's neck. Mary tuts but allows her to continue. She rubs it in, considering Mary's skin. It is soft, a little like running her fingers across the scattered tissue-paper petals of a peony.

This weekend means Rosie missing her trip to the market.

It was a suggestion from her therapist, to chart out the week. To plan a trip into a busy environment that would result in a reward. And she was right – Diane – it did seem to be working. In fact she finds herself looking forward to it, excited about it. She can't understand why she loves it, how it could possibly soothe her to be pushed and squashed between shoulders and elbows as everyone fights for the opportunity to buy a cut-priced rubber plant or hydrangea, but it does. Maybe she's just getting better at being in close proximity to strangers, but you could say the same thing about trains, and she still can't travel on them without having a full-blown panic attack, so it must have something to do with the market itself; the smell of the plants, the reassuring appearance of the stalls every weekend, come rain or shine.

But this weekend is different. It's Mary's special day. And she wants, more than anything, for Mary to be happy.

'All factor-thirty'd up.'

She wipes the last of the sun cream onto her bare belly, then dries her hands on the material of her bikini bottoms.

She works with Mary then. They fall into a quiet rhythm, side by side, carefully smoothing each seam over the tables. It reminds her of that first autumn here, when she used to help Mary to set the table. She would play a game with herself to see if she could pick up the right amount of cutlery without counting. Five sets on weeknights. Seven on Saturdays, adding Liz and Iain.

Somewhere nearby a lawnmower hums.

The noise pushes an image into her mind like a snapshot.

A hand, the colour of the flesh distorted, all wrong. She can almost taste the smell of it. The antiseptic, the acrid tang of burnt hair, the disconcertingly familiar scent of seared flesh, the sound of the bone saw. She had tried to avert her eyes as much as possible. She'd focused on her monitors, the pattern of the patient's heartbeat, the rhythm of their breath, but she still saw it, couldn't avoid it in order to do her job.

There had been a time when her perspective on the human body had been purely objective. It used to be that patients' bodies had been completely absent of emotional charge. She wasn't without empathy – she still saw the patient, she cared for the human – but the actual bodies, the parts of them that she watched the surgeons open up, remove, sew back together, were nothing more than work, as mechanical as the pictures in an anatomy book. Then, out of nowhere, it all caught up with her – her childhood, her mum, all those things she never talks about – something shifted, and all she could see was the red flesh, the gleaming white bones, the peeled back skin. Suddenly she was acutely aware that these were parts of a person, someone with hopes and dreams, a tangible part of a being who loved and was loved. And everything had become so, so much harder.

'Doesn't matter that the tables are all different heights, does it?'

'The wonkiness adds to the charm. Very bohemian.'

Mary claps her hands then makes her way across the grass, and back towards the house. Rosie watches her go, pulling at the belt around her waist, cinching in her dressing gown, and feels an enormous surge of tenderness. An urge to protect her.

Why did the wedding have to be this weekend? During one of Diane's rare holidays? She'll have to talk it through with

Danyal instead. That's if he's still talking to her after being roped in to help her dad all morning.

Rosie adjusts her bikini top. It is twisted at the back, digging into her flesh. The bikini is ancient, losing its elastic and meant for breasts larger than her own. But she hadn't thought to bring a bikini when she was packing to come to a wedding in September. She should have checked the weather earlier in the week. She hadn't noticed that it was still so warm until they were halfway down the A14. The hospital seems to have its own microclimate when you've been there for so long.

She looks up at the four windows that face the garden. The bathroom and their bedrooms, Phoebe's and Emma's with hers – the smallest – wedged between. It's almost exactly as she always thinks of it, but her early memories always include the wisteria: those beautiful purple-blue flowers that had framed the windows of the entire back of the house for the first four summers that she lived here, before Phoebe tried to use it as a ladder and the whole thing had to be cut down.

Michael appears at the conservatory door and raises his hand in greeting.

'I've been tasked with digging out the festoon lights!'

She gives him the thumbs-up. As he walks towards the back door of the garage, Rosie watches him. The breadth of his back, the way the material of his shorts hangs from his buttocks.

Rosie has never really understood why Michael is thought of as a sex symbol. He's an all right actor – Rosie has even enjoyed a couple of his films – but as for being physically attractive? He's just a bit . . . obvious. When people find out about the connection it's always, 'You're related to Michael Regis?! *The* Michael Regis?!' and then – particularly the older women and the gay men – mime fanning themselves and say, 'How do you control yourself? Don't you just spend all of Christmas Day drooling over your mince pies?' And Rosie always replies, 'Nope, not my type.'

She watches him now, disappearing into the dark of the garage. It is undeniable that he's handsome, even if it is in a Disney prince sort of way. Maybe, if she hadn't known him since he was a slightly gawky teenager, maybe, if she had met him when he was a fully-formed film star, she too would be overwhelmed by his presence?

What is she doing? Weighing up the possibility of finding Michael attractive?

Immediately Rosie closes her eyes and places one hand, spread wide, beneath her collar bone and the other just below her belly button. She inhales through her nose, holds it for four seconds, then exhales. It's amazing how quickly it works. Human physiology is something that she is still astonished by.

At the table, placing her hands on her hips, she considers the heap of bunting. A big knotty mess to untangle. She allows herself a little sigh, then gets to it. She will untangle it knot by knot using her teeth on the particularly tricky ones. A process not dissimilar to her sessions with Diane.

She tips her head back and looks through the still branches of the tree, the sunlight shining in perfect shafts through the leaves. There are more leaves on the ground and in the pond, more brown and gold amongst the green of those still on the branches than would be usual for this early into autumn. She'd read about it just last week on Instagram – one of her friends from XR had posted about it – 'early drop' they call it. Apparently it's to do with the drought, it's the tree's attempt at self-preservation. Maybe if all the trees die, people will wake up.

A horrible thought. She loves trees. She loves this tree particularly.

It's one of the things she remembers most clearly about that first summer here. She used to sit at her bedroom window and watch it. It was reassuring, that it was there every morning, when so much else in her life had changed. Twenty-five years ago it was, that she first moved to this house. A whole quarter of a century. And yet, she can still remember that feeling.

The absolute confusion.

The disbelief that her mum was really gone.

Four

Rosie closed the dictionary and slid it back onto the shelf above the desk, between the thesaurus and the *Complete Works of Shakespeare*.

So that was that. To be an orphan, you needed to be completely parentless. It seemed all sources were in agreement on the matter. And though he was showing little inclination to be so, her dad was still very much alive. So calling herself an orphan was out.

The same would be true for those boys.

There should really be some sort of term for it, some word that provides an explanation without having to explain it. 'Orphan' was a code word, a signal to draw a line under a subject. She couldn't remember the Artful Dodger asking too much about what happened to Oliver's parents when he turned up at Fagin's, and the Big Friendly Giant didn't stick his giant nose into what happened to Sophie's parents, did he? It would be so much easier to say, 'I'm an orphan,' and have people look a little shocked, then sad-eyed, and not ask her any more questions.

Anything would be better than saying those metallic-tasting words: 'My mum's dead.' Words that make her mouth feel as though it's been painted on the inside with nail varnish, her tongue stiff and sticky. It's a sentence that she didn't want to have to say ever again. Because when she did say it, she was almost always asked, 'What happened?' And that, that, is something she *really* didn't want to talk about.

If she were allowed to say, 'I'm an orphan,' then the need to explain would magically disappear.

Maybe she could call herself a 'half-orphan'? But that would mean further questions, and she doesn't want to get into talking about her dad.

It would be so much easier for her, starting at the new school.

Hi I'm Rosie. My favourite Spice Girl is Mel C. And I'm an orphan.

They'd nod sympathetically after a statement as confident as that. It might make people understand that she was heaving around this big ball of sadness in her chest. That every morning she felt like her heart was breaking all over again when she realised she could smell her mum's perfume because, the night before, she'd sprayed it on her pillow to help her sleep. That she'd be willing to do anything – to suffer physical pain, to give away all her books, to never dance ever again – anything, just to feel the soft warm skin of her mum's hand wrapped around her own for five minutes more.

If she could call herself an orphan, everyone would know that they should be kind to her.

Rosie picked up the school tie that was lying on top of the other parts of her new uniform, stiff on their hangers, draped over the bed. She held the tie up under her chin and looked in the mirror. The colours didn't suit her. Her mum always told her she should avoid yellow. She looped the tie around her neck and pulled her hair out of the way so it sat, scratchy against her skin. She had no idea what came next. She didn't have a clue how to begin tying a tie.

In the changing rooms of the hot stuffy shop, when they'd emerged from behind the curtain for Mary's appraisal, Phoebe's tie had been securely knotted and taut beneath her chin. She'd looked at Rosie in the mirror and raised one eyebrow, smiling that tight smile that wasn't really a smile at all. Mary shook her head and pushed Phoebe back into the dressing room, carefully looping the striped material around Rosie's neck into a knot, saying something about a rabbit going through the hole and chasing a fox. She wasn't really listening to the words Mary was saying, but was focusing instead on the ups and downs of her accent. She still wasn't used to it, it sounded so foreign to her ears. Foreign but soothing.

Until just a few months ago she'd only ever met Mary a handful of times. Nearly everything she'd known about her came second-hand, through her dad, her half-sisters. Sometimes, when her parents argued, her mum would say, 'Oh, I'm so sorry if I'm not living up to the standards set by your first wife,' or sometimes something a bit ruder.

Mary hardly ever swore. Her accent wasn't as jaggedy as her mum's either. She always sounded soft and sweet. Even when she was angry at Phoebe and her voice was raised, she sounded relaxed and calm, almost as if she might break out in song. This house not only had a different smell to her home back in London, but it had a different melody too, it was smoother, more constant. The hum of the big fridge in the kitchen, the birdsong through any open window, the constant radio playing somewhere in the house. All nice noises, but a constant reminder that the place she was supposed to be calling home now, wasn't.

A burning sensation seared across Rosie's chest. Did she really miss the sounds of home? The almighty shrieks that used to rattle through the door when her mum locked herself in the bathroom. Did she really want to hold on to them? Those howls that made her feel so helpless, that made her dad's eyes film with tears as he held her on the sofa and told her that 'Mummy will be all right soon, Petal. She's just feeling a bit sad.'

A bit sad.

Rosie looked in the mirror and tried to tie the tie once more. For a moment, she thought she'd mastered it, but then as she tightened it, it slid apart, back into uneven lengths.

She considered for a second knocking on the door of the bedroom next to hers, nudging it open and asking Phoebe if she could show her how to do it, since she was such an expert. But almost immediately, she shook her head and pulled the tie from around her neck.

If Emma had been at home then she'd have happily knocked on her door and asked her. Emma had been lovely to her. Had always been kind to her. But she was at Lee's. As usual.

She couldn't bear the idea of asking Phoebe and facing those pursed lips and the refusal to help, but she'd have to work it out by Monday. She'd ask Mary to write down that little rhyme for her, or draw her a diagram.

She threw the tie onto the bed. Her bed.

She couldn't get used to it.

Was it ungrateful to still be wanting to go home?

Mary had tried her best, she knew she had.

One morning at the beginning of the summer – when she'd been quietly moving the bloated Rice Krispies around the bowl, scraping the spoon on the floral pattern that peeped through the swirling milk – Mary had placed a hand on her shoulder and asked her what her favourite colours were. Then, a few days later when she'd managed to extricate herself from watching the soap that they all watched that wasn't *EastEnders* – oh, how she missed *EastEnders* – she'd wished everyone goodnight, kissed her dad, who smelled of beer, and picked her way up the creaky stairs. She'd gone to her room and found new turquoise curtains hanging in the window, and a fresh pink duvet cover too.

She'd cried then, though she wasn't sure why at the time, because it was a lovely thing for Mary to have done and she should have been grateful rather than crying herself to sleep. It was probably because it was then that she'd realised. That was the moment it had really sunk in: this was her bedroom. And if this was her bedroom, then she wouldn't be going home to wake up in her actual bedroom, because this wasn't a horrible nightmare but her real life.

Rosie looked out of the window. It was the last day of August, three whole months since her mum had died. One and a half since her dad had called Mary and she'd arrived in London two hours later. One and a half months that Rosie had been looking at this view. Such a different view from the one she was used to.

At home, in London, her room was right at the top of the house, up three flights of stairs. She'd loved the way at night, when the lights came on across the city, from her bedroom it seemed as if she could see all of London, a patchwork of pinprick orange and white lights. At sunset, she'd watch the tiny buildings in the distance change colour; sometimes she thought that she could even see the glint of sunlight on the Thames itself.

The view from her new bedroom window was quite different. Here her room was at the back of the house, looking over the garden, the tree and the pond beneath it that, around midday, reflected the sunlight onto the ceiling of her room. And beyond the little picket fence at the end of the lawn, as far as the eye could see, was a sea of brown churned mud, punctuated by corrugated metal huts, and big hulking, snorting, farting, stinking pigs.

At night, other than the faint orange glow of light from the nearest town, it was just a wide expanse of black. But she could still hear them. Smell them.

When she was younger, she'd loved pigs. She'd had little figurines and cuddly toys of pigs in all shapes and sizes lined up on her shelves in front of her books. She'd even petitioned her parents to get a pot-bellied one as a pet. She'd so desperately wanted to be around pigs – their little snuffly noises, their funny curly tails – all the time.

Little did she know that one day she'd wish with every fibre of her being that she could get away from them.

When it was hot a couple of weeks ago, she'd left the window open and slept in just her knickers and T-shirt without a duvet, as she'd done in London. At first she'd enjoyed the sound of the breeze rippling through the leaves of the big tree outside, the way moonlight filtered through its branches creating patterns on her bedroom wall. But then, the wind must have shifted direction, because suddenly, all she could smell was pig poo. She'd got up and closed the window, and even though it'd been shut ever since and she'd sprayed every possession she owned with Impulse, she could still smell it.

The garden was pretty, she had to admit, even if the pigs made it stink.

She looked out of the window. In the late afternoon sun, the tree seemed to be dancing, the silvery-green leaves were glowing in the sunset as if autumn had already arrived, the red and orange reflections on the pond beneath making it look more like fire than water. Another day was ending.

She thought again of those two boys. The two princes.

Where would they be sleeping that night?

She wished there was a way she could contact them. She would tell them that they shouldn't feel bad if they didn't feel like crying. That it didn't mean that they didn't love their mum. That it might just take a little while for their brains to catch up. Maybe she'd write them a letter.

Those first few days after her mum died had felt like an odd sort of dream, and now they were the strangest sort of memory. She felt as though she had watched it in a film or read about it in a book, not that it had happened in her own life, that it had happened to her. What she did remember clearly, though, was repeatedly thinking that she should be crying. Her dad was, and so was Auntie Yas – who kept hugging her and making her feel weird because she not only looked a bit like her mum but smelled the same: perfume and Dove soap. But, for some reason, for weeks, Rosie hadn't shed a single tear.

Were those boys crying into their pillows tonight? Or would it take someone making them a new set of curtains for the tears to start falling?

Mary had cried that morning when the boys' mum died, and Emma too. Phoebe hadn't, but she'd sat next to her as they watched the news, which, considering how she treated her for the last six weeks, was remarkable in itself.

Rosie had come down to find the kitchen deserted. That alerted her to something being wrong: for the whole summer, not a day had passed where she hadn't woken to the smell of coffee and pastry working its way through the floorboards.

She was still struggling to get her head around the production that every meal in this house seemed to be. It was confusing; so formal, yet weirdly relaxed. Proper fabric napkins folded into a little tent on top of each plate, yet everyone was wearing their pyjamas, their hair still ruffled from the pillow. Or in the evenings, lighting candles and waiting until everyone had sat down to start eating, but no one batting an eyelid at Emma reading at the table. She'd never been allowed to read at the table at home on the rare occasions they'd sat at it – and breakfast had normally been a bowl of cereal in front of the TV.

But this morning, she'd come down to find the table unlaid and everyone, even her dad, in the lounge staring slack-mouthed at the television as images of cars with blacked-out windows slid past.

'There's been a car crash.' Mary's eyes were red and puffy from the tears they'd already shed. 'Princess Diana, she's been killed.'

Rosie's first thought was that she hadn't seen Mary cry before. Her second was about those boys, Lady Di's sons, the princes.

How did they find out that their mum had died?

She'd had an immediate vision of their father, telling them as hers had told her. A film-like image of the two princes, in epauletted little suits, sitting on a leather sofa, just as she had, their father sitting next to them, and then the long slow exhale, as if he were deflating. Prince Charles, the future king of this country, crumpled into a ball and not telling them, but repeatedly calling out their mother's name in strangled sobs, just like her dad had when he'd told her.

It was all wrong, of course. They were probably told by their nannies or their governess, or whoever looked after them. And they certainly wouldn't have been told in the lounge of a three-bed semi in North London.

It was strange, but she didn't feel quite so alone, knowing that somewhere, out there – beyond the tree and the fields full of stinking pigs, lit copper by the setting sun – those two boys knew exactly how she felt.

Rosie stood at the window and opened it, for the first time in weeks.

The air had a bit of a chill to it and she could smell a hint of woodsmoke mixed in with the ever present animal stench. The scent of the smoke stirred something in Rosie's chest. Despite it all – her sadness, her missing her mum – there was something hopeful about the change of seasons, the new start. Soon the leaves on the tree that were being turned orange by the sunset will really be bronze. Many of the others she'd seen as she rode her bike around the village were already starting to show the first signs of colour.

It was a really nice tree. She was glad she could see it from her room. Mary had given her the choice: the big room facing the front, or this little one. She didn't want the one overlooking the lane, where people passing might be able to see her looking out. So she'd chosen this one, where she could hear Phoebe and Emma through the walls on either side. She had thought then that it would only be for the summer. Maybe she'd have chosen differently if she knew it was going to be permanent.

'We're going to stay here a bit longer, Petal.'

Her dad was standing in the doorway to her room, leaning against the frame. His hair was wet from the shower and he was smelling strongly of aftershave.

'Mary's going to look after us both. Just for a bit. Just until I work out where we're going to live.'

'But, Dad, what about dancing? I've got exams. And all my things? My room? And school? What about school?'

'School's sorted. Phoebs will be able to show you the ropes. It'll be great having a sister in the year above. And Emma in the sixth form too! You'll be untouchable!'

Her dad had looked at her then. He must've seen the look of horror on her face.

'I'm sorry, Petal. I just can't go back to that house yet. I'm sorry.'

And then he turned away, and before she had a chance to protest, or suggest that she stay with her Auntie Yas, her dad's back was shaking with sobs and she knew that if her dad wanted her to stay here, then that was what she was going to do.

The last few months had been the saddest months of Rosie's life, but she still hurt for her dad. Just knowing that her mum was dead made her chest feel as if it was caving in with pain, but her dad had seen it, her dad had found her – her mum, lying in that cold bath. Rosie shook her head, and tried to turn away from the images that bubbled up in her imagination.

Sometimes, she wondered if she had actually seen it, because the images she had in her mind were so clear. So real. But she hadn't been there. The last time she saw her mum was when she'd dropped her at Auntie Yas's house with a quick kiss on the cheek and told her to 'make her proud'. She hadn't thought anything of it at the time. She thought she meant to do her best in ballet. But now it was like that phrase was on repeat in her head.

'Make me proud.'

Rosie leaned out to pull the window closed. As she did so her eye was drawn to a movement at the end of the garden. Someone was unlatching the gate. She watched the hooded figure open it then cut through onto the path behind the house. She could see then, it was Phoebe; she could tell by the silhouette: she was slightly shorter than their older sister, and anyway, Emma would never wear all black. She watched Phoebe pick her way along the path. She was moving quickly, away from the house, between the fields towards the village. Even under the baggy jeans and sweatshirt there was an elegance to her movement. A womanliness.

Little women!

Laurie. That was another straightforward orphan from one of her favourite books. She'd read it last summer, on their holiday to Greece. And then again during half-term. She loved it so much that when her dad asked her if she had any ideas for Christmas presents for her half-sisters she'd known exactly what to get them. She'd wrapped them herself, curling the ribbon with the side of the scissors like her mum had shown her. Then at their Granny's on Boxing Day, she had been so excited, she'd had butterflies in her stomach as she watched Emma carefully slide her finger beneath the Sellotape and fold back the wrapping paper.

'*Little Women*. Thank you Rosebud. I haven't read this one.'

Emma had leaned across and given her a squeeze. She'd looked across at Phoebe then. She was leafing through the pages, a mess of ripped wrapping paper on her knee.

Phoebe sighed, then turned to their dad.

'If I take it back to the shop, will they give me a book token? Or will I need a receipt?'

Emma turned to Phoebe and snatched the book out of her hand.

'Say thank you to Rosie, Phoebe.'

That had been the only good thing about this summer. Living with Emma. Emma called her Rosebud and knocked on her bedroom door to say goodnight. She let her choose what to put on the TV, and then plaited her hair while they watched it together.

Phoebe, however, always took control of the remote, the second she entered the lounge. Or if she was there first, she'd move from the sofa to the floor if Rosie dared to sit next to her. And earlier in the summer – when they'd been driving back from swimming in Felixstowe with Mary and Lizzie – Phoebe had pinched herself so hard it had left a red mark, and then she'd screamed out, pretending that Rosie had done it, and Mary had had to pull the car over on the main road.

Rosie watched as Phoebe disappeared in the gloom of the encroaching dusk. It would be dark soon. Where was she going? She could still hear that dirge that Phoebe called music coming from her bedroom next door. A decoy? Or maybe she'd just gone for a walk?

There was a lot of 'going for walks' here. Lizzie and Mary walked around the village together every night, before dinner, as part of their 'keep fit'. Even her dad had occasionally put his head around the door and told her that he was just popping out to stretch his legs. Another difference: at home, walking was only ever a means of reaching a destination.

Shivering, Rosie closed the window and turned back to the bed and the uniform that was lying on the pink duvet, the tie strewn over it.

How strange that her mum would never see her in this uniform.

Five

Phoebe stands in the conservatory, swaying. Her infant son on her shoulder, the heat of him making her dress stick to her skin.

She squints, trying to make out a movement at the far end of the garden. Beneath the tree, Rosie is bent over, concentrating on something on the lawn. The sun shines through the tree above, making her skin appear dappled – an animal, crouched in the grass – but then, she stands, stretches, and climbs onto a chair at the far end of the table. She is on her tiptoes, raising one end of a string of bunting up into the low-hanging branches of the tree.

The baby snorts, readjusts himself, and pulls his bare legs further in, towards his belly. His back arches against her palm, a perfect tortoise shell. She whispers soothing noises against the dark, soft down of his head. It tickles her nose and she scrunches up her face to stave off a sneeze.

He ought to be in the carrycot upstairs, next to his sister on the air-mattress, dead to the world, clutching that semi-deflated balloon as if it were a prize teddy. But selfishly, once he had finished feeding – and she felt the suction from his mouth loosen, her nipple sliding from his mouth, a trail of milky saliva around his lips – she had watched the consciousness wash from him as he became heavy in her arms, and she couldn't bring herself to put him down. She wanted the smell of him near her, the movement of his little lungs against her chest. She needed it, the weight of him against her like a talisman, an evil eye. When there is a baby asleep on your shoulder, it is difficult for anyone to pick a fight with you. And though she knows that fights are strictly prohibited this weekend, there's something about the suffocating quality of this heat, the thickness of the anticipation, combined with the pockets of activity around the house – the just being in this house – that makes her sure, positive, that before the day is out, there will be a fight, prohibited or not. She can almost taste it in the air.

She takes a sip of lemonade – the glass cold in her hand, the ice cubes clinking – and slips on the sandals that sit on the coir mat inside the door.

She's had the same sized feet as Mary since she was about fourteen. It only recently occurred to her that, as a teenager living in this house, she had the pick of three people's shoes. She'd never taken advantage of it. She wouldn't have been seen dead in any of Emma's things. Mary's shoes hadn't held much allure for her either back then. She thought they were all ugly too, though a different sort of ugly to the patent sheen and spindly heels that Emma favoured. It wasn't until she was mid-pregnancy when her feet had swollen like water balloons and her extensive collection of shoes became objects of torture, that – like a flash of sunlight through parted clouds – she understood Mary's propensity for utilitarian footwear. Birkenstocks, and even Crocs, morphed from attire she wouldn't be seen dead in to something she'd spend sleepless nights compulsively ordering, her face lit up by the phone as she scrolled and clicked and added to cart and entered the memorised digits of Michael's credit card. All with him sleeping, oblivious, beside her.

Phoebe walks across the lawn. The grass is so dry after these months with no rain, it is more like straw: it crackles a little each time she places a foot down. She pinches her toes as she lifts her feet, increasingly aware that the impressions in the insoles of the sandals do not quite match the curve of her foot.

'Hey.'

Rosie wobbles on the chair at the sound of Phoebe's voice. She extends an arm to catch her balance, and turns, an echo of a pirouette. She gives her a look that she has rarely seen on Rosie's perpetually smiling face, but then, with a speed that makes Phoebe want to snort with laughter, the scowl disappears. It dissolves as Rosie remembers Mary's directive, and Phoebe watches – head cocked, eyebrow arched – as Rosie tries to mask her prohibited facial expression.

'*Shh* – Granny's sleeping.'

Rosie jumps off the chair. Her landing causes her hair to fly outwards. Briefly, her curls are suspended, a halo around her head. Then it falls again and her face unfurls into the smile she knows so well.

'I've got about three hours untangling ahead of me before I can put it up.' Rosie motions to the heap of string and golden flags. 'Should be done just before it's time to take them down.'

'Is Granny all right there, do you think? Isn't it too hot?'

'There isn't anywhere left to sit indoors, so I helped her out here. At least she's getting some fresh air.'

Rosie sits back onto a dining chair, her fingers working another knot in the bunting.

'Can you pull that chair with the arms further into the shade for me?'

Phoebe gestures to the Ercol carver that usually sits in the hall covered in junk mail.

'Just because we're back here doesn't mean I'm going to be your dogsbody.'

'I don't want him to get too much sun.'

Rosie sighs and gets up, grabbing the high back of the wooden chair and dragging it towards Phoebe, into the deepest shade of the tree. She positions it close to the fence that surrounds the pond, next to the armchair where their grandmother is snoring. Then swiftly takes her glass, holds out her hand for Phoebe to take as she sits, then hands back her drink and bends to stroke the sleeping baby's head, all in one smooth motion.

'Sorry to snap, Phoebs.'

'Well, I did spend the best part of a decade treating you as my personal servant. Sorry, I'm starting to get a bit nervous.'

Rosie pats the back of her hand.

'It's going to be fine.'

Phoebe nods. It helps to nod; if her body believes it's going to be okay, maybe her brain will too. A rivulet of sweat trickles from her hairline down her forehead, she catches it at her temple and swipes it away.

'Ugh, I'm so hot!'

Rosie glances over at her.

'Why do you always wear black?'

'"I'm in mourning for my life."'

'What accent is that supposed to be?'

'It's from a play. Ignore me. Like I said: nervous.'

Rosie shakes her head and takes on one of the knots with her teeth.

The baby shifts and Phoebe looks down at his serious little face. She'd wanted to call him Masha, if he had been a girl. Michael had been against it, said he always thought Masha was the most annoying of the *Three Sisters*. She didn't mean that Masha though, she meant the one from *The Seagull*, the first play she'd ever seen at the National Theatre. Lizzie had taken them to see a Saturday matinee, when she was about thirteen. It was framed as a treat, but she understands now it was primarily to give their mum the chance of some time to herself in London. Whatever the reason, it was a transformative experience. She'd left that theatre knowing she wanted to be an actor, and that if she ever had a daughter, she'd call her Masha. As it happened, acting turned out not to be her calling, and when she had a daughter, she'd been very happy to name her after the extraordinary woman who brought Michael up.

She settles her hand around the perfect curve of her son's head, and then she is marvelling again at his beautiful nostrils, the dapple of tiny hairs across his brow.

'I thought you were going to nap too?'

Phoebe tears her eyes away from Albie's face and settles them on Rosie's.

'I couldn't. It needs to rain.'

'So depressing isn't it?'

'I keep lying awake in the heat, worrying about what it's going to be like for the children.'

'Where's the other, louder one?'

'Clara *is* napping. Zonked. My fault, having her up so late. I'm going to try and get her down early tonight, so I can have a bit of fun.'

She sees, from the corner of her eye, Rosie pause and give her a look. But she ignores it and sips her lemonade, surveying the scene: the mismatched chairs, the uneven surface of the tables under the tablecloths, the trail of glittery bunting strewn across the grass.

'Well, this all looks sufficiently eccentric.'

'I rather like it. It's like the Mad Hatter's tea party. It's sweet.'

'Let's hope that the sweetness extends to the whole event.'

Rosie busies herself again with untangling, and starts to hum, then stops abruptly.

'We need some tunes.'

Rosie walks towards the house, the trail of bunting abandoned on the grass behind her.

Phoebe relaxes into the seat and considers the two high-backed chairs at the far end of the table. They stick out like sore thumbs amongst the familiar higgledy-piggledy mess of the other furniture. Their gilded brocade upholstery, ostentatious and, well, naff. Phoebe can only think that it's some in-joke that she isn't privy to, because when the delivery men had unloaded them from the van this morning, Mary had become helpless with laughter, to the point that Michael had to sign for them as Mary had excused herself to go and find a tissue and calm down.

Well, whatever the joke, her mum certainly deserves a laugh, and if it takes ugly brocade thrones to do it, so be it.

She can hear the faint melody of a theme tune from the radio inside, another programme starting. Time is marching on; she ought to think about waking up Clara, or put the baby down too, have a quick shower while they're both asleep. Or she could just wait till Michael is finished with the lights and she can hand the kids over to him. If one of them wakes when she's halfway through, she'll undoubtedly have to abandon her ablutions, and end up greeting people she hasn't seen in years with one smooth leg, and one simian one.

Phoebe looks at the house: this building that she grew up in. How strange and sad that this is the last weekend they'll ever be here. Neither of her children will remember it. Until her mum had called her, a few months ago, she'd somehow thought that it would always be there, their home. And of course it will still be here, just without them in it. It seems impossible that it could belong to some other family. But it will, in just over a week's time. You'd have thought that by now she'd have learned that there is no such thing as permanence. Life certainly seems insistent on hammering home the lesson.

Her eye is drawn to a flash of red and yellow in the conservatory.

For a moment, Phoebe has the odd sensation that she is watching herself. Not just herself 'in twenty-five years' time' as people generously say when they see Mary and her side by side, but for a fraction of a second she thinks: *How can I be there, if I'm here?* Then her mind catches up and she realises, of course, it is her mum, in her new dressing gown, stacking boxes.

She watches her disappear back into the house as she brings the baby to her face again and inhales the doughy scent of him, trying to stimulate her oxytocin.

She knows that all she ought to be feeling today is happiness for her mum. That today is about celebrating, about being grateful that they can be together – all of them. But she can't help but feel sad about what they are leaving behind. And she knows this roiling feeling in her stomach is not just sadness. It's fear too. She has been scared about today's approach for months. Scared of what it will be like to see Emma. Scared of what will happen. Scared of how she'll feel. Scared of how she'll cope with those feelings.

She swills the ice in her glass. It is melting rapidly in the heat, watering down the cloudy lemonade so it is almost transparent. She tips up the glass and empties it into her mouth, crunching what remains of the ice. A sharp pain streaks through her head, across her eyes, as the cold constricts the blood flow through her head.

'Found it!'

Rosie is shouting out of her bedroom window.

'Fuck's sake, Rosie!'

She says it under her breath, but the baby still startles, flinches as if he is falling, and Phoebe holds him tighter against her, shushes him and rubs her hand over his back in a circular motion.

How is it that no one in this family understands how difficult it is to get small children to sleep? Everyone knows it, don't they? They've watched TV, they've got friends who have kids? Her mum had kids, and yet, last night, she and Rosie had a lengthy discussion on the landing, as if they were trying to be heard over an approaching helicopter. Did they really need to discuss the fucking bunting at gone midnight, directly outside the room where her children were sleeping?

Rosie slams the window to her room and then quickly appears at the window next to it.

'You're supposed to keep windows closed during the day, open at night. That's why it's so hot in here. Want me to shut yours?'

Phoebe shakes her head, points exaggeratedly towards the room where Clara sleeps, and brings a finger to her lips.

'Oh, right. Sorry!' Rosie closes the window to Emma's room, drawing the curtains inside.

Phoebe has only peeked around the door of Emma's room since they arrived. It didn't feel right, somehow, going in when she would be sleeping there tonight. It felt as if she were trespassing on their former selves. Instead, she'd just reached up above the door to take down the little framed embroidery that had hung there ever since she could remember, and dusted it with the hem of her dress before hanging it back onto its hook and straightening it with her forefinger.

She had been braced for a certain amount of nostalgia this weekend. It's only to be expected that being back in your childhood home, saying farewell to all the nooks and crannies of the place where you became the person you are, is always going to invoke memories. She just hadn't been prepared for which memories they might be, and how, remembering those moments, would feel like living it all over again.

Six

Phoebe squeezed her eyes shut and let a smile spread across her sweaty face.

It's like, she thought, *coming round after a concussion.*

She laughed. A noise that was muted because her face was pressed into his chest.

Sex is like a concussion? Quite a statement. Probably not one she'd voice aloud.

Not any old sex. Not all the sex that she used to have that she can barely remember.

But great sex, with someone you really want to have sex with. Great sex with someone you've loved for as long as she's loved Michael Regis.

They could have been doing this for years. If she'd just told him that she loved him that night in Bangkok.

She'd forgotten it. The lucidity of thought that comes directly after. This is when she ought to write. In the moments after orgasm, ideas that have been dancing on the periphery, that have been bobbing in the flow of her daily stream of thoughts, become clear.

The drinking had helped that too. That was one of the many things that she'd loved about it. The booze. She'd said that in Group once. She remembered saying it, though she couldn't remember where; which city, which group, during which one of her many attempts to get sober.

'It slows down the river.' She'd sobbed. And they'd all looked at her blankly. And suddenly that 'safe space' didn't feel very safe at all.

Michael understood. Had always understood.

She'd told him that long ago, soon after they first met. They'd been smoking, lying next to each other on the grass on Parker's Piece.

'I think weed is the best at it.'

She trailed her fingers back and forth above them, watching them leave a momentary shadow as her optic nerves struggled to relay the message.

'The best at what?'

She could feel the vibration of his voice in her left arm where it touched him.

'At slowing the river.'

'Yeah, it's like it mutes the noise.'

Michael understood.

That was all it came down to really, wasn't it? 'Connection.' Understanding without the requirement to explain. He understood that she meant the fast-flowing, cloudy-watered river that hurtled through her consciousness. The glowing ideas and thoughts and things she really had to do which – if she looked away for longer than a second, if she didn't reach out immediately and grab them – would dip down beneath the surface into the murky depths, never to be seen again.

It was often when she was walking that Phoebe became aware of the velocity of her thoughts. When she was moving forward and didn't look at her phone or put on her headphones and listen to the jibing and probing of her favourite podcasts, she was particularly aware of them. They surrounded her, enveloped her, they hung around her head like cartoon thought bubbles that appeared and popped and multiplied like dividing cells. It was like that, from the moment she cracked her eyes to let the day stream in, to when she fell into sleep at the day's end, always had been. It was only then, when sleep took her, that they slowed. But occasionally they even punctuated her rest; jolting her awake with their persistence.

It was little wonder she so often felt exhausted.

But, during sex, good sex, they just . . . went.

Before, however, it's different. At even the merest suggestion of sex, her thoughts are at their loudest.

Tonight, for example, when she opened the door and saw him with the bag at his feet and his eyes rimmed with red, she'd ushered him in without a word. But inside her head, an orchestra was tuning up.

She deposited him on the couch with a mug of tea. Then she quickly opened the window in the spare room, made the bed and started the bath running. She unwrapped a fresh tablet of soap and placed it by the taps. She hid the little pot of hair-lightening cream that she used on her upper lip in the cupboard beneath the sink, then paused for a second and wondered why. But in that stillness the thoughts rushed at her, so she shook her head and went back into the lounge and handed him the largest towel she had, apologising that it wasn't softer.

While he bathed, she opened the fridge, then the cupboards, then opened the delivery app on her phone before opening the fridge again, staring into the light of it as though it might hold the answers. Why wasn't he in a hotel? Why wasn't he at the bloody Ritz? Why hadn't he asked his assistant, the production manager, the producers, to find him somewhere? Surely he could've found somewhere more appropriate than her semi-decorated Catford flat?

She waved her hand in front of her face, batting away the thoughts as if they were a cloud of circling flies.

From the bathroom, the sound of a rush of water as he pulled the plug spurred her to action; she boiled salted water on the hob, removed the bright green sprout from the centre of the shrivelled clove of garlic, crushing it with the side of her knife and chopping it finely before peeling the wrinkled skins off the two tomatoes and chopping those too.

A synthetic almond smell entered the kitchen with him, and she thought of marzipan and then cyanide; she shook her head and apologised for there not being a drop of alcohol in the house.

He poured them a glass of tap water each, found the cutlery, laid it on the battered coffee table.

'Wasn't this table in the Cambridge house?'

'Recovered from the depths of Mum's garage when I came back from New York. It's a bit nineties, but it'll do till I start making proper money again.'

She placed plates of spaghetti before them both. It glistened with olive oil, speckles of nutmeg on the swiftly dissolving curls of cheese.

They sat on the floor to eat. Her with the sofa at her back. Him opposite, the table between them. He asked her about what she was writing. She told him she thought she was, maybe, writing a book, a sort of memoir. She asked him about the film. He told her that he hated the director.

The realisation that they were a reflection of their younger selves – eating hundreds of almost identical meals from this very table – settled into her chest like indigestion.

Had there ever been a time she hadn't wanted him?

Maybe, at first.

There had been the breath of a moment when she'd thought him straight-laced. A little boring, if she was honest. She hadn't liked his shoes, she remembered. She'd enjoyed his company, had been grateful for it in those first few strange weeks, but she had felt the need to seek out new friends, more friends, friends who would let her into the inner circle; she'd felt as though her friendship with Michael was partially about keeping each other company as they hung around beyond its circumference.

Then, there'd been that churning fury when she'd arrived at the auditions, signed herself in on the little clipboard and seen his name on the line two above hers. She'd walked into the auditorium and he'd waved at her, articulating the tips of his fingers, his lips rolled in against each other: a cheeky admission of guilt. She'd felt claustrophobic, angry, to have had him follow her there. It was her thing, her bid for independence, her chance to meet new people. To have helped her to learn her speech but not let on that he too intended to audition – to audition for *Hamlet*! – himself. He'd sat opposite her for weeks in cafes, on the end of her bed as she did her make-up, as they walked their bikes along the wet pavements from college to the pub, listening to her reciting the speech, nodding when she'd got it right, and he'd never said a word. It would have been so easy for him to have told her. He could have mentioned it at any time. As he corrected her on the order of the flowers in her speech, or as he listened to her practise that little song over and over. It would have been so easy to have just slipped it into the conversation.

It still irked her a little now to think that he didn't tell her. Nearly twenty years later.

She remembered the audition as clearly as any event in her life. His audition.

How for a moment everything was suspended. She remembered – so vividly – how her breath, her heart, both seemed to still, and there was a quality to the air as if she, the room, everyone in it were held in aspic. Michael started speaking and he was someone else entirely, yet more him than she'd ever seen before. She understood what he meant, not just Michael, but Hamlet, Shakespeare! She understood a little more about herself. She understood more about everyone she knew, everyone she had ever met.

Was it then that she had first wanted him? In that scruffy studio theatre that smelled of coffee, and dust burning on the lights?

Was it at that moment, sitting on the raised seating, her scarf folded across her knees, that the course of her life was altered entirely? Maybe. She did know that afterwards, as they stood in the alley, their breath making clouds in the late November afternoon air, that she noticed for the first time the threads of gold in his eyes as he leaned forward to light his cigarette from her Zippo.

She had hunted for them earlier that evening, as they ate their garlic and tomato covered spaghetti. Turning her fork on her plate, aware that his focus was on the food, she looked up, while he wasn't looking directly at her, to see if those golden threads still existed.

For all the time they hadn't seen each other, she'd convinced herself that she'd made them up. That they were part of the tragic fairy tale she'd woven for herself about how she'd fallen in love with him, how she'd been usurped, or on her more generous days, how she had missed her chance by keeping her feelings a secret.

But as he looked up this evening, she saw them.

It was as if his irises had been embroidered with gold filigree. He frowned then, smiling as he did so, questioning her stare, the sides of his eyes crinkling. She inhaled sharply to see that, when his face relaxed and he continued to eat, the creases around his eyes didn't disappear. How was it possible that the young man with the horrible shoes was ageing? That Michael – who helped her dad to carry her boxes up from the car to her student room, and then – once her dad had instructed her to 'Be good, Button' – had offered her one of his warm cans of beer and pretended not to notice her trying to hold back the tears – was getting old? It made sense; at thirty-four, she sometimes felt as though she had lived several decades – but Michael was ageing, too? Surely Nature should have some sort of strategy to protect the finest specimens of each species from decay?

When she finished eating, she put her fork down onto her empty plate and pulled her knee up in between her breasts.

The noise inside her head, the river of her thoughts, was almost unbearable, and she was about to stand, to suggest that they go for a walk.

And then she noticed the tilt to his head, and she knew.

As soon as she recognised it, he was moving towards her. He was crawling around the table, like a big cat. Then his head was resting on her shoulder. And she put her hand on his head. And then. Then he pushed himself up to face her and kissed her.

He kissed *her*.

He was lying on top of her now. He was holding her, but his body was heavy, pinning her down. They weren't moving. Her head was pounding. Hot.

Maybe she had actually hit her head as they fell to the floor?

She spider-crawled her fingers across the rug and finally came across the hard, metal leg of the coffee table. She'd kicked at it to push it out of the way so she could make room for them on the floor. No, she hadn't hit her head. It was just like the bit after the concussion. The coming round. The waking up and the realisation of what they'd done.

She had her eyes closed, but still she could tell his quiet wasn't because he'd fallen asleep. He was awake. She could feel the realisation creeping into him, just as it was into her. His body was no longer soft and heavy, but tense, coiled.

He wasn't inside her, but he was close enough that she could feel every shift in his body. Other than her left sock, they were both completely naked, her thigh wet. The rug was bunched up at her back and she could feel the gaps in the floorboards against it. Those 'beautiful' floorboards that hadn't been quite so beautiful when she'd ripped up the ugly, burgundy-swirled carpets to find them battered and stained. Was she ever going to be able to look at her beloved floorboards again without imagining her back, naked against them, with Michael lying on top of her?

There it was.

The headache, the hangover, the comedown. The dark dark shame that followed giving in to the lure of escape. What goes up must come down. It was the very reason she'd worked so hard at getting sober.

She knew sex was dangerous ground for addicts. But surely sex with Michael Regis didn't count? Surely there was something sacred about finding escape in the arms of her oldest, dearest friend?

She pressed her eyes shut until little coloured stars danced on the inside of her eyelids.

She'd imagined it would be something profound, if it ever happened. And it was, in a way. But it was also human. Ridiculous. The tangle of them falling to the floor. Their knees superfluous, flailing, with nowhere to go.

And it had been scary at first. The vulnerability of it. But that fear was counterbalanced by the shift in the frenzy of her thoughts. The more he touched her, the more she touched him, the more the torrent slowed until there was nothing but a trickle.

Bliss.

But that was gone now. And there they were, naked on her livingroom floor, her nose pressed against the warm cyanide-scented skin of his chest. And her head was crowded with thoughts, with images; with the image of one particular face. There was no way back from here. None. None at all.

'Fuck!'

She didn't say it, so much as breathe it.

'I know.'

His voice was muted too. His chin dipped against her scalp, his face in her hair, his breath hot on her crown. Still he didn't move.

'Fuck.'

'Please. Please can you stop saying that.'

'What now Mike? Fuck. Sorry.'

He did move then. Tipped his chest to roll off her. And she rolled too, onto her front, the floorboards cold against her ribs. He sat up and put his head in his hands and a noise started to vibrate from him, hollow and familiar. It was painful to hear it. It was painful to know she held some responsibility for it.

Another moan. And she knew immediately why it was familiar.

That summer that Rosie's mum committed suicide. Her dad wandering around the house, his bloodshot eyes blank, unseeing. She remembered distinctly the repetition of him picking up a cup and then, almost immediately, without even taking a sip of the cold tea within, putting it down again, and how, on those rare occasions they found laughter, his chuckle would mutate into sobs, and Mum would put her hand on his forearm and even hold him as the deep groans shook his body. And

Rosie, she'd been so quiet, so sucked into herself. The containment, the control had made Phoebe furious, and she was horrible to her, that little eleven-year-old who had just lost her mum.

It made her burn with shame to think of it.

Another time in her life that she wouldn't be winning any Best Sister awards for.

He was rocking – back and forth – his moans starting to form the words he himself told her not to say. She rubbed his naked back, the ribs visible through the skin like a ladder from the patch of hair at the base of his spine, to the neat point at his neck.

'Fuck. Oh fuck. Fuck.'

There was something about the noise, the sadness, that repulsed her, that made her want to run away. She chastised herself as she thought it, but she couldn't help it. She could easily stand, grab her jeans, her bra and her other sock, and move to her bedroom. Give him some privacy, let him get out what he needed to get out. But she didn't do that. Instead, though every cell of her was telling her to run, she leaned towards him.

That at least was progress.

She got up from the floorboards onto her knees and crawled on the rug, feeling the rough fabric scraping at her skin. She came over to where he was scrunched up, rocking, repeating the same words over and over, and she draped herself over him.

Paper covers stone.

She always used to be the scissors, when they were kids. Paper. Scissors. Stone. Their mum had used the game to settle squabbles. She knew that Emma would choose paper and so she would always choose scissors.

It wasn't until recently that she had realised that her sister was probably letting her win.

Her stomach pitched. But then a flare of indignant rage blotted it out, and she wrapped her arms around her best friend, trying to soothe him, to shoulder some of his hurt. She held him for a long time, her breasts against his heaving back, her head alongside his, and she let herself rock with him, an inversion of their positions mere moments before. Together they rocked, back and forward, forward and back.

Seven

Michael feels a twinge in his lower back as he lifts the plastic boxes to his chest. His back has been bothering him for a couple of weeks now, since that fight scene.

They'd called the doctor to set right away, who referred him to a physio who drove in from Belfast by the time it was getting light. She twisted his legs around a bit, massaged his glutes, then gently suggested that doing his own stunts was probably something he'd want to wrap up before long if he wanted to be able to lift his grandkids when they came along. He'd laughed.

'I've only just turned forty. My eldest is three years old!'

'Up to you, stick with the Lycra till you're in the knackers' yard if that's what you want.'

She shrugged and continued to knead his quad.

'You give this same pep talk to Tom Cruise?'

He laughed. She blushed.

'I just think –' she paused, putting pressure on his thigh, twisting it across his body '– I saw you in that play. The one with the oil. It blew my mind, and it just seems a shame, that's all. That you're just . . . punching bad guys in the face.'

'Decrepit *and* a sell-out!'

She shrugged again, but she didn't blush that time.

* * *

He finished the film, with a double having to step in for both a fight and a sex scene. But there'd still be a queue of people ready to give him a hard time if they'd seen him helping to move the furniture around this morning.

He looks towards the gap in the hedge. It's been a while since he's done anything interesting enough to warrant paparazzi hiding in the bushes, but it would be just his luck if they happened to get a snap of him lugging around sofas and climbing up ladders. It was hard enough getting his agent to agree to their coming to Mary's without security; his life wouldn't be worth living if she knew he was risking the shoot. She's right, of course, he should be resting ahead of filming. The muscles at the base of his spine have been complaining all morning, and he's going to have to ride and sword-fight in this one.

He can just imagine how that would have gone down with Richard.

'I'm afraid I can't help. I've got to protect my back so I can play King Arthur.'

No, he'd rather throw his back out and lose the gig than give Richard Roberts that opportunity.

Michael places the boxes onto the end of the table with a grunt and bends backwards, his hands against the base of his spine. He can feel the muscles beneath his palm, bunched, tight, pulling his bones closer to each other, like a marionette whose strings have been tied into a knot. Something makes a delicious clunk and he groans with pleasure.

'Back?'

'Clara's not as light as she used to be. Just need a massage.'

'Are you sure that you should be doing the Bulgaria job?'

Michael doesn't answer, but bends over the box and rips off the lid.

He lets out a long groan.

'Mike! If it's that bad you need to see someone!'

'Phoebs, it's not my back. This box. It's a complete mess. Whoever packed the lights away didn't coil them.'

'That's unlike this family; everything else in this house is so spick and span.'

She gives him a cheeky smile and he allows himself to smile back. He runs his palm across his forehead, wiping away the sheen of perspiration that has gathered there, then checks his watch. One thirty-three. Less than an hour and a half to get this shit sorted. Mary's impressed upon him, several times, that she wants everything to be set up by the time Emma arrives.

His stomach drops. Emma. Here.

He is aware that Phoebe's eyes are still on him. He swallows, then sets about yanking the wire, unscrewing each bulb and carefully laying them on the tablecloth one by one.

'What sort of vibe d'you reckon Mum's going for here?' Phoebe is waving the hand that is free of the baby towards the table. 'House clearance meets country fete?'

'I love a dinner under the tree. Reminds me of your twenty-first.'

'Not my finest hour.'

He sends her a wink. She blows him a kiss. The baby stirs.

'How many is it?' Phoebe whispers, rubbing Albie's back. 'Forty-two and the two babies? It's going to feel so weird, everyone being here.'

'It'll all be over in less than twelve hours, and then, tomorrow, if you want, we can go home.'

She smiles, nods, and closes her eyes, her head resting against the chair behind her.

He's won a few awards in his career, but none of his performances were more deserving of recognition than the one he's been putting on since they arrived here in Mouser Lane. He's exhausted from all the pretending already, and Emma isn't even here yet.

The air lies still across them, a blanket scented with the smell of fresh-cut grass.

'I don't get why we're sitting down. It's a thing you eat on your lap really, isn't it? I thought the whole thing was "low-key". A fuck-off dining table with a couple of thrones is hardly what I'd call low-key.'

Michael shrugs, turning back to the lights.

'If it's what your mum wants . . .'

'You know Dad's got Rosie's new boyfriend out there man-handling the bloody pig?'

'Yeah.'

'So pathetically macho. Hazing him, seeing if he passes muster.'

'Does he? He's pretty dishy, don't you think?'

'No comment.'

Phoebe sips her lemonade.

'Wise woman.'

A strimmer starts up in a garden nearby, a mechanical squeal that blocks out the melodious orchestra of birdsong.

'I'm just glad your dad didn't ask me. Can you imagine? He'd probably try and skewer me instead of the pig.'

'You'd have had to hold Clara in front of you, like a human shield.'

They both laugh.

There is a frustration though, in Richard's breezy disinterest in him. If Michael is honest, he's never been sure that he much liked him, but he never used to care. Now, when some might argue that Richard has good reason to hate him, he just seems non-committal, and Michael finds it almost unbearably irritating. He doesn't even like *him*. In his opinion, Richard Roberts is the root cause of every single problem this family has ever had. Though that's something he'll almost definitely never voice, even to Phoebe.

Another thing to add to the list of things he absolutely must not say this evening. He'd better not drink too much.

Michael unravels the thick coils of electric cord, pulling them into great lengths, laying them on the grass beside the length of the table, replacing the bulbs one by one.

'What time is Emma getting here?' Rosie arrives, bringing with her a scent of coconut and something falsely floral. She places a small retro-looking stereo on the table, dropping several tape cassettes in their plastic boxes next to it with a clatter.

'Hello?' Rosie is waving her hands above her head, as if she were calling to shore for rescue. 'Am I on mute? I asked what time our sister is arriving?'

She looks pointedly at Phoebe. Phoebe shrugs at her, crinkles her nose. Rosie shakes her head.

'Mike?'

By his calculations, Emma will have just collected the car at the hire place.

'Your dad had that flight scan thingy up on his laptop in the kitchen. Said she was flying over Iceland about –' he looks at the giant face of his watch '– three hours ago. So she shouldn't be that far off. Hour and a half?'

'The waiting is stressing me out.'

Rosie disappears into the garage.

Michael looks at Phoebe. She has her eyes closed, her nose nuzzled in their son's hair.

'You okay, Roberts?'

She opens her eyes and smiles at him.

'It's Mum's day.'

'Yes, today is about Mary. It is Mary's special day.' He says it rote, his voice robotic, moving his arms mechanically up and down like an android, the same way they have been saying it to each other for months in the safety of their own home.

'Watch it, Regis.'

She smiles at him, her eyes sparkling.

Rosie appears from the garage carrying a stepladder and thumps it down on the grass next to him with a crash.

'Actually, Mike, why aren't you helping Dad with the pig?'

Rosie's head is on a tilt.

'Mary asked me to do the lights.'

She purses her lips, raises her eyebrows.

'I can put you a string up while I'm at it, if you like. Hanging down from the tree, one at each end of the table so you can hang the bunting evenly?'

'Thank you.'

Rosie melts into a smile. If only forgiveness for all his sins could be so easily gained.

With a clunk, Rosie loads a tape into the stereo. It whirs into action as she presses 'play'. A brief moment of static and then an electronic piano.

'Do we have to listen to old people's music? We'll be subjected to enough of it tonight.'

'Phoebs, you know we are the old people now, right?'

Rosie saunters towards the table, trailing the little embroidered flags behind her, and sits on one of the ratty cane chairs. She leans back and stretches her legs out, wriggling her bare feet against the dry grass. She works along the string of the bunting, her fingers moving deftly, then she raises it to her mouth, tugs at the string with her teeth.

'Anyway, it's Paul Simon. Weren't you waxing lyrical about Paul Simon last night, Michael?'

'I was just saying I associate him with this house. Paul Simon. Prince. Fleetwood Mac. Rolling Stones, when your dad was around, and, actually, The Libertines. If I hear any of them, I think of this place, and everyone shouting over each other as music played in the background.'

Phoebe and Rosie both laugh.

'What's that quote Mary says, Phoebs? Something about the gift to see ourselves as others see us.'

'It's Burns. "To a Louse". "Oh wad some Power the giftie gie us, to see oursels as ithers see us."' Phoebe's Scottish accent is appalling.

'What must you have thought when you first came here, Michael?'

'I can't really remember.' He climbs the ladder and lifts the festoons to cable-tie them to the branch. 'It was a long time ago.'

And it was, a long time ago. A lifetime ago. But he does remember.

Eight

Michael had been waiting over an hour by the time he heard the rattle of the engine. A noise he could have identified blindfold as Phoebe's Fiesta. She beeped the horn and leaned out of the window.

'Oi! Oi! Don't get many of you to the pound!'

Phoebe was in her habitual black, but she looked different. Her hair was tied up – which was unusual – and her skin looked strangely shiny and clean, as if she'd been scrubbed. But that wasn't it.

'Where the hell have you been?' He hoisted his bag onto his shoulder.

'Apologies, your highness, but I had a late one and forgot to plug my phone in. You're lucky that Mum likes to play the radio at around 1000 decibels, or I wouldn't be here now.'

He shoved his rucksack onto the back seat and walked around the car.

It had only been a week or so since he'd last been a passenger in this car, but the seat had already been moved. He fumbled around beneath it and managed to push it back so his knees were no longer around his ears. He held up his mobile.

'Well, even if you'd charged your phone it would have been pointless – the reception is non-existent. Not a single bar!'

'Ah, you see, we only use them there things for playin' Snake 'round these parts.'

He laughed. It might've been his first trip to Suffolk, but even he could hear that her accent was appalling. Phoebe took a final drag on her rollie, then stubbed it out into the overflowing ashtray and put the car into gear.

'Well, I hope you're ready for this, Regis. It's the whole circus, you know. Even the Ringmaster's coming to town.'

'Ah, Richard Roberts, my biggest fan.'

She winked at him as she shoved the car up a gear and he realised that the reason she looked different was that she wasn't wearing any eye make-up. Then she pulled away from the station, the wheels skidding on the loose asphalt as she accelerated too fast.

He hadn't been this far east before. He'd been north, when he did the Duke of Edinburgh awards, and he'd been south to Brighton a few times with his nan, and he'd been to Bristol for the Summer School, but until today he'd never been further east than Cambridge.

On the train, he'd watched the landscape change. The city dissolved fast enough, and then soon after, there was a name he recognised – Colchester – he'd been there once on a school trip when they were studying the Romans. After that the land became waterlogged, and then, beyond Ipswich, it became more like the countryside he'd imagined he was headed for. The fields spread from the side of the tracks, gold and green flashing past the windows.

He assumed that Phoebe was driving him through farmland now too, it certainly smelled like it, but he couldn't see over the hedges that bordered each side of the road. Phoebe was speeding, as usual, singing along to Eminem, getting almost every word wrong. All he could see through the dirty windscreen was the blue sky, where the road met in a point of perspective ahead. The multicoloured flowers on the overgrown verges to either side became smears of white, green and red as they passed.

The animal stench got stronger. It seemed to be lodged in his throat. Farmyard smells were to be expected out in the country, but this was overwhelming.

'What is that smell?'

Phoebe inhaled and exhaled performatively.

'That, my friend, is the smell of my childhood. Breathe it in! The Countryside.'

She inhaled and started to sing in a vibrato baritone.

'And did those feet in ancient time . . .'

'Jerusalem'. With Marshall Mathers III providing the backing track.

He thought it was a joke when Phoebe pulled up outside the house. But then she turned into a gravel path alongside the house and onto a square of tarmac, surrounded by tall hedges. There, parked already, was an Audi A4 and a Toyota that he immediately recognised as Phoebe's mum's from the time she gave him a lift across Cambridge.

So it wasn't a joke? This place was Phoebe's house? And Phoebe's house had a car park?

She reversed into the space between the two stationary cars and cut the engine, then made a sweeping gesture towards the house in front of them.

'Home Sweet Home.'

It was massive. A big grey house like the ones Inspector Morse went to, to arrest murderous Oxford dons.

'Regis? You look like you want to run.'

Phoebe, her door open, her foot already out of the car, was twisted in the seat, her sunglasses on the end of her nose, watching him.

'Phoebs, I thought you said you were "scraping at middle class"?'

She wrinkled her nose.

'Erm, you grew up in a mansion?'

'Oh shut up Regis.'

She rolled her eyes and shook her head, but he could see a blush starting to creep up her neck.

'It's really not that big when you're inside. There aren't even enough bedrooms when people come to stay now Mum's commandeered the guest room as her "studio". You're going to be on the sofa. Anyway, it's my parents' house, not mine, and they bought it in the eighties, so it probably cost them about as much as this piece of shit car cost me.'

She got out of the driver's seat and slammed the door and was stalking past the car, along the side of the house.

'We're back!' She walked towards the house, twizzling her keys on her forefinger, then stopped and looked back at him. 'Well chop chop Regis, we're catching a ferry in twenty-four hours.'

He followed Phoebe through a door at the side of the house, with peeling paint and a cat flap that looked big enough for a child to make an escape through.

It was a small room, a utility, alive with the sound of washing clothes. The tumble dryer gave the space a humid quality that instantly made him feel claustrophobic – there was barely room for the two of them – particularly as he couldn't turn, thanks to his backpack. He was so close to Phoebe that he could smell the trace of *Golden Virginia* and *Herbal Essence* that he had come to recognise as her scent, over the powerful washing powder smell that pervaded the room.

Phoebe dropped down to sit on a plastic foot stool, pulling at the laces of her *DMs*. Then she chucked them onto a pile of miscellaneous battered footwear in front of what seemed to be some sort of filing cabinet, repurposed for storing shoes.

'Just dump your stuff.' She was shouting to be heard above the spin cycle of the washing machine. She turned and walked away from him, continuing to shout. 'Hello? Mum? Emma? Anyone? Mum, where are you?'

He took off his backpack and placed it next to the rattling washing machine. Then he unlaced his shoes and placed them together, neatly, next to the piles of sandals and trainers. He turned to close the door and discovered the reason it had been unable to open fully: coats. Seemingly hundreds of them, hanging one over the other, defying the laws of physics, and sense.

There was no sign of Phoebe in the kitchen.

A kettle on the stove top started to whistle and he grabbed a tea towel from the bar in front of the hob and took it off the heat. He spent a few seconds searching for the knob to turn the cooker off, before realising that it was some sort of old-fashioned oven where you just closed the lid.

It was a lovely kitchen. A long room, with cupboards along one side, and work surfaces the other. It smelled of spices and cooking and the same lemon-scented cleaner his nan used in a kitchen that was quite a lot smaller than this one. There was a mound of foam in the washing-up bowl, and beneath the drama that was booming out of the radio on the windowsill, was the drone of a dishwasher, presumably hidden behind one of the cupboard doors.

He poked his head through the double doors on the left, into a dining room – the table piled high with papers and books – and then walked through into the light of a conservatory. Here, there were more newspapers, folded on the glass-topped table and in several stacks on the windowsills, between bottles of sun cream and desiccated flies.

He walked to the open doors and looked out into the garden. There was a patio, paved in a sort of brick parquet, and then some raised planters, filled with purple flowers. Beyond, was a great expanse of lawn, and beyond that a field with neat rows of small green plants, spaced evenly in furrows that seemed to converge as they neared the horizon. Above the fields, a great expanse of perfectly blue sky.

He inhaled, filling his lungs. It no longer smelled like a farmyard, but of lavender and freshly cut grass. This was what he had been expecting.

His eye was drawn then, to a movement, the shift of something in the shadow beneath the tree. It was difficult to see because the sun was reflecting on the pond beside it, so he put his hand above his eyes to shade them and squinted. It was a woman. A blonde woman. A blonde wearing very few clothes.

'Do you want to borrow some binoculars?'

Her voice made him jump, but he tried to hide it. He swung around, his eyes wide.

'Nice garden, Roberts.'

'Yeah, I guess. If you like that sort of thing. I refer to both the blonde and the dahlias.'

He could feel his face burning.

'Michael!' Phoebe's mum, Mary, appeared in the conservatory too, arms outstretched. She was smiling, her lips a shiny shade of pink that matched her dress. He noticed, as she leaned in to hug him, a smear of the same colour on one of her front teeth. She held him at arm's length, appraising him.

'I'm so pleased you could make the party. Everyone's so keen to meet you properly before the two of you go off adventuring.'

She hugged him again.

Phoebe, smiling at him over her shoulder, rolled her eyes.

'Mum – you're freaking him out. It's not a party. Just dinner. You know. For my birthday. Mum is big on birthdays.'

'You are only nineteen once, Phoebe.'

Mary looped her arm around Phoebe's neck and kissed her ear. Phoebe shrugged and stuck her tongue out, but – he noticed – she stayed in the crook of her mother's arm.

'I put the kettle on. Thought you'd want a cuppa after your journey. Or is it too hot for tea, for you? Em's made some iced stuff, I think. But I'm for a brew myself. We'd drink tea in a sauna in Glasgow.'

'Tea would be lovely, Mrs Roberts. Thank you very much.'

'Oh gosh. Mary – please. I didn't like being called Mrs Roberts even when I was married to Phoebe's father.'

'Oh, sorry. I didn't realise you'd changed—'

'She hasn't.' Phoebe waved her hand in front of her face, batting away his embarrassment.

'My subtle way of letting you know I'm single, Michael.' Mary winked and gave Phoebe a nudge with her elbow.

'Honestly, Mother.'

'Well, Phoebe, you aren't the only one who can see how handsome Michael is, you know?' Phoebe made a swipe at her mum and Mary laughed, a surprising sort of squawk, just like Phoebe's. 'Right, three teas.' She backed away from them, into the kitchen.

'Ugh, I need a smoke already. Shall we "take a walk"?'

Phoebe stepped out of the conservatory, onto the patio.

'Oh, my shoes.'

'You and those bloody shoes—' She stopped herself, smiled at him, then pointed to a pair of shoes that looked like cut-down wellies. 'Just put on Dad's garden shoes, we won't be long.'

He slid his feet into the rubber shoes, his heels hanging over the ends.

'They're a bit small, Phoebs.'

'Ah, stop moaning.'

She picked one of the purple flowers from the edge of the patio and brought it up to her nose, closing her eyes. He quickly discovered the shoes were pretty uncomfortable to walk in, and a shriek of laughter pierced the air.

'You don't have to walk on tiptoes! You look like you're about to dance *Swan Lake*!'

And with that, he brought his arms above his head, rising onto his tiptoes and spinning in a perfect pirouette.

Phoebe's laughter morphed then, from the bird-like shriek into the laugh that he loved, one where the sound left and she was just shaking silently, her face contorted with unbridled mirth, and then he laughed too as she took his arm and led him down the garden.

'This, as you can see, is my sister.' Phoebe extended her arm to indicate the girl in the pink bikini beneath the tree. 'Emmaline. Emma. Em.'

'Hello Emmaline Emma Em. I'm Michael.' He put his hand up to shade his eyes so he could see her face.

'Hello.'

The girl raised herself on her elbow and lifted her sunglasses onto her head. She looked just like Phoebe. Phoebe, but with long blonde hair and – although he was doing his absolute best not to look at it – the sort of body he'd only seen on the cover of *FHM*.

'Okay, so you've met. Come on, I'll show you the escape routes.'

She tugged at his arm and he raised his eyebrows in apology to Emma, before following Phoebe up the garden, out of the gate and onto a dirt path that ran along the edge of the field.

Phoebe showed him around the village.

'This is where I smoked my first cigarette.'

'This is where I kissed my first girl.'

'This is where I let sexy Peter Follen finger me.'

'Phoebe!'

'Don't be a prude, Regis.'

'This is where I lost my virginity.'

'In a graveyard?'

'Yes.'

They smoked a joint lying on the grass near the children's swings, and then, without warning, Phoebe snatched the rubber shoes from his feet and hurled them over a fence, into someone's garden. He had to walk all the way back to the house barefoot, the pair of them bent over double in hysterics, laughing about absolutely nothing.

He wasn't sure if it was the effect of the weed, or if it was due to every room being so crowded, with both possessions and people, but already the house seemed smaller to him than when he'd first encountered it.

He followed Phoebe into the kitchen again, where she pointed out the noticeboard. Beneath the newspaper clippings and postcards of recent years, edges of children's paintings were visible, despite being produced by Phoebe and her sisters long ago. He'd been lucky if his nan had kept any of his creations stuck to the fridge for longer than a week.

He met the kittens. Garfield, a tiny ball of ginger fur, and Lasagne, a tabby with white paws, wrapped themselves around Phoebe's ankles, mewling for food.

'Shoo.' Phoebe pushed the insistent kittens away from her with the side of her foot. 'Mum says she got them cos she's sick of foxes getting the chickens. But I think they're her replacement children. In preparation for Rosie's departure.'

She led him through to the dining room – now strung with multicoloured bunting – where a pretty girl with a mass of ringlets was blowing up balloons.

'You're not supposed to come in here, Phoebe!'

'I'll act surprised. Rosie, this is Michael.'

She hugged him so tightly that he found himself blushing again.

'Michael! I've heard so much about you! I'm Phoebe's little sister.'

'Half.'

'Phoebe's little half-sister.'

She cleared her throat and then smiled broadly and touched his arm as she apologised for not coming to see the play.

'I was a total hermit during my exams.'

'Swot.'

'You might be able to breeze straight As on three hours' sleep Phoebs, but most of us need to revise. Anyway, I was gutted; *Hamlet*'s my favourite. So, I'm told you live in Clapham?'

Rosie's questioning was lengthy, but he was gratified to deduce from the specificity of the questions that Phoebe had indeed been talking about him in rather a lot of detail.

Phoebe showed him the lounge, the walls covered in framed artwork that could possibly have been the Roberts' girls' masterpieces too. There was a wall of books, a record player with shelves of vinyl above it but, looking around, he realised he couldn't see a TV.

'Where's the telly?'

'Oh mostly after dinner we play bridge, or Ma-ma plays the piano and we all sing.'

He wasn't quite sure whether to believe her, even though she was doing a posh voice – but then she pointed a remote control above the fireplace and a huge wall-mounted screen came to life.

'Dad bought it so he can watch the cricket when he's here.'

Phoebe sat on the sofa, then swivelled to lie on it. Her T-shirt caught as she did so, and revealed a section of her midriff. He looked back to the TV where the muted news showed Roman Abramovich shaking hands with some men in suits.

'You'll probably sleep here. Depending on whether Dad is drinking. If he isn't, then he'll probably want to get back to London and you'll be able to take the fold-out in the office.'

She indicated a door with a glass panel at the end of the room.

She showed him the downstairs loo.

'Check it out: Cringe Central.'

He stepped into the tiny pea-green room and saw that the multiple frames adorning the walls were all for awards and prizes, from swimming to full attendance.

'Dad started it when the paper won the BPA. But, as you can see, after he left, Mum continued the tradition. Most of them are Emma's because she's a competitive arsehole. But who knows, maybe one day, if I apply myself, I'll get my own bog full of dusty awards too.'

She stood at the bottom of the stairs and pointed in a circular motion above her head.

'Mum, Em, Rosie, Me, Mum's studio-slash-junk-room-you-can-barely-open-the-door-to, and the bathroom,' she said, then she looked at her watch. 'Right, shall we have a drink on the patio, before we get changed for dinner?'

And again, he found himself wondering if he'd somehow wandered into a Noel Coward play.

It was starting to get dark before dinner was mentioned, and he was so hungry that he was beginning to get anxious. He was fairly inebriated too.

After the joint, they'd had a gin and tonic, just him and Phoebe in the late afternoon sun, laughing as she told him stories about growing up in this house. How she'd once tried to climb down the wisteria to escape being confined to her room and pulled the entire thing clean off the wall. How Emma had once nearly drowned in the pond 'like Ophelia' because she was trying to save a shoe from the weedy depths. At which point, Emma, who was making her way to the house, still in her bikini, wrapped her arms around Phoebe's shoulders and informed him that another way to frame the story would be that she had nearly drowned because Phoebe had thrown her shoe into the pond and screamed until she went in to fish it out.

'So it's a habit?'

And Phoebe had stuck her tongue out at him and Emma had kissed the top of Phoebe's head and wandered into the conservatory.

Then Mary joined them. She made them cocktails: some disgusting red Italian spirit that she mixed with ice and fizzy water. It was bitter and fruity and the way it settled in his stomach reminded him of the time he'd tried to drink an entire bottle of squeezy lemon juice to try and impress his sister's mates. It was at that point that the Lizzie and Iain, about whom he had heard so much, turned up. She had cropped red hair and an incredible smile, he had a strong Scottish accent and a very firm handshake. They both had incredible tans and a couple of bottles of sparkling wine, all of which had recently arrived from the Amalfi coast. After a flurry of cheek kissing and hugs, they sat down and started firing questions at him.

Mary disappeared into the house, and the radio – which he realised had been on ever since he arrived – changed to music, a song he quickly recognised as early Prince. She returned to them with a tray of champagne flutes and Rosie carrying a selection of little bowls filled with nuts and olives and little cracker things.

'Something to put us on.'

That was when they all turned their heads at the sound of a loud motor and the spray of gravel behind the hedges.

'Great.'

'Great.'

Phoebe and Emma seemed to speak in unison.

'Behave.' Mary pointedly tilted her prosecco towards each of them.

Phoebe's dad emerged through the hedge, his Ray-Bans on top of his head, carrying a clanking Waitrose bag.

'Happy Birthday, Button!'

That was when things started to get confusing.

'There is some animal testing. It's unavoidable.'

'The thing about Blair . . .'

'It's barbaric.'

'So you live with your grandmother, is that right?'

'Mostly mice and rats.'

'My sister and I have lived with Nan since we were two.'

'We've got forty minutes to make the connection in Paris. Which means running for the Metro or Dad slipping me twenty quid so we can get a taxi.'

'Top up?'

'It's the dogs and monkeys people really get excited about.'

'Try and stop me!'

'Why is it always me? Why not your mother?'

'Yeah. Just my nan.'

'It's science.'

'So, have you got your eyes firmly set on the stage?'

'If I had to choose between Liz and a dog, I'd choose the dog.'

'She must be very proud of you.'

'You've caught the sun, Bunny. Suits you.'

'And that's why you've always been my favourite.'

'Would you like to be on *EastEnders*?'

Everyone seemed to be having two conversations at once.

An argument then, about whether it was in France or Italy that Emma had fallen asleep in the sun and ended up in hospital, which merged into a debate about the success of *The Da Vinci Code*. Thankfully, just as he wondered if fists were going to be thrown, Phoebe's gran, Irene, arrived. She appeared, heavily made-up and on the arm of a man who looked to be around half her age and who Phoebe and Emma seemed to have a prearranged agreement to call 'Grandad' at every opportunity, much to his embarrassment.

'Stop it you two.' He only heard Mary whispering it to them because he was sitting between them.

Quickly, the conversation moved back into a confusing jumble. Iain decrying the commercialisation of Glastonbury to the unlikely audience of Irene.

'Showers, Irene! Showers!'

Rosie telling Liz her plans for October.

'If I get what I need, then I'm hoping, Glasgow.'

Irene's boyfriend was talking about the development of the old livestock market into shops.

'There'll be something for everyone. You young ladies might be interested to know that The Top Shop has secured a unit.'

A comment that didn't seem to warrant the gales of laughter it received.

At the same time, Richard was giving Emma his review of Beyoncé's first solo album.

'I hope it doesn't mean the end for Destiny's Child, that's all I'm saying!'

It was chaos. Glorious, loud, confusing chaos.

He knew that it was partly to do with having eaten nothing but breadsticks and a few olives since the can of chocolate Nurishment he'd had on the train, but at that moment, listening to the raised voices and laughter, he wasn't sure when he'd ever felt so happy, so at home.

After dinner, they all sat at the table, drinking coffee – black from the cafetière with little uneven brown sugar lumps straight from the box – watching as Phoebe opened her cards and presents. He rarely got gifts from his nan that weren't clothes he'd asked for, or the money to buy them. And he found he was enjoying himself. There was a ceremony to it that appealed to his sense of the theatrical; the way the carefully wrapped parcels were presented to Phoebe, how she opened each one as they all watched expectantly, the expressions of surprise and delight from both Phoebe and the onlookers as she unwrapped variously a library of Harold Pinter plays, a *MAC* lipstick, a jeroboam of Prosecco and a stack of CDs, some camping cutlery that slotted together, a dress, a shirt, a pair of trousers, all black, a gold 'P' on a thin chain necklace – that he noticed was the same as the 'E' around Emma's neck – and, somewhat incredibly, a brand new laptop. Finally, Phoebe held up two crisp ten-pound notes that had fallen out of the card she'd just opened.

If he could pinpoint it, he'd say that was the moment things started to go a bit south.

'You can use that to buy me a new pair of gardening shoes!'

'Shut up, Dad. Thank you, Granny.'

'Your mother said I should get you euros for your trip. But it was like they were queuing for rations in the post office, so I didn't bother.'

'I really am sorry about your shoes, Mr Roberts. I'll happily replace them.'

'No you won't, Mike.' He could feel the warmth of Phoebe's hand on his back, through his shirt. 'Dad, get over it.'

He knew Richard Roberts wasn't his greatest fan, ever since he insisted on paying for his own meal when they went for dinner after *Hamlet*, but now he was in danger of forever being labelled 'the shoe thief'.

'Dad's perfectly entitled to be annoyed that you lost his shoes, Phoebe.'

'We didn't lose them, Emma. I threw them into somebody's garden.'

Mortifying.

'Erm, Granny?' Emma leaned across Michael to pick up the birthday card. She was wearing a very strong perfume. '*Who's* your favourite?'

To my favourite Granddaughter the card said in a gold swirl on the front.

'Oh, it's all I had in my drawer. I think I must have bought it for your twenty-first Emmaline.'

'Okay.' Mary quickly stood up. 'Shall we do cake in the living room?'

It must have been somewhere between the dining room and the lounge that Iraq was mentioned. He didn't hear who'd brought it up, because he was helping Mary and Liz to load the dishwasher, an activity that involved a lot of laughing. But, as he followed Mary into the lounge, he realised the voices that they'd heard over the frenetic music that was playing, really rather loudly, were not raised in mirth, but anger.

In the ten months he'd known her, he'd seen Phoebe get annoyed on several occasions. He'd seen her debating in the pub, and telling drunk men at gigs to keep their hands to themselves, and, having walked alongside her in the sea of protesters moving along Piccadilly in February, he knew how strongly she felt about the war. He hadn't, however, seen her this angry, this out of control.

She looked crazed. She was pulling at her hair with frustration, her eyes wet, her face covered in smears of black mascara.

'You can't believe that!' Phoebe's voice was higher in pitch than he'd ever heard it. In the background, Pete Doherty and Carl Barât were still singing. 'You think we should just shrug and let him get on with it?'

Emma, in complete contrast to Phoebe, seemed quite calm.

'It's just my opinion, Phoebs. I don't know why you take it so personally.'

'Politics is personal.'

As she gesticulated, her wine was sloshing onto the patterned rug that stretched the length of the room.

'You should be able to have a debate without getting so het up. Aren't you learning anything at Cambridge?'

Phoebe let out a scream of indignation.

'All right, all right! Enough!'

Mary was beside him, putting the tray of cake down on the coffee table, gesturing for Liz to turn off the music. The Libertines were silenced and, though the shouting continued momentarily, it quickly silenced at the high-pitched whistle that Mary emitted, her fingers in the corners of her mouth, almost deafening him.

'Right. No more politics. At least not until after I've gone to bed.'

And, surprisingly, that seemed to be that.

Michael felt unsure if he should check in to see if Phoebe was okay, but by the time they'd sung and she'd blown out her candles and he'd handed out the slices of chocolate cake that Mary had plated for everyone, he saw that Phoebe seemed to be fine. In fact, she was laughing at a story her father was telling about when he and Lizzie were at school together. She was sitting next to Emma, who was laughing too. Her face still bore the marks of upset from just moments before – her eyes blood-shot and glassy from the tears that had smudged her make-up – but they were sitting quite calmly next to one another, eating their slices of cake with one hand, their other hands inter-twined, resting on the sofa between them, the gold of their matching necklaces glinting around their necks.

Nine

Mary unhooks the bucket from her arm and places it on the table with a slosh. A blaze of yellow. The dappled saucer-faces of three dozen sunflowers shuddering as the table continues to vibrate from the impact of the bucket.

'They're gorgeous, Mum.'

'Wow, Mary!'

She rubs at the inside of her elbow, where the handle of the bucket has been digging in, enjoying the gentle thrill that comes from the girls' admiration of the flowers.

'From seed.'

She'd started growing them in April. A bit late, but she didn't want them to flower too early. It was an act of faith, a request to the universe, God, that this year, this time, the wedding was actually going to happen.

She sowed a single seed to each little terracotta pot. Forty of them. They took up the entire length of the windowsills in the kitchen and the conservatory. Each morning she inspected them as she waited for the kettle to boil. Every time she was at the sink – washing dishes, filling a glass of water for Irene to take her pills – she would watch them, sometimes even talking to them, willing them on. Manifestation. That's what Emma called it, wasn't it? Mary's still got that sanctimonious little book she gave her in LA. The one, that – in its essence – told you that if you were unhappy, there was no one to blame but yourself.

But it was manifesting, wasn't it? To imagine something you want and then tend to your dream with careful, daily steps. That is what Mary felt she was doing for all those months she watered them and fed them and squirted them with her home-made garlic spray to keep the aphids off. All that time, she was anticipating that moment yesterday morning, not long after dawn, when she'd walked down the garden, taking her shears to the neat rows of stalks with their yellow frilled heads and cutting them, plunging them first into recently boiled water and then into cold, in the buckets they are in now.

She picks one out of the water. The thick, ridged stem is rough in her fingers and she turns it, considering the vivacity of it, the dense swirl of the seeds. Yes, she had manifested this. These sunflowers – and this day.

Mary places the sunflower back into the bucket, the bloom quickly losing its singularity and becoming part of the array of surprisingly varied shades of petals. She'd thought, when she planted them, that they were all the same. But as they grew, she recognised they were different, and then, just a few weeks ago when they started to flower, she'd been delighted to see that there were three different varieties. Two yellow ones and some of those fluffy teddy bear ones – just like in the Van Gogh.

Visiting those paintings were two of her favourite ever trips. Munich was much more interesting than she'd expected, and they'd had a couple of lovely meals. And Amsterdam, well, she's not sure she's ever laughed as much as that weekend in Amsterdam, and that was even before Lizzie talked her into visiting a coffee shop.

* * *

Mary places a hand to her chest.

Maybe one day, now the world has reopened, they'll visit the only version she hasn't seen yet, in Tokyo.

Maybe next year? A delayed honeymoon?

She's getting ahead of herself. Wedding first, honeymoon later. And for now, she has these sunflowers to deal with.

She considers the collection of glassware in the boxes before her. The vases are not quite a match for the painting, but they'll more than do. Plus, they match the drinking glasses she's dug out from the garage – which saved them a fair bit in hire costs. She casts her eyes over the plastic boxes filled with glasses. Immediately she can see a lipstick mark on the rim of one. When did they last use these? It must have been her sixtieth – that was the last party they'd had here in the garden because that was when the arsehole at number six had reported them for a disturbance of the peace. For years, they'd worried about how long it would take Emergency Services to reach the village – but the police had arrived not long after midnight. There hasn't been much cause to have any parties since – but it was a small joy to post a packet of earplugs through Number Six's door yesterday. She'd attached a Post-it with a flourish. *You'll need these on Saturday. We're having a big party – I'm getting married.*

She holds up the glass to the light, trying to discern the colour of the lipstick. It's hard to tell, it could be pink or red – surprising there's any pigment left in it at all after all this time. That was a great party. They'd hired a band – just some lads – the son of one of Lizzie's colleagues. She'd told him that Mary loved the Eurythmics – they'd laughed with delight, her and Liz, as they danced to the suited young lead singer giving Annie Lennox a run for her money on the high notes. The whole marquee had smelled of fresh mint. Phoebe and her girlfriend at the time came over from New York to run the bar, made mojitos till the police called time on the whole affair.

She looks up at the sky. Scanning for clouds. She's still a bit nervous about their decision to cancel the marquee for today. The forecast is adamant that there is no rain until next week at the earliest. But this odd humidity, this heavy air, is making her doubt it. It wouldn't be the first time they've got it wrong.

She is really sweating now and feels trussed up in this dressing gown. She darts a glance to the gap in the hedge to reassure herself that it is only Phoebe, Michael, Rosie, her sleeping mother-in-law and the cat who might see her, then pulls at the belt of her dressing gown, and quickly yanks it off, throws it over the piano stool.

'*Swit-swoo* Mum! Is that a new slip?'

Mary feels her irritation at Phoebe swell. Can't she have nice things? Why should the fact she's bought herself some new underwear be notable? Was there ever a bride who didn't consider what knickers were best to wear beneath her dress? She turns to her to say as much, but is distracted by Phoebe's feet.

'There my bloody sandals are! You can't leave things alone for one second with you about!'

She pulls out the chopping board and knife from the box and bashes them down onto the table. She sets about trimming the ends of the sunflowers, carefully arranging them in the vases.

Out of the corner of her eye, she sees a look pass between Phoebe and Michael. A shrug from Phoebe. A shake of the head from him in return. A surge of guilt rises in her chest. She needs to stick to her own rules. If she's expecting all of them to put much bigger issues aside so the day can be harmonious, then she should be able to navigate the irritation of Phoebe borrowing her battered old sandals.

'Sorry to snap. I fear my nerves might be getting the better of me.'

'You've nothing to be nervous about Mum.'

The music cuts out and there is a staccato drum roll that Mary immediately recognises as Paul Simon. The recording has a slightly elastic quality to it, as if the tape is warping in the heat, but it is more likely that it has been stretched by gravity and time, just like the skin on her soft bits.

Her last ever mixtape.

It's the one made for their drive up to Edinburgh for the Festival, to see Phoebe in that awful play with all the fake blood.

'If you're going to be the taxi driver, I'll be DJ.'

Mary wasn't sure she was up for a five-hour drive with Liz's music choices blaring out of the speakers. But, as it turned out, Cyndi Lauper had been as punk as her compilation got.

'I contain multitudes, Mary. Before I met Iain, I even owned some ABBA on vinyl.'

They'd walked up Arthur's Seat on that trip. It took them an age and they'd had to stop for a sit down several times on both their ascent and descent. But it had been worth it. To see that view. To see Lizzie smiling like that as they ate their reward Tunnock's, her face lit the colour of Turkish delight by the setting sun.

Mary closes her eyes.

She is struggling to place the song. Then the distinctive timbre of Paul Simon's voice triggers something.

'Leave Your Lover!'

She shouts it, as if she were on one of those interminable game shows that haunt her throughout the short daylight hours of winter, filtering through from the lounge where Irene sits, mostly asleep.

'*Fifty Ways To* Leave Your Lover.'

Michael's deep voice filters down through the willow branches, from where he stands at the top of the ladder.

He's right. She knows. And it's probably because she's so hot and sticky and nervous about everything, but something about it – his interference, his confidence, his just being there – snaps something in her. She wants to get rid of him, wants to send him away. Just for a bit, just until Emma arrives and settles in.

'Oh!' She brings her hands to her cheeks, then quickly drops them. She needs to be careful not to overplay it.

'What?' Rosie freezes, her arm in the air, passing Michael the next length of the festoon lights.

'The candles!' She carefully avoids Phoebe's eye. 'I've forgotten the candles!'

'What candles, Mum?'

'For the table! I meant to get some yellow candles yesterday in town, but then you arrived, Phoebe, and I had to sort the blow-up mattress and the cot, and your dad was fussing. Oh dear!'

'Is it something I can help with Mary?'

She feels a stab of guilt then, for her little plan. He's a good lad really, he'd probably absent himself if she asked him to. But Phoebe would never allow it. And so she perseveres.

'Oh, could you Michael? Would you mind popping to town? I've thirty lovely little storm vase holder things I ordered online. Thirty's quite a lot. But I did see the right colour in Waitrose and, even better, in that little shop with the plant pots in the window, next to the toy shop, opposite the new posh coffee place. I'll get you some cash. Or better to write down my PIN?'

'No, no, Mary.' He taps his back pocket then pulls out his wallet. 'I'll just grab my phone. Do we need anything else while I'm there?'

'Mum, don't you have, like, a drawer of candles in the dining room?'

'Not yellow candles, Phoebe. The plan has always been to have yellow, to match the sunflowers.'

'What about the lights?' Rosie is still holding the flex above her head, the bulbs hanging from it snaking into the grass. 'I thought you said you wanted it done by the time Emma arrived.'

'Oh, we'll cope with the lights, Rosie. Thank you, Michael, I don't think there's anything else we need.'

'Right then, see you in a bit.' He leans down and kisses Phoebe's hair, strokes the baby's head, then jogs into the house.

Phoebe is watching her, she can feel her gaze. She's always been able to read her like a book.

It's a good job she pushed the three boxes out of the way and into the top of her wardrobe last night. She thinks of the rows of dinner candles packed tightly inside them, the way the beautiful wax graduates from vivid yellow to deep, sunset orange. She ordered them at the same time as the holders, months ago, just the right height for the storm vases. She can just see them on the table, among the sunflowers. She can picture how, as the sun set, the glow of their flames would have thrown light on her guests, casting flickering shadows across the faces she's spent a lifetime loving. It's a sort of mourning, the loss of those candles – and the waste of the hours she spent trawling the Internet for them. But, it's worth it, just to get that man out of the way for an hour or so.

'Well, I guess that it's me putting up the bloody lights then. I better get some more cable ties.'

Out of the corner of her eye, Mary looks at Phoebe watching Rosie walk towards the garage. Phoebe is waiting to speak, Mary knows. And when Phoebe draws a breath, she knows that she is going to pass judgement, to say something she wouldn't in front of Rosie. Phoebe has been giving her unsolicited opinions ever since she could speak. She's even managed to find a way to turn it into a way of making money. The opinion columns. The memoir. Sometimes she'd happily pay Phoebe to keep her opinions to herself.

'Did you know that Dad's roped Danyal in to help with the pig? Classic Richard Roberts.'

Mary smiles brightly.

'Yes, nice to see them getting on.'

Not the response Phoebe was fishing for, she knows. But she is resolved not to get pulled into Phoebe's sniping about Richard. For all his failings she couldn't have done without him over the last few years; the least she can do is show him the respect of not talking about him behind his back.

'Do you think Dan'll be able to lift it? He's not exactly hench, is he? Not Rosie's usual type—'

Mary holds her palm out towards Phoebe to stop her.

'If you've got something to say about Rosie's lovely new boyfriend, Phoebe, say it to her face.'

'Mum I was just—'

'Well, don't "just"!'

'Sorry, Mum.'

She looks at Phoebe. There is a tension around her mouth that Mary recognises instantly. She couldn't bear tears, not before the party has even begun.

'That's okay, darling.'

The tape deck clicks and silence falls. Around them the birds call to each other, occasionally swooping through the garden. A blue tit hangs onto a branch of the willow, pecking at an insect. The sound of Michael's engine purring to life on the other side of the hedges is followed by the rattle of the gravel as he drives away.

Mary swallows and throws her arms open, extending them to the garden, to the tables, the chairs and smiles at Phoebe, a real smile this time.

'Exciting, isn't it? I can't tell you how excited I am. How grateful I am that I get to have you all together.'

'I'm glad to be here, Mum. We all are.'

She doesn't look at Phoebe, but concentrates on the flowers, placing them into the vase and shifting them so they sit evenly. She can feel, though, Phoebe still waiting to speak.

'Mum?'

'*Mmm-hmm*?' Mary still doesn't turn.

'Are we okay?'

Mary pauses and closes her eyes. Tightens her lips. The temptation to reply truthfully is strong.

'I don't think we need to bother with the spit roast, just put the pig in the garage. It's like a nuclear reactor in there.' Rosie emerges from the garage, walking backwards, unrolling an extension lead.

It is hardly an original observation. Ever since the children descended on the house, they've been arriving in one room or another making exaggerated metaphors about the heat, the mess. But rather than groan, or roll her eyes, or get annoyed, she grasps at Rosie's awful joke, as if it were a rope thrown down a ravine. Here is an opportunity to haul herself away from a conversation she doesn't want to continue.

She laughs. It sounds tinny, horribly fake.

'It'll be perfect later.' Mary fans herself.

'I'm glad it's going to be nice for you, Mum. But I've got to be honest, I'm starting to find this perpetual summer profoundly depressing.'

'I'll be interested to see what Em has to say about it. Even she will struggle to deny that it's normal for September—'

'Girls—'

Mary shoots a warning look towards them. Though it had occurred to her that it might be one of the trickier areas of conversation for them to navigate, on seeing the kitchen thermometer pushing 25 at ten this morning.

'Sorry.'

Phoebe mimes zipping her lips.

'I need Liz here to keep you all in line.'

Mary stops and places a hand to her chest. The feeling she has been working so hard to suppress all day spreads across her ribcage and threatens to constrict her throat.

'Nerves?'

She looks down at the chopping board and grips the handle of the knife a little harder. She can feel their eyes boring into her, but she keeps her own eyes trained on the stalk of the sunflower. She watches the knife slicing through the thick, sinuous stalk to reveal a fresh dappled green circle. She picks the flower up and drops it into one of the glass vases.

'A little. I'll admit I am ever so slightly nervous.'

Rosie's hand rests lightly on her back, her voice is close behind her.

'It's going to be okay, Mary. Everything is going to be okay.'

Ten

Mary inhaled suddenly and sat bolt upright in the empty bed.

Was she dreaming? Was it something from a dream that woke her?

No, it was that noise. Those birds in the garden. It was as though there was someone out there, laughing at her.

Yaakka, yakka, yakka.

Mary looked towards the window. The curtains gaped where she had yanked them shut before falling into bed, and she could see the sky starting to lighten. It was early, the cusp of night and day.

Richard wasn't beside her, so that made it a weekday. Yesterday was market day, because Irene had grudgingly delivered a striped carrier bag full of vegetables. That must mean it was Thursday today.

Thursday, one more day before Richard is home. One more day just her, alone with the baby.

She could do it. Just one more day.

She lay back down and looked up at the ceiling. She still hadn't managed to sort out a light shade for the bedroom. Just looking at the bare bulb hanging from its twisted flex makes her feel on edge, aware of the lists and lists of things they had to do before this house would feel truly theirs.

She cast her eyes over to the windows. The curtains that Richard brought back from Habitat looked so out of place. It was a lovely gesture though, uncharacteristically thoughtful, and they were exactly the sort of thing she'd have chosen herself. A plain, simple, brightly coloured geometric design that would look lovely when they'd repainted and ripped up this godawful carpet.

From the moment the estate agent had opened the front door to them, it was evident that the previous owners weren't afraid of experimental decor, but the master bedroom was particularly hideous.

'Blimey, you didn't say the house used to be owned by Barbara Cartland!'

Everything was pink. The carpets, the walls, the ceiling, even the skirting boards. She'd told Richard that if it was to be their bedroom then they had to redecorate it before they moved in or they might never get around to it. But then it had been a rush to move around Richard's work and the baby, and it was the only room with an en suite, and so here she was, a fully grown woman with a bedroom straight out of *Barbie Dreamhouse*.

Outside, she could hear an engine: the sound of a car approaching the house. It was still dark enough for the headlights to be on; she saw them swish across the curtains as the car turned into the lane. The hum of the motor got louder as it neared. It came to a pause on the road outside her bedroom window. She cocked her head, her heart lifting. Could it be Richard, surprising her with an early return? She held her breath, waiting for the sound of the gravel as the car turned into the drive. But then the engine turned over and it drove away. A bit early for nosey parkers. Must've been someone from the village trying to get a look at what they'd done with the old place as they passed on their way to work.

They'd barely made a dent in her plans for redecorating, but she'd happily have given anyone who was interested a tour, even if they were only coming to gawp. Honestly, at that point she'd have ushered in anyone who would have been willing to talk to her rather than scream at the top of their lungs.

Mary had been living in the village for nearly a month and she still hadn't met any of the neighbours. She'd said hello to a woman with a sleeping toddler in a pushchair when she was out trying to get Emma to settle, and she'd raised a hand to the odd silver-haired gardener tending their borders, but she hadn't got as far as asking anyone if she could borrow a cup of sugar. Yes, Lizzie and Iain were on the other side of the church – one of the deciding factors in their purchase – but they both worked during the day, and anyway, it would've been good to make some new friends. Maybe another new mum. She needed to make making friends a priority. She didn't want to end up like Irene.

It had taken Mary a while of living with her parents-in-law to realise that the few visitors to the house were there to see Bert; most were acquaintances from the Rotary Club, or people he'd invited in the name of business. If any women came to the house, they were always the invitee's wife or secretary. It was then that she realised that Irene's conversation was populated by people from the war, or before that in London, and every so often strangers that she thought scandalous or pitiful. Mary even found herself feeling a bit sorry for her. Imagine living in a place for more than thirty years and not really making any friends. She'd go mad if Richard was the only person she could have a proper conversation with. There's not a day goes by that she doesn't send up a little prayer of thanks for those pigs running into her and bringing Lizzie and Iain into her life.

Mary yawned and moved her head from side to side on the pillow, stretching out her neck.

At least if it was Thursday that meant the weekend was nigh. Yes, that brought with it the numbing routine of the roast at Irene's, but it also meant curry on Saturday night with Lizzie and Iain. No cooking all weekend. And she'd have two whole mornings where waking up would be entirely at her leisure while Richard tended to Emma's cry.

That was if her body would allow her to sleep. These frustrating wakeful mornings had become more and more frequent recently.

The birds in the garden chattered again and, softly behind it, she could hear the gentle rustle of the willow leaves, like a sigh. She held her breath and listened to it. Her tree; it even *sounded* beautiful.

Beyond it she could hear a distant engine: farm machinery working in a nearby field. There was the coo of wood pigeons, the occasional piercing squawk of a distant pheasant. Her ears tuned in to the sounds of the house then. Bubbles in the radiator on the landing. The drip of the tap in the bath. But no human sound. Just beautiful, glorious silence.

Next door Emma was asleep. Mary pictured her little face, twitching as she dreamed.

Dreams. How she missed dreams. You had to sleep, sleep deeply, in order to dream. But here she was, awake, once again.

Yakka, yakka, yakka, yakka.

She pulled back the duvet. She might as well get up.

She picked up the clock from the bedside table. It was less than three hours since she'd slid her feet out of the slippers she was ramming them into. The last alarm had been at 2 a.m.; the pre-emptive strike with a missile of milk.

It helped if she imagined it was a game. The baby was a little car. The game was never to let the tank run dry. It was her mission to do all she could to refill it in good time, to prevent a sputtering engine, at all costs.

She checked that she had set the travel alarm correctly when she'd fumbled with it in the semi-dark, and seeing she had, dropped the little clock into her pyjama pocket, and patted it gratefully. Her little ally.

She walked across the detested carpet over to her dressing table and appraised herself in the oval mirror.

She looked scunnered.

She squirted a glob of pink moisturiser from the uncapped bottle of Oil of Ulay and massaged it into her skin. Now, she looked knackered and moisturised. She picked up the lipstick that was lying, uncapped, next to it and touched it to her lips, rubbing them together before dotting it on her cheeks and pinching them. She smiled at her reflection, sighed and took a swig from the mug of cold tea that was nestled amongst her toiletries. Immediately she pulled a face and took a proper look in the cup: the surface of the tea was speckled with dust. How long had it been on the table? She paused for a second before draining the cup. She pulled her dressing gown from the landslide of clothes on the chair and left the room, swearing softly as she stubbed her toe on the pile of boxes by the door, still unpacked after the move.

She walked across the worn carpet of the landing slowly, running her hand along the wall, feeling the raised swirls of the wallpaper. Another job that lay ahead of her: stripping the hideous textured wallpapers. Most of the rooms had escaped this treatment, but the landing, the entrance and hallway, and the downstairs loo all had a psychedelic embossing that stood out in relief under the pea-green paint. There was something about the texture of it that fascinated her – she'd found that it was soothing to stroke – but if she looked at it too long it could make her feel a bit nauseous. She couldn't use the downstairs loo without keeping her eyes down, or a sort of rocking seasickness took hold. Though that could have been due to exhaustion.

She'd read an article while she was still living at Irene and Bert's, a study on the use of sleep deprivation as torture. How, if you deprived your body – your brain – of sleep, you started to lose all sense of reason. A healthy brain needed sufficient time in all the states of sleep to function. REM. NREM. Delta Waves, Theta Waves, Alpha Waves. 'Optimal cognitive function' the article had stated.

'Ha.' She'd said it out loud, without laughing. 'Ha. Ha. Ha.'

'I've asked before that you don't read at the dining table please, Mary.'

And she'd imagined tightly rolling the newspaper in her hands into a baton, standing, walking over to Irene, and bringing it down, heavily, upon her head. But then, the baby had called out and she'd stood, leaving the paper on the table, and when she'd returned, the article and the newspaper had disappeared.

No, she didn't miss living with Irene.

Mary walked along the landing towards her daughter's room. The 'nursery', the one room they had decorated. Simple, everything white, with a scattering of little yellow ducks printed on the curtains she'd stayed up until the wee hours sewing. The room looked out onto the back garden, and in the afternoon it got the beautiful reflected shimmer of the tree. The embroidered sign that Irene had made hung above the door. 'Emma' in blue cross stitch, purple wisteria, like the flowers that adorned the back of the house, coiling around the E.

She paused outside the door and considered pushing on it to widen the crack enough to peek into the room. She closed her eyes, listening.

It was a surprise to Mary, how often she felt the urge to check on her daughter's breathing. She knew, logically, that her constant checking wasn't prevention, but still she regularly found herself with a gently placed hand on the chest of her sleeping child, her own breath slowing as she acknowledged its rapid rise and fall.

She hadn't anticipated being the sort of mother who obsessed over such things. It's not as if she'd had much of a role model in her own mother. It's not as if she'd even been sure she wanted a baby at all. Maybe it was that: guilt. Maybe she was worried that, because she hadn't been sure about keeping her, that she might be punished by having her taken away? Or maybe it was because mothering took every ounce of her energy that she felt so possessive of her? So fearful that she might just stop . . . being? She couldn't rationalise it, she hadn't expected it, but she was so in love with this child that it scared her.

Mary quickly pinpointed the sound she was searching for, the rapid, soft inhale and exhale.

Exhaling herself, she pulled the door to.

Descending the stairs, she mentally ran through the day that lay ahead. She just needed to get to lunch time and then Irene would come to be with the baby for a while and she could do some washing. If only she could put Emma down for a few minutes without her screaming blue murder. Then maybe she would be less reliant on Irene. Maybe then she could even go longer than twenty-four hours without seeing her.

She knew she shouldn't have anything but kind thoughts towards Irene. God knows she couldn't have coped without her over the last four months. But, in her more frazzled moments she did reflect that when she signed the papers in the registry office, she had been agreeing to spend her life with Richard, not his mother.

'No one tells you you're marrying their family.'

It had become a bit of a routine to meet Liz in the library cafe on a Saturday morning, before her weekly market shop. Mary had laughed, and rocked the pram to and fro, enjoying the sideways looks that the patrons of surrounding tables cast their way as Liz blithely added more hot water to the stainless steel teapot

She'd got used to it now, the looks that came with spending time with someone who dressed like Liz, and she found she rather liked it. She felt that she was somehow subversive by association, and there was a thrill in it. It was even more exciting on the occasions that Iain joined them. It made her feel special, interesting, to be friends with people who stood out from the grey, conformist crowd. She revelled in the attention, the sly glances, the gaping mouths of those who stared so blatantly. In fact, the only reactions to Iain and Liz that Mary had been disappointed by were from Richard and, even more surprisingly, Irene.

For weeks, she'd been telling Richard about her 'new friends'. She rambled on about Lizzie and Iain, Iain and Liz. She'd felt like a schoolgirl with a crush, finding every opportunity to use their names. But she kept the details of their appearance close, held the tantalising particulars of their chosen attire to herself. 'Iain, my new friend Iain, he wears lipstick!' she wanted to blurt out over the kippers. 'Liz, my friend Lizzie, wears a bike chain as a necklace! An actual chain from a bike.' But she'd withheld it, for she discovered the real pleasure came from biting her tongue on the details and anticipating the shock she would witness on Richard's face when he discovered that she, Mary, who only occasionally wore a bit of mousse in her hair, had made friends with two real-life punk rockers.

She had been in her habitual position, pinned beneath the baby, on Irene's burgundy sofa, when the doorbell rang. Richard bounded to the door, and then, after a fumble of locks, the hallway filled with jovial exclamations.

'You didn't tell me that the Liz you've been banging on about was Elizabeth Dunn!' Richard turned back to Liz, who had entered the room behind him. 'Elizabeth bloody-brainbox Dunn!'

'Actually Rick, it's Lizzie King now.' Liz motioned to Iain, behind her, who was ducking as he entered the room in order to accommodate his hairstyle. 'My husband, Iain.'

Richard didn't so much as raise an eyebrow.

'Iain! Richard, Richard Roberts. A pleasure to meet you. Liz and I go way back. Don't let her tell you I broke her heart – it was quite the other way around.' Richard vigorously shook his hand then turned to the kitchen, raising his voice. 'Mum! Come and see who's come for tea. You won't believe it!'

So it was true, Mary thought – exchanging a look with Iain as Irene took Liz into an embrace – everyone really did know everyone around here.

It still wasn't quite light enough to see properly in the kitchen. It was one of the only rooms in this house that suffered from a lack of light. The windows faced the wrong direction for both the morning and the evening sun. Atmospheric in the evening, when the light of the setting sun filtered in from the conservatory, but not so ideal for early mornings. There'd be no sunny breakfasts in this kitchen, which is why she was petitioning Richard to install a patio in the front as well as one leading from the conservatory to the garden. She'd long wished for a home where she could read the supplements and eat hot toast with the sun on her face. Seeing as she couldn't do that in the kitchen, then May to September al fresco would have to do.

The fridge hummed in the corner, and from the utility room she could hear the whir of the boiler, the morning heating kicking on. She pulled her dressing gown tighter at the waist and flipped the light switch.

The chaos of the kitchen was illuminated: the crockery that she had used yesterday piled by the sink, cornflakes stuck to the sides of the bowl, smears of tomato sauce on the plate, several knives, a fork, two spoons piled on a chopping board coated in crumbs, a few mugs too, their insides darkened with the scum of undrunk tea. She'd have to wash up before Irene arrived, or face the silent judgement.

Mary squirted washing-up liquid into the bowl and turned the tap on, watching a heap of bubbles start to form. She fished in her pocket and checked the travel alarm, placing it on the windowsill behind the sink. According to the little red hand, she still had at least forty minutes until the next refill was due.

Forty whole minutes until she could wake her little Emma.

It washed over her again, that surprising sense of longing she felt for this baby that she also wished so often to be free of.

When she was with her, there was little she thought of other than getting away. She daydreamed about going shopping or to a museum or reading a book uninterrupted. But then, as soon as the baby was asleep, she wanted to pick her up, to squeeze her perfect soft legs, to smell her. That little being. This stranger who was now her constant companion. Her Emmaline, her Emma. Who was she? Who would she become?

Yaakka, yakka, yakkka.

Those birds again. It really did sound like laughter.

She pulled her hands from the suds and dried them on the sunflower print tea towel that Liz had given her as a house-warming gift.

She used her hip against the door to open it to the conservatory, the hinges creaking as it gave to her weight, and she squinted as she stepped into the light of the morning. She pulled her arms to her chest. It was a good few degrees cooler than the kitchen and her feet were immediately cold, even through her bed socks. She inhaled, a ripple of pleasure spreading across her collarbone.

Her garden.

The hope for the future that this expanse of grass and soil and water stirred in her.

The greenhouse that she would put over there. The flowers she would grow. The picnics they would eat – the three of them, sprawled on a tablecloth spread on the manicured lawn – laughing with Emma as she showed her knickers turning cartwheels on the grass. The tree. The pond. The lawn. The way it just seemed to keep going to the horizon, as if the tilled earth of the fields beyond the legal perimeter of their land belonged to them too.

She couldn't wait for the summer. She could just imagine sitting out there, feet up in the shade of the willow, a Campari and orange juice in her hand, watching a waving sea of wheat turn from gold to pink as the sun set.

Though they'd probably need to put a fence up, so Emma wouldn't venture off along the footpath, or worse, into the fields during the harvest. A little picket one would do the job, and it wouldn't spoil the view too much. She wouldn't be able to let her play out there unsupervised anyway; unless she gave way on fencing the pond off. Richard has already mooted filling it in, so she'd have to find a compromise before she woke up one Saturday to find him out there with a cement mixer. She would still have her bench though – fenced off or not. From the moment she saw the tree she could just see herself there, next to the pond, under the willow, sitting quietly with her thoughts and a book, looking up at the blue, blue sky filtered through the willow's criss-cross of branches.

The sky was quickly turning from navy to a pale delphinium blue. It was going to be another clear day. That was one of the things she loved about living in Suffolk, it was either raining or it was sunny. Those grey, weatherless days that she had grown used to in London rarely made an appearance here. Outside now, the morning mist had evaporated. The light was already filtering through the branches of the tree, skimming the water underneath. Glittering.

It was going to be a beautiful day.

Tea, she thought, and turned back into the kitchen to fill the kettle.

She scalded the teabag then added milk, removing the bag and cradling the cup in her palms, blowing on the tea to cool it. She looked towards the radio, contemplating switching it on. Despite longing for it in the interminable months when she was subjected to the constant noise of the local station at Irene's, Mary had become a bit wary of Radio 4. Though it provided company when she was ironing or folding the laundry on those long weeknights when Richard was away, she was finding it increasingly discombobulating. The routine of the baby and spending so much time with Irene, both of whom rarely looked further than their own immediate circumference, meant that the squabbles of Westminster were – for the most part – on the periphery of her awareness too. When she caught anything other than *The Archers* or *Book of the Week*, it could be a bit of a jolt to be pulled out of her swaddle, to be reminded that life was continuing out there without her.

It was on the radio, just a few days after her return from hospital, that she had first heard that Ronald Reagan had been elected President of the USA.

Mary had been lying in bed, feeding Emma. She could hear Richard singing to himself in the kitchen downstairs. Mary leaned over to turn on the radio. America had elected an ex actor as their president. She'd looked down at Emma – her little nostrils flaring slightly as she exhaled – and felt goose pimples rise along her forearms: what sort of a world had she brought this child into?

She took her tea into the conservatory and sat on one of her new peacock chairs. The rattan gave a little sigh as it took her weight. She let her head, her neck, relax against the high back, and raised her shoulders with pleasure. Lady Muck. That's what her dad would say if he could see her sipping her Earl Grey in her country house, surveying her garden, like someone out of a Forster novel. Well, he never would. James McDonald hadn't been south of the border since he was demobbed in '46. If his only daughter's wedding and the birth of his sole granddaughter wouldn't lure him, then a trip to inspect her new conservatory furniture was unlikely to.

Howard's End!

'Robert's End.' Her voice echoed into the quiet of the conservatory.

She wrinkled her nose. That wasn't right either. Sounded as if she was willing on Richard's death, or Irene's, or – she realised – her own.

Mary had been searching for a name for the house since they'd exchanged. It seemed preposterous that a house as big and imposing as this should only be known as Number 4, Mouser Lane.

Mouser's End?

She shook her head.

She would've liked to have gone for something with a Scottish inference, but she knew Richard wouldn't allow it. She'd had her heart set on *The Willows*, but then Richard had started saying 'Beep, Beep' whenever they drove up to the house and calling her 'Badger'. Maybe a literary reference wasn't totally ridiculous though; they were both English graduates, after all. She just needed to find the right one. It'd come to her.

A movement on the lawn caught her eye. A white and black bird. A magpie?

The bird seemed to be looking directly at her. Both its beady eyes, though on either side of its very slender head, appeared to be trained on her.

She stared back.

The bird opened its beak then and a cackle emerged. It seemed impossible that such a noise could come from such a small creature. The noise echoed from above. Mary's eyes searched the mass of bare branches studded with buds. Some were already starting to unfurl, a new year of greenery about to unravel. Among the new leaves, perched on the branches, sat several more birds. Magpies, she was sure now. She counted them. Seven. Six sitting on the branches. Two more on the grass. Eight for a wish.

She closed her eyes tightly and attempted to hold an image in her mind of this house. Not as it is – cold, quiet and horribly decorated – but as she longs for it to be. Full of life and friends and laughter.

Her ear was drawn to another sound then. The angry cough and splutter of a waking baby, swiftly followed by a piercing cry that seemed to penetrate her deepest thoughts and shatter them.

Mary sighed and pushed herself to stand.

'Coming Sweetheart, Mummy's here.'

And she hurried towards the scream of her baby echoing through her big empty house.

Eleven

Richard rounds the corner of the house from the patio and wipes his hands on his jeans.

He can smell it. The pig. It's all over him; the moisture it emitted.

His stomach rolls dangerously.

There'd been a couple of times – lifting the thing – that he'd thought it was going to happen, that he was actually going to be sick. He'd only stopped it by sheer force of will. At one point he had to gulp it down, the repulsive tide of half-digested breakfast that was rising in his throat. It was sheer determination that had stopped him heaving a soup of orange juice, coffee and masticated toast all over this new bloke of Rosie's.

It was all right for him, this Dan, he was used to prodding about with bodies.

Richard though, was increasingly finding meat – particularly the uncooked stuff – difficult to separate from what it once was.

It was hard to put a finger on when it had started happening.

He remembers a leg of lamb, the year before last, or maybe longer ago than that. He'd peeled the plastic off: all fine. He'd scored it with a knife, started tucking cloves of garlic into the meat, inserting the little spears of rosemary he'd pre-prepared. It was a routine he'd performed surely tens, if not hundreds, of times over the course of his life, but then he hooked his finger into the flesh to allow room to slide in the little bouquet of herbs and he saw it: an image of the animal in a field, its downy pelt still covering these muscles into which he'd stuck his knife. He saw it like a movie in his mind: a little lamb, running, gambolling. Then, he had a horrifyingly clear sense of the sinews of its joints, expanding and contracting. And then he actually thought he heard its bleat, its sweet little voice, calling out to its mother.

On that occasion – the last Easter there'd been more than the four of them – he'd feigned a bad tum to get out of eating it.

'Reflux. Too many chocolate eggs.'

Everyone had rolled their eyes, but that was just at him being a glutton. Since then it'd got progressively worse.

It was easier once it was cooked. If someone else cooks it then he can just about manage to close his mind to it. It was as frustrating as it was inconvenient, this new aversion to meat. He's spent his life eating the stuff, and he grew up in a market town with livestock auctions almost audible from their front doorstep twice a week.

When the kids were little, he always explained that pork was in fact pig, beef: cow, and happily fielded questions as to why chickens didn't deserve the same dignity as their mammalian cousins in being afforded an alternative title when they were no longer alive. He'd posed for photos eating a bloody burger during the Mad Cow crisis, for Christ's sake. But then, for some unknowable reason, everything changed.

He wonders if that isn't partly Mary's reason for choosing a hog roast today. She claimed it's for the spectacle of it, for the celebratory show, for the ease of feeding so many, and, she'd said, it's a nice little project for you. You said you wanted to help, she'd said, you did say you wanted to make a contribution, to do the food, as a gift, she'd said. I thought you'd enjoy the performance of it. And, I've always loved roast pork, she'd said.

There was something in the way she'd looked at him that told him it was a test.

She's done it a lot, over the years, set up these little traps. These games of chicken, where she's put him in a position that would push him to breaking point. Nearly always it resulted in his capitulation, and he would have to apologise, to grovel, to admit that yes, he was a hypocrite, yes, he was wrong, or yes, once again he'd been hiding something from her.

He understands. She's meting out punishment. And, honestly, he probably deserves it.

And so, when she asked for a hog on a spit, he'd set about it.

Every step of the process has been gruelling. The planning, the fitful hours lying awake, wondering whether he'd made the right decision, ordering it with the head on. Loading it into the boot of his car at the butcher's, the heft of it in his arms made him think of that film where Richard Gere had to dispose of the body of his wife's lover. And just now, the work of impaling it with the aid of Rosie's creepily polite, overdressed new boyfriend.

The effort of trying not to vomit when he saw the inside of its ribcage, gagging when he noted the absence of teeth as he forced the pole through its mouth, thinking of that nursery rhyme – wee, wee, wee, all the way home – as he turned the handle, set the coals, closed the lid of the roaster – all of it, all of it was penance.

His penance will never be complete.

He looks out across the garden now. Rosie is crossing the grass, carrying a tray of glasses, a big jug of lemonade balanced among them. Her long limbs glisten with recently applied sun cream as she walks.

She's so like her mother now. If he squints, he can imagine for a moment that it is Dee, standing there at the table in an ugly old bikini, pouring drinks, nodding along to – who is that? Paul Simon?

He hasn't listened to that album in years.

Richard puts a hand to his chest, then moves it to his forehead and runs his fingers through his hair, pushing it back, noting that it is damp at the temples.

It's so bloody hot.

Mary's got the right idea, in that floaty dress thing, under the shade of the tree. She looks quite girlish, her hair in rollers, her face without a scrap of make-up, fiddling about with the flowers.

Ta-ta sunflowers!

He saw her lopping them down yesterday morning through the open bathroom window. Then, as he was folding away his sofa bed, performing the daily transformation of his bedroom back to Mary's studio, he realised that he was beaming. Quite ridiculous, to hold a grudge against some flowers for monopolising Mary's time. Particularly when there are several *people* more deserving of his resentment. But each day – each hour – he's increasingly aware that the time he has to spend with her is trickling away.

He raises a hand to his Adam's apple and feels the bristles beneath his palm. He needs a wet shave; another thing to do before the ceremony.

As he walks across the patio he notices Phoebe, sitting in the shade. The baby in a little white vest asleep on her shoulder. Little Albie. His grandson. Phoebe and Michael's son.

His skin bristles at the very thought of Michael. Where is he? He hasn't seen hide nor hair of him for hours. He is supposed to be out here, helping Mary with the decorating, and he'd also said he'd set up the disco stuff. Probably off for another of his runs, flashing his muscles around the village, hoping that a paparazzo'll jump out and 'catch him unawares'. He swears the vanity of the man has increased exponentially with his success.

Well, at least the fool has given him his little chicken. His joy! He scans the garden for Clara, then checks his watch. Nap time. Not for much longer though, soon he'll be able to nip in and wake her up. That's his favourite bit, when she's all groggy and cuddly.

His mother is napping too, he sees. Asleep in the armchair he heaved outside this morning.

It's strange to see the contents of the house spread across the lawn like this. It'll be stranger still to see them packed away into the lorries next week. Each item a moment in their lives.

It'll be forty-five years in September. Forty-five years since he sat down in that Cardiff pub and turned to see who that laugh belonged to.

Forty-five years.

'Pig's in!'

They all turn to look at him. Phoebe, frowning, brings her forefinger to her lips. His mother jolts in the armchair. She wakes up, sits up straight and catches her thumb to the side of her mouth, to clear the spittle.

He walks up to Mary and takes the almost empty glass from her hand. He drinks the remaining lemonade before refilling the glass from the jug on the table and emptying the glass again, gulping down the lemonade in one.

'Thirsty work that.'

He hits his chest and his oesophagus yields a satisfyingly prolonged burp.

'Poor piggy wig.' Rosie is pouting at the far end of the table.

'It was grown to be food, Petal.'

He can feel Mary watching him, her eyebrows raised. He avoids her gaze and fills another glass, takes it over to his mother.

'You should drink something, Mother. You'll shrivel up like a raisin if you don't.'

Irene takes the glass and sips it.

'Oh no, it's too sweet. I haven't held on to all my teeth to have them fall out because of a glass of pop.'

'Suit yourself.'

He takes the glass and drains it.

'Are we really still sharing glasses in this house? Yuck.'

Richard winks at Phoebe and she rolls her eyes at him, smiling.

'Where's Danyal?'

'Your boyfriend's gone to freshen up.' Richard smiles at Rosie as he refills his glass, the ice cubes jangling as he pours. 'I think he found working on the pig a bit . . . shall we say, strenuous?'

'Honestly Dad!'

Rosie turns towards the house, shaking her head as she walks away.

'He offered!'

'You're a shit, Dad.'

'I was open to offers. And he offered. Didn't hear your partner volunteering his services. He slithered out of it, didn't he?

'Mum *asked* Mike to go into town. I'm sure he'd have helped otherwise.'

'I didn't hear any of you feminists offering up your services, either.'

'I am looking after your grandson. I'd have happily helped were I not thus encumbered. Also, I don't identify as a feminist.'

'Yes. Well, it's quite some time since I tried to keep up with how you *identify*, my sweet.'

Mary catches his eye, a warning. And he nods, draws a breath, takes a mouthful of the ice at the bottom of his glass and crunches it.

'Dan's used to cutting up bodies, Phoebe. Surely that makes him the perfect man for the job?'

'I'm sorry, but if you're working on the premise that we're doing the jobs to which we're most suited, then choosing the vegan to aid in impaling a pig onto a spit makes little sense.'

'Well, he's going to help me with the salads now, so that'll make up for it. There'll be more cucumbers and peppers than he can shake his vegan stick at.'

'Richard.'

'You are a dick, Dad.'

'Any chance of getting a bit of respect around here, do you think?'

His question is met by a trill of laughter: the two of them, heads thrown back, laughing at him, united in their mirth.

He's aware then of the feeling he occasionally has, where he knows the power for the day to continue happily is entirely in his hands. The way he responds to their laughter – an obvious mark of disrespect in response to his request for the opposite – could make or break the whole day. Take it on the chin, and the day progresses: they continue the preparations; he goes to the kitchen and makes the salads, Mary and the kids finish up out here, then they all get ready, Emma arrives, and they all have a drink together, clink a glass before they trail off to the church, and then, this evening, they will drink and laugh and dance.

But, it could also go the other way.

He could do that. He has done it before. He has the power to destroy it all.

And right now, with Mary and Phoebe laughing like that, that is precisely what he wants to do. The desire to unleash chaos sits in his stomach like hunger. He wants to flip the table. He wants to ruin the wedding, he wants to wreck Mary's special day. He wants to tell his grown-up children, with their grown-up bloody partners, to go back to their own bloody houses. He wants to shout at Mary. He wants to throw this glass and smash it. He wants to say: I've changed my mind, you sanctimonious cow. Enough with the punishment. I had an affair. It was years ago! Get over it!

It's not like she's a bloody saint.

But he doesn't say any of this. Instead, Richard laughs.

He pushes them down, those horrible thoughts, and he joins in with them – his ex-wife and his daughter – and he laughs at himself.

'What's the big joke?' His mother's voice crackles, static on a poor line. She grunts with effort as she pushes herself forward and appears, from the depths of the armchair, peering around the corner of its wing.

'Granny! Did you have a nice sleep?' Phoebe's voice is still laced with mirth.

'I wasn't asleep, I just had my eyes closed. I'll be up in a minute. I'm not like these lazy folk who spend all day sitting around.'

'An attitude I haven't inherited. I bloody love sitting around.'

Richard pulls out one of the dining chairs from the table and leans back into it, folds his hands behind his head and angles his face towards the sun.

'Yes, well. The devil makes work for idle hands, Richard.'

Irene inhales sharply. Rubs at her thigh. Her skirt bunches up and Richard sees the crooked lump of his mother's knee. It reminds him of the pig: the transparent skin, the pale hairs, catching the light. He averts his eyes and tries to mask a shudder.

'This hip. I fell you know, Phoebe. I had to have an operation.'

Richard rolls his eyes at Mary. She keeps her face neutral and looks back towards the flowers.

'Yes. I know, Granny.'

'It gives me a lot of bother. I think it was better before the operation.'

'I don't think it was, Mother.'

Irene ignores his response and looks at the baby dozing on Phoebe's shoulder.

'Little Albie. Your grandad would have liked to have met him. Your grandad, my first husband, he was called Albert you know, Phoebe. He died just before you were born. I called him Bert. Albie is the same name isn't it? Albert, like your grandad.'

'What a coincidence!' Richard, his back to his mother, rolls his eyes at Phoebe.

'I named him after Grandad, Granny.'

'Did you? Oh! How nice.' Irene wets her lips. 'He was drunk when I met him, you know.'

'Explains a lot.' Mary's sotto comment goes unnoticed other than by Richard, who lets it work through him – with a thrill of disloyal glee – and settle about the corner of his lips in a momentary smirk.

'We were sweethearts, me and Bert. Just kids when we met. Like you and your Michael.'

Richard shares a glance over the table with Mary, and they both quickly avert their eyes, steering away from the rocks.

'I had a few foreign boyfriends too – you know, Phoebe – during the war. I've always been open-minded.'

'Granny, Michael's British.'

'Oh yes, I had a lot of boyfriends, from all over. I've been on "dates" too. You girls didn't invent them, though you like to think you did. Lots of boyfriends, before and after your grandad. We all did in the war.'

'Imagine if you'd married the Canadian one, Irene.' Richard recognises that Mary is feeding her a line, engaging his mother in one of their circular conversations. He wonders again at Mary's patience. He's watched her over the last few years: so easily, so patiently conversing with this woman, this stranger he barely recognises as the woman who brought him up .

'You'd have all been Canadians.'

'Doesn't quite work like that, Mother.'

'Well, you're the expert Richard. If anyone knows about having families all over the place, it's you.'

Richard's eyes dart to Mary. He could swear she is smirking, her head bowed.

This, he won't miss.

'It's all great expanses out there, plains and mountains, isn't it? I wouldn't have liked to have lived in Canada though, what with all the bears and wild animals. You probably have family there Mary. Do you know of any?'

'None that I'm aware of.'

'There are a lot of Scots in Canada. They went for the gold, you know. Always a nose for money, the Scots.'

It's Richard's turn to smirk now. Looking at Mary, he sees hers has been replaced by pursed lips.

'But I'm a townie, me, always have been. I don't like the countryside. Too many yokels. Everyone involved in each other's business. That's why I'm fine with this little plan you've all hatched, now I've got used to the idea. It's not been easy for me, living in the middle of the countryside, hardly able to walk anywhere. If I'd had my way, I'd have gone back to the East End after my Bert died, Phoebe. But, there was a call on me then, with you girls, your mother needed me. And then Richard having the affair and Rosie's mum doing herself in.' She pauses and closes her eyes. 'Yes, I always . . .' her voice trails off and she is still suddenly, as if the batteries have run down mid-sentence. But then she draws a breath. 'I won't come tonight. Thank you for the invitation though, Mary.' His mother's eyes are still closed.

'You're bloody coming, Mother.'

'For heaven's sake, Irene. It's here! The wedding party is here, in this garden! You live here.'

'Not for much longer. You're all packing me off. Excuse me if I don't feel like celebrating it.'

'Granny!'

'There's no need to shout at me.' She crosses her hands in her lap. 'I'll just have supper in my room.'

He watches. Mary draws a deep breath, her eyes closed. He is waiting, he realises, to see if Mary will break her own rules. But then she exhales, opens her eyes, nods to herself, and smiles as she picks up the chopping board, tipping it so the ends of the stems she has sliced from the sunflowers drop into the bucket with a splash.

'Please yourself, Irene. Nothing is going to spoil my day.'

She is still smiling as she picks up the bucket and walks into the house.

'Granny, you know it's more like a hotel than a home, and it's near Dad. You should think of it as that move back to London you've always wanted.'

'Don't pester me, Phoebe.'

'Oh, little fella's awake.' Richard moves to his daughter and scoops the child from her shoulder, bringing him expertly onto his own.

'You feeling all right about tonight, Button?'

'I hadn't really believed that she would come.' She scratches at a seam of dried milky vomit on her shoulder. 'She does know we're all here, doesn't she?'

'She does.'

Phoebe exhales heavily. She leans forward on the chair, resting her elbows on her knees, her hands cradling her forehead, rocking.

'It's not about you two tonight. It's not about you, or your sister, or Michael, or Rosie, or me.' He turns to Irene. 'And it's not even about you, Mother. It's about Mary.'

Phoebe folds forward, her head now wedged between her knees, her reply muffled through her hair and hands.

'I know, I know.'

From the house, a high-pitched screech pierces the air. Phoebe sits bolt upright as if several volts of electricity have been charged into her spine.

'Mummy! Mummy! Mummy!'

Clara's forlorn cry filters through the open window from the bedroom. It pushes Phoebe to standing and, in one smooth motion, immediately she is next to her father, attempting to pluck the baby from his chest. But he steps back, holds out his hand.

'I'll go, Button.'

'Are you sure? He needs changing and Clara will want a snack and I usually let her watch one episode of . . .'

'I'm quite capable of changing a nappy and doling out some *Mini Cheddars*. No matter what your mother says.'

'Today's about Mum, remember!'

'Yes, yes, it's your mother's day. Absolutely. No fights. No politics. Everyone smiling. Everyone friends. Orders understood.' He salutes as he retreats. He is halfway to the house by the time Clara's second cry cracks the still afternoon air into a thousand pieces, an opera singer breaking a glass through song.

Twelve

Richard couldn't see her face from the driver's seat, only the top of her little head bobbing up and down in the mirror. He could see flashes of her new tracksuit. The turquoise velour with white detail: a white border of elastic around each ankle and wrist, white trim around the hood, and a fat white plastic zip that interlocked down the front. His little treat for her, a prize for becoming a big sister. He'd bought it for her in Lillywhites on Thursday afternoon.

He'd filed early and was walking to St Paul's to hop on the tube when he suddenly felt flattened with heaviness, breathless with guilt, and so, when he got to Oxford Circus, he didn't change to the Victoria Line but emerged from the steps into the grey afternoon and turned down Regent's Street. Spending money never failed to make Richard feel better.

He'd browsed the ground floor in Liberty for almost an hour before selecting a gold necklace and a small bottle of perfume for Mary, then he'd ascended the dark wooden staircase and had the assistant help him select a white flannel Babygro with a teddy bear embroidered on the collar. She'd wrapped it in tissue, tied the ribbon on the little purple bag, and rung it up before he asked her if she wouldn't mind wrapping another just the same. He put his hand up as she'd started to untie the ribbon.

'No, I'll need a separate bag.'

The guilt followed him down to Piccadilly. It followed him wherever he went these days. It was as if he dragged it behind him, his leg faltering occasionally at the weight of it, pulling him back.

He'd selected the tracksuit for Emma in Lillywhites and then went to a pub, downed two pints, and got on the tube. The ache in his bladder a just punishment all the way back to the flat.

Behind him now, Emma had quietened down; she was singing softly to herself, drawing invisible patterns on the inside of the window.

When he'd picked her up from the nursery it had been like wrestling a feral cat into the back seat. She had refused point blank to put on her seat belt. Her scream had been at such a high pitch that he'd grabbed her arm and put his hand over her mouth before he realised a woman in the car opposite was watching him.

At the house, he'd plonked her down in front of a VHS of some Disney film – one of the several he'd begged off Alison on the Arts Desk; he knew there was a possibility of being home alone with Emma for some time, if her own birth was anything to go by. There was hardly any food in the fridge, but Emma had seemed happy enough with a soft cheese triangle and a Mars bar. He'd felt prouder of himself than he knew he had the right to be for such a small act of caregiving, but still, as he sat beside his daughter – chocolate smeared around her laughing mouth – he felt the foreign sensation of relaxation flooding through him.

He'd woken to an empty couch and the final credits of the film with the blast of a rousing brass ensemble version of a song sung earlier by two animated animals. He was confused for a moment as to why he should be here, in this house that smelled of washing powder and cooking oil. He had a painful yearning for the smell of Dee's hair, a desire to run his hand over the nape of her neck when it was tied up on her crown.

Then Emma was calling from the downstairs loo to get her bum wiped, and he rubbed his hand over his face.

'Coming!'

No one had warned him about the incessant bum-wiping that parenthood involved. He'd thought that it was something that would go with the nappies. But, despite spending three-quarters of the week where the call of 'READY!' didn't reach him, he still found himself wiping a bum other than his own multiple times a week. And soon, he'd be wiping more.

Two more bums.

What had he got himself into?

He pulled the car to a stop at the lights and flicked on his indicator. He checked his watch – only five minutes into visiting hours, thank God.

It had been a real scramble to find all the things on Mary's list, get Emma changed out of her chocolate-and-paint-covered clothes, and wrestle her onto the booster seat. He felt as though he'd done a round in the ring with Muhammad Ali by the time he turned the key in the ignition.

He had a huge amount of respect for Mary, doing this all on her own for much of the week. His mother helped, of course, but still he knew that he couldn't do it. He'd have packed his bags and been off years ago. Though, isn't that what he had done anyway?

There hadn't been a decision really. He'd just kept his job. Somebody had to work, to pay the mortgage, to pay the bills, to keep them all dressed and fed. Shortly after Emma was born, there'd been that brief flirtation with Anglia Television, but print journalism was where his heart was. He'd always been told that he had what it took for television, but he'd thought it more likely Mary would go in that direction. People would switch on to see someone with a face like Mary's, even since she'd gained a few pounds, whereas there had been more than one occasion when a colleague had joked about him having a 'face for radio'. No, if he was heading anywhere, it was Westminster. A prospect that was seeming more feasible by the day, more possible with every conversation and every handshake. Well, almost every conversation.

'Nothing that you want to disclose now, is there Richard? Before we take this any further?'

He had smiled his broadest smile, the one he'd been practising as much as he had his public speaking.

'Don't you worry about that, Minister. It's the bones jangling in your closet that I'm here to see to.'

Maybe he ought to have taken the job at Anglia? Then he wouldn't be in this mess.

He liked to think that his relationship with Dee was a twist of fate. A case of being in the wrong place at the wrong time, of an attraction so strong he couldn't resist it. But he knew in his heart of hearts that if it hadn't happened with Dee, it would have happened with someone else. Let's face it, it had happened with someone else, and someone else before that. But none of those indiscretions were anything like what he felt for Dee.

Dee.

If he thought about her for too long, if he pictured her now, it hurt. It actually, physically, caused him pain. He pictured her as he'd left her, lying on the bed on her side, the white sheet draped over her hip, the dark circle of her nipple. Her face was resting on her hand, a generous smile spread across it. A smile that was willing him on, telling him that he went with her blessing, that she was with him in the whole mess of it all. The diamond earrings he'd put in her ears the night before glinted at him as their facets caught the early-morning light through her bedroom window.

He hated that house she lived in, with the flatmates in tie-dyed sacks who looked at him as if he were an ancient, even though he was barely a decade older than them. But her room, the pile of books by the bed, the mattress on the floor, the twist of her clothes across the carpet, the scent that hung in the air of the place, joss sticks, cocoa butter, the patchouli she dabbed on her wrists. He loved that room.

He loved her.

And he still loved Mary. Didn't he? He'd certainly told her so just yesterday as he'd leaned forward to kiss her damp brow, and again four hours later, when he'd wept at the warmth of their squalling daughter against his chest just minutes after her entry into this world.

He checked the mirror as he took the corner and saw a smear of green paint on Emma's forehead.

Whilst he'd been asleep, she'd managed to cover herself in the finger paints that he ought to have put somewhere out of her reach before collecting her from nursery.

Mary had wrapped the little pots of paints just minutes before they left for the hospital. Giving Richard strict instructions to give them to Emma when he first brought her to meet the baby.

'You're bribing her?'

He'd watched her break the Sellotape with her teeth and then pause, breathing to allow a contraction to pass, before sticking the end of the parcel closed.

'It's a gift to mark the occasion, to imprint it as a celebration, rather than a life-altering change that she should fear.'

'Are you wrapping me a present too, then?'

She'd shot him one of her looks.

Mary often said it was like having another child to look after when he came home at the weekend. It just didn't seem to occur to her that maybe it was because she treated him like a child, he behaved like one. She was always one step ahead of him. Putting his socks in the washing while he was in the loo. Pouring the hot water from the kettle on to the waiting teabag when he'd nipped next door to check the cricket score. She'd even started changing the light bulbs.

It wasn't like that with Dee. She liked him to choose the wine. *She* thought it was charming that he opened doors for her.

He'd considered putting the paints back in the box and rewrapping them, but he hadn't had time, and Emma was already covered in the bloody stuff. So he'd just packed the other things Mary had asked for and chalked it up to one more thing that Mary could add to the long list of things she was annoyed at him for. She hadn't wanted another child, and she held him entirely responsible for their having one; he expected that arriving with their daughter covered in finger paints, rather than excitedly clutching the wrapped box containing them, was likely to pale into insignificance.

* * *

At the lights, he craned his neck to look over his shoulder.

Emma had stopped singing now and was looking out of the window, her right hand idly stroking the soft fabric that covered her thigh. Her booster seat only just allowed her to see out of the window; if anything it made her seem smaller, more vulnerable. The seat belt didn't help either. Too high, it cut across the top of her chest just beneath her chin. He should get some adapters for his car really, or just let her wobble around without one, as she did in Mary's Volvo. Still, it made Richard feel better to have her strapped in. It was one of the many benefits of having such a new model: seat belts in the back.

He remembered sitting in the back of his dad's Morris Minor. How he would often slide off the seat and sit in the footwell, feeling the vibrations of the engine in his groin. He would close his eyes and focus on the fizzy warmth between his legs as his penis stiffened. It was, when he thought about it, his first awareness that he could get an erection; something that he still found miraculous. An unending source of fascination that would forever have an inseverable association with motor engines.

The lights changed and he pulled away from the junction, taking a left, turning towards the hospital.

He yawned loudly, prompting a giggle from the back seat.

'Are you going to sleep in the car, Daddy?'

'That wouldn't be a good idea. Would it, Bunny?'

Richard felt as though he had been awake for weeks, though really it was only three days since Mary went in. Hopefully she'd be out by Sunday and they could take the baby over to his mum's for the roast. 'Mum's'. Not 'Mum and Dad's'. He still wasn't used to it.

His memory of his dad was progressively becoming more of a feeling than an image. When he thought of him, it was as though he could hear his voice, smell the cigar smoke on his jumper, see his face as it had been when Richard was young and in those days before he died – all at once. It was as if Bert had become a composite of all his memories, rather than the man who used to pat him on the head when he returned from school, the person who had shown him how to peel an apple with a knife so that the skin came off in one big coil of green and white. Barely six months had passed, and yet one of the people who had caused him to be had been reduced to no more than a jumble of sensations.

Richard bit at his bottom lip and checked the rear-view mirror as he indicated to pull into the hospital car park. As he turned, the top of Emma's head appeared in the mirror and he had to bite harder as he thought of how his dad doted on that little girl. How he'd let her sit on his knee and make clip-clop noises as they 'rode to market'.

It had been part of the argument with Mary, that they ought to try for another. He'd wanted to give his father a grandson too. The best gift a man could give his father, an assurance that the family name would live on. He ought to have known better than to voice that reason in Mary's presence.

'You wanted to do all this all over again for the sake of your name? What about my career? What about my body? What about my bloody sanity?'

But then there was that Friday night ten months ago when he'd arrived back from London to find her pink-cheeked and giggling at the kitchen table with Lizzie King. There was an empty bottle between them, another uncorked next to it.

'Richard! My darling husband is home. Join us for a large one?'

And for the next few hours, it was as if she was the girl he'd first met in Cardiff, flushed and tactile and laughing. It was as if he could see her properly for the first time in three years. He'd forgotten how pretty she was, how she glowed in the presence of others, and then later, in the bedroom, how surprisingly forthright she could be, how unashamed to ask for what she wanted.

She hadn't wanted the baby. But abortion had never been an option for Mary. And so he had made a silent prayer of thanks to the god he didn't believe in but she did, that a grandson for his father might be on the way after all. He couldn't have done it right though, the prayer, because just a few days after Mary's first scan, his dad had died.

The hospital was much quieter than when he'd left earlier that afternoon. Although it was visiting hours, parking was easy and the corridors were relatively unpopulated.

The cafe was already shut as they passed; his stomach gave an involuntary gurgle. Though Mary had done little but complain about the indistinguishable casseroles that she'd been offered in the maternity ward, Richard had become rather fond of the hospital canteen; their cheese scones, in particular. A foodstuff that until recently he'd associated with pensioners – scones – but actually, he'd discovered that they made a rather good snack, and with enough butter they were quite delicious.

Another sign of the inexorable descent into decrepitude, a fondness for scones?

He checked his watch. They were already late and Emma's stride was so short it'd be a while before they got to the ward, but the hunger, combined with the fatigue, was making him irritable. He tugged at Emma's arm to try to hurry her along.

'Ouch, Daddy! Too hard!'

'Sorry, Bunny.'

He stopped and looked down at his daughter. Her eyes were wide, open to wherever he might lead her next. It would not be a good idea to arrive late and in a bad mood. That would be the perfect recipe for a row.

'Come on, Bunny. Let's get Daddy a snack.'

Richard wiped his hand on his jeans as they entered the ward, carefully folding the foil peanut bag into a small square, tucking it into his back pocket. He turned to look for Emma. She was some metres behind him, her mouth pursed, concentrating as she sucked the salt off the peanut he had given her. As she approached him, he got down onto one knee and held out his palm towards her.

'Spit.'

Emma let one half of the wet peanut fall from her mouth into her father's palm. A long trail of spit spun from her lips to his hand like a spider's thread. He shook his hand to detach it. She smiled up at him, then opened her mouth, the other half of the nut balancing like a little beige boat on the pink sea of her tongue. Then, with a swift gulp, she swallowed the nut and opened her mouth wide once again.

'All gone.'

Why was it that Mary didn't give her nuts?

Was it the risk of choking or was she allergic? There had been something about allergies when she was tiny. Something about a rash. It was what they had thought caused all that ceaseless screaming. But what was the rash caused by, and was it still something that happened?

'Yummy!'

Well, she seemed fine. And they were in a hospital, after all.

Mary was sitting up in the bed with her eyes shut when they arrived on the ward. She still looked as tired as she had when he'd left her, but less sweaty. More 'Mary'. She'd brushed her hair, and she had a new nightie on too, he noticed.

Emma became shy as they approached her. She looked around, taking in the other raised beds filled with strange women, some with curtains pulled around them. She gripped his hand as they stood next to the metal-framed bed.

'Look who's come to see you, Mummy!'

'Well hello there! Look at that tracksuit. Don't you look grown up?'

Emma relaxed in response to her mother's smile. She leaned against the metal strut of the bed and extended her arms upwards. Richard lifted her, and she scrambled over Mary, causing a sharp intake of breath, pain crossing Mary's face like a cloud, before she righted herself and became the ever-smiling mother once more.

'Where's my baby sister?'

Emma was peering over Mary in the direction of the Perspex bassinet.

'You've changed your tune.' Richard looked down at the mass of purple-hued skin that was his new daughter. 'She asked earlier if we could send her back.'

Mary laughed and hugged Emma.

'She's here to stay I'm afraid. But don't worry. We're going to have a lot of fun with her.'

'I love her. I love her the most.'

Emma was leaning over Mary now, stretching her arms out to reach towards Richard, who was cradling the baby in his arms.

His daughter. Not a grandson for his father, after all. Not a son. Another daughter.

*   *   *

Richard was proud to have been present at the births of his children. Prouder still to have accompanied Mary for many of the hospital appointments, for all of the scans. It was something that had only been encouraged by his mother's horror at the idea of his being involved in such things.

'They're my offspring too, Mother. Times have changed.'

But he hadn't been there for Dee, not for that first scan. Because at the time Dee went for her first scan, she hadn't even told him that she was pregnant.

As with so much in Richard's life, it all just seemed such horrible timing. Mary falling pregnant, the subsequent weeks of rowing. Then his dad and all of that; the sorting things out with his mother, the surprising force of his own grief. And then, the first whispers of the possibility of a new opportunity, that boozy lunch at The Carlton, and the clarity that he'd woken with, that morning in Dee's bed. They couldn't do it any more, he'd told her. He couldn't do it. He needed to be a better man. For his daughter. For the son that his wife might be carrying.

He didn't know that even then, as Dee set her jaw, pulled her jeans on and buttoned a creased shirt over her beautiful soft nipples, that cells – from both him and her – were multiplying inside her, dividing and growing and creating a complication that – though he saw now he really ought to have – he hadn't even considered.

The baby opened her eyes, her irises seemed black, still, unable to focus. Her face was swollen, the skin mottled from the violence of birth, her hair stuck to her head with white vernix.

'Yuck!' Emma recoiled in horror. 'She's so ugly!'

Mary smiled at Richard. This is what she'd been warning him about – the sibling rejection.

'Newborn babies are all a bit ugly. You were too, all squashed.'

He crinkled his face up to demonstrate. Mary tutted. Emma laughed at him. At least someone appreciated his jokes.

'I was yellow when I was born.'

'And very grumpy. You wouldn't let me put you down.' Emma glowed with pleasure as Mary squeezed her to her chest.

Richard looked down at the baby. Emma wasn't wrong, she was a funny little thing. Her eyes, too big for her head, a mass of matted hair, deep furrows across her forehead. She looked a bit like an old man.

His throat tightened.

She looked a bit like his dad.

He managed four months' cold turkey before he'd given in and called Dee.

Four months of living the life that his wife, his mother, his colleagues, had believed him to have been living for the last three years. Driving to London on a Monday morning, driving back to Suffolk on a Friday evening, sometimes a Saturday if a story broke late. He ate at the flat – scrambled eggs on toast, beans on toast, the occasional pie at the pub, the odd night of nothing but crisps, pork scratchings and bitter for dinner and, of course, those increasingly frequent meals around Whitehall, discussing 'possibilities' and 'spitballing' strategy. But then, there came a Friday when he had woken up and the need to be touched, to be wanted, was so acute that he'd dressed and called Mary before he'd even left for work.

'A flat tyre. And I've a day from hell ahead of me. I'll have to stay in London tonight, to get it fixed in the morning. Don't worry, I'll be back in time for our soirée with the Kings.'

But he hadn't been. In fact, he didn't make it back to Suffolk until the following weekend. Because it was that Friday that he'd looked up from his paper as Dee walked into the gallery foyer wearing a tight purple dress. And as he'd watched her turn – and seen the subtle change in the curves of her body – everything Richard thought he knew about what life had in store for him changed.

Since then – since he had first placed his hands on the hard expansion of Dee's abdomen – he'd given up any idea he had of giving her up. He hadn't considered giving Mary up either. He'd just let it happen: the flow between his two lives, his family and his pregnant wife here, his work and his pregnant girlfriend there, and most of the time, it was okay. Most of the time – as long as he didn't think about the future, and just dealt with the situation right in front of him – everything was fine.

But since just past 2 a.m. this morning, when this bundle of life came sliding into the world, the enormity of the mess he was in surrounded him like cellophane, wrapping itself tighter and tighter with every moment that passed.

He inhaled, forcing his brain to take him elsewhere, to change the subject.

'What's Friday's child?'

'Friday's child?' Mary was concentrating on plaiting Emma's hair.

'You know, "Monday's child is fair of face, Tuesday's child is full of grace," . . . this child was born at two something or other, on a Friday. So what's Friday's child?'

'I think – I always get mixed up with the ending:

Monday's child is fair of face,
Tuesday's child is full of grace,
Wednesday's child is full of woe,
Thursday's child has far to go,

Friday's child is loving and giving,
Saturday's child works hard for a living,
But the child that is born on the Sabbath day is . . .

I don't remember that bit, is something and something, loving and gay, I think.'

'Sabbath?'

'It's an old-fashioned word for Sunday. It means rest.'

'So, that means that your new little sister is loving and giving.'

Mary's wide mouth stretched into a smile.

'Loving and giving. That's perfect isn't it, Em?'

'What day was I born, Mummy?'

'Wednesday!' He smiled at Mary, a dog expecting a treat for good behaviour, but Mary pulled a face at him that he couldn't understand.

'What is Wednesday's child?'

'It's just a silly rhyme, Em. What did you have for lunch at nursery?'

Richard frowned at Mary, changing the subject.

'Monday's child is fair of face, Tuesday's child is full of grace, Wednesday's child is full of woe . . .'

Ah, he thought.

'What's woe?' Emma's little brow creased.

'Well . . .' Mary looked even more tired than when they'd arrived now. Richard could see the bags under her eyes. '. . . it is only a poem, but what it means is that Wednesday's child will have a lot of challenges.'

'Like competitions?'

'Exactly.' He turned purposefully, bringing the baby around the bed so he was on the same side as Emma, then perched gently on the edge of the mattress. He could feel the polyester of the blanket rubbing against the stiff, starched sheets beneath them. Richard tilted the baby, angling her towards Emma. She was still cocooned beneath her mother's arm, shyly nuzzling into the space between Mary's breast and the propped-up pillow behind her.

'Emma? Would you like to give baby Phoebe a kiss?'

He watched her burrow her face deeper behind her mother's back.

'Come on Em-em. Remember what we talked about.' Mary stroked her daughter's hair where it was pulled tightly against her head into uneven plaits.

Richard carefully raised the sleeping baby to her.

'Give her a kiss, Em. Tell Phoebe what a good job you're going to make of being her big sister.'

The little girl weighed up his words for a second, then nodded and leaned forward.

'Gently.'

Emma softly kissed her sister's cheek, then ducked her head slightly, whispering.

'I'm going to look after you. Always.'

Thirteen

Phoebe stands and fiddles about with the flowers on the table, straightening the stems in each vase. She stands back, trying to evaluate whether she has made them look better or worse. She hasn't a clue about any of this sort of thing. She's always preferred attending a party to hosting one. Even those celebrating her milestones were rarely arranged by her. The only thing she'd ever really got involved with was the running of the bar, and that is no longer deemed appropriate.

She looks at the flex for the festoons lying in the grass, next to the length of Rosie's untangled bunting: the evidence of others' labour. She hasn't done anything to help set up other than tie a few flowers to the pews in the church. That's partly down to the children, but it's also because it just all seems to be happening without her. Everyone seems to know what they ought to be doing, whereas she really doesn't have a clue. A running theme in her life. She's always felt as though everyone had made plans at some meeting she hadn't been invited to.

Maybe that's why her mum seems slightly off with her.

She's aware that she has a tendency to take other people's moods personally. But she can't shake the feeling that, other than the obvious nerves about her forthcoming nuptials, her mum is still nursing some sort of grievance. Could it be the memoir? Surely she can't *still* be angry about her book? She thought they'd had all that out during that delightful fortnight last summer.

She couldn't have read today's paper already, could she?

Phoebe had known that writing about the wedding in her column might ruffle a few feathers, but she'd figured everyone would be too busy today to read it, and by the time they got to it – if they got to it – it would all be water under the bridge, and they could laugh about it. It was, she thought, one of her funnier pieces. But, if her mum had read it, that might explain the tight smiles and evasion of eye contact. After all, she had made a promise that today would be harmonious; it could possibly be said that putting her fears of all that could go wrong into black and white in a national newspaper wasn't upholding that. Well, you can't take back words that are in print. You just have to find a way to make up for it. She might not be laying the table, or stringing up the lights, but she can give her all to making sure the wedding goes off without a hitch. That everyone is there, celebrating together, just like her mum wants.

'Granny, you know that Emma is coming today?'

'Emma? ' Irene's smooth brow crinkles.

'Emmaline, Granny. Your granddaughter? Your favourite. My sister. Emma.'

'Emmaline!'

'Exactly. If Emmaline's coming all this way, then don't you think you could try to come? Just for a bit, at least? Mum really wants you there. It's a really special occasion. An important one.'

'I'm not stupid, you know.'

'I wasn't saying that, Granny.'

'You used to be so slender, Phoebe. Have you tried grapefruit for breakfast?'

Phoebe draws a breath and sits down on the piano stool.

'If you're not going to come to the church, promise me you're going to come to the party.'

'A church wedding. I'm surprised they're allowing it.'

'Why wouldn't they?'

'Those arms of yours will burn out here, Phoebe. We didn't have sunscreen when I was young. We used to use cooking oil.'

'Granny.'

'I used to like the sun, but that was before people knew about skin cancer. I've never taken to sunbathing though. All that lying around. I like to be active. If it wasn't for this hip.'

Phoebe scrutinises her grandmother. She's always been an objectionable woman, someone who found a way to insert her obtuse opinions into the most benign of conversations; so it is difficult to know whether these increasingly frequent non sequiturs are a sign of senility.

'That handsome film star husband of yours won't find it difficult to find a lithe new model, you know.'

'We aren't married, Granny.'

'All the more reason to look after yourself. They do that, you know. Men. Wandering eyes. I tried to warn your mother, but she wouldn't listen. No one to blame but herself that your father strayed.'

'Granny!'

Phoebe's shout is like a dog barking. Irene puts a hand to her chest.

'Granny, don't cry. You can't talk about people's bodies like that. I've told you a hundred times.'

'You shouted at me!'

'You just called me fat, so I think that makes us square.'

Phoebe walks to the table, plucks another tissue from the box and hands it to Irene, then rests a hand on her shoulder. How has her mother lived with this woman for the last three years without killing her? She knows there wasn't much choice involved. She's started to wonder recently how many choices anyone really gets to make in their life. It seems that one event follows another, and then one morning you wake up and find yourself living a day-to-day that is nothing like the future you envisioned for yourself. It doesn't take much. Some curtains that need washing. A chair with a dodgy leg. A broken hip. A house sale that is delayed by a global pandemic. And suddenly you find yourself living with and caring for your ex-husband's mother. Mind you, it probably wasn't the final act her rather fierce, opinionated grandmother had been expecting either.

Compassion. That's how she's going to get through this weekend. Compassion.

'Sorry, Granny.'

'I'm sorry too, Phoebe.' Her granny dabs at her eyes.

'Mummy! Grampy let me have an orange lolly!'

Clara is at the conservatory door, barefoot, and dressed only in a grubby vest, hugging her balloon to her chest, sucking on an orange ice lolly. She has orange juice dribbling all down the white of her vest, the lolly melting faster than she can eat it.

'Did you go to the toilet Clara?'

'Not yet. Grampy said I can have a lolly first.'

'Well, Grampy's not always right, Poppet. Go on, go and have a wee.'

The child smiles, but doesn't budge, continuing to lick at her ice stick.

'Come on mucky pup, let's clean you up.' At the conservatory door, Richard, the baby in one arm, reaches his hand out for Clara's.

'Thanks, Daddy!' Phoebe watches her dad usher Clara through to the kitchen, his head bent down as he talks to her.

She walks to the table and pours herself another glass of lemonade, then collapses into one of her mum's Merchant Ivory chairs from the conservatory.

'You always were a daddy's girl.'

'That was Emma, Granny.'

'Daddy's little Bunny he called you.'

'That was Emma. I was Button. Rarely.'

'You've got a bond, you two, like I did with my dad. Though, I never called my dad Daddy.'

'I don't think I've called him Daddy since I was about four until just now. But anyone who takes the kids off my hands for a few minutes can be called whatever they like.'

'Hello, erm, Rosie said there might be something to drink out here?'

Her Granny cranes her neck around her armchair, following the direction of the voice. Phoebe turns too and sees that it is Danyal. Rosie's new boyfriend. His face slick with sweat, his shirt is seemingly two-tone, darker in spreading circles under his arms, and a diamond shape across his chest.

'On the table, young man.' Irene points towards the almost-empty jug.

He sidesteps towards the table, smiling broadly. It must be serious: Phoebe can remember only one other boyfriend of Rosie's who'd been a guest at Mouser Lane, the muscly one with the very precise facial hair. That was for a big family event too, though she can't remember which one.

Whatever happened to him?

The light through the willow is creating a shimmer across his specs that obscures his eyes.

'Watch those lovely teeth of yours, though, it's full of sugar.'

Phoebe places her forefingers to her temples and cringes. Then smiles at Danyal.

'Rosie made it. So she barely sweetened it. But it's cold and wet.'

'Oh that's perfect. Just right. Lovely. Delicious. Thanks, thanks so much.'

He pours the lemonade into the remaining glass. Ice cubes tumble out of the jug and clatter onto the tray.

'Oh, whoopsie. Gosh. Sorry.' He is chasing the ice cubes around the tray now, scrambling to transfer them one by one to his glass. As each slides out of his reach or flips out of his fingers into the grass he exclaims. 'Whoopsie. Oops. Oh dear.'

Unable to bear watching him struggle further, Phoebe approaches him.

'Let me.'

She takes the tray from the table and, in one smooth action, pours the remaining ice cubes back into the jug.

'Oh, cheers. Thanks. Thanks so much.'

'What sort of doctor was it that Rosie said you were young man? Forgive me, I forget your name.'

'Danyal. And, erm, I'm a surgeon. A paediatric surgeon.'

'Feet?'

'Ah – children.'

'Dan. I'll remember your name now. I always used to be Reenie, you know, before I got old. One day, you'll notice that everyone's started calling you Daniel, then you'll know that you've got old too.'

'Danyal.'

'Sorry?'

He clears his throat, smiles. Phoebe, her back still to her granny, mouths to him, *Sorry*.

He shakes his head; a tiny movement that Phoebe wouldn't have seen if she weren't so close.

'Thirsty work.' He drinks deep, pointing in the direction of the front of the house.

'Sorry about Dad.'

'No, no. No problem at all. It was a good opportunity to get to know him. A bit surreal, I've seen him on *Newsnight* so many times, and then, there I am wrestling a dead pig with him. Lovely to meet him, though. Lovely to meet you all. Thanks for having me.'

'Dead pig?' Confusion is creasing Irene's face.

'The hog roast. I was helping Richard get the hog ready for tonight's feast.'

He places his glass back on the tray and takes off his glasses. He is very handsome, Phoebe sees, without them. He breathes on the lenses and polishes them on his hanky.

'I'd better find Richard, er, your dad.' He slides his spectacles back onto his nose, folding the hanky before tucking it back into his pocket. 'He wants to see my "knife skills". I'm afraid unless he's got a scalpel to chop the lettuce, he's going to be disappointed.'

'If you watch a lot of *Newsnight*, you'll know our father is a notorious bully. You should ask Michael for tips, he's been handling Dad for the best part of two decades.'

'Honestly, it's only marginally more stressful than a kidney transplant. Nothing I can't handle!'

'I haven't the faintest idea what you two are jabbering on about, but I'd be grateful if one of you might be able to help me into the house.'

Immediately, Danyal is extending his hands to her, offering his help.

'Well, I bet you're a hit with the mothers as much as you are the children.'

He blushes.

'Ready?'

Phoebe watches as he gently holds her granny's hands as she finds her balance.

'Madam, may I escort you into the house?'

'Call me Reenie, young man. Dan, wasn't it?'

'Dan's fine, Reenie.'

Phoebe's eyebrows raise to hear a trill of laughter escaping from her grandmother.

She sits down in the armchair that her grandmother just vacated; she can feel the warmth of the recently departed body in the upholstery beneath her. She watches Danyal and Irene make their slow progress towards the house. Irene is laughing at something, patting his bicep. They meet Rosie at the door of the conservatory and she helps to support her grandmother as she takes the step, before gliding across the garden to the table, picking up the bunting from the ground as she passes.

'Well, looks like Granny's in love.'

'He's cute, Rosie. Are you going to keep him?'

Rosie doesn't say anything but climbs the ladder, pulling at the cord Michael tied in the tree, testing it.

Rosie not responding to her question is not surprising. She's always employed the art of silence to great effect; keeping her thoughts and feelings to herself has always been one of the many ways that she and her half-sister have differed. It used to drive Phoebe mad. She'd use all sorts of tactics to try and get a response out of her. Often, cruel tactics that would rightly earn her a grounding from her mum or one of those long walks around the village with Liz. Memories of some of her behaviour still haunt her, even though her sobriety has demanded she sought forgiveness both from Rosie and herself. All those times she snidely clarified Rosie's relationship terms – the constant reminders that Mary wasn't even her stepmother, never mind her mum – as if Rosie could have forgotten that. And that horrible time, in this very garden, when they were all celebrating Phoebe's twenty-first birthday, just days after Rosie had been through an ordeal she can't begin to imagine, and she'd told her obviously traumatised half-sister to 'stop being a party-pooper'.

Well, she can't change the past. But she can try to change this very moment.

'How's work, Rose? Mum said you . . .'

Rosie turns her back to her. 'You work for a newspaper. Don't you ever look at the front page?'

'I meant how's work for you—'

'It's really hard Phoebe.'

'Could you take a break? A sabbatical? You could rent out your place and go travelling or something?'

Rosie turns and looks at Phoebe. Her eyes are narrowed and Phoebe braces herself to be told off, but then Rosie shakes her head and walks back to the house.

Phoebe wipes her hands down her face.

She's been so focused on seeing Emma that she hadn't really considered the magnitude of the work she has to do on this relationship. They'd seen each other on the occasional family *Zoom*, and Rosie had come down with Mum to meet Albie when he was born, and she'd sort of assumed they were okay. But recently she's realised that she hadn't given enough thought to how everything must have affected Rosie. She could blame the lockdowns, the distance, the stress of being a new mum during a pandemic, but, deep down, she knows it would all be an excuse. Of course, there had been moments when she'd wondered how Rosie was getting on, had sent her a text, or a funny video of Clara with the rainbow she had helped her paint for the window, but she hadn't really thought about her. Hadn't considered what it must have been like for Rosie day to day. If she's truly honest: she hadn't *wanted* to consider it.

In the conservatory, Rosie threads a coiled heap of flex through the open top window, then walks back across the patio, the blue flex snaking across the lawn behind her.

'If you do manage to get some time off, you should come and stay with us. You and Danyal. We've loads of room.'

Rosie presses the plug into the socket, and the criss-cross of lights that Michael rigged earlier illuminates. It seems as though they are part of the tree, the iridescent fruit of the silvery willow.

'That sounds nice.'

'Don't get too excited. I'd expect at least a night of babysitting as payment for your board.'

Phoebe tilts her head, waiting for Rosie to respond to her stupid joke, but she stands, appraising the lights. Phoebe reaches out her bare foot and makes contact with the back of her half-sister's knee.

'I've missed you.'

Rosie turns and looks at her directly, a half-smile.

'It's good to see you too, Phoebs.'

'Oh! It looks wonderful all lit up, even now! I do hope Michael finds those candles!'

Her mum is striding across the patio, Danyal trailing in her wake carrying two crates, one stacked upon the other. He is wearing one of her mum's aprons now, sweating even more profusely than he was when he was last out here.

'Just stack them there, thank you, Dan.'

Her mum is still in just her slip, her rollers still sitting tightly against her head, her face still un-made-up and radiant.

Sometimes Phoebe feels as though the past few years have aged her so much that she is enjoying the very last of her beauty now, at the very beginning of her thirty-seventh year. For a while she's had a passing concern that she won't get to enjoy the sideways glances that still come Mary's way whenever she is out in public. She knows that the early mornings and the broken nights have taken their toll.

That's another thing she's dreading about seeing Emma. She doesn't know if she can bear to witness her sister's response to the physical change in her. But there is a small part of her, the morbidly curious part of her, that wants to see how, or if, the last few years have changed her sister to the degree they have her.

That feeling again. It's as though her tongue is too big for her mouth; a sea creature rooted in her jaw, pulsating against the roof of her mouth. She swallows a gulp of the warm air to try to dispel the feeling. How ridiculous that she feels this way about seeing someone whose approval she has never sought. Someone she's spent so much of her life trying to separate from.

Maybe Emma's changed radically too.

She hasn't even seen any photos of her from the last four years.

On her darker days, she's looked. She's held her breath and typed her name into search engines or social media apps, but she hasn't been able to penetrate the fortress of her sister's digital life. Even if she had, it is unlikely that she'd have much more of an idea. She's always been camera shy, Em, even before she worked out how to use the Internet to make money from everyone else's personal details without sharing her own.

She knows, through their mum, that she is safe. That she is 'doing well'. But there hasn't been a single word from her. No call. No text. Nothing since the last official letters and her pointed departure from the family message group. 'Emmaline has left the conversation.' Isn't that the truth?

'Phoebe!' Her mum's voice startles her and she realises that she must have briefly succumbed to sleep. 'You've got two children in there that need you. Your father's trying to entertain them while preparing salad for forty.'

'Poor Danyal is in the kitchen in a pinny. I heard Dad telling him off for dicing the cucumber.' Rosie is unloading champagne glasses from a crate, Mary is sorting through a tray of cutlery.

'Ugh, when does the drinking start?' Phoebe asks, hauling herself out of the armchair.

Mary and Rosie stop what they are doing and stare at her.

'Oh my God. Not when do *I* start drinking! When do *you* start drinking. I'm just readying myself.'

'Just come and find me, Phoebs. If you feel . . .'

'I know how to navigate a party. Concentrate on Mum. It's your day, Mum.'

Rosie nods and smiles, motioning to the lights strung through the boughs above them.

'You're getting married, Mary!'

Her mum claps her hands, and laughs. She looks so happy. Suddenly Phoebe thinks she might cry.

How did they get here? When did everything change? Why didn't she notice the time passing so quickly?

To some degree the answer to those questions is drinking. But still, she feels as though there are not just nights, but years that she can't account for. She hadn't been entirely physically absent, she'd visited home often, even when she'd been living in New York, but she's come to realise that, for quite a period of time, she'd been so wrapped up in herself, she just hadn't noticed things. She'd been so busy worrying about her career, money, men, filling the void any which way she could – that she'd missed so much. Granny getting old. Lizzie. She'd even missed her mum falling in love.

It's funny – how there is so much she can't remember. And yet, there are single mornings, phone calls – a phone call – that stand out with such clarity, still even now she can almost smell the air of where she was standing at that very moment.

Fourteen

Phoebe handed over the ten-dollar bill, then took her change and dropped it into the cup by the register. She smiled at the server without lifting her sunglasses, then pulled the paper end off the straw and sucked. The effect was almost immediate: a cooling relief in her dry throat, the reassuring knowledge that soon caffeine would be flooding her system.

All through the meeting she'd been fantasising about an iced coffee. Cold brew with a drizzle of *Half and Half* and a single shot of hazelnut syrup. She'd felt the want as if it were under her skin, and she'd had to keep pulling her attention back to what Raylynne was saying.

The two hours in that office felt like a full working day. Two hours of nodding furiously, focusing on Raylynne's mouth, but then realising she'd stopped listening and was focusing not on the words coming out of the mouth, but on the perfect teeth within it. So she switched focus to her eyes, but then found herself entranced by her own reflection in Raylynne's heavy-rimmed spectacles, and so tried concentrating on another feature. And on and on.

When she'd first started meeting Raylynne for editorial on Thursdays, there'd been a fresh breakfast buffet – at the least coffee and croissants, sometimes fruit cups, sandwiches – but recently the table between them had been adorned with nothing but two glasses, a bottle of sparkling water covered in condensation and a saucer of lemon slices. Evidently the catering had been to woo her. Either that, or she was further out of favour than she'd realised.

Her skipping breakfast hadn't really been a choice that morning. As seemed to be happening increasingly, she'd woken late and had to scramble to leave the apartment.

The first subway had been a jam of bodies, and, though she'd managed to wedge herself in, she'd jumped out at the next stop, claustrophobia starting to make her vision cloud. All this meant there wasn't time to grab a coffee from a bodega before the meeting, despite her legging it at 14th Street to make her connection – something she hoped no one she knew had seen. Phoebe had discovered in her time living here that if there was one thing New Yorkers hated more than a dawdler on the subway, it was a runner. So earlier, with no choice, she'd turned her music up and run, trying not to make eye contact and tuning out the shouts from those whose elbows or bags her sprinting form made contact with. Better not to say anything than say sorry and further induce ire with the round vowels and flat 'r's that gave her away as a Brit.

It pains her to admit it, but accents had never been her strong suit. In fact it had been after one particularly mortifying audition for an Arthur Miller that she'd called her dad and asked if he still had any contacts at the paper. But after nearly two years of living in Manhattan, she felt her accent was almost passable. It wasn't perfect, not like the one that had brought Michael his legion of fans. His Boston accent was so spot on that, until the show got its Emmy nominations, the majority of viewers assumed Michael was, in fact, a Maryland native. It was only when the publicity tour stepped up a gear that he was outed as a Brit. The late-night chat shows gave over a large percentage of any interview to getting him to speak in other regional accents and showing clips of him onstage in the UK: something with which – Michael told Phoebe – the female co-star, sitting next to him on the chat show couch, had been less than impressed. They'd both had a good laugh about that.

Even though Phoebe's accent was decidedly mediocre, sometimes she went whole days speaking in the odd transatlantic drawl she'd cooked up, and no one batted an eyelid. That was one of the many things she loved about being in New York: hardly anyone noticed that she was there at all.

She'd been up for making friends at first, but it seemed impossible to establish anything meaningful. The texts cancelling meetings came so frequently – often when she was already on the subway or in the bar or restaurant – that, occasionally, she had to question whether she ought to be taking it personally, even if she wasn't. Over time, though, she'd realised that this flakiness suited her. She was a free agent, able to do what she wanted, when she wanted.

The caffeine was starting to course through her system now. The painkillers she had taken when she left the offices were kicking in too, the sharp daggers at her temples easing.

She continued to walk downtown. She walked past the theatre where the Chekhov that'd been getting such great reviews was on and pulled out her phone to add an alarm for the following day to try and get up in time for Rush tickets, then smiled to herself and took a left at the next junction heading towards Times Square. A man jumped in front of her, grinning from ear to ear, doing his best to force her to take a flyer for a comedy show that evening. She flashed her most tolerant smile to decline – she can still remember the soul-destroying repetition of flyering on the Royal Mile every day of that sodden August they did *Titus Andronicus* – but he wouldn't leave her alone, so she firmly shook her head, then ducked into the open electric doors of a store.

She wandered around the front display of vividly coloured make-up, enjoying the cool air of the AC that was beating down from above. She tried a couple of lipsticks on the back of her hand and sprayed perfume onto her pulse points. It was nice, heavy, like wandering around a garden at night when the jasmine is in full bloom. She turned the little red bottle around in her hands as she wiggled her wrist to let it dry, waiting to see how it settled on her skin. As she raised her wrist to sniff it again, she noticed a bruise on her inner arm. She prodded it with her forefinger and withdrew her hand with a jolt. It was extremely tender. Immediately she lifted her other arm and saw, beside the flock of ink birds swooping down her bicep, an identical bruise on that inner arm too. She closed her eyes tightly and licked her lips. Then, with a nod of her head, she opened her eyes and pulled one of the little cellophane covered cubes from the shelf before her, the perfume bottle within it rattling as she carried it to the till.

Leaving the shop, she found the sidewalk congested with Broadway matinee tourists flooding towards the darkened theatres that were about to spring alive. She checked for cars, then stepped to the edge, placing one foot in the road, and pulled her phone out to check the time. It was just past one, which meant Michael might be awake, even though his flight had got in late last night. Checking again that she wasn't going to be taken out by a bus, she held her phone out at arm's length and rotated the camera so it was facing her. She pouted and turned to the side, adjusting the framing before using her thumb to capture the image. She brought down her phone and turned, so she was no longer squinting into the sun. The picture was perfect. At the angle she took it, it appeared as if her head and Michael's, on the billboard behind her, were the same size. From the tilt of her head and the pout of her lips, it seemed that he was looking down at her, and she was waiting patiently for him to kiss her.

'Ain't that the truth,' she said to herself in her weird, fake accent.

Then she cleared her throat, opened her messages, and sent the photo to *Regis US Mob.* She tapped out a message.

Missing you mate. How's the jet lag? Going to find a café to work, call me when you're compos mentis. xo

Beside her, a group of young women, late teens, early twenties? were also standing with one foot in the road, angling their cameras, pouting their lips and taking photos.

'Oh. My. God. He is just the hottest?'

'Have you heard his accent? I just die for British men! It's like: stop, Michael. Too much.'

'I know, right? It should be an offence to be that beautiful.'

Phoebe smiled to herself and slid her phone into her back pocket, shifting her bag on her shoulder.

She was about to enter the yellow maw of the subway entrance, reaching her hand into her bag to find her headphones, when the noise of a helicopter flying above made her look up. The sky was a clear, clear blue and she was aware, suddenly, of the perfect temperature of the air on the bare skin of her limbs. And then, despite the movement of people, vehicles, all around her, the noise of motors, sirens, conversations, she recognised, with delight, the distinct stillness of her own thoughts.

She pulled her hand from her bag and turned away from the subway entrance and continued to walk downtown. She passed a bus waiting at the intersection. Inside, she caught sight of the same white-jacketed doctor that she'd seen in advertisements all over the MTA system. He looked too polished, too beautiful to be a real doctor. But then she thought of Rosie and all the beautiful men she posts pictures of herself with online, and revised that assumption. It seemed odd that simply thinking about doctors could do it, but immediately she felt her breath become shallow and a palpable ache settled itself in the centre of her chest.

She reached for her phone and typed as she walked.

How are things, Mum? x

Then another message.

Can we speak this weekend? When would be a good time to call? Px

As soon as she pressed send her phone sprang to life in her hand and her stomach flipped to see Michael's name lit up. She slid her thumb across the screen and swallowed as she brought the phone to her ear.

'Thanks for all the voice messages, Roberts. How's the hangover?'

His voice seemed far away, tinny. Surely he ought to sound closer now they were on the same landmass?

'Messages?'

'Well, they were more like recordings from the inside of your pocket. I think the cool kids call them "butt dials". Anyway, it was a fascinating insight into your secret New York life.'

'It's hardly a secret, you are welcome to visit me any time.'

Phoebe felt unstable, suddenly, as though she were sliding down a hill of gravel, her feet slipping.

'And who, pray tell, is the gent with the baritone laugh?'

Again she put her left hand to the tender inside of the arm that was holding the phone. She remembered then, there had been a man. But what was his name?

Fear catches at her. A fear that felt as if her stomach had dropped out, an elevator freefalling down a shaft.

She couldn't remember his name. But she did now – suddenly, vividly – remember the sex.

'Phoebs?'

'Hi, hi, yeah, still here.'

She drew a breath, pushed away the memory of the man kneeling at the end of the bed. There was a condom, at least. She remembered then, checking it when he'd gone, wrapping it in toilet roll, flushing it down the loo.

Jerome! That was his name. The bartender.

It was always the bartenders.

The relief of remembering was short-lived. She was trying to listen to what Michael was saying, about the wig fitting that morning when he could barely see straight with tiredness. But the shame was enveloping her now, constricting her throat, pulling her shoulders closer to her ears.

'Well, anyway. Your drunken misdials are not the juiciest goss I've got.'

Despite the blanket of horror that was threatening to smother her, a smile tugged at the corner of Phoebe's mouth. Michael's joy in gossip was one of her absolute favourite things about him, one of the many passions they shared.

'Go on . . .'

'Guess who was next to me on the plane? Nah, I'll tell you right now, 'cos you will never guess it. You. Will. Never. Guess.'

'Is it someone you love?'

'Erm, no. It's not someone famous. But it's someone you love, or, well – I've never really understood the deal with you two.'

A cold feeling settled across Phoebe's shoulders.

'Em? You sat next to Emmaline?'

'*Ding ding ding*! It was so weird—'

On some level, Phoebe was aware that Michael was still talking. She nodded her head, she made little noises – '*uh-huh*' 'yeah' – as he was speaking, but to say she was listening to him, really hearing what he was saying, would be untrue.

How could this be? What were the odds of her sister being sat next to her best friend on a transatlantic flight?

'How was she?' She had interrupted Michael, she knew, but the question leapt out of her mouth before she'd been aware that she was speaking.

He laughed, the tinny sound to the line returning.

'Like I said, good, she was good. It was weird. I always have found it a bit . . . weird spending time with Emma. It's like I was on a flight with you, but it wasn't you. Weird. Anyway, we're meeting tonight. There's a dinner, I said she should come too. There'll be other Brits. Should be fun, I reckon. I'm picking her up later. She's in West Hollywood too. Did you know she's got work here? She wouldn't give me details, it was all very secretive. Maybe she's a spy.'

'Maybe she just doesn't want everyone who works on the Paramount lot to know her business? Gossip McGossipface.'

'Ha, ha. Anyway, I thought it was a nice thing to do. Invite her out. Seeing as she doesn't know anyone in LA. Ought I not to have? Do you want me to rescind the invitation?'

Yes, Phoebe thought. *Rescind, rescind, rescind*. But she didn't say that, instead she blew air through her lips.

'Don't be silly. It's nothing to do with me. You can hang out with whoever you want, Regis. Even my boring sister.'

The familiar bellow of Michael's laughter echoed down the phone.

'Phoebe! You are, hands down, the harshest person I know.'

In the background she heard the sound of a door opening, a woman's voice speaking to him.

'Sure thing, I'll be right there.' Momentarily his voice was distant as he spoke away from the phone, and then, he was back. 'Gotta go, Phoebs, Hollywood needs me.'

'Duty calls.'

'Exactly, mate. Exactly.'

She could hear his breathing change as he stood, and she had an image of him in his trailer, raising his hands above his head, stretching in the way he always did when he was about to leave a room.

'Phoebs?' His tone was softer now. 'Do you have a message for her? For Emma?'

Phoebe shook her head, scratched her neck and inhaled.

'I don't know. You could say I said hi? I guess?'

'You're a wordsmith, Roberts.'

'Have fun.'

'I'll text. Love you, mate.'

'Love you too, Regis.'

Michael ended the call and she came to an abrupt halt on the sidewalk. At once the front of someone's shoulder collided with the back of her own and with a yell of, 'Move!' she was back on the streets of New York.

Her stomach churned, empty other than for the iced coffee. She felt as if there was an energy fizzing around her, an aura of shame that she wanted to pluck off her skin in handfuls to be rid of it.

Ridiculous.

Why is she worried? She should be happy that two people she loves are keeping each other company. The thing is, when two people keep each other company and those two people have a person in common, that person tends to be the subject of at least one thread of their conversation.

Michael could tell Emma about the deep-voiced bartender who she can't really remember getting intimate with last night. Or that she was on shaky ground with the paper. Or that she'd called him more than once in the last month so drunk he'd had to order her an Uber from his phone in London by asking her to read out the signs on the nearest junction. All stuff that likely wouldn't surprise Emma, but in Emma's hands would undoubtedly get back to their mum or, worse, prompting Emma to make another of her 'little trips' to New York to check in on her.

But what Michael might reveal to Emma is nowhere near as horrifying as what Emma could tell Michael. She could just imagine it. Emma, nodding as Michael spoke. Elegantly taking a sip of her drink, or that infuriating habit of hers, sucking the salt from a single peanut. And then, a slight shrug of her left shoulder and that slow blink she does before she speaks. It needn't be salacious, and knowing Emma it wouldn't be. Anything she said about Phoebe behind her back would be just as true as anything she said to her face, but it would be just that: true. Small truths. Tiny truths that she hadn't so much hidden from Michael over their nine years of friendship, as edited. And if he talks to Emma . . . just thinking of it, she wants to crunch herself up into a tiny ball right here on the sidewalk. A woodlouse of shame, coiled against the gum stains and filth of a billion feet.

It was looking up from the sidewalk that she became aware she'd walked much further than she'd planned. She'd missed the turning for the library, and the station to catch the L. But she shrugged and continued to let the flow of people propel her, tilting her face upwards to catch the sun. She tried to focus on the noise, the fumes, the heat, the hum of other beings moving around her. Anything but the question that was screaming inside her head.

What if they like each other more than they like me?

She looked across the road and saw a bar with a neon *Pabst Blue Ribbon* sign glowing in its window: white, red and blue. Her laptop banged against her hip as she rushed to make the crossing. She had work to do, a lot of work if she was going to file the changes Raylynne wanted by this evening. She shrugged and pulled the handle on the black-tinted glass door.

What was the difference between working in a bar and working in a cafe, really?

The girl on the other side of the bar straightened up to greet her from where she was bending down to the fridge beneath the counter. She swept a shock of blonde hair away from her eyes, and Phoebe noted its greasiness, but then the bartender's green eyes caught hers and she smiled and revealed incisors that were particularly sharp.

'What can I do for you?' Phoebe noticed the sinews in the bartender's forearms as she flipped the bar towel over her shoulder and pushed her hair behind her ear.

'I'll take a Maker's.' Phoebe smiled as she slid onto the bar stool. 'Large. On the rocks.'

Fifteen

Mary pats her rollers and grabs a fistful of spoons from the crate on the chair beside her. She circles the table behind Rosie and Phoebe, laying a spoon next to the fork and knife that Rosie has already placed on every rectangle of yellow napkin.

Phoebe laughs at something Rosie is saying and it makes Mary jump. The loud and surprising burst of it, the very echo of her own. Odd, but there is something foreign about hearing it in this space. Phoebe's laugh – all of her girls' laughter – has been absent from this garden for such a long time.

At some point, they'd discussed having a dry wedding. Whatever happened to that idea? If the wedding had been when they'd originally planned it, then it would have been easier. Phoebe would have been pregnant and even the guests who didn't know all of the ins and outs of their family history would have noticed if a heavily pregnant woman was sneaking glasses of champagne, or making off to the loo with a purloined bottle of Gavi.

Phoebe has turned so much around, Mary doesn't want to be the one responsible, she doesn't want to be the cause of her breaking her sobriety.

But is she asking too much?

She phoned Michael last week, in a sudden panic. Was he sure Phoebe would be okay around the booze? Was he absolutely sure that she was still sober? She could be hiding it, she said, she had before. He told her to talk to Phoebe. But that seemed impossible, and so she talked to Richard. And Richard promised her that every single drop of booze would be accounted for, that he would do his best to ensure that their daughter was not exposed to undue temptation.

'It's all under lock and key. Try and trust me just this once.'

And so she just has to trust him. And Phoebe.

She has to trust Phoebe and Richard.

She circles the table. Forty-four seems so many places to set after nearly two years of just the four of them around the same bloody dining room table.

Forty-two guests. Or forty-one, if Irene digs her heels in. A table full of people she loves. People who love her. The swell of panic rises in her.

It's too much. Can she really expect everyone to get on, just so she can have her wedding day? Should they have just done a quickie? It was good enough for her last wedding.

Although, was it really? Hadn't she always wanted the church, the special dress, God and her family watching as she said, 'I do.'

Last time, there wasn't a single member of her family in the registry office. Both of the witnesses had been Richard's friends from the paper. But today, every single person in that church will be hers in some way.

Rosie is holding the end of the bunting between her teeth, dragging it behind her like a dog running away from a butcher with a stolen string of sausages. She watches as Rosie mounts the chair; it creaks dangerously as she does so, and then wobbles precariously as she reaches up into the tree and grabs hold of the dangling ribbon.

'Careful.'

'Always.' Rosie ties the end of the bunting string to the hanging ribbon in a single easy motion.

Mary returns to the crate for the steaming mug that she'd wedged in the corner and unfurls the folded dishcloth beside it, throwing it over her bare shoulder. The smell of the malt vinegar she added to the water fills her nostrils, and her mouth moistens.

Chips on the beach. In a polystyrene tray from the pier in Southwold, the twice-cooked ones in Aldeburgh, the ones cooked in lard in Felixstowe, the ones in a cone in Lowestoft. All of them drenched in vinegar, covered in grains of salt.

'The best part of sea swimming, in my opinion.'

Liz licking the salt from her forefinger before picking up another chip. She never used the little wooden fork.

'Oh aye, you wouldn't catch me in there without the promise of chips.'

She really ought to eat something soon or she'll be fantasising about hot buttered toast at the altar.

Her stomach flips again. Altar. Her church wedding.

They all went there yesterday afternoon for the rehearsal. It was chaos from start to finish: Clara running around the font at the side of the church, Michael trying to catch her whilst soothing the crying baby on his shoulder at the same time; Phoebe and Rosie fussing over how best to tie the sunflowers to the end of the pews. It was difficult to hear herself think, to concentrate on what she ought to be doing, following the instructions the rector was giving. But then everyone flooded out of the church and the rector was in the nave talking to Joan Butterworth, the church warden, who made no qualms about letting them know she mightily disapproved of the union happening in her church. And for a moment it was just the two of them holding hands, and the afternoon light was flooding through the stained glass above the altar, casting a rainbow of colour across their faces. She'd felt her lungs expand, as if she had been beneath water and had just breached the surface, finally able to breathe.

Rosie is holding glasses up, checking them in the light before polishing them with a tea towel and placing them back onto the table.

'Is it going to be all right, do you think, Phoebs? You feeling okay?'

Phoebe draws a breath through her teeth like a mechanic evaluating the extent of the damage to a car. And Mary raises her palm to head off her daughter's answer.

'Emma wouldn't be flying all this way for a scrap. She is coming of her own accord. She wants to be here, she wants to see us all.'

'I know you're trying to stay positive, Mum. But I think "us all" is pushing it.' Phoebe's head is tilted at an enraging angle.

'Oh for goodness' sake! If the last few years have taught us anything, then surely it's that life is too short for silly disagreements.'

'You don't need to tell me that, Mum.'

Rosie draws a deep breath and raises her eyebrows, but doesn't take her eyes from the glass she is polishing.

'There comes a point, girls, where you have to let bygones be bygones and move on. Just look at me and your dad.'

Mary sees a look pass between Rosie and Phoebe, their faces taut with the effort of suppressing their response. Then, Phoebe catches Mary's eye and she can hold it in no longer. A smile cracks across her face.

'Yeah, just look at you!'

Phoebe and Rosie's shoulders bounce as they let their sniggers turn into cackles.

'Ah, weesht. We do all right, considering.'

Phoebe holds up her hands in a truce and Rosie mimes zipping her lips, but they continue to smile to themselves as they polish the final glasses and position them.

And then, in a moment of quiet, the table is set.

The three women pause.

It looks magical already, even in the daylight. The glow of the lights in the branches of the willow is barely visible in the glare, but their positioning hints at what an impact they will have once the sun is setting; already their reflection in the surface of the pond is magical. The mismatch of furniture seems more uniform now the table is dressed, as if the array of chairs were purposeful, part of the design. The length of the table is in shade but dappled with sunlight, which filters through the canopy of the willow above them and shimmers up from the pond beside it. Here and there the shafts of light catch on glass and bounce at an angle across the tablecloth, creating pools of white. Reflections twinkle from the polished blade of a knife, the dipped bowl of a spoon, and these tiny spotlights are cast upwards, catching on the bright yellow of the sunflowers' crinkled petals.

Mary casts her eyes about the table for anything out of place.

'It looks stunning, Mum.' Phoebe's arm is cool against the skin of her back as she drapes it over her shoulders.

'It's beautiful Mary.'

Rosie leans in and kisses her cheek, and Mary can smell her sun cream, but also that perfume, the one Rosie's mother wore. The one that she'd smelled on Richard's clothes for months before she knew about the affair. How distant that time seems now. A whole lifetime since the pain and shock of Richard's secret life in London, his secret child. This woman whose arm is looped through her own now.

Mary lets her head incline to rest against Rosie's and the mass of her hair tickles at her ear. Soon Emma will be here too. Her girls all together. And then, later, everyone that she loves will be here.

Everyone, with one glaring omission.

'Oh dear.' Mary pushes at the tear that is tracing its way down her cheek with the heel of her hand. 'I promised myself I wouldn't cry, at least until the vows.'

'You deserve happiness, Mary.'

' "Deserve" is a—' Phoebe pauses, shakes her head. 'It's going to be a great day.'

'Rosie's right, Mum. You do.' A new voice rings out behind them, and all three turn to follow it.

Mary squints against the glare of the sun, trying to see who is speaking, but of course, she knows – they all know, because the voice is as familiar to each of them as their own. It's just that it's been so long. It had somehow seemed impossible that she would really be there, even though she had promised that she would be.

'Emma!'

Her eldest daughter, standing at the end of the garden, on the wrong side of the gate, her hand hovering over the latch.

'Hello.'

She pushes her sunglasses onto her head. Without her glasses, despite the make-up and subtle non-surgical enhancements, it is clear that this is her daughter, Phoebe's sister, the woman who was once the girl who used to lie on this lawn, playing with her little sister, their feet in the air, pretending to walk on the branches of the willow above them.

Emma presses on the metal latch and walks through the gate, closing it behind her with a gentle click.

'Darling!' Mary exhales, the sting of tears threatening once more.

'Em!'

Rosie is running ahead of her then, barefoot over the parched lawn, her long, bare legs jumping over an empty plastic box, and then she is wrapping her arms around Emma. And then, just as abruptly, she is standing back, holding her at arm's length. 'You've changed your hair! For a second I didn't recognise you. It suits you!'

'Hello Rosebud.'

Rosie laughs, a hoot of joy to hear the childhood nickname spoken by Emma, but then her face folds in on itself and she starts to cry.

'Oh . . . oh, don't make me break my promise to Mum before I'm even over the threshold,' says Emma, drawing Rosie into a hug.

Rosie laughs through her tears.

'It's not you. I'm so glad you're here. I'm so glad we're all here.' She wipes at her face and stands back to allow Mary access to her daughter.

Mary places her hands on her Emma's shoulders.

'How was the journey?'

'Awful.'

'Thank you.' She pulls Emma against her. It's the warmth of her body, the smell of her, the way Mary instantly recognises the way her neck isn't quite long enough to rest her head over Emma's shoulder – all of this – that sets the tears that have been threatening, falling.

'It's been too long.'

Emma's chest vibrates as she laughs.

'We talk every day.'

Mary holds Emma at arms' length again.

'It's not the same. Let me look at you.'

'Is this all you've brought? Shall I get your bag from the car? Where have you parked?' Rosie lifts the small leather holdall from Emma's shoulder and carries it over to the table, hanging it over the back of one of the thrones. 'You're staying aren't you? We made your bed. You have to stay for the packing, or Phoebe will take all of the good stuff.'

'Hi.'

Mary turns to see Phoebe is still back by the table, one hand resting on it, almost as if it were holding her up. She looks back to Emma. And then to Phoebe again. And back to Emma.

'Hello, Phoebe.' There is the briefest of eye contact between them before she turns back to Mary. 'So where's your betrothed?'

'We're not seeing each other until the church.'

'Such a pair of romantics.'

'And Dad?'

'Inside. Everyone's inside. Oh, I want you to meet Danyal, right now. And Granny! Everyone!'

Rosie turns back to Emma and kisses her swiftly on the cheek, then runs back towards the house.

'Everyone! Em's here! Emma's home!'

'It looks beautiful out here Mum. Love the flowers. And the bunting.'

'Rosie made it, hasn't she done a lovely job?'

Emma loops her arm through Mary's and they both look up at the little multicoloured flags that hang in a sweep, the length of the table. Gold thread shimmers on the edge of each of the yellow appliqué sunflowers, reflecting those in the vases beneath them. The little triangles are embroidered on both sides so the message of the central eleven panels will be visible to the guests along either side of the table.

'Mary and Iain.' Emma reads aloud from the embroidered bunting.

'Should we have done it the other way around, do you think? Iain and Mary? It'd look less like "Marianne" then wouldn't it?'

Emma snorts and strokes Mary's forearm that is threaded through her own.

'Mummy! Nana!'

Emma stiffens at the sound of Clara's voice. Mary has a sudden urge to try to block the child from her daughter's view, to stand in front of her to screen her from seeing this beautiful, perfect child whose parentage is evident in her every feature, her expressions, the way even that she runs as she is doing now.

'Hello little mucky pup, what's that Grampy of yours been feeding you?'

'Lollies.'

Clara grins, the sticky residue of her treat surrounding her beautiful mouth.

'Lollies? Plural?'

Phoebe is standing now. Mary can hear the effort in her voice. The false brightness in order to mask her emotions in front of Clara.

'Who are you?'

Clara is standing but a metre from Emma, her arm extended in an accusatory point.

'That's your Auntie Emma, Clara. Remember, we told you she was coming? She's come all the way from America for Nana's wedding.'

Clara looks at Mary, calculating something, and then turns back to Emma.

'You came in an aeroplane and you live on the beach.'

Emma nods.

'That's right.'

'I'm going to lead Nana and Grandad Iain down the aisle. We practised yesterday. I have to walk like this.' Clara steps towards Emma, bringing her feet together before stepping out once again. 'I have to throw flower petals onto the floor, but I'm allowed to hold my balloon too, because it's yellow like the petals.'

'Clara's our flower girl.'

'We're having a party here tonight, and I'm allowed to stay up until it's dark. But Albie will have to go to bed. We're going to have dinner here, in the garden, next to the pond.'

'Well, that sounds fun. Doesn't it?'

'You have to stay this side of the fence though, because the pond is more dangerous than it looks.'

'Oh, okay. I'll try to remember that.'

'Albie doesn't eat dinner, only booboo. But I'm going to sit on a big girl's chair and eat the chocolate cake. There's a little sign with my name on in curly writing so no one takes my seat. Don't worry you'll have one too so you know where to sit. Nana is going to make sure you and Mummy are at opposite ends of the table to keep the peace.'

'Clara, shall we go and get you in the bath so you can put your dress on?'

Phoebe is up and pulling the little girl into her arms.

'I've got a yellow dress.' The little girl calls back to them over Phoebe's shoulder as she's carried away. 'Yellow, like my balloon!' She smiles back at them as her mother marches her into the conservatory.

Mary watches them disappear and then turns to Emma, and takes her hand. 'Well done, sweetheart.'

Emma nods.

'It means the world to have you here.' She feels Emma pulse her hand in hers.

'Does Phoebe know I'm giving you away?'

Mary nods.

'Everyone does.'

The high-pitched pips of the radio in the kitchen slice through the air.

Panic surges through Mary like an electric shock.

'Is that— Is that the time? I've got to get ready.'

'You've plenty of time.'

'But all these boxes! We need to tidy up! The chairs need straightening, and—'

'I'll do it, it's fine. Look at the weather you've got. It's going to be fine. No –' Emma squeezes her hand '– it's going to be perfect.'

'I just want it over and done with now.'

And she does. That is her overriding feeling. She wants the ring on her finger, the papers signed, the party over and done with. Because, then comes the hard bit. The packing up, the saying goodbye. But then, then, when they're in the car winding their way up the spine of this country, when they cross the border, she might just be able to breathe.

Mary feels Emma's hand tighten on her forearm.

'Try and enjoy it, Mum.'

'I know. I will. But I think I'm going to need a drink, and the sun's still high in the sky!'

'I might join you.'

'Oh?'

'Come on, you go in and get started on your hair. You've got loads of time. Loads. I'll follow you up. I can help with make-up, if you want.'

'Thank you.'

Mary moves closer to Emma, then pulls her into her chest. It is uncomfortable to be so close to another body in this heat, but she holds on for a few seconds longer before releasing her and placing her hand on her cheek.

'Thank you.'

'Go on. You've been waiting for this day for a long time.'

'Yes.' Mary consciously fills her lungs and slowly exhales. 'Such a long time.'

Sixteen

Mary gripped the receiver in her left hand, the coiled flex dangling between her and the phone like an umbilical cord. The metallic ringing down the line made her mouth dry, instantly. She took a chewed biro from the occasional table and determinedly scratched out one of the numbers on the list beside the phone. The 0s were formed like little squares, the 7s struck through, like a pound sign; the name – his name – written in his ugly scrawl. 'Richard – London'. She gritted her teeth and yanked the whole sheet of paper from the wall. Although the Sellotape was browning at the edges, it still managed to take a jagged disk of the hideous green paintwork with it. Beneath it, swirls of white and orange wallpaper peeped out and she let out a grunt of frustration just as the tone on the phone changed.

'Hello?'

'Iain. I'm so sorry to bother you.'

It was last Tuesday morning when Mary had first noticed it.

It was lodged in the crook of the window, curled up, coiled, hiding. A mottled brown-black lump, not much bigger than a chickpea or a peanut, pushed up into the very corner, between the rubber seal and the frame.

It was the movement that had drawn her attention. The extension of a crustacean-like little leg, articulated at each joint.

Thicker than a pin, thinner than a matchstick. A leg that unfurled and then seemed to probe – like a hand emerging from the duvet to seek out the button and silence the radio alarm.

She unwound the toilet roll gently, watching it the whole time, that brown pebble in the corner, obvious now against the white of the window frame. She imagined herself reflected in its mass of eyes. She remembered something about them having eight. Or was it eight eyes on each side? However many it was, it was too many.

She flushed, awkwardly manoeuvring her hand behind her. An uncomfortable contortion, but she didn't want to turn her back on it. She wanted to keep it in her eyeline at all times.

It must have come in when she opened the window on Sunday.

She'd taken to putting the two of them in the tub together in a tangle of small limbs. It was quicker, marginally, but it was also much, much noisier. A debate about who got the tap end, the squawking hilarity of a stream of bubbles trailing from Phoebe's perfect little bottom. A shriek from Emma that she 'Didn't want to sit in a bath full of farts.'

Mary had just needed a moment.

She'd opened the window and inhaled.

She could taste autumn in the air, and its freshness made her realise just how hot it was in the bathroom.

The thermostat, that was another thing she'd have to try to understand.

The leaves of the willow that still clung to the branches were mustard yellow, their edges nibbled by brown, orange, red, the undulating silver waves of summer long gone. The mass of fallen leaves beneath the tree spread out, like rust, across the grass.

Lawnmower. She needed to get petrol for the lawnmower.

'Mummy, is it a hair-wash day?'

'Yes. Can you be a big girl and help Phoebe, please?' Mary leaned a little further out of the window, closing her eyes and focusing on the lick of the breeze on her face, the vegetal smell of approaching rain.

It was sixteen days since she'd watched the tail lights of Richard's Mazda recede down the road, and, overall, she'd held it together.

She'd cried when she couldn't get the petrol pump to work. She'd cried when she turned the corner to the school – Emma trailing behind, her satchel dangling from her shoulder, Phoebe, whining in the pushchair – found the gates closed, locked with a chain and padlock, and realised it was Saturday. She'd cried until she'd fallen asleep on the sofa on Thursday; when Liz had turned up with a white oval ovenproof dish covered in tinfoil in one hand and a full bottle of vodka in the other. And again on Saturday, when Iain had discreetly absented himself from their usual curry night so Lizzie could help her to search for the solution to men at the bottom of two bottles of Riesling.

But on the whole, she hadn't cried very much. The answer to not crying, she'd discovered, was to decide not to. To keep busy and not think about it. To try not to think about anything at all, really. There were clothes to wash and noses to wipe and food to prepare and squabbles to settle. Keeping busy, when your bigamist husband had left you with two children, a five-bedroom house, and four chickens to look after, wasn't an issue.

Mary had discovered, however, that a by-product of purposefully not thinking about something is that you stop thinking too hard about anything. And that was why, when she took a deep breath and turned around to rinse the shampoo out of the girls' hair and stop Phoebe drinking cup after cup of the murky bathwater, she'd left the window open.

Later, she'd woken to the sound of raindrops whipping against glass and realised she had once again fallen asleep on the carpet next to Phoebe's bed, whilst waiting for her to go to sleep. She'd heaved herself up and pulled the duvet up to her daughter's chin, then gone to clean her teeth. The bathroom was frigid and the floor wet, rain making its way in through the open window. She closed it firmly and shook her head as she gingerly mopped up the spatters of rain with an old flannel that she threw straight in the pedal bin. She shook her head again. She'd been really careful about keeping windows open for too long ever since Chernobyl. As it turned out, potentially radioactive rainwater wasn't the only thing that had made its way into her.bathroom.

It was ridiculous, she knew, to be afraid of spiders. She was a capable woman. She owned a drill, she could even change a tyre, if pushed. But for some reason spiders just undid her.

Her first strategy was to open the window again; let it out the way it had come in. It was a brave thing, to approach the window with it there in the corner, watching her. But she extended her arm and lifted the window's catch, using the full length of her fingers to jab at the window, once, twice, until it swung open.

'Go on, off you go.'

Then she closed the bathroom door behind her, going down to cut the crusts off cheese sandwiches.

After lunch, when she'd happily set up Phoebe with some crayons, she'd made her way back upstairs and gingerly pushed the door open. It was still there. In the crook of the window. The gossamer strings of a web stretched between the corner and the frame surrounding the pane that was swinging out into the October afternoon. She'd decided then that she'd have to be brutal. She pulled the window closed with a *thunk*. She tried not to picture the crushed limbs, the tiny crunch that its exoskeleton must have made as the window slammed against it, squashing it into the corner of the frame.

But then, the next morning, as she squeezed pea-sized dots of pink, strawberry toothpaste onto the two small toothbrushes held out to her, she saw it again. It was the same one, she was sure. She recognised the colouring, the particularly sharp look of its feet. Only seven legs now, she noted. And she imagined she heard the slam the window had made the previous night echo in the room.

It was on the rim of the bath, dancing towards the taps.

'Shit!'

'Shit's a bad word, Mummy.'

'Yes, it is. Don't you say it.'

She reached for the shower head, closely watching the spider's attempts to scale the chrome. With a flick of her fingers, the shower sprang to life, a thick spray of water cascading into the bath. Mary aimed. The spider hung on at first, but then the force of the jet seemed to loosen its grip and it was scrabbling, desperate to hang on, and it was falling, its seven legs reaching and then contracting, and it was a small, dark mass again, a pebble, circling the plughole, and then, gone. It was gone.

Mary continued to aim the shower at the plug, watching the water swirl and disappear, and then she turned off the taps, placed the shower head back into its cradle, and wiped her hands on her dress.

She was going to be fine. She could handle whatever life threw at her. She was tough.

'Come on girls, spit. It's time for Emma to get to school.'

Sitting at one end of her long kitchen table now, worrying her thumbnail with her front teeth, Mary shook her head at her earlier hubris. Tough? Is that why she's waiting for her best friend's husband to come and catch a spider for her?

She started at a noise from outside. It was dark, it had been for several hours now. Soon the clocks would go back and it would be even darker.

Standing in the conservatory, she felt that she was surrounded by a force field, protected from the squall of the weather outside. Rain was lashing the windows now: leaves, small sticks, swept up by gusts of wind, sticking to the wet panes. Her eyes adjusted to the dark and she saw that her little chicken coop was safely battened down. Down the garden the long arms of the willow were whipping back and forth in the wind; a black silhouette against the orange glow of the night sky. She considered for a moment the tree's proximity to the house. She knew that this storm wasn't going to be as bad as first predicted – she had watched the weather forecast earlier – but she couldn't help assessing the possibilities for accidents. Disaster mitigation was a skill that really sharpened with parenthood. Richard had arrived home with all those fire extinguishers a couple of weeks after Phoebe was born.

She felt her chest tighten at the thought of him.

She was still very angry. So angry that she worried she might never not be angry again. She'd said as much to Lizzie on Saturday night.

* * *

'You've plenty to be angry about.'

Lizzie refilled their glasses.

'How he had the energy. That's what I don't understand.'

Mary felt a heat across her cheeks.

'Well, actually. There hasn't been much energy expended in our bedroom for quite some time.'

Lizzie cackled and placed her hand on Mary's forearm.

'I didn't mean that, but even if that's the case, it's not a reason. There is no planet on which having two families is okay because you aren't getting regular blowjobs.'

Mary covered her face with her hands.

'Another drink?'

She didn't say anything, in case she sobbed, but she'd allowed herself to when Liz had drawn her into her chest.

What she kept coming back to was how she hadn't noticed. Three years. Three years at least because the girl, Richard's daughter, was only six months younger than Phoebe. A detail that made her feel slightly sick.

It hadn't been right with Richard for a long time, but no matter how many times she went over it, she couldn't think of any changes in him that she could have picked up on. What did that say about her?

'It says that you are busy. It says that you have been raising two kids. It says that he's a bloody pillock who's – sorry Mary, but remember I've known him a very long time – never been able to keep, his not particularly large, dick in his trousers.'

She laughed then. For the first time in two weeks. It wasn't even that funny. It was puerile and unfair, but combined with the wine, it peeled back an even deeper layer of disclosure.

'In many ways it feels like a relief.'

She hadn't realised it until she said it, but once it was out there, she knew it was true, and then she couldn't stop. She told Liz how, recently, she'd found herself increasingly irritated at his appearance on Friday – how she dreaded the rev of his car engine on the drive, how it seemed to interrupt her flow, and unsettled the girls. She told her that often when he was away she would catch them when they didn't know she was looking, curled up watching TV together like a pair of kittens, or Emma reading patiently to Phoebe, stoically accepting her third cup of invisible tea at a teddy bears' picnic. But at the weekends there seemed to be constant screaming. Disagreements over who got the most cereal or who should have help to take their wellies off first. She sighed then, realising that was only likely to get worse now his presence was going to be even more sporadic.

Lizzie licked her thumb and wiped it under each of Mary's eyes; an action so intimate it made Mary intensely aware of a need to swallow.

'It's going to be messy for a bit. But you're young, you're gorgeous. You won't be single for long.'

A noise pulled Mary away from the dark outline of the tree. Her name was being called, a deep voice from within the house. Her stomach pitched and she pushed her hair back from her face, turning to see Iain entering the kitchen, pulling off his leather jacket, shining with moisture.

'I'm afraid I've dripped all the way through the hallway, like a wet dog!'

He smiled, running his hands over his head, water dripping from the lengths of his ponytail.

His hair was much more conventional than when they'd first met. He kept the sides grown in now, rather than wet-shaven, and the colour was an uneven brown. He'd cut the last of the peroxide blonde from it not long after she'd met him. Liz's hair was all grown out now too, no sign of her previous hairstyle. It had been a messy bleached blonde bob for a while, a hairstyle that made Liz look even more like Debbie Harry than when they'd first met.

Mary handed Iain a hand towel from the rail on the front of the cooker. His thumb touched the back of her hand as he took it from her.

'I'm sorry to be such a wuss. It's just Richard has always dealt with them. I'd hoover it up, but the vacuum's broken.' She rambled on as he ran the towel over his face, around his neck. 'If I'd known the wind was going to get so bad—'

'We said to call any time. It's nae bother, we're a stone's throw, aren't we?' He folded the towel neatly and placed it on the corner of the table. 'So where is the fearsome beastie?'

Iain mounted the stairs ahead of her. His socks were worn at the heel and she could see the pink of his skin peeping through the white weft of the cotton. She felt her cheeks warm. She had got to get a hold of herself. She was lonely, yes, but she couldn't start getting worked up by a glimpse of her best friend's husband's heel – it was beyond desperate.

She followed him into the bathroom and caught sight of herself in the mirror. What a state. Her hair pulled back in one of Emma's rainbow scrunchies, her cheeks flushed with the shame of her inappropriate thoughts.

'I washed it down, I washed it down, and it came back up. It came back up twice.'

'Yep, they do that.' He sealed the arachnid into its jam-jar cage with a coaster. 'Incy wincy spider, climbed up the water spout. And all that.' He stopped suddenly, pulled a face. 'Sorry, they're asleep are they?' He was whispering, pointing in the direction of the girls' bedrooms with his eyes.

'Out for the count.'

There was an odd silence. A pause in their conversation that felt like the buzz of static, and she was suddenly acutely aware that she had never been alone with Iain ever before.

The spider was frantic in the trap. It tried to mount the walls of its cell to no avail, its seven legs whirring against the glass and making a faint tapping noise.

'We'd better set our prisoner loose. She's a bigun. No wonder you needed to call in the reserves.'

Mary recoiled slightly as he held the glass up to inspect it.

He smiled then. Winked. And Mary felt a familiar wash of warmth threatening to lap over her. She turned abruptly and headed down the stairs.

'Let's put her out the front, so she doesn't hang around in the garden.'

She opened the front door and was almost blown back in. Turning directly into Iain's chest.

'I thought they said it was going to blow itself out.'

Maybe it was the speed at which she'd come down the stairs, but for some reason Mary felt as though she couldn't quite catch her breath.

The phone rang. And Mary sidestepped Iain to answer it.

'Hello?'

'Mary. Is Iain there?'

Lizzie.

'Just leaving. I feel so silly for calling now. I've never been good with spiders.'

'We said you should. I'm glad you called. Spiders are absolute knobheads, I hate them. Listen, can you tell Iain I'll be staying here?'

'In the lab?'

Lizzie's throaty laughter echoed down the phone and Mary

felt that odd glow of pride that she always did when she made her laugh.

'A colleague – lives right next door – has offered me their spare room. It'd be mad to drive back. It's mayhem, apparently. Trees all over the roads. I should have knocked off on time, but they said it was going to blow itself out. Anyway, I'm going to be fed and watered, so actually it feels like a bit of a treat. Don't tell Iain I said that!'

The front door banged shut and Mary jumped. Then something hit the kitchen window with an almighty smack. She turned, sharply, expecting to see a crack in the pane, but only saw a length of willow branch against the glass, long yellow and orange leaves stuck to the window as if applied with glue.

Mary rotated to face Iain. Too late she realised she had turned full circle, the phone cord now wrapped around her neck.

'You two should batten down the hatches and open a bottle. Have a glass for me, yeah? Put him on, would you, Mary?'

'Oh, yes.' Her voice didn't seem to be her own. 'Hang on, he's just here.'

She unwound herself from the wire and handed the receiver to Iain. Then stepped into the kitchen to give him some privacy. Though even if she had wanted to listen in on their conversation, she wasn't sure she would have been able to, the blood in her ears was rushing so loudly. A drink, alone with Iain? What would they talk about? She wasn't sure that even she could blather on about spiders all night.

'Well, there I was thinking that the walk home through this was going to be rewarded by hot steak and chips on the table.' Iain was standing just on the other side of the door frame between the kitchen and the hall.

Mary had an odd urge to shut the door on him.

'Steak, lucky you. I was just going to have cheese on toast.'

'Oh, manna of heaven! We used to make it with a bit of diced onion.'

He kisses the tips of his fingers.

'Me too! I mean, it was one of about four meals in my dad's repertoire! I made it for Richard when we first met. He said it was worse than putting salt in my porridge.'

'Ah, yes. Well, Richard has always struck me as the sort of bloke who'd opt for honey.' He shook his head, gravely serious. 'There's no helping some people.'

He winked at her. Then frowned, concerned.

'So, Liz said it wasn't just the spider that's been causing you bother. Apparently, you've a bottle that's got a cork stuck in it?'

She laughed and opened the cutlery drawer, scrabbling to locate the corkscrew, then held it towards him.

'I'm afraid I can only offer payment in molten cheddar and diced onion on less-than-fresh Mighty White.'

'Deal.'

He smiled, entering the kitchen now and extending his hand. Mary shook it, considering how rare it was that she was made to feel as petite as she did at that moment.

Outside, with a crack, a branch of the willow was wrenched away from its trunk and fell, with a splash, into the ink-black water of the pond beneath it.

Seventeen

Emma watches her mum walking into the house. She searches for her response to seeing the place she grew up in.

'Hello.'

Barely a whisper. She isn't saying it to the people inside. She's saying it to the place, to the tree, the grey bricks.

What does she *feel*?

Not much, through the slight haze of the jet lag and the Ambien she took at take-off. Just what she has felt since making the decision to come: to be here for her mum, whilst being determined to engage in the absolute minimum and get out of here without burning the place to the ground.

A bead of sweat runs from her hairline and around the curve of her cheekbone. She had the air-con on full for the whole journey and it hasn't occurred to her until now that her outfit might be too warm for the weather.

She rolls her shoulders, stiff from the journey and carrying her bag. She turns to see it hanging over the back of the – *What are those hideous chairs?* She looks around the table, recognition flaring at every other piece of furniture. Battered and worn stuff that she would rather die than have in her own home, but all recognisable as things that belong to her mother. These brocade monstrosities must be new additions. Rosie had told her that her mother was different. Is this what she meant?

The sound of tyres on gravel. Another car pulling up at the side of the house.

How funny that a noise like that should provoke such an overwhelming feeling of nostalgia. She's heard a million cars come to a standstill on gravel in her lifetime, but that particular noise, the duration of it, the way the tyres have to curve against the stones before stopping, that is a noise that immediately pulls her back to the late 90s – the three of them scrambling to look as though they'd been doing homework as Mum arrived back from work, or bracing themselves for the brittle conversation between their parents when their dad had arrived to take them to their grandmother's on his allotted weekends.

The slam of a car door and she dabs at her forehead, readies herself to greet whoever it is that is about to appear at the side of the house.

'Victory!' Michael rounds the side of the house brandishing two brown paper carrier bags before him like trophies.

Michael.

He doesn't look at her, but continues to talk as he walks towards the table, towards her.

'I know we're all supposed to be playing nicey nicey, Phoebs. But she was absolutely setting me up to fail. Thirty fucking yellow candles? I was spotted too. Had to smile for selfies in the Waitrose car park. She might as well have just said, "Fuck off Michael, you're not welcome here. Go and get mobbed, it's what you deserve." ' He pauses, looking at the table. 'Or maybe it really was to match the sunflowers? Whatever. I found the bastard things!'

He laughs triumphantly and finally looks up from the table, meeting Emma's eyes for the first time. Momentarily his smile broadens, his eyes widen on seeing her face, and then it drops like a curtain. His features are no longer lit up by the pathetic pleasure of getting one over on his mother-in-law; instead his face is slack and distinctly greying.

'Hello.'

She has prepared for this moment for years. Practised it in the mirror every time she cleaned her teeth since the day she agreed to come. And then again today, over and over, as she lay reclined in the semi-dark, speeding across the Atlantic.

'I thought you were—' He clears his throat. 'You've changed your hair.'

She doesn't move a muscle or say a word. But watches him searching for the thing that he ought to say.

There is pleasure in it, more than she was expecting. But she doesn't let it show through the practised mask that is her face. Her 'work face', her 'game face'. She is used to people squirming when she uses it, but seeing Michael Regis squirm is more gratifying than she could have hoped.

He presses his lips together, raises his eyebrows.

'You're here!'

She doesn't move at once, but slowly. Just as she planned. She raises an eyebrow, pouts and looks down at herself, patting her hands down her chest, her thighs, and then looks back at him, game face still in place.

'So it would seem.'

'I wasn't sure—' He swallows. 'You're here.'

He smiles then. The smile that he's known for. The smile that she's avoided for four long years, that she's turned away from at news-stands, that she's changed channels because of, that she took a different route to avoid for the three long months it was on that huge billboard on the junction of Laurel and Melrose.

'I came for Mum.'

He holds the paper bags out towards her.

'I've been in town, for your mum. She asked me to go. To buy candles. Yellow candles.'

'To match the sunflowers.'

He nods, places the paper bags onto the table. The handles are wrinkled from where he has been gripping them so tightly. He lets out a long exhale, then fans his face.

'You brought the LA weather with you!'

She doesn't give him anything. Just as she planned. Not a flicker.

He shakes his head.

Good, she thinks, good. *I want you to struggle. This shouldn't be easy for you. Struggle away.*

He rubs his hand across his forehead. She can see the beads of perspiration appear almost immediately when he removes it. But then he looks at her again and inhales decisively, and takes a step towards her. It takes all her concentration not to flinch, not to step back. But her discomfort must show in some way for he pauses and nods, raising his hands, letting her know he's staying where he is, he isn't going to encroach on her personal space any further.

He smacks his mouth. Swallows.

'Really good to see you, Emma.'

She fishes a packet of cigarettes out of her bag, and swiftly places one between her lips, lighting it in one smooth motion.

'You smoke?'

Emma shrugs.

'You used to.'

'I gave up. Remember?'

She stares at him then. Glares at him with the full force of her hatred, just for a second, before she switches it off and breaks their eye contact.

'You go ahead. Tell them I'll be in in a minute.'

He nods and turns, walking towards the house. But as he reaches the patio, he pauses. Emma watches him as he stands still, his back to her until he inhales and turns so fast, she thinks he might lose his balance and topple over.

'I've missed you, Em.' He sounds out of breath.

Emma, keeping his eye contact, inhales deeply on the cigarette. Then she purses her lips and blows three perfect smoke rings, each one into the centre of the last.

They both watch them expand and disperse.

'Right.' And with a decisive nod he turns and walks into the house.

Emma walks toward the table and trails her hand across the tablecloth. It's a bit of an odd set-up, the mismatch of chairs, the higgledy-piggledy cutlery and glassware. But it is beautiful. With the light from the pond, and the festoons and the sunflowers. So many sunflowers, all along the table and on the bunting too.

What's that about? Something to do with Ukraine? She's never known them to be a particular favourite of her mum's. Or maybe it's to do with that painting?

Her stomach churns, the cigarette smoke suddenly feeling horribly foreign in her lungs, and she coughs violently. She tosses the cigarette onto the grass and puts it out under the ball of her foot, then takes off her jacket and throws it into the armchair. She does a double take: it's that horrible threadbare old thing from Granny's ancient three-piece suite. Why on earth did they allow her to bring that here? There ought to have been some sort of sacrificial burning of it when they packed up her house and shipped her over to Mouser Lane. Maybe Emma could instigate it this evening.

There's still a part of her that's itching for destruction.

Her eye falls on the crumpled paper bags where Michael left them. She can see that the brown paper handles are damp. Michael's hands must have been sweating when he was talking to her.

Good, she thinks. *I hope he's sweating. I hope he's shitting himself.*

A baby's cry rings out from the house and she stiffens.

The baby. Michael and Phoebe's new baby. A little boy. Named after Grandad.

She's always loved that name. Bertie.

She pulls a candle out of one of the bags. Immediately she can see that they are the wrong colour yellow, a dark ochre, almost brown. Not even close to the vivid yellow of the sunflowers that she knows her mum would have envisaged if she asked Michael to find yellow candles.

That's going to go down like a ton of bricks.

She smiles to herself, remembering how pleased Michael seemed when he was chatting away to her, before he realised that she wasn't Phoebe.

Leaning across the table, she pulls one of the candlesticks towards her and wedges the diarrhoea-coloured candle into it, then pulls her lighter from her pocket. She curves the palm of her hand around it. The flame catches, she can feel the heat of it against her palm, and as she removes her hand it barely flickers but just burns yellow, orange, blue and green at its very centre.

There isn't a whisper of wind. She didn't notice before, but now she has, she can't imagine why she didn't immediately. The place is so still. The tree is motionless, the straw-like grass, the golden stubble of the wheat in the field beyond, all still, waiting, holding their breath.

Emma places the candle onto the table and closes her eyes, and, for a second, she is as still as everything around her.

Then she inhales, puts her handbag over her shoulder, and turns towards the house.

Eighteen

Emma slipped out of the foyer, letting the door click behind her, and descended the white steps onto the pavement. It was still light, but it would only be so at this time of day for a few more weeks. Already she was favouring closed toes over open, tea over chilled drinks. She paused for a second, wondering whether to remount the stairs to the flat and grab the pashmina hanging over the arm of the sofa.

She looked up at the sky: it was grey, of course, but the weather wasn't cold.

Emma wasn't entirely sure that she was ready for an English winter. Not just because a winter on these islands gave them little excuse not to attend a family Christmas, but also because of the relentless grey. At home, even if the air took on a chill that required a cardigan or a light jacket, the skies remained blue all the way from October to February. She'd been known to lie out in a bikini when carved pumpkins adorned driveways and apply sunscreen even when the first signs of festive decorations began to appear. A winter in England would mean leaning into the crackle of open fires, the cashmere jumpers and socks, the long Sunday walks by the river, she would have to remember how to find joy in the shifting colours of the leaves once again.

Emma hadn't lived in London since Lehman collapsed. In fact, the last three weeks were the longest she'd spent in the UK in nearly ten years. Michael had been back, of course, for premières, for interviews and photoshoots and, on occasion, she'd come along for the ride too; visited her dad, her mum, Liz and Iain, spent time with her granny. But for the most part, she let Michael do his job and she'd got on with hers. Acting, as she often reminded him, was his job, and just because she'd married him it didn't mean it was going to become hers. This was the first time she'd broken that rule and was joining him in London for the duration of the show.

In retrospect, maybe she ought to have followed him around a bit more when they'd first got together. She could have taken advantage of the hotel rooms he barely spent any time in, explored the cities that he saw as fragmented locations before dawn. Maybe, if they'd slept in the same bed more often when her body, and his, had been just that bit younger, then maybe they wouldn't have had to go through the last eighteen months.

She inhaled and turned onto Marylebone High Street.

In the bookshop, she turned the carousel of greetings cards looking for something appropriate. Each one she considered made her cringe with how it might be conceived as a metaphor. A blooming flower? Nope. Fruit? Absolutely not. A tree? Not quite as bad.

She decided, in the end, on a simple line drawing of the London skyline. She borrowed a pen from the cashier and wrote his name then paused on the message. She bit her lip and quickly wrote.

We are so proud of you. Break a leg. See you on the other side.
All my love.

Would he notice it? The use of the plural?

She knew superstition prevented him opening any cards until he came offstage, so, either way, it shouldn't throw him.

She hovered the gummed edge of the envelope near her lips then drew a decisive breath and tucked the flap into itself – just in case she changed her mind – then scrawled his name on the front and handed the pen back to the cashier.

'I'm always buying cards on my way to parties, too!' The woman smiled conspiratorially.

It's funny how people said Londoners were unfriendly. Emma had found it to be quite the opposite. People hadn't stopped talking to her since she'd arrived at Heathrow. In the queue for passport control, someone had asked her if her bag was a real Birkin, the driver had chatted non-stop from Hounslow to Hammersmith, and everywhere she went people seemed to want to tell her their life stories. Everyone seemed desperate to make random observations about the weather or their opinion on Brexit or – if she let slip that she lived in the States – the President. In LA people might send a smiley greeting to each person they passed, but nobody nosed in on your business the second you ordered a coffee. Angelinos didn't seem to feel the same urge to share their political opinions with the person on the next Pilates reformer.

Even today, when she lay on that bed with her heart in her mouth, the sonographer had yakked on and on about how they were going to apply for an Irish passport thanks to a dead grandparent. Ordinarily, Emma was quick to let it be known which way she'd cast her vote, particularly when someone had assumed her stance on the matter, but, on this occasion, she hadn't bothered to disabuse them because there, on the screen, was a dancing form. Two legs. Two arms. A head, and – the chatty sonographer assured her – just the right amount of thickness at the back of its neck.

Years.

Years she had been waiting to hear those words.

Yes, there were other words too:

'As far as we can see . . .' 'There are no guarantees . . .' 'At your age, we'd still recommend . . .'

But she hadn't listened to them. She'd just heard: 'It's all looking good. It looks like a healthy foetus.'

Emma smiled back at the cashier and thanked her for the pen.

'It's not for a birthday, actually. My husband's in a play at the National. It's opening night, and I'm going to tell him that I'm pregnant.'

The woman's eyes widened in surprise.

Emma felt a thrill run through her. It was something she'd always revelled in, her ability to upend the atmosphere merely by stating the facts. Like when she used to wait for one of Phoebe's crusty Cambridge mates to stop bashing on about Iraq before reeling off the litany of human rights abuses that Saddam Hussein was responsible for. Or how at dinner parties in the Hollywood Hills when someone inevitably mentioned The Wall, she'd get just as high as all of those around her vaping their legally acquired dope, by calmly stating she wasn't surprised that everyone around the table was against it, seeing as the running of all their households was reliant on the cheap labour that lax immigration allowed.

'You're married to Michael Regis?'

Emma was suddenly aware of the craning heads in the queue behind her.

'Yes.'

She felt the smile she'd learned to display in these situations tightening her lips.

'I thought I recognised you from somewhere. Michael Regis? I just love him.'

'Yes,' said Emma. 'Me too.'

By the time she got to Marylebone Lane, her shoes were starting to pinch. She extended her arm and hailed a cab. It was much slower to cross the city in a taxi, but she knew several hours lay between her and the removal of her heels.

There was something so reassuring about the purr of a black cab. The way the engine puttered when it came to a standstill. The Plexiglas partition between her and the driver making disengaging from any conversation so wonderfully easy. Cabs were one of the things she did enjoy about London. She rarely took cars in LA, unless they had been organised for Michael. She hated the eerie glide of the hybrid cars that Uber and Lyft drivers favoured; they seemed to slide down the hills, hover along the avenues. Anyway, she liked driving, always had, and since she rarely drank she was generally more than happy to take on the role of designated driver.

The car turned on Wigmore Street, taking her in the opposite direction to the way she'd been walking. She leaned forward and tapped on the divide between her and the driver, the fuzz of the intercom bursting into life.

'I said the National? The National Theatre?'

'Yes, love. Traffic's a bit sticky, what with Crossrail. Best to go down Park Lane, cut across at Westminster.'

'Oh, okay. Thanks.'

She sat back in her seat. Westminster. She ought to call her dad. She'd been in London now for the best part of a month. Perhaps now that she had some reassurance, perhaps now that she no longer felt like a hen sitting on a secret egg, she'd be a bit more confident to venture beyond the confines of the flat. Now that the show was up, Michael would be at the theatre nearly every evening, and then, no doubt, buffeting around the members' clubs of Soho until the early hours. It would be nice to treat her dad to a meal out, to meet whatever woman he had hanging on to his credit card at present. She should try and get up to Birmingham to visit Rosie, or maybe arrange to meet her mum for lunch in Cambridge. But could she afford the stress of it all? Yes, twelve weeks was a milestone, and her ribs were expanding more freely with each breath, but still, there was no need for unnecessary stress. And meeting up with her family was definitely classed as unnecessary stress. She certainly didn't need a repeat of the last time they were all gathered, and there'd be Christmas to deal with before too long. Being in this country would make it nigh-on impossible to excuse themselves.

If only Michael had a family.

The taxi stuttered across Green Park, sweeping around the front of Buckingham Palace, the dregs of summer tourists posing with their backs to the building, selfie-sticks extended.

Guilt. An awful thing, to wish her husband had close relatives just so she could avoid spending a single day with hers. She didn't ask him about it and he rarely discussed it. A year or so ago, there had been the to-do with his sister, but there was still a considerable sum of money that left their UK account on the first of each month in her name. Sometimes, when Emma was venting her frustration over one member of her family or another, she noticed that his nod had become restrained because he was thinking, 'How lucky you are to get to complain about such things.' She knew that because, before, he used to say it out loud. Before they started the treatment he wouldn't nod, but would tell her. 'You have the best family in the world Emma,' and then the argument she'd had with her mother would pale into insignificance, because inevitably the subject of Phoebe would arise, and soon they would be arguing too.

For all the heartache and physical pain of the last three years, one of the benefits had been that their arguments were a thing of the past. In fact, there had been points when she'd wondered if their marriage would have weathered 2016, if they hadn't been trying for a baby. She swore that Michael would have loved to be out there alongside her sister, amongst the swarms of angry women in his own knitted pink hat with cat ears, or on the streets of London, waving a blue flag with yellow stars. But he hadn't. He'd been right there beside her. Holding her hand through every one of their relentless losses. He'd been right there alongside her for the blood in innumerable hotel bathrooms. He'd listened with her to the recordings of heartbeats on her phone before bed as if they were nightly prayers. Those same heartbeats that just disappeared, as if they had been figments of their imagination.

These had been the hardest, worst years of her life, but if nothing else, they had made her marriage stronger. The pain they'd shared had brought her and Michael closer, and now – at last – it seemed that they might be able to put that pain behind them.

The cab slipped through the terrorist deterrent bollards and down Birdcage Walk, skimming the edge of St James's Park. The light was fading already and a gust of wind blew a flock of early fallen leaves in front of the car. They swirled like brown birds, looping, then taking flight.

She placed her hands over her abdomen and closed her eyes.

She shouldn't have thought about their losses. It felt dangerous, as though remembering her pain might invoke more. She tried, instead, to turn her thoughts towards hope. Towards the manifesting that her friends in LA were such advocates of. She focused on their home, on the future.

The late afternoon light would be streaming through the windows, a soft clean scent filling the house. She would be looking out at the sea at sunset, a warm bundle on her shoulder, the smell of onions cooking, Michael humming at the kitchen island behind her. She tried to see small footprints on the beach, a laughing child swinging between her and Michael – '1,2,3, wee . . .'. Her mother smiling as small shoes tapped their way up the path to her hollyhock-surrounded front door, the noise she would make as she lifted her first grandchild and swung her around, and the bare, skinny legs flying out as she turned her, around and around.

It was always a girl she imagined when she did this, when she tried to picture their future, and she mustn't, because, from what she'd been told, from what she'd read, manifesting could become confused if you were too specific. Though she'd also read that it wouldn't work if you weren't specific enough.

She used to roll her eyes at such things. Manifesting. She would have laughed out of the room anyone who suggested such a notion. Her life had been moulded around numbers – analytics, data – not feelings and illogical concepts with no scientific basis. But six years in Hollywood could do things to a person. More and more, she found herself reaching for the smooth teardrop of rose quartz that she wore around her neck, or writing in her journal about a future that didn't yet exist, and ending her entry with 'So it is'. She'd dissolve with embarrassment if any one of her friends from the City or her colleagues across the world read those journals, but they had helped her. And so had the manifesting, she thought, stroking her lower belly.

She was surprised to find that, really, she didn't have a preference of sex, even if her imagination kept leaning in one particular direction. That was another thing she never used to buy. Those women who would rub their bulging stomachs and singsong, 'Honestly? We really don't mind, as long as it's healthy.' She used to smile, but inside she was thinking, 'You liar,' because she'd thought then, that of course they had a preference. Of course they did. Everyone did. But, now, at just three months pregnant, she had discovered that she didn't. Honestly? She just wanted a healthy baby.

She leaned across the back seat of the cab and tilted her head up to see Big Ben. The scaffolding surrounded it now, hiding its majesty behind a brace of metal and swathes of plastic. She could still see the face though, the time still clear. 6.40 p.m. She'd have to go straight to the stage door to try and get the card to Michael by the half. She inhaled deeply at the prospect of having to work her way through the fans. He wouldn't read it till after, so maybe she'd spare herself and give it to him in the bar.

She'd never understood it. Fame. The pursuit of it, or, as she'd discovered over the last six years, the practicalities of it. She'd never aspired to be famous. Even when they were little, Phoebe would say that she wanted to be a rock star or a film star or the prime minister or a famous writer, but to Emma, the very idea of it made her feel nauseous. So it came as something of a surprise that in order to be with the man she loved she had to navigate fame every single day of her life. For the most part, she pretended it wasn't happening. She tried to focus on the benefits of Michael's success, of her own success; their beautiful home, the travel, the money. Those were things she'd always hoped for. But there were moments she couldn't avoid it: stage doors being one of them. There had been a period of time in

LA, before they moved to Malibu, when young women had crowded the sidewalk outside their West Hollywood apartment and her mum had called to say she'd seen her in Granny's copy of *Hello!* But when he proposed she'd told him, yes, she would marry him, but she wasn't going to marry the world's press. He'd kissed her hand and slid the ring on. Then as he got up from where he was kneeling, he said, 'Funny, Phoebs has always said that the exposure was the only thing she would marry me for.' And there she was, even on the night of her engagement, her little sister somehow managing to cast her shadow. Just as she had for her entire life.

There was a chance that Phoebe would be there tonight. They had a 'thing', her and Michael, about being on the front row for opening night. Or they had had, before Phoebe packed in the acting for writing about her sex life in the world press. Emma hadn't had much time to think about it, but now, as the cab passed over the bridge and started to wend its way closer to the theatre, there was a fizz in her stomach at the idea of spending the evening with her sister.

Emma had seen Phoebe only once in the last year, when they'd come over in early spring for Michael's promo interviews for the play.

She had known that Phoebe was waiting for them in the hotel lobby. But still, she was surprised how quickly she had picked her out when the doors of the elevator opened. There she was, all in black, dark hair that fell to her shoulders, the same as ever, but she was altered too. Her cheekbones were more prominent than they'd ever been, her eyes seemed sunken, with darkened dents beneath them.

Even before last year's fall out, it had been a long time since Emma had allowed herself to worry about Phoebe's drinking. Years had passed since the days when she was willing to stick her fingers down her sister's throat or direct a cold shower at her unresponsive form slumped in the bathtub. But it was a shock seeing her like that, a pulse of latent love caused her heart to thump in her chest and made her want to reach out and shake her sister until she stopped hurting herself. Until she stopped breaking her heart.

Michael had charged across the room and embraced Phoebe in his signature lumbering bear hug, but Emma had hung back and averted her eyes as they held each other, and not just because she was angry. She had always tried, as best she could, to keep out of their friendship. She knew that, despite Phoebe's protestations, she'd been hit hard by her and Michael getting together. To be honest, it wasn't until things had progressed to the point of no return that Emma had realised how involved they were in each other's lives, even when they hardly saw each other. Even now, after four years of marriage, if Emma thought about it too much – their shared history, their in-jokes, their shorthand conversation that made her feel as though they were speaking another language – she felt left out, jealous from every angle. And so she separated herself from it and let them continue their silly text conversations and gossipy sharing of tweets by people they loved to hate. After all, it was her that he went to bed with each night. It was her that he'd asked to be his wife. It was her whose hand he had held through every retrieval and embryo transfer, every Big Fat Negative, every hope obliterating loss.

When Michael released her from his embrace, Phoebe had turned to her, the sides of her mouth raising in a semi-smile.

'Hey Em.'

The briefest of nods in the way of greeting.

'Hello, Phoebe.'

It was cold, she knew, but she wasn't going to pretend that everything was fixed between them just because her sister had seen fit to swallow a packet of paracetamol with her nightly bottle of vodka.

The meal had been eerily quiet. Mostly it was Michael talking, trying to fill the air that seemed to have settled around them, thick, like smoke.

She'd watched Phoebe stutter when she ordered her meal, how she'd blushed when she talked about how much London had changed, how lucky she was to have her new column thanks to an old friend of their dad's, how she was thinking of trying to write something more long-form. And Emma realised that so much of the ebullience she'd always taken for granted as being Phoebe's personality had come from the depths of a bottle. It had been so long, that it was an alien feeling to pity her; but there – in that dimly lit, sparsely furnished restaurant that was air-conditioned to within an inch of its life – Emma felt sorry for her sister.

The taxi drew alongside the grass next to the London Eye. Emma held on to the yellow bar next to the window, bracing herself as the taxi jerked and pushed her forward, the driver braking, pausing for the oblivious pedestrians, surprised by a vehicle on the road.

They passed the BFI. She looked out of the back to see it, the long windows, the swarms of people streaming to the Southbank, many heading to watch her husband on the opening night of his play. Her eyes continued to scan the crowd for Phoebe until the taxi drew into the curb and the intercom buzzed to life, the taxi driver telling her what she owed.

The lights dimmed in the theatre and the noise of the audience's chatter waned. A percussive note beat once, twice, three times, and then the lights went out completely, the entire theatre was plunged into darkness. Every human in the room was holding their breath, their eyes open blindly in the dark, waiting.

Beside Emma there was an empty seat and that felt like a let-down as much as it did a reprieve. She inhaled and drew her legs beneath her, crossing them at the ankles; the bare skin of the front of one foot resting against the soft leather at the heel of the other.

The lights came up and there was Michael, centre stage. He appeared to be completely naked, but Emma knew that beneath the black liquid at his waist, he was wearing trunks. It was an arresting image, just as he'd told her it would be. An iconic image. A stage that was nothing but an expanse of black liquid, him alone in the centre of it, a man bathed in blue-green light semi-submerged in a rippling sea of glistening oil.

It would be on several front pages tomorrow, she knew already. The image of Michael's hand clenched in its final fist before it disappeared beneath the glossy surface would be on the cover of every weekend arts supplement.

She had read the play; knew it was good, clever. The language danced like poetry, and it was absolutely the right choice for Michael to take it, even though it meant her having this last embryo transfer alone in LA while he rehearsed in London. It could be – as his agent had kept repeating on that first video call – 'career-defining'. It was bound to be a hit, the next crest in a wave of art that seemed to pander to a collective desire for self-flagellation in the face of a rise in global temperature.

She looked around the blue-tinged faces that populated the auditorium. Would they feel better for watching her husband disappear beneath the shimmering surface? Would his last gasps, his performed drowning – in what she knew to be a very small amount of liquid polyresin coating a membrane, taut above the surface of the stage like a parachute – spur them to action? She didn't believe for a second that the renewed vigour with which they recycled their bottles of their French mineral water would last longer than the play's run.

Maybe it was the prospect of being a parent, but until recently, she really hadn't been convinced that the shift in their climate was man-made. It wasn't 'belligerent denialism', as Rosie had so delightfully put it. She recognised that the climate was changing, that temperatures were rising, ice caps melting, the sea levels rising, but she hadn't found any facts that made it clear that it wasn't some cyclical thing; after all, hadn't there been heatwaves since records began? Hadn't there been an Ice Age? She had to admit though, some of the recent data about emissions was quite compelling.

Still, she didn't see how the few people privileged enough to see a play like this, changing their habits for a couple of weeks, would make any impact. If the problem really did exist, then systemic change was needed. People needed to believe that it was in their interest to take action, to use their voice, their money, their vote, to make meaningful change. The persuasion required to enact such mass rethinking was the sort of challenge that appealed to her. But from her experience everyone on that side of the political spectrum got a bit uncomfortable when you started to talk about influential campaigning. And anyway, they never had the same sort of finance as the other guys.

She curved her forearm across her belly as she watched the father of her child on the stage. It was nearing the end of the play; she recognised it from his constant recitation over the last six months. Only his face was visible now, floating on the surface. Above, a tilted mirror reflected what was below it: his face, slowly becoming part of the oil slick.

'We were just trying to be happy.' Michael's voice echoed through the auditorium. 'We didn't know it would come at such a cost.'

And then, a choking noise as he slipped beneath the surface.

The audience sucked in a collective breath, and she too – though she knew the only liquid he would have swallowed would be the smallest amount of honey, tinted black with food dye – felt a lump in her throat, her eyes smarting with the arrival of tears.

It must've been the hormones. She wasn't ordinarily so easily manipulated by performance.

As the audience stood, raising their clapping hands above their heads, Michael jogged onto the skirt of the stage, smiling. He was free now of the glistening liquid behind him and had pulled on a pair of baggy tracksuit bottoms. A towel hung around his neck, but dark smears of the dyed honey still shone as they caught the light, on the side of his jaw, the inside of his arm.

Emma stood then too, clapping. Her face, wet. Her heart, pounding with pride.

He was searching her side of the audience, his eyes tracing in the dark as he came up from his bow. Then they settled on her and his smile widened to see her and she felt that shock of electricity course through her. The same one she'd felt years ago in her mum's garden, under the willow.

She'd been sunbathing, well, lying in the shade of the tree in a bikini. It was a few days before Phoebe's birthday, early July, and it was hot. It seemed particularly so to her, after months of tepid wet spring in Manchester, followed by those first busy months in the City. She was exhausted, she remembered, relieved to be home for a weekend, away from the new life in London that she wasn't entirely sure had been the right move.

She remembered, very specifically, that she was a few chapters into *The Time Traveler's Wife* and drinking a sweet iced tea when she'd first heard a male laugh mingling with Phoebe's parrot-like squawk. And then they'd appeared from the conservatory, Phoebe and this friend of hers who was coming to stay the night before they caught the ferry to start a two-month rail tour of Europe. That was the first time she'd seen Michael. She didn't, at that point, even know his name, but she was astounded at her body's response, the energy that surged through her; a lightning strike of lust.

'This, as you can see, is my sister,' said Phoebe, extending her arm to indicate Emma, but without making eye contact with her, 'Emmaline. Emma. Em.'

'Hello Emmaline Emma Em. I'm Michael.'

'Hello.'

She'd lifted her sunglasses onto her head, aware that her face was probably red and sweaty from too long in the sun. And then he'd smiled, and that same energy had snaked up her spine. An electrocution. An ache in her bones that told her this moment was important, pivotal.

'Okay, so you've met. Come on, I'll show you the escape routes.'

Phoebe had tugged at Michael's arm, and he'd raised an eyebrow at Emma before following Phoebe up the garden and out of the gate and onto the path. Emma had lain back down on the blanket she had spread on the grass and listened to her sister's voice growing quieter, Michael's deep laugh receding, as they walked down the path. And even after their voices had completely dissolved into the rustle of the willow branches in the afternoon breeze, she had stayed there, stock still, her eyes open, as she wondered at the sensation that was still vibrating through her.

* * *

She watched Michael jog off the stage for the second time, and then the house lights came up. Around her, the audience stood, the noise of slapping chairs and exclamations of praise filling the auditorium. Emma stayed seated and watched as several groups of people wandered to the front of the stage, trying to reach out their hands to touch its glistening surface. But they couldn't reach it over the wide circular skirt where Michael had taken his bow.

The auditorium was almost empty by then, just a few stragglers chatting. Emma gripped her bag to her as she stood. She twisted the gold latch on the front and flipped back the top flap, reaching into a pocket. She pulled out the photo, the image of the 3-D scan they'd given her earlier in Harley Street, and slid it into the envelope before licking the flap and sealing it.

'Come on baby, let's go and find that clever daddy of yours.'

In a row of seats, about halfway up the auditorium, a woman was bending over, filling a black plastic bag with rubbish that the audience had left beneath their seats. She stood as Emma approached and smiled at her.

'Incredible wasn't it? I've been looking forward to this one. I'm totally in love with him.' The woman was fanning herself with her hand as if she were overheating.

'Yes,' said Emma. 'Me too.'

Interlude

Clara runs her hands through the basket of yellow petals. She stirs her hand around and around, as if she is mixing a flower soup.

Behind her, the big wooden door of the church is pulled closed with a clunk and they are plunged into darkness.

She turns and looks up, towards Nana. As her eyes adjust to the gloom she comes into focus. She looks really pretty. Her hair is curly and sticking up at the top, a bit like she is wearing a crown of her own hair. And there is a lovely smell coming from her that is stronger now the door is closed; she smells of flowers and wood and cake.

Her nana turns to her side to say something to her new auntie from America. They are whispering to each other; her auntie gently touches bits at the front of Nana's hair and then she takes out a lipstick from her pocket, pulls the lid off and dots it on Nana's lips, rubbing it in with her little finger.

Clara reaches out and runs her hand over the silky material of the skirt of Nana's dress. She traces her finger along the line of one of the red stripes that crisses and crosses the green and white and black squares.

'Come on, sweetheart.'

Auntie Rosie is crouching down, beckoning to her from the other side of the arch that leads into the church.

'Are you ready?'

She looks behind her again, back to her nana. She is looking at her now, smiling, her eyes all shiny, like she might be about to cry.

'Good girl, Clara. I'll be watching.'

Clara turns back to Auntie Rosie and nods. She is ready.

She steps out into the light of the church.

Auntie Rosie, still crouching down, places her hands on Clara's shoulders.

'So, remember: when the music starts, I'll hold your hand and walk you to there.' She points out in front of them, to the gap between the rows of benches where Clara needs to turn and walk towards Grandad Iain. 'And then, just like we practised. One step. Two step. One step. Throwing flowers all the way. Okay?'

Clara doesn't have time to nod because the music starts. It is loud and has a funny wheezing sound behind it, a bit like Grandad Iain when he came to stay with them last summer. She recognises the tune from when they practised yesterday. But also from the song that Daddy played really loudly in the kitchen earlier to test the speakers.

Auntie Rosie holds out her hand. Clara gently pats her balloon to make sure it is properly tied to her basket, and then reaches out to have her hand taken.

As Clara turns to face the front of the church, Auntie Rosie lets go of her hand and the music changes to the chorus that everyone was singing as they all walked up to the church. Then everyone starts laughing and for a second she feels a bit wobbly and she wants to run away. But then, among all the faces looking at her, she sees her mummy and her daddy, down at the front, smiling at her. Mummy is nodding at her – and pointing. Clara follows her finger to see Grandad Iain. He is standing at the front of the church, just like yesterday, but this time, without his stick. He is wearing a lovely skirt; it has the same sort of chequered pattern as her nana's dress but in different colours. Next to him, the vicar man they practised with yesterday is wearing a lovely coloured dress too. Clara smiles back at them and starts to walk.

She is enjoying everyone looking at her now.

There is that man with the orange hair in a ponytail her mummy was speaking to in the sunshine outside. And there is the man that was here yesterday, the one that speaks the same as Nana and Grandad Iain too. There's her Auntie Rosie's boyfriend, Danyal, who is a doctor for children like her, but who are ill.

She scatters the petals on the grey stone floor, just as she was shown. And then, when she reaches the front, the music changes again and Mummy scoops her up and whispers into her ear.

'You did so well. I'm so proud of you.'

And then, there is Nana, her arm hooked through her American auntie's arm, walking over the petals Clara spread on the floor, holding a huge bunch of sunflowers and smiling the biggest smile she has ever seen. Nana winks at her as she passes, but her auntie just keeps looking straight ahead without smiling, just like she did on the walk to the church.

When Nana is at the top of the path, standing opposite Grandad Iain, the music stops and for a while, they just stand there, smiling at each other. She notices a funny noise and looks up to see her mummy is crying, her tears falling onto Albie's head. And then she notices Daddy is crying too. And the lady on the bench behind them – she keeps wiping her eyes with a hankie that is starting to turn black from her eye make-up.

The church man starts talking loudly at the front, and then there is a rustling of papers and everyone stands up and sings a song about loving big and small animals. Then, when they've stopped singing and the wheezing music stops, everyone shuffles to sit down. Daddy lifts her to sit on a hard cushion that he's put on the seat so she can see Nana at the front. The church man is saying lots of things now, about God and families, reading it all out from a book in a big booming voice. It didn't take this long in the rehearsal yesterday. She tugs on Daddy's sleeve and asks him how long it will be before they get to eat the chocolate cake. She only whispers, but still, he tells her to shush. She can feel her brow creasing, her bottom lip jutting, but then he unties the string of her balloon from the basket on the floor and gives it to her.

'Now, sit nicely.'

She holds it against her chest, squishing the air inside it from one side to the other, as Nana and Grandad Iain take it in turns to copy what the church man says.

And then, everyone is cheering. And Nana and Grandad Iain are kissing. A long kiss. And everyone starts laughing again. Daddy puts his fingers in his mouth and does one of his loud whistles and Mummy says, 'Mike!' and Albie starts crying.

It is very hot outside, after the cool of the church. Everyone is talking very loudly and some people bend down and talk to her. One man even shakes her hand.

'Well done, young lady.'

'Well, didn't you do a grand job.'

'*Oooh*, I bet your granny's proud of you.'

'She's my nana.'

'*Oh-hoo*, opinions already. A chip off the old block, eh?'

Everyone is talking and talking and she is starting to feel really quite hungry now. She sits on the step of the church, next to where Daddy is bouncing Albie up and down, trying to make him stop crying. She runs her hand over her knee. The dress is silky under her hand. She loves her dress. It's just like the one Belle has in *Beauty and the Beast*.

She has a funny feeling then, like a buzzing in her chest. She looks up and she sees that her American auntie is watching her. Staring at her. She is standing a bit away from everyone, in the grass among all the wonky gravestones, a trail of smoke rising from her hand. Clara smiles at her, waves. But she doesn't wave back. She just keeps looking at her. The buzzing in her chest gets stronger. It is starting to make her feel a bit sick.

Then Nana and Grandad Iain appear in the doorway of the church behind her and everybody cheers again. And the air around her is filled with swirling yellow petals.

Nineteen

They sit, the two of them, on the thrones at the head of the table, chuckling.

'They none of them get it, you know? These chairs. Our thrones.'

'Ah, it's not for them to get, is it?'

'No, I suppose not.'

Mary's left hand rests comfortably in his right. She squeezes his hand, a brief pulse.

She leans in towards him and he leans in to her. His lips are soft and warm against hers.

She smiles at him, then sits back, lifts her glass and takes a sip.

'This wine really is fantastic isn't it? Takes me right back. A liquid time machine.'

He nods, lifts his glass and takes a sip too.

'Aye.' His eyes are closed. 'A couple of sad sacks twirling our forks in our pasta.'

'I've never thanked you, I don't think, for taking my hand over that table.'

She takes another sip of her wine.

'That pasta was simply the best meal of my entire life.'

He laughs.

They clink their glasses.

It is cooler now the sun has set. Not so cold that bare shoulders can't be borne, but chill enough that clothes no longer stick to the smalls of backs.

Mary's dress is just as she'd hoped it would be. Long, flowing, perfect. The blue, green and red of the MacDonald tartan perfectly swathes her curves. There had been a moment, earlier on in the day, when she'd worried it was too revealing, that she would look like a semi-dressed tomato as she walked down the aisle, the dress sticking to her in all the wrong places, her face as red as the scarlet checks in the material. But it was perfect.

Her church wedding.

Another thing she loves about this man: his allowing her the time and space to work on that important relationship that, for much of the last forty years, somehow got sidelined by all her others. She's grateful that, unlike Richard used to, Iain doesn't raise a smirk as she kisses his cheek before she leaves on a Sunday morning.

'You've got Jesus and I've got The Clash. We don't have to agree on everything to love one another.'

Perfect.

She doesn't want to say it out loud and tempt fate, but she's willing to dare to think it.

The whole day has been perfect.

And now it's cooler, the perfect temperature for dancing.

Everyone is dancing!

Music blasts out from the entire lower level of the house. The dining room, the lounge, the kitchen all transformed into a dance floor. All the rooms are unrecognisable as the spaces that this family have cooked, eaten, fought and loved in for four decades. The kitchen, the room she's always liked the least, is a discotheque; the lights low, a glitter ball turning. There are flashing lights plugged in at the socket that ordinarily powers the toaster. Smartly shod feet rhythmically beat the lino that has barely seen any shoes until now.

Mary had demanded from the off that it was a 'no-shoe house'. At the time it was a rebellion against her mother-in-law, but it stuck, and these days even Irene asks for help to remove her shoes at the threshold. Ex-mother-in-law. She is now mother-in-law free. Although, will she ever really be free of Irene?

Iain shifts, sighs, squeezes her fingers once more.

'Got your puff back?' She runs her thumb across the back of his hand.

'Dinnae fuss.'

She nods, takes a deep drink of her wine.

'What a perfect day for it! I thought for sure when we agreed on September we'd all have brollies at the ready. But your man up there is smiling down on us.'

Mary cringes.

'It's still not over. Can you wait to profess perfection until tomorrow?'

'You're worried I'll jinx it?'

'Just until midnight, at least? Or tomorrow? Or maybe a few days, when everyone's gone home without a scrap?'

He laughs, lifts her hand and places his lips to her skin. Pleasure crawls up her arm.

'A foolish man that doesn't heed the request of his wife.'

Wife. *Mary King*. She could jump for joy.

It might be cooler, but the air is still heavy with the unnatural heat of the day. The air is thick with the scent of the Daphne, its pink clusters of flowers in the pots by the shed spreading their perfume all the way to where they sit. Both the diffusion of this sweet scent and the drop in temperature are down, in part, to a light breeze. Autumn stirring, Nature trying to reclaim its rightful season. Despite her expensive hurricane lamps, the breeze has guttered the candles, making the wax spill and some of the flames extinguish. The spread of wax, splattered across the table, secretly adheres the tablecloths to the tables beneath.

They'll lose their deposit, she thinks. Then shrugs and leans her head on her husband's shoulder.

The wax is not the only spillage that the cloths have sustained. Circles of red wine – up and down the table – splatters of apple sauce, smears of chocolate are dotted across the length of it, but are particularly condensed in the area where Clara sat, before Phoebe had declared it 'Bedtime for ratbags' and the little girl had grimly administered kisses as instructed, before being bundled off to bed by Michael.

Mary would have liked them to stay, the little ones. She'd had a vision of dancing with Clara, her little granddaughter bouncing on her hip as they moved to Bowie and Jagger. But she bit her tongue and let Phoebe get on with it.

Mary rolls her head on Iain's shoulder and looks up into the branches of the tree.

The willow looks more itself now; moving as it is in the breeze.

God, she'll miss this tree.

The festoon lights seem to dance in the tree's branches. The leaves reflect their glow and project it onto the surface of the pond; the light dances on the stained cloth, the chairs, the two of them.

It is only a light breeze though, no wind. Not like that first night they had stayed up talking by candlelight until the early hours.

The sway of the branches is subtle, only noticeable from the oscillation of the shadows on the table. Recognising its movement is similar to an awareness that the person beside you is inhaling and exhaling – something you do not consider but inherently know and is only truly discernible when you place a hand on their chest.

She does that now, places her hand on his chest. Beneath her palm she can feel the *dah-dum* of his heart. It's slower now than when they slipped out here.

'Okay?'

'Oh yes. More than.'

She does that a lot, she knows. Places her hand on his chest. She does it sometimes when he's sleeping. Checking for the thrum of that ball of sinewy muscle in his chest, for the rise and fall of his breath.

Iain places his hand over hers where it rests.

'Still livin'.'

She's wondered whether it irritates him, her constant observations of these, the most basic of his bodily functions. She's asked him as much. 'It doesn't,' he replies, smiling, shaking his head. It's something that makes him adore her all the more, he told her, a tender quirk that reveals how much she cares.

There'll come a day, she knows, where she'll lay her hand on him and find his chest still. She imagines her rapping her knuckles on his chest, a hollow '*dung, dung, dung*' echoing back at her, the barrel of his chest as empty as the tin man's.

Or, maybe she won't. Maybe Mary will go first. Maybe he'll be like Irene, making the lives of his new stepdaughters as complicated as Irene does Mary's.

She's come to realise that she'll miss Irene when they're up in Scotland. Richard too. Iain has even said the same. A real surprise, that. She knows he's always thought Richard a bit of a pompous arse. So full of himself, with the designer gear and the slicked back hair, and a 'secret Tory' to boot. 'They all are, these Liberals,' Iain says. 'At least have the guts to be right wing.'

Like Emma, she thinks. She wears her beliefs like a badge of honour. There's a bravery in that, at least. It's been one of the most interesting discoveries of her life, loving Emma just as much, despite her attitudes: the revelation that the fierceness of love you feel for your child surpasses even the most polarising political views.

The chairs that surround the table now sit at odd angles, abandoned by their occupants when the first notes of the first dance began and all of those still at the table hastily discarded the last of their desserts, running inside to see Mary and Iain take their first turn around the kitchen tiles as a married couple.

They danced to Donna Summer, another joke that had seemed funnier when they'd planned it in the depths of winter, the first dance being to 'Last Dance'. Everyone enjoyed it though. The song choice was met with whoops of surprise. Those who had known them long enough were probably expecting something with a few more guitars.

They didn't do a routine or anything. He was game, but Mary said any attempts would have likely ended up with her ripping the seam of her dress or tripping on her own feet. That wasn't the real reason, but even if he knew it was because she was worried it might be too much for him, he didn't let on. It was the right choice though, there was something so much more intimate about a dance without choreography. There was a give-and-take between them that felt like an agreement. I'll let you turn me. We'll move away from each other now, play to the crowd, and then they were together, just the two of them, the entire world fading into the background as she felt the warmth of his body against her own.

There will be a lot of dancing in their marriage, she had decided.

Iain's stomach gurgles. A noise loud enough for Mary to hear it. She laughs.

'You can't still be hungry?'

'Ah, I reckon I could manage to fit another sliver or two of that pork. He did a great job, didn't he?'

'He did. I told you he would.'

'You did.'

Truth is, she too had been slightly suspicious of Richard's offer to cater the wedding. Yes, there was much about the nuptials that was unconventional, but having the bride's ex-husband handing out the canapés felt a little much, even when the groom has the anarchy symbol tattooed on his left bicep.

There is something about it though, the organisation of the wedding breakfast, that has felt like her last project with Richard. For months, while they discussed whether the potato salad ought to have a mayonnaise or yoghurt dressing, she'd watched Iain's brow crinkle, trying to fathom their obsession with such details. It had been particularly funny to watch him feign interest as Richard talked him through his plan to turn a reclaimed oil barrel into a giant barbeque.

'What's in it for him?' Iain had whispered to her in bed. 'Why not pay for external caterers? He can afford it. Why spend so much time planning, organising, preparing?'

All fair questions. It was true that, in most situations orchestrated by Richard, there was, at their heart, something in it for Richard. Mary had ticked Iain off, told him to stop being so 'bloody suspicious'. Partly that was because she couldn't quite shake her own suspicions. But, it would seem, it wasn't some sort of elaborate plan to ruin their wedding day. He really had just wanted to do something nice for them. To do something that showed he gave his blessing. It was his way of telling her that he loved her.

Now, the feast Richard put so much love and energy into is decimated. A few lumps of gelatinous potato stick to the side of otherwise empty glass bowls, tomato seeds cluster like frog-spawn in an oregano-flecked soup of olive oil and lemon juice at the bottom of wide porcelain dishes, and wilted leaves swim in dressing in the blue ceramic serving bowls Mary had bought on her honeymoon in Tunisia in the late 70s.

The pig, its eyes closed, still appears to be sleeping, but it is less animal now and even more horrific. The meat has been almost completely removed. A few scraps lie on the platter beneath, but the majority has been eaten. Thick slices, crammed into a buttered brioche bun, smothered in mustard and apple sauce, swilled down with champagne and the Gavi that she had fallen in love with when she and Iain so astoundingly got together in Italy. The wine was another gift from Richard. Possibly the most thoughtful gift he'd given her in all of the forty-five years they'd known one another.

She sips her wine.

'Summer in a glass.'

'The last of the Summer Wine.'

'The wine of the last normal summer.'

The last summer they spent abroad. The last before the world shut down. And for a while, for those horrible six months that Iain had been in hospital, she'd thought that it might have been Iain's last summer full stop. She shakes her head and takes another sip of the wine. A morbid thought for her wedding day. Still, still, even with this ring on her hand, the girls playing nice, something, something just won't let her settle. Maybe she just needs to get blind drunk? That'll stop her fretting.

In the kitchen, the song changes. A woman's voice, an electronic beat, recognisable to the majority of the guests it would seem, as voices rise in a cheer. Squeals of joy. Whoops of delight.

The lyrics slide into the garden, voices singing along, the fervour increasing as the song surges into its rhapsodical chorus.

'*Esch.*' Iain sighs performatively. 'I suppose you'll be wanting to dance to this racket.'

'You know it.' She offers her hand to him, but he shakes his head.

He pauses a moment, preparing himself, and then finds his own way to his feet. She gently touches her hand to his elbow, but he waves it away.

'Dunnae fuss.' He leans in to her and kisses her cheek. 'I'm feeling good. Just bracing myself for the dance floor. Warming up.'

He moves his arms up and down, lifting an invisible dumbbell. Shakes his arms in a strongman position.

'As ready as I'll ever be to take on Dave Stewart and his synth-pop horrors.'

She laughs. The sound echoes around the garden.

'You really have the most beautiful laugh, Mary.' His face is more serious than she's seen it all day. 'I noticed it, you know. When we met. When you were almost taken out by those two pigs.'

'I'm so glad of those pigs.'

He looks over at the remains of the hog roast.

'They'll have been bacon long since.'

'You're not going all funny about meat like Richard, are you?'

His turn to laugh now. The initial bellow of it quickly turning to wheezing and coughing. He leans on the table to catch his breath; her hand rests on his back and he lets her leave it there.

'Are you sure you're up to it?'

He nods his head, but doesn't move. His eyes are fixed on the sunflowers that still glow a fierce yellow in their vases down the centre of the table.

He looks to her then, that glazed look that frightens her dissolving as quickly as it appeared. He smiles.

'Sorry. Liz was with me there for a moment.'

'Ah.' She moves her hand on his back, rubbing in decreasing circles. 'Yes. She's been with me for much of the day, too.'

'Watching over us.' He extends his hand to tuck a wild strand of hair behind her ear. 'You've done her proud with the sunflowers.'

'They were her favourite.'

'I know.' He takes her hand. 'Come on, we'll miss dancing to this dreadful song of yours.'

She feels the laugh well up and escape her mouth. Oh, how she loves laughing. There's going to be lots of laughter to accompany the dancing.

He is smiling at her now, extending the crook of his arm to her. Even with the weight loss and pallor that he still hasn't shaken since leaving hospital, he is the most beautiful man she's ever seen. She loves the tiny dip in his nostril where the piercing once sat, the dent on either side of his eyebrow from the hoop that hung there too. The skin of his shaved head is reflecting the lights above. The faded blue tattoo above his ear, the only one that's visible with his suit on. She'd always been so impressed by that, the way that both Iain and Liz were able to transform themselves back to 'norms' as they'd called it. How, with their Mohicans down and their shirts buttoned at collar and cuff, they were just two of the many people who wore lab coats in that particular part of Cambridge.

She slides her arm through his and they walk across the lawn arm in arm.

'There you are!' Richard appears at the door, his tie loosened around his neck. 'We've been looking for you! Annie's on: time to tear up the dance floor, Mary!'

'That's the plan.'

He laughs, ushers them inside, his movements fluid and a little louche now he's approaching drunkenness.

'Even my mother's tapping her foot!'

'Well, we can't let ourselves be outdone by Irene.' She winks at Iain as she takes his hand and pulls him behind her into the conservatory.

Twenty

Mary wasn't sure if it was the dawn light streaming through the open shutters that woke her. Or perhaps it was an unconscious reaction to the slow asphyxiation caused by one of Phoebe's splayed arms across her throat.

It took her a moment to orientate herself. The mental tick list hovering in her mind's eye: what did the day hold? How many lunches needed to be packed? Were there after-school arrangements to be made? Did she need to be in the office?

But then she opened her eyes and saw the cracked plaster of the ceiling. It wasn't pink. She wasn't in her bedroom. She inhaled deeply: the air smelled of salt, citronella, sunscreen. Her entire body softened.

She was on holiday.

She gently lifted Phoebe's arm and placed it on the pillow beside her head. She could smell the ghost of chlorine as she placed her lips to the edge of her daughter's fingers and kissed them.

A swim. She'd have the pool to herself at that time, the sunloungers too. She could just lie there uninterrupted before the sun got too hot, before they woke and started demanding things of her.

She sat up and stretched her arms above her head, then leaned over Phoebe, reaching across to where Emma lay beside her, and gently brushed her hair from her face so she could get a better look at her.

She'd thought the days of her daughters crawling in to join her in the middle of the night were long behind her. Though she used to complain about the way they'd find their way into her bed by morning, she missed it. In those months after Richard left, when she was particularly at sea, it had felt like a life raft on the ocean of her loneliness, the small snoring bodies wedged against the curves of her own, keeping her afloat.

These days, the odd nightmare made Phoebe call on her midnight cocoa-making skills, but it was rare for either her or Emma to express any such vulnerabilities. So it was a surprise to Mary that, since they'd arrived in France, her bed had been graced by at least one nocturnal visitor every night.

On the first night, Emma had woken her as she slid beneath the cool white sheet, her recently-shaved legs smooth and hot beside her own spiky ones. She'd complained that Phoebe was snoring, but then, in the dark, she'd reached out for Mary's hand as she was falling asleep. And yesterday she'd woken to a foot on the pillow beside her, and quickly identified it by the poorly applied turquoise polish as Phoebe's. Now, this morning, the two of them. Phoebe, inadvertently throttling her with one of her rapidly-lengthening limbs, the other wrapped around Emma, whose head was nestled on her shoulder. When she saw them like this – wrapped around one another, as if they were a single organism – she couldn't help but feel aggrieved that she'd never had a sister.

She did, however, have Lizzie. Lizzie, with whom she'd spent the whole day laughing yesterday.

Mary smiled as she contorted herself to squeeze into her swimming costume.

Although she'd been grateful when Liz had suggested that they go on holiday together, she had been worried that she might feel like a bit of a gooseberry, or that the girls would get into one of their fights and make Iain and Liz regret ever asking. But so far, it had been pretty idyllic, and exactly what she needed.

The gîte wasn't huge. There was enough room to escape each other, but it was small enough to feel as though they were together, even when apart. A small pool that the girls had spent every daylight hour either jumping in and out of or floating on. A big kitchen with a flagstone floor that was cool underfoot. Shuttered windows, so beautiful from the outside, and the perfect complement to an afternoon nap brought on by one too many white wines with lunch. The vine that grew over the pergola on the back patio meant that even with her sensitive skin she could sit out and read, or doze in the shade in the late afternoon.

The location was ideal too. It was just a short drive to Avignon and, though it felt as though they were in absolute isolation, surrounded by fields full of vines and sunflowers, it only took a leisurely stroll down a very quiet road to arrive in a small but well-populated town square.

Yesterday morning, she and Lizzie had filled their jute bags until they bulged with the extraordinary fruit and vegetables that the Saturday market offered. She'd felt like Lesley Duncan in that BBC series as she swept from stall to stall in her floaty summer dress, picking up green figs that were weeping pink juice and sniffing them, fondling the fronds of slim fragrant fennels, salivating over the misshapen tomatoes. The whole market was a kaleidoscope of colours; even the mushrooms came in every shade, from pink-edged white, through ochre yellow, to deep purply-black. There was a tranquillity too; there wasn't the cacophony of the market traders she was used to back at home, nor was there the background squeal of the livestock, but just the mumble of the traders and the quack and cluck of a few caged ducks and hens.

Even when the market wasn't there, there were more amenities than were to be found in the village at home. Here, there was the *tabac*, with its typically lax policy on age, happily providing her fifteen-year-old daughter with *Gauloises* that made her cough like her dad used to. The *boulangerie*, with its long spears of perfectly crispy bread, and croissants that seem as tough as old leather when you tear them, but just dissolve to nothing the second they touch your tongue.

She smiled to herself as she descended the stone stairs into the kitchen and recalled that it was Sunday. A Sunday where she doesn't have to concoct an excuse in order to avoid lunch at Irene's. Nearly eight years she'd been separated from Richard, and yet, still she found it almost impossible to get out of the weekly commitment.

She stood for a second by the open door onto the patio and closed her eyes. She'd been living in Suffolk for sixteen years and there were fifty-two weeks in a year. Fifty-two multiplied by sixteen was – she'd spent more than two years of her life having Sunday lunch with Irene. And now it was even worse: she was not just having lunch with Irene, but invariably with whichever man-friend of hers was flavour of the month too.

Mary still couldn't quite get her head around how active Irene's love life had become. When Irene had started attending parish council meetings to protest the pedestrianisation of a street that she didn't even live on, Mary had shaken her head and thought of all the ways she'd spend her free time, if she had as much as Irene. But then, she discovered that there seemed to be a perk to Irene's new-found activism. When the first gentleman had joined them for roast beef and spuds, she'd passed it off as a phase, that Irene was enjoying the flattery of being trailed around by someone quite a bit younger than herself. But then, a few weeks later, another, different, gentleman joined them for chicken, mash and green beans, and so she'd had to put in a call. Richard had been flabbergasted. That part of it had been quite funny. While Mary found Irene's rotation of relationships rather surprising, you'd think that his seventy-two-year-old mother had taken up abseiling from the way Richard received the news.

'It's the speed of it, Mary.'

Richard had run his hands through his hair as he sat at the dining table, waiting for the girls to appear with their bags packed for the weekend. 'And I just don't see what's in it for them? I know love is blind and all that but can the over 50s of East Anglia really be finding my mother so irresistible? They don't—' Richard mimed a retch. 'Is there sexual activity, do you think?'

'Have you considered that maybe it's the "sexual activity" that's the draw for her? She's in her early seventies. Don't you think there's a slim chance that you'll still want to have sex when you're her age, Richard?'

'Mary!'

The look on his face still made her chuckle, but she was surprised to recognise a glimmer of envy in herself. Though none of the men that had passed her the gravy boat over the past few years held any attraction for Mary herself, if she were completely truthful, she was a little put out that Irene's love life was so much more active than her own.

She told herself it was because she hadn't tried. But that wasn't quite true.

A few years ago, egged on by Lizzie, she'd even answered a few ads. According to *The Guardian*'s back pages, there was actually a heartening number of men in their mid/late 40s with GSOHs claiming that they WLTM a woman with a GSOH in her late 30s/early 40s in the region of East Anglia. There had been a pleasing number of responses too. And Lizzie had practically dressed her, applied her blusher, and pushed her out of the door on the handful of occasions that the letters resulted in a date.

There had been one, in Cambridge – did something at Addenbrookes on the admin side – that she'd actually quite liked. Paul. They'd had a couple of lunches, then a couple of dinners, and then, thanks to Lizzie and Iain playing babysitter, a surprisingly satisfying night in a hotel in Newmarket. But then it just fizzled out. She wasn't sure if it was because he didn't want to meet the children, or she didn't want him to meet them, or she just didn't have time for him with work and the girls and the house, but at some point one or the other of them had stopped calling. It was a shame really. He'd had kind eyes and was really quite funny after half a bottle of wine.

She thought, when she started at the paper, that she quite liked one of the reporters. He smoked, but he had a lovely deep voice, was recently divorced, and had joint custody of his eight-year-old daughter whom he collected from school every other day and so had to leave the office early. But then she'd overheard him calling her 'Big Mary', and she'd gone right off him.

She would have quite liked to have met someone though. Not multiple people like Irene. Just one nice one would do.

It wasn't that she was unhappy. Her life was busy and richly populated. She enjoyed her job. She loved her garden. She was busy with her girls and surrounded by people she adored – and another few that she was *surprised* to find she cared a great deal about. But there was still loneliness, despite it all.

There was still a deep-rooted desire for companionship.

She had Lizzie. A companion the like of which she had never known until now. She couldn't imagine finding someone who would make her roar with laughter, or catch her tears without judgement, as Lizzie did. But she was aware, particularly when she watched Lizzie and Iain together, as she had been doing on this holiday, that there was a space in her life for someone else, a vacuum that she'd quite like to fill. Someone to talk to first thing in the morning. Someone to remove her reading glasses and turn off the bedside lamp when she fell asleep with a novel still in her hands.

That was what she couldn't understand about Irene's rotating door of gentlemen callers. What intimacy could they provide her with, when each relationship was so short-lived?

She remembered Bert so fondly, his softly spoken kindness, the quietly caring actions, the smell of the dry cleaners on him when he returned home in the evening. Surely none of these flings of Irene's gave her anything near to what she had with Bert?

It must be the sex. Mary couldn't think of any reason for Irene's actions but the sex.

Fair enough. She missed sex too. Sometimes she wondered if she'd ever have it again.

In the kitchen, she opened the fridge and took out the bottle of expensive mineral water that Phoebe had gagged on when she drank from it, claiming it 'tasted like seawater'. Mary filled a glass from the draining tray and gulped the water down. She pulled a face. Her daughter was quite right, it tasted as though someone had dissolved a spoonful of salt in it. It was probably the right thing to be drinking, though, considering the weather; it was barely past seven and she was already damp with perspiration.

The heatwave didn't seem to be showing any sign of abating. The drive down to Dover had been horrendous; they'd been stuck in traffic practically all the way from Canterbury. On the ferry they'd all stood on the deck enjoying the cool of the forewind, the sweat of their T-shirts drying into faint salty circles under their arms. She'd hoped that it might be cooler in France, but from the moment they'd clanked off the ship in Calais it had been fiercely hot.

The drive to their hotel in Reims had been the hardest of her life. The concentration she'd had to give to staying on the wrong side of the road. Phoebe, reading the map. Emma sulking since her sister's front seat position also meant control of the tape deck; her Wet Wet Wet album had been replaced with the wild guitars of Nirvana and Pearl Jam. She'd needed the loo all the way from the turn-off to Amiens, but Mary was scared to turn off to the services in case she lost sight of the red flash of Iain's car ahead.

The next day, as they charged towards their destination and she tried to defuse an argument between Emma and Phoebe about Joan of Arc, she had noted that the fields were arid, the plants and vines yellowed, wilting or scorched, and still, ever since they'd arrived, the days were fierce and the nights still and heavy. It reminded her of that summer of '76 when she'd just finished university and it had felt as if the whole world was on fire. It had felt eerie then, but now, with the news full of the hole in the ozone layer and the possibility of global warming, the unrelenting nature of the heat had really put her on edge.

She had called Irene from the phone box in the village square on the evening of their arrival. Irene had put in a request for such a call; to reassure her of the children's safe arrival, by which, Mary could only assume she wasn't too bothered about the health of their chauffeur. It was only as Irene answered the phone that Mary realised the pastis they'd been drinking outside the cafe from where she'd spotted the phone box was somewhat affecting her motor skills. Most of Mary's conversations with Irene were tricky in one way or another, but this one was made additionally so due to static on the line causing parts of sentences to disappear; lost for ever somewhere over the Channel like one of Irene's mythologised boyfriends from the war.

According to Irene, the heatwave was even worse in the UK.

'It's our fault you know. It's the Greenhouse Effect. Mrs Thatcher warned us all. Ask Lizzie.'

Mary rolled her eyes.

'Lizzie's a medical research scientist.'

'Well, she's always been a bright spark, even when Richard and her knocked about together. Anyway, if you're calling about the garden, I'm afraid—'

The line crackled fiercely.

'Irene?'

'—I'm not sure even my best efforts will keep them alive.'

Mary had then spent the rest of the time her two francs bought her trying to get reassurance that Irene meant the tomatoes not the chickens, a task that wasn't aided by her slight inebriation.

Mary wasn't sure that she had been entirely sober since. She really wasn't used to drinking so much wine. But Lizzie was adamant that, when in France, it was the done thing to have wine with lunch.

'If you can't get drunk during daylight hours when you're on holiday, when can you?'

She had to admit, the casual attitude to alcohol consumption had helped her relax faster than she'd anticipated. She'd been so stressed when they left, but she'd discovered it was much easier to forget the long list of worries waiting for her back at home when the day was punctuated by one little drink, swiftly followed by another. A glass with lunch, another by the pool to aid digestion, a gin and tonic while the three of them prepared the dinner, and then a special bottle with dinner, and then after – when the kids had receded to the TV room to watch a fuzzy old VHS, their semi-dressed bodies lounging across the sagging sofas, completely unaware of their beauty – the three of them, Lizzie, Iain and her sat and talked and talked, the flickering candles lighting their features. Inevitably, another bottle was opened.

No wonder that by the time she did make her way to bed she was completely unaware of her daughters clambering in beside her.

In the kitchen now, she reached for the key to unlock the door, but found it swinging open onto the patio with only the slightest pressure of her touch. Iain and Liz must have forgotten to lock it when they went to bed.

It had been late when she left them. The children, scorched by the sun and stuffed with white bread and sausages, had already made their way to their rooms, and Mary had been so enjoying the conversation that she hadn't noticed how late it was until the grandfather clock in the hallway had chimed.

'Is that one? One in the morning?'

'*Uh-oh*, Cinderella. Looks like you'll be going up to your bed in a pumpkin tonight.'

'Aye, very funny. I've promised Phoebe I'll take her into Avignon so she can nose around the festival. If I don't get some sleep I'll be driving on the left.'

'Oh, have another Mary. Don't leave me alone with him!'

'You sleep well, Mary.'

She reached to grab the glasses and the bottle, to clear the table, but Lizzie raised her hand.

'I think we'll finish the bottle, won't we?'

Liz inclined the half-full bottle towards her husband. He nodded and held out his glass.

'We'll not be long behind you, Mary.'

As Mary stepped out into the cool early morning air, she saw there were glasses, now empty, still spread across the table. The bottle that they had been drinking was empty as promised, and the brandy that they'd bought on the ferry was there too, its contents somewhat diminished.

The chimes of the clock in the hallway. Half past seven? Emma would wake soon, strapping on her trainers and circling the village before it got too hot.

Mary hastened along the path, around the side of the house to the pool. She tucked the towel into itself at her chest so it wouldn't fall, and then adjusted the elastic of her swimsuit on her bottom. Just then, she heard a voice. She stopped abruptly and tilted her head, trying to tune in to the sound. It was the low murmur of a male voice. Iain. And then it was joined by another: Lizzie's, lowered, whispering. Strange that they should be up so early when they went to bed so late.

She turned the corner of the house so that the pool was in full view. Her friends were sitting on the far edge, their feet dangling in the water, their hair wet, their bodies wrapped in towels. They hadn't noticed her arrival. Their focus was lowered towards the water, their expressions serious. Even from this distance, Mary could see the furrow of Liz's brow, Iain nodding his head. A slow, heavy nod.

At once, Mary knew she was intruding on a private moment and she stepped back to try to return from whence she came without drawing their attention. It was then that she noticed the trail of clothes that led from where she was standing to the grass by the pool.

She was really intruding.

Quickly she turned to leave. But as she did so her towel loosened. It started to drop and she let out a small yelp.

'Mary?'

She grabbed at the towel, covering herself as best she could, and turned back to her friends.

'Sorry. I'm disturbing you. I just thought I'd have a swim to wake myself up, but – I'll just go in and make myself a tea. Sorry.'

'No, No—'

'Mary, don't be a numpty, come here.'

She saw then that Lizzie had been crying. Her eyes were puffy and red. She wiped her nose on the back of her hand and sniffed loudly.

'We watched the sunrise.'

Lizzie patted the space next to her. Mary walked around the pool, so she was beside Lizzie, and eased herself to sit beside her.

'How was it?' Mary flushed, raised her hands to her face. 'The sunrise!'

Lizzie chuckled.

'It was fairly unremarkable. I shan't be making a habit of it.'

Mary lowered her feet into the water. It was surprisingly warm, still retaining the heat of yesterday's sun. And then, Mary felt the pressure of Lizzie's arm against her own, before she rested her damp head on her shoulder. It was an unfamiliar sensation, the warmth of another adult's body, so close to her own. There was something about the tenderness of it that made her almost tearful. She inhaled, and followed suit, leaning in to her friend, letting her head rest against Lizzie's.

'I saw you tucked into the brandy.'

Iain nodded and held up his empty glass.

Again, that feeling of intrusion. Something had happened here. Was this the afterglow of an aquatic lovemaking session? But then, why the tears? She didn't know what it was, and she wasn't sure she wanted to know.

'Mary—' Liz cut herself off and lifted her head from her shoulder. She looked at her then, pressing her lips together, and ran her hands through her hair. Lizzie had been her natural auburn for a few years then. It was more feminine than any of the styles she'd sported since Mary'd known her. The perm that she had had in spring had dropped to nothing, but crinkled waves now fell to her pronounced clavicle and it just suited her perfectly.

Mary watched as Liz glanced at Iain. They exchanged a look before she turned back to Mary.

Oh god, Mary thought, *Richard was right, they have been after a threesome all this time.*

But then, she saw that Lizzie was really crying now, her cheeks wet with tears as she tried to hold Mary's gaze.

'I'm sick, Mary. Really very unwell.'

Twenty-one

Richard ambles into the garden. Listing slightly, swaying to the music as he crosses the patio. He lets his feet drag a little as he shuffles across the lawn to the decimated remains of the buffet. Months of work demolished. Yet the empty plates and bowls stir a swell of pride in his chest.

Despite the horrible sunflower print plastic tablecloth Mary had insisted on, the food looked spectacular when he first laid it all out.

Earlier, as soon as the house fell quiet – the chattering voices and clicking heels fading as the wedding party made their way into the village and up to the church – Richard had stretched out his shoulders and then put on his oven gloves and wheeled the cooling hog roast from the side of the house, over the patio and, with some effort, onto the lawn next to the table. It would have been much easier to have cooked it in situ; he wouldn't have had to bother about attaching wheels to the bloody roasting contraption either. But, he'd worried about roasting it under the tree. Everything was tinder dry with the drought, and if that thing were to go up in smoke then it was likely the house sale would too. The young couple buying the place had no doubt fallen in love with the tree, just as he and Mary had. Richard had every confidence that the oil drum was safe, but he thought it best to keep it out of harm's way while hot fat was dripping onto white hot coals.

Sweating, he manoeuvred the roaster so it was in pride of place alongside the buffet table, next to the pond. After all, what was the point in having such a spectacle for a meal if it wasn't at the very centre of the festivities? He laid out the multiple bowls of salads, the baskets of pre-sliced brioche buns, the glistening bowls of apple sauce. Then he looked at his watch in alarm, ran into the lounge, quickly checking that his mother was still breathing, and rushed upstairs to jump into the shower.

As he rubbed the menthol-scented shampoo through his hair, he considered, for a moment, that this shower would be one of the final few that he would ever take in this bathroom. He paused, the water cascading over him, hot on his shoulders, his scalp, the minty shampoo stinging his eyes, as the last forty years sped past his mind's eye.

A maudlin thought jabbed at him: how many more showers did he have ahead of him, full stop?

He allowed himself a moment then. A short burst of feeling sorry for himself. That this should be his life. With Mary marrying Iain today, the responsibility of his mother's care was entirely on his shoulders. The best of his life was behind him. His children grown. His sex life non-existent. And what was left of his career, really? The odd *Zoom* into *Peston* to give his opinion on the latest bad behaviour in Westminster.

Then he shuddered and wiped his eyes, tilted his head up into the spray of water and let it fill his mouth.

He dressed in what he still thought of as 'Mary's Studio', but truly had been his bedroom – and office – for the best part of three years. If that God of Mary's did exist, he certainly had a sense of humour. Just three years ago Richard's life had been almost unrecognisable to the one he is living now. He had been free and single. In his late sixties, no one would have referred to him as young but as many of his contemporaries were shutting up shop, off the back of Brexit he'd found himself more and more in demand as a pundit.

He combed his hair back from his forehead, feeling that same flush of satisfaction that he always did when he acknowledged how little it had receded over the years. Then he tucked the silver lengths of it behind each ear and set about dressing in his new suit. He couldn't remember ever having waited so long to wear a new purchase. Particularly when it was so perfect. Straw-coloured linen. A little treat to himself on his last trip to Milan. At the time, it hadn't even crossed his mind that one day he'd be wearing it to Mary's wedding.

He dabbed a little *Joop* onto his palms, then patted his hands over his cheeks and the sides of his neck. He was appraising his linen-bedecked reflection in the free-standing mirror when his eye was drawn to a flash of colour through the window, outside, along the road. Then his ear caught voices raised in jubilation. Michael's bellowing laugh, the squeal of little Clara being carried on his shoulders.

The noise of his granddaughter's laughter had unsettled him for a moment, made him feel unsteady, dizzy almost. He still couldn't conceive of the depth of affection he felt for the child – would things have been different if he had felt this way about his own? This wasn't the time for reflection, for now the figures were visible at the end of the road; the first of the guests were returning.

It was nearly crunch time.

He didn't doubt that there would have been a few raised eyebrows at his absence in the church, but when they saw his gift, the feast he'd prepared in the couple's honour, no one could doubt his support of the union.

Navigating the crowd, shimmering in their summer wedding wear, he ducked beneath the brims of hats, smiling greetings as he went. At the table he pulled the bead-weighted covers he'd purchased for the occasion from the multiple bowls of salads – rich dark leaves jewelled with pomegranate and pumpkin seeds, glistening with a sheen of oil; Greek salad with huge cubes of organic feta, sprinkled with fresh oregano from Mary's herb pots; new potatoes, slathered in his signature Dijonnaise, with slivers of spring onions, capers and dill; and the apple sauce, a beautiful jelly with chunks of fruit in it, with a sweet aroma of honey and sage.

Then he took off his jacket and hung it over the back of the rickety old chair that usually sits in the porch covered in discarded gloves and scarves, and pulled his apron on, tying it twice around his slender waist.

Raising his knife above his head, he called out, requesting an audience. His eyes searched the onlooking faces until they fell upon Mary's and then, sending her a grin, he pulled back the lid of the roaster and posed as everyone whipped out their phones to capture the moment.

The air was too warm for a puff of steam to be visible, but the scent that immediately pervaded the air was extraordinary. There was a gratifying group intake of breath at the sight of it.

The skin, scored deeply as if the animal had been flayed before its fiery end, was charred in places – the tips of its ears, the corners of the diamonds etched into its skin – but otherwise it was a perfect, deep orange hue. It shone, glistened, in the afternoon light.

Somehow, now cooked, its position on the spit made it seem as if it were leaping, dancing, gambolling, and Richard found himself gulping and averting his eyes. Once again, he worried that he ought to have had the head removed by the butchers, or he should have listened to Michael's suggestion of trying to remove it with a hacksaw. But even as he thought it, he knew he wouldn't have been able to do it. For when he looked down at the roasted hog to start carving it, it had taken everything he had to get on with the task in hand.

He found the best thing was to look just at his knife, not to let his eyes veer anywhere near the head. With its eyes closed so peacefully, all he could see was an image of his granddaughter – of Clara – asleep on his chest yesterday afternoon.

He looked up, back to Mary, and searched her face for a response. She had been watching him, and for a second he wondered if she really did know how it made him feel, the meat, the grotesqueness of it all.

She nodded at him, smiled and winked. He smiled back at her, his oldest friend, and then, as he looked back down at the meat to slice it, he was surprised to acknowledge that his nausea had subsided somewhat.

Now, the meat is almost entirely removed from the carcass. All that is left between the immobile, black-eared head and its sinewy haunches are the snaking shards of meat that surround the spine and, hanging below it, the curved bones of the surprisingly small ribcage. Still, he feels his stomach lurch as he looks at it, so he turns and swipes a glass from the table, filling it with red and gulping it down.

He wanders over to his mother's old armchair and collapses into it. He sighs. It's a relief to be off his feet. He contentedly stretches his legs before him. He is bone-tired, he realises, he could fall asleep right then and there. He really is turning into his mother.

He lets out a nasal chuckle, his eyes still closed.

She looked very funny earlier, sitting at the table in this chair. He laughs at the memory. It was ideal really, her chin only a little above the table's edge, a preventative to the dribbles of food that generally make their way down the front of her clothing.

It is a miracle that she was at the table at all. She is as stubborn as a mule when she's made up her mind. A trait he has inherited. Rosie worked a wonder getting her to join them for the meal. She'd been adamant that she wouldn't go to the church, but Rosie bargained with her to at least put on a clean dress and a fresh coat of lipstick, 'in case she decided to pop her head in to the party later'. He was livid, seeing her there, all made-up but refusing to budge. But Rosie told him to calm down, she said that curiosity would get the better of her, that his mother would never be able to stay in the house when there were potential dramas to be gawped at in the garden. And, as was often the case, Rosie was right, for as Richard had welcomed the first of the guests and directed them to the waiting crate bar he'd erected on the patio, he saw his mother appear in the conservatory, neck craning for an assistant to help her dismount the step onto the patio.

She certainly seemed to have enjoyed herself too, sitting in her armchair, alternating between holding court and listening in on conversations. He hasn't seen her this lively in years. And he's never seen her eat so much. She made short work of not one, but two, brioche buns stuffed with hog roast, and he was rendered speechless by witnessing her washing it all down with a generous glass of red wine. He expressed his surprise as he helped her through the onlookers to watch Mary and Iain disco their way through their first dance in the kitchen. She arched an eyebrow and said, 'Yes, well, I thought I'd better make the most of my last gasp of freedom.'

It was like a sharp jab to his gut.

How did she manage to time these things so well?

For a long time now, Richard has considered himself impermeable to criticism from the majority of the world's population, but, somehow, his mother's measured sideswipes always seem to catch him when he's off his guard.

Why should he feel this guilt?

He knows that what he is doing is the right thing. The best choice. In many ways the only choice.

What are his other options now that Mary is off, anyway? Move his mother into his central London third-floor flat? The idea of getting her up the stairs alone is utterly preposterous. If they managed it, what then? Doesn't he deserve a life?

He hadn't thought about any of this until her fall. It hadn't even tickled at his thoughts. Maybe it's because he just hadn't seen anyone close to him deal with old age. His dad, Dee, Lizzie all there one minute and then gone the next, and before their time. He'd always thought that theirs was a family that wasn't lucky – or unlucky? – enough to have to deal with the difficulties of advanced years.

Had he really been so blinkered? So focused on himself and the moment he was living in, striving in, that his thoughts just didn't wander to the future? You'd think, as an only child, he'd have considered it. But until Mary phoned him and told him that his mother had broken her hip and she couldn't see any option other than to move her into the house until she was recovered, he hadn't for a second considered that the day was approaching when he'd have to care for his mother, or at least, make decisions about her care.

If he thought about it at all, it was in the abstract: you get old, you go into a home. But it isn't abstract any more, it is his mother. But that really isn't the only issue. The real issue is that, as much as he hadn't considered the logistics of his mother's advancing years, he certainly hasn't considered his own. It won't be long before his children will be making decisions about him.

What will they do with him?

The music inside shifts. The Rolling Stones, he recognises. He had this song on a cassette that he often listened to on his weekly drives up and down from London.

How many times has he driven that route? Forty years they've lived here, and for many of them he drove up and down the M11 twice a week.

Over the last couple of years, he's barely driven at all. For the first time in his life he's been in one place. He felt trapped at first. Annoyed at Mary for that call, just before lockdown, saying that he needed to come. It wasn't fair that she and Iain had to care for his mother, and anyway, if it really was going to kick off, then she didn't like the idea of him being stuck in London with no outside space, and she had enough to worry about, without worrying about him.

That first week, he'd thought he was going to go insane – not just having to fulfil his mother's demands, but living back in this house. He'd stayed the night on numerous occasions over the years, but being here, living here; it couldn't help but remind him of those awful months after Dee's death. Then Iain started to feel odd. They dismissed it for a couple of days, assuming it was just the stress of having to move his lessons online. Besides, he didn't have a cough or a temperature. Then, they'd got a call from the head at Iain's school – two other teachers had been hospitalised. He could see the panic in Mary's eyes. To be honest, he'd felt pretty panicked himself. And then, faster than seemed possible, Iain was in hospital and he was trying to hold Mary together whilst making his enraging mother cups of tea that were an acceptable shade of beige. They were a tough few months, but once the worry of everything had settled down and Iain was off the ventilator, their new isolated lives found a rhythm. Then, the slow trickle of leaks out of Downing Street had started and he'd been in quite a bit of demand. Nearly every night he'd be called on to give his view on one scandal or another. He'd been so busy he'd bought himself a ring light and ordered a few important titles to slide between the other books on Mary's shelves. Slowly, he realised that he was more content than he had been in years.

This place has always been his home really. But in just over a week it'll be someone else's.

He didn't want to be in when people came to have a look around. He made sure that he was out, walking around the village, doing the shop, just going for a drive. Mary had absented herself too, taken Iain for a trundle about the local National Trust in his wheelchair. The agents had reported back, and his mother too. They'd mostly been people looking for a renovation opportunity. With the new housing estate on the other side of the village and the amenities that went with it, a property such as theirs was ripe for developers. You could tell them, his mother said, the ones that wanted to flatten it or carve it up into flats. In the end it went to a young family.

'They were quite nice,' his mother reported back to them over dinner. 'Noisy children. She's a businesswoman, lovely nails. I didn't catch what he did – seemed a bit snooty, if you ask me.'

The couple were moving up from London, the agent told them. They wanted a garden for their children to play in, fresh air for their little lungs to breathe, and more space for them to work from home.

Richard agreed with Mary; he was pleased that it was going to a family rather than a developer, but it had also sparked a fierce nostalgia that he hadn't seen coming. Nostalgia, but also regret.

It is his general opinion that there is no point in looking back and bemoaning what might have been. You can't change things, so what's the point of it? But, there was something about the sale of the house, about these huge changes in all of their lives, that felt so seismic. It would be very odd if any of them, particularly him and Mary, didn't take a moment to consider what had happened in the time their family had lived in this house. This home.

As he considered the years that had passed since he and Mary first pulled up alongside this house, he recognised that there'd been happy memories, yes. But he also felt an overwhelming sense of self-loathing. He'd been the luckiest man alive, and yet he'd never, ever, been satisfied. He was always looking ahead to what was next, what he could grab and he never took the time to notice how good he had it. He'd missed so much of his children growing up because of it. He'd missed the warning signs with Dee. He hadn't been a good husband. But most of all, worst of all, he didn't speak up when he realised that, after everything, he was still in love with Mary and always would be.

He's drunk, he realises, his eyes still closed.

Drunk and on the brink of sleep.

Richard rubs the palms of his hands over his face, as if he is washing it.

Laughter comes from the kitchen. More Eurythmics. 'Sweet Dreams.' Mary's absolute favourite. Released the year his dad died. Soon after he met Dee. He remembers Mary humming it around the house – it had driven him barmy.

Well, she won't be driving him up the wall any more. And he's no one to blame but himself.

Twenty-two

Richard carefully wedged the case of wine between his suitcase and the two large yellow bags, stuffed with gifts. He'd had everything all wrapped when he'd bought them. Not very personal, but at least he'd chosen the gifts himself. Most of his colleagues got their secretaries or, more often these days, their secretaries' assistants to order everything.

He got into the car and checked the essentials. He tapped his pocket to check that the bulk of his wallet was in place, unclipped his phone from his belt and angled it in the well by the gear stick, and leaned forward to look out of the windscreen. He squinted up at the flat, double-checking the lights were off, then started the engine, put the car into gear, and pulled out into the street.

'Driving home for Christmas . . .'

Those were the only lyrics he knew, but he made a good approximation of the rest, humming the tune where innovation failed him as he turned onto Millbank.

Home? Did he still think of Mouser Lane as his home?

He had a flat now. The dream bachelor pad of his younger self. Surely that was his home?

Home is where the heart is. Where was his heart?

He shifted a little in his seat, adjusting himself. He considered, briefly, whether to undo the top button of his trousers. He'd put on weight recently, and that was before the onslaught of non-stop eating that was a Christmas at Mary's. Well, he'd just have to splash out on some new suits. He'd been too thin for too long.

There had been a point, in those months after Dee, when he'd caught sight of himself in the mirror in the spare room back at Mary's, and hadn't recognised himself. He'd studied himself, fascinated. He looked like an anatomical drawing: he could see each of his ribs in relief, the jut of his hips, and then, turning, the long pearl necklace of his spine, the wings of his shoulder blades. He wouldn't have been surprised if he were able to see his internal organs too, so transparent, so pale was his skin. He remembered very clearly that odd sensation of realising that he still had a body. It was almost a surprise for, from the moment he'd found Dee in that bath, with its water so dark with blood that it almost looked solid, he'd felt as if he'd ceased to be a complete human. Just a brain full of regret and memories, and a heart so heavy, so painful, that it was like lugging around a jar of pennies in his chest.

The traffic around Westminster was almost at a standstill; worse, even, than it usually was on a Friday night. He'd considered delaying the drive till the morning – the roads were bound to be clear early on a Saturday – but he wanted to spend as much time with the girls as possible, and, with a house full, Mary would be needing his help. Besides, he'd have to get up early on Saturday to get to the market. He'd got a turkey on order from the butcher, so that was all sorted, but he still needed all the veg, and there'd be other bits that Mary would have missed, being so busy with that new fancy job of hers and helping Iain to ferry Lizzie back and forth to the hospital.

It was going to be a happy Christmas, he could feel it. They all needed it after such a tumultuous year. He really hoped the kids would all stay in for New Year's Eve, but he feared those days had gone.

Last year Rosie was the only one who'd stayed for dinner. Emma had gone back to Manchester early to celebrate with uni mates, and he'd dropped Phoebe at a sleepover earlier that evening, turning a blind eye to the clank of bottles as she'd slung her bag over her shoulder and slammed the car door. He'd cooked a very successful beef wellington with dauphinoise potatoes, but Rosie had opted for bed after 'Auld Lang Syne', leaving the four of them enjoying the Priorat that Liz, Iain and Mary had brought back from Spain. Then, at around 2 a.m., Mary – a little tiddly – had showed them her stockpiles.

'I was positive that the bug was going to do for us all on the stroke of midnight last year.'

She'd given them a tour of all her hiding places, and they'd become increasingly helpless. The cupboard under the stairs stacked with toilet rolls, plastic crates in the garage filled with bags and bags of dried pulses and grains, and – he and Liz had really lost it at this – she'd filled the entire chest of drawers in the hallway with candles. He couldn't remember the last time he'd laughed that hard. Iain had told them both off. And he was right, really, Mary was only – just as she always was – trying to look out for them all. And, though the lights had stayed on, she hadn't been totally wrong to worry about what the next millennium might usher in.

That morning in September was never far from his thoughts.

First, there was the call from Mary. He'd been in meetings all morning, and around eleven, he'd grabbed his phone as he headed out to Pret. He'd been alarmed to see several missed calls from Mary. *Mother*, he remembered thinking. But when he called back he discovered, between Mary's choked sobs, that it wasn't his mother. Mary had been calling about Lizzie. She'd been admitted to hospital. It had set him reeling. The news, but Mary's reaction too.

He'd often wondered about it, the tight-knit friendship the three of them had, Mary, Lizzie and Iain. He'd watched *Jules et Jim*. And just a few months ago he'd taken himself to see *Y Tu Mamá También* at the cinema, to see what all the fuss was about.

He'd mentioned his suspicions to Emma when she last came down to London and he'd taken her for dinner. She'd rolled her eyes at him.

'Dad. Why are you so predictable?'

So he'd kept his mouth shut since, but those niggles about Mary's closeness to the Kings still occasionally raised their heads.

They'd been on the phone for a good half hour. He'd walked as far as the river and watched the light bounce off the water as she spoke to him about the operation that was coming, about the treatment that was likely to make Lizzie lose her mobility, at least for a bit.

'We had a drink last night and she showed me the pictures of the wheelchair they've got in the garage. I was okay, holding it together, and then when she went home this morning, I just lost it. I needed to talk to someone, and you were the first person I thought of.'

A thrill ran through him when she said that. And it was then, there, looking at the surface of the Thames reflecting the light in a way that reminded him of Hockney's water paintings, that he'd realised.

It had come as quite a surprise. He hadn't thought about the opposite sex, or indeed sex at all, in more than three years. And yet there he was standing by the Thames, beaming because Mary had called him. Because he was the first person she'd thought of.

He'd walked back to the office in a daze. He was giddy. Like a teenager with a crush.

He'd been so lost in his own world that it had taken him a few moments to notice anything amiss when he arrived back in the office. He'd almost made it back to his desk when he realised that everyone in the whole place was stock-still and staring open-mouthed at the bank of screens in the far corner.

He still saw it sometimes, when he closed his eyes. That image of a person, of people, jumping. Then the noise, the collective gasp, as the first tower fell.

There was a little congestion as the North Circular merged into the M11, but then once he'd passed the cameras, the traffic thinned out and he took the car into top gear, finding a steady pace. He liked to sit just below 75, speeding safely.

He pressed the car phone button and the screen lit up. He scrolled down to 'Home' and pressed the little green phone icon.

'Hello? Eight, Four, Two – Two, Oh, Six. Mary speaking.'

His stomach flipped at the sound of her voice. She sounded so Scottish on the phone. He never noticed her accent face to face.

'Just me, letting you know I'm on the M11.'

'Don't use the car phone Richard, you know it scares me stiff.'

His stomach flipped again. She worried about him!

'Okay okay!' He laughed. 'I just wanted you to know I should be home in time for dinner, so lay me a place.'

She laughed now.

'Oh, Richard. There's no dinner. We've been at the hospital all day. I'm just in from helping get Lizzie settled in her new bed. It would appear Phoebe's out. I was just trying to talk one of the girls into running into town for a takeaway.'

'Well, tell them my vote is for curry.'

'Okay, okay.' She was distracted now, he could hear it in her voice. 'Drive safely.'

The car phone screen lit up as she hung up and his heart sank. Of course she had other priorities. Long gone were the days where he'd return on a Friday night to freshly-bathed children and a home-made meal keeping warm in the oven. He'd forfeited his rights to all of that, he knew. But he was so looking forward to seeing her that he couldn't help but feel a little deflated that she'd not been anticipating his arrival too.

He felt a pang of jealousy and then immediately chided himself. How ridiculous, to be jealous of Mary's sick best friend – and his good friend for years. But he knew what it was like to be cared for by Mary. He absolutely wouldn't have made it through the months, the year – years – after Dee's death without her.

She'd welcomed them both back into her home. Him and his daughter by another woman. Yes, he still owned half of the house, but she would have been well within her rights to tell him to sod off. She hadn't though. She had looked after him, she had looked after him *and* Rosie. She had fed them and made their beds and washed their clothes and, once, she'd even washed him. She hadn't asked him what had happened. She hadn't asked him if he wanted to talk about it. She had just been there.

She had always been there. For him. For the kids. Even for his mother.

Mary.

What a woman she was.

Why had it taken him so long to realise it?

Twenty-three

Emma emerges from the conservatory into the cool of the evening. The kitchen, the dining room, were starting to make her feel a bit claustrophobic, everyone around her jiggling, gyrating and sweating to songs whose opening bars fire up instant memories of her childhood. She's been standing in the corner, by the door to the utility room, for the last hour, fighting the urge to walk through it and out into the night, leaving altogether. She's done her bit. She walked her mum down the aisle. Posed for the photos. Made small talk with Iain's family. Nodded and smiled throughout the meal. All while doing her best to avoid Phoebe's gaze, and trying even harder not to watch that little girl's every movement.

As she crosses the patio she realises there is a barely perceptible tilt to her movement. There is a full glass of champagne in her hand and, as a few drops splatter onto the patio, she concentrates her efforts to walk in a straight line.

At the table, she takes a seat on one of the high-backed rattan chairs that ordinarily reside in the conservatory. She eases herself into it until the creaking ceases, and then she exhales and feels, for the first time that day, the muscles across her shoulders relaxing. Her head lolls against the back of the chair and she rolls it from side to side, stretching out her neck. A fine concoction, jet lag, anxiety medication and champagne. She feels as though she is dreaming, everything exaggerated and yet oddly at a distance. Her eyes trace the length of the table, past the tree and out to the buffet, across to the carcass of the pig. She shudders. It's like the site of some sort of ritual sacrifice.

She lets her head rest back against the chair once more and tilts her chin up, watching the lights moving in the branches of the willow.

'How are you enjoying the party, Bunny?'

Emma jumps, clutching her champagne glass to her chest. She sits forward in the chair, looking around to follow the voice. Her dad appears from behind the winged side of her granny's old armchair and wiggles his fingers in a coy wave.

'I thought everyone was dancing.'

'Ah, you're never alone in this house,' he pauses, rubs at his eye, shakes his head. 'I was going to say, "you know that". But, I suppose it's been long enough that you mightn't remember.'

They sit in silence. Inside 'Who Runs The World' starts to play.

'One of my requests.' He nods towards the flashing lights spilling into the conservatory.

'You've forgiven her for Destiny's Child?'

'Life, it would seem, Bunny, is about letting things go.'

A breeze whips across them. The flames on the candles momentarily disappear, then reignite. A napkin flies off the back of a chair and lands a few metres away on the grass. The surface of the pond ripples, distorting for a second the perfect reflection of the glowing festoon of lights in the willow's branches above.

'Come home more often, Bunny.'

'My home's in California, Dad.'

The noise of footsteps draws their attention to the patio. Rosie's new man, looking at his phone, smiling to himself. He is really rather handsome, in a slim, tidy sort of way. His shirt is perfectly pressed, as if he has just put it on. The only sign that he might have been wearing the outfit longer than a few minutes is the knot of his skinny blue tie being slightly off centre. She saw, from her vantage point in the back corner of the kitchen, that he was reluctantly led to the dance floor more than once over the last several hours. But he can move, even if he didn't want to. His blue straight-legged trousers make the suit jacket hanging on the back of the dining chair next to her instantly recognisable as his. On the chair next to that, a shiny beaded shawl glitters under the lights – she recognised it earlier and couldn't place it – but then, with a roll of her stomach, she realises that it's the same one that Rosie wore when she and Michael got married.

Dan pauses his stride and taps something into his phone, then looks up. He draws back slightly on seeing them. Then, as if it hasn't happened, he smiles and walks towards them. Her dad tilts his head, then inhales deeply and pulls himself to standing and walks to the table, to fill up his wine glass. When he turns back, Emma notices that he is swaying slightly.

'How are you enjoying the party, Doc?'

'Everyone's having a great time.'

'Well, I'd better get in there and put a stop to that.'

'Actually, Rich, Rosie's looking for you.'

Her dad sips his wine, regards him as he does so. Then, swallowing, he nods.

'Do me a favour, son. Don't call me Rich.'

'Oh, sorry. I thought I heard Iain . . . sorry.'

Her dad winks, then turns and walks with a slight list, towards the house.

'He should consider himself lucky you shortened it to Rich. Most people opt for the more fitting diminutive.'

Emma places a cigarette between her lips, lights it, then looks up. She smiles at him, exhaling smoke through her nostrils.

'You're not much of a dancer, either?'

'Just taking a breather.'

'Yeah, me too.'

Emma smiles at him and inhales deeply on the cigarette.

He sits on the piano stool. She raises her eyebrows and holds out the packet of cigarettes towards him. He shakes his head. She nods, brings the cigarette back to her lips and inhales.

'You know, actually, I do quite fancy one. Do you mind?'

Emma shrugs and throws the packet at him. He ducks and it sails past him, landing on the buffet table with a clatter of cutlery.

'Ball games are not my sport.' He laughs, that nervous laugh she'd heard so much through the meal. He rises and retrieves the white packet and slides a cigarette out of it.

'Sorry, Phoebe. Oh no! I mean Emma. Sorry! Or is it Emmeline?'

'Yes, I'm the one that Mum rather hopefully named after Pankhurst. But my friends call me Em.'

Emma beckons him to her, holding out the lighter aflame. He leans in, angling the end of the cigarette towards her. She can smell his aftershave. Oud. She'd have won that bet, if she'd have placed it.

'I think you've got it.'

She pulls the lighter away. They make eye contact.

'Rosie always says she couldn't ever touch a fag again after seeing what they do to your insides.'

She drags hard on the cigarette, tilts her chin up and blows a stream of smoke up into the low hanging branches of the tree.

'Well, my patients don't tend to be smokers, so it's a little easier to pretend to myself I'm not making a horrible choice.

Anyway, one won't make a difference, we live in the city centre so we're practically smoking ten a day, anyway.'

'Gross.'

'Yep.'

Halfway through the cigarette, the smoke seems to change flavour. She imagines it, coating her throat, the white wisps of it settling in the villi of her lungs, immediately transforming to gluey black and orange tar. Her lungs are going to look like the skin of that pig did earlier, glossy and orange, flecked with black. Decisively she throws the half-smoked cigarette onto the grass and grinds it out with the sole of her new heels.

'I don't really smoke. I bought them at the airport. Thought it might help me get through the day.'

'Is it working?'

'Not really.'

She shrugs and reaches for her champagne glass. Empty. Standing, she scours the table and locates a half-full bottle of red wine. She fills her champagne flute, almost to the top, and then drinks it down. One, two, three gulps. She gasps for breath.

Dan is watching her.

'I'm not the alcoholic. That's Phoebe.'

He smiles. Annoyance flares. She grasps for something, anything to wipe that patronising look off his face.

'So, are you going to make an honest woman out of my baby sister, young man?'

'That's the plan.'

Emma cocks her head.

'There's a plan?'

'Yes, I asked your dad this afternoon when we were, erm. When we were . . .' he nods towards the carcass of the pig, but doesn't look at it, avoids doing so, in fact.

'You asked his permission?'

'Yes.'

She laughs then.

'What? Is that funny?'

'I mean it's quite old-fashioned!'

'Well, I am a bit.'

'So she'll have to convert?'

He frowns. And then he blinks, slowly.

'I'm not religious.'

A heat rises from the pit of her stomach to the crown of her head. She stands, quickly, to try to shift the awkward silence.

'Congratulations!' She leans in and hugs him. He feels stiff in her arms.

She releases him and laughs, awkwardly. Then she walks back to the table and refills her glass, turns back to him and raises it.

'Well, here's to you and Rosie!'

He smiles, then leans over and pulls his suit jacket from the back of the neighbouring chair, reaches into the inside pocket and pulls out a small velvet box. He flicks it open.

'I've been waiting for a moment. I know, from the way she talks about you all, that asking her with all of her family around will mean the world to her.'

It's a pretty engagement ring. Simple. Not a patch on hers.

'Lucky girl.'

'I'm hoping she'll agree.'

She mimes drawing a big tick in the air before her.

'Oh, and your mum knows too, and Iain. But no one else, so . . .'

He places a finger to his lips. She nods.

Dan smiles at her and looks down at the ring before he snaps the box shut and slips it back in his jacket pocket.

'And you? How are you getting on?'

'I'm trying not to drink too much and stay at the opposite side of the room.'

She turns her wrist to look at her watch. She squints, struggling to make out the time; maybe she needs to put a little more effort into the 'not drinking too much' thing.

'And there's only twenty-three minutes of the night left!'

'It can't be easy for you.'

'It's not. Thanks.'

She smiles at him, then at once it feels they've been holding eye contact too long. She averts her eyes and then points in the direction of the pig.

'He's got it worse than me though. Poor thing.'

The animal's burnt skin is now stripped away. Its flesh too. The arch of its ribs is visible, the column of its spine.

'We think we're so sophisticated, don't we? With our iPhones and our electric cars, but beneath it all we're still just as shackled to the food chain as any other beast.'

'Delicious, though.'

'I'm a veggie.'

'Of course.'

He frowns. Her cheeks smart with the immediacy of her embarrassment.

'I just mean that, it makes sense that Dad made you carve with him if you don't eat meat. If there's one thing my father can't abide, it's a vegetarian.' She laughs. 'I— sorry. I'm drunk. My mouth doesn't seem quite connected to my brain.'

He still doesn't smile.

'We were vegetarians for a bit. All three of us. That back field –' she sweeps her arm towards the darkness that lies beyond the reach of the lights in the tree '– it used to be full of them. Pigs. Big, noisy, stinky pigs, and all these cute little piglets. Hundreds of them. Put you right off your sausages.'

'I can't imagine being a kid with all this space.' Dan is looking at the house now, shaking his head. 'What a place to grow up! You were so lucky.'

She looks back at the house. The way it is lit up from within, a doll's house full of music and laughter.

'I don't really remember being a kid. I mean, I do, I remember playing over there, or eating porridge in the kitchen or whatever. But a lot of the memories that linger are, well. Let's say that we *were* lucky. But some of us were luckier than others.'

Twenty-four

Emma looked at the clock. She needed to try calling her dad again. He wouldn't be awake yet; it was only six, and there was a long day ahead of her. She'd drink the coffee first. She sipped it and winced. She'd already burnt the roof of her mouth twice trying to keep herself awake with the pitiful offerings of the machine in the corridor.

It was just the three of them in the waiting room now.

Phoebe was fast asleep, hunched over in the wheelchair. Her bare limbs were covered in scratches; one of her arms in a sling across her chest, a leg sticking out in front of her, braced on the foot rest. Her ankle had become increasingly deformed over the hours they'd been in the waiting room and was now a vivid shade of purple. In the chair opposite, Rosie slept, her head lolling to one side, her pyjamas obvious beneath the fleece she'd grabbed as a last-minute thought. She somehow looked ten years the junior of Phoebe, in her cut-off jeans and hoodie, despite there being less than five months between them.

It had been thrumming when they'd arrived in the early hours: bustling with diverse injuries, including a toddler who had proudly announced that he'd 'got a pen lid up my nose', a woman with a burn to her hand that was wrapped in a wet bath towel, another woman with a very pale face but no discernible injuries, and a young man in a Norwich City football shirt who was crying in a wheelchair.

As Phoebe was being assessed, she could hear the sound of vomiting, groans of pain: someone who was very obviously even drunker than Phoebe had been when she found her in the bus stop earlier that week. There was also the occasional fuzz of a police walkie-talkie.

The presence of the police had made her heart thump and caused her to give both of her sisters a hard stare, reminding them to stick to the story.

Looking back on the events of the previous twenty-four hours, it would be easy to question why Emma hadn't taken up her mum's offer of a month in the Balearics with the Kings, but when she'd made the decision, there had seemed to be no option.

'Well, that was not the response I was expecting! Most children would jump at the chance of a month in the sun, all expenses paid.'

Her mum had the printout of a white villa covered in pink flowers in front of her.

'We aren't children.' Phoebe was twizzling her fork in her spaghetti. 'I'm staying here with Dad. Youth Theatre are doing *Chicago*, and they owe me a good part after last year.'

'Oh fine. Be like that. What about you, Rosie?'

'Is it till the end of August? Cos I was kind of hoping to stay with Auntie Yas for Carnival, like last year. It sounds fun, though.'

'Em?'

She'd avoided her mum's gaze for a moment.

'One last trip away with your old mum before you desert me for the city of dreaming spires?'

'I'm sorry Mum. I'd love to, but I really want to be here to collect my results in person.'

That part was true enough. They'd been in Italy two years earlier, and she'd had to get her GCSE results read down the phone by her granny, who seemed to think that pretending her run of straight A*s were a collection of C, D and E grades was a prank that would go down in the annals of history. That had been stressful enough, but then she'd returned to the UK, ready to celebrate her incredible success, to find out that Lee had cheated on her, snogging Louise Peters from the lower sixth at a party so memorable, people were still referring to it as 'The Party'.

So yes, she wanted to see her A-level results with her own eyes, but her main concern was that she wouldn't miss the celebrations. Particularly as Sarah's boyfriend Justin had confided that his friend from the local private school, who had booked the area for them all at Club Allegro, thought she was 'fit'.

'Oh, what a shame. Well, at least Lizzie and I'll be able to let our hair down when we hit Café del Mar for sundowners!'

'Oh Mum, cringe.' Phoebe covered her face with her hands.

'*Ach*, you know it's not my thing. But it's on The Bucket List.'

They'd all gone quiet then, pushing the last shreds of spaghetti around their plates, making contemporary art with the swirls of pesto.

'You'll have to behave for your dad though, all of you. I don't want to be getting phone calls to some bar in San Antonio because you're all running wild.'

They hadn't run wild. Not to start with anyway.

For the week after Mary left, everything was as tranquil as it got for Mouser Lane. Phoebe had been out of the house from almost the crack of dawn, rehearsing for *Chicago*. She hadn't got the part she wanted, but after a few days she'd come round to the idea. Apparently it was better to just have 'one good song' in which she had a solo, because it meant she could spend more time 'socialising' backstage. Rosie was her usual amenable self, making up her little dance routines in the garden and watching TV with their dad in the evening, and Emma had been busy too. After her exams finished, she'd got a job in a little cafe next to the cathedral that served cream teas to tourists. It was easy work and surprisingly well paid thanks to the tips, which bolstered her hopes of not needing to work during term time in the coming year at Oxford.

In some ways it was that peaceful week, that lull of false security, that had made what followed worse.

She'd been fast asleep when her father had tapped on her door.

'Bunny?'

She opened her eyes and struggled to make sense of where she was. The smell of her dad's aftershave reached her, and even in the semi-dark of her room with its still-closed curtains she could see he was wearing a suit. He hadn't worn a suit since he came back to live here after Rosie's mum died.

'Are you okay, Dad?'

'I need to ask you a little favour, Bunny.'

They'd been alone in the house before on several occasions, but never overnight, but that was mainly because Mary rarely went anywhere they weren't invited too. She could see why, when the call came, her dad had barely given it a second's thought. She knew he'd been talking to people at the BBC and ITN for months, and he could hardly turn down the opportunity just because there was a chance his daughters couldn't behave themselves for a few days. After all, Emma was legally an adult, Rosie – the youngest at fourteen – was allowed to be left unsupervised, and anyway, if there was an actual problem, Granny was only fifteen minutes away.

The hardest thing she'd anticipated about the arrangement was the likelihood of having to act as her sisters' taxi service and, really, that had been the only irritation. Until the night Phoebe's play opened.

She'd waited for her in the car outside the theatre, listening to a programme about the impending solar eclipse. She watched the audience trickle out, and then, some time later, from the gate at the side of the theatre over which 'Stage Door' was painted, dribs and drabs of young people in baggy black clothes emerged, their faces still caked with stage make-up. She scoured the faces looking for Phoebe but she couldn't find her. Then she watched as the lights in the theatre's foyer went off, and a man with long hair down to his waist locked the gate at the side of the theatre.

Eventually, after visiting almost every establishment that was open past nightfall, she'd found Phoebe, in the beer garden of a pub she'd never been to. She was talking to a table of men well into their fifties. She was with that dreadful Frances and Bea, and two other girls Emma had never seen before, but who were obviously in the play – a fact that was evident by the kohl around their eyes and the matching fishnets that they were wearing.

'Phoebe.'

'*Uh-oh*, here come the fun police.'

She had waited right outside the stage door for the rest of the week, a tactic that had proved successful until the final night, when Phoebe had somehow managed to bypass her. She'd given up, knowing that dragging her away from the last night party would mean more hassle than it was worth, and went to bed, with the house phone on her bedside table. At some point she'd be woken by the inevitable call from Phoebe summoning her for a lift home, so she could sleep off the litres of Archers and lemonade she'd undoubtedly been poisoning herself with. But she'd woken to Rosie bringing her a mug of Earl Grey, asking where Phoebe was. She had thought she was going to vomit, so destabilising was the fear she felt at that moment. But then, just as she was dialling their grandmother's number, a car pulled up on the gravel at the side of the house, blaring out Foo Fighters, and delivered Phoebe, stinking of cigarettes and with a trail of blossoming love bites along her neck.

Their dad had come home soon after, vibrating with the excitement of a week in a television studio.

'They've asked me to do another week. So, I'll do a shop and then shoot back to town. You'll be okay, won't you Bunny? I'll be back on Friday. And I'll bring a bottle of fizz to celebrate your results.'

She wanted to tell him that, actually, she wasn't sure that she would be okay for another week. That, actually, she didn't want the responsibility of looking after Phoebe, that she wanted to enjoy these last weeks before university. She wanted to say that the events that morning – when she had realised that Phoebe wasn't in the house and something awful might have happened to her when she was supposed to be protecting her from harm – had made her feel old and angry and scared and – worst of all – a bit relieved that she wouldn't have to worry about her any more. But her dad was glowing. He was smiling, humming to himself as he loaded clothes into the washing machine. And it had been years since she'd seen him like that, years since she'd seen him this close to being happy, to being the dad she remembered. So she didn't say any of those things, she just put on her running shoes and broke her personal best for three laps of the village. And then, after a shower, she had waved him off from the front path, with Rosie and an unusually quiet and ashen Phoebe by her side.

'Phoebe Roberts?'

A doctor with sandy coloured hair and round tortoiseshell glasses stood in the door of the waiting room with a Manila folder in his hand.

'Yes.' Emma stood and unlocked the break of the wheelchair in which Phoebe was groaning as she woke. 'It's her, my sister. Has she broken something?'

'If you could follow me.'

'Can we all come?'

Rosie was sitting up now too, yawning, the side of her face red where it had been pressed against the vinyl of the waiting room chair cushion.

'No, erm – adults with you?'

'I'm eighteen.' Emma straightened her back and stared directly in the doctor's eyes. 'But our dad will be here soon.'

'Well, it's only a little room. But yes, I suppose you'd better all come.'

'So, that little line there is a break, I'm afraid. And there too, you can see. The foot, not the ankle. But still we'll have to set it. Which will mean no showers, swimming or weight-bearing for a good few weeks. And mobility will be tricky, as crutches are off the table. How did this happen again?'

Phoebe looked at Emma and she made the tiniest of movements of her head, the whisper of a shake.

'I fell.' Phoebe shrugged, then winced at the evident pain of the movement. 'I basically misjudged the distance that I was trying to jump.'

The doctor looked at Phoebe for a moment, and then looked at Emma, before inhaling deeply, shaking his head and scribbling something into his notes.

It had been a spilt-second decision to lock the door. And as soon as she'd turned the key, something in Emma's gut told her she'd crossed a line. She'd actually put her hand out to unlock it, but at the same moment Phoebe had tried to open the door and, discovering it was locked, she had let out a scream so unholy and crazed, that Emma decided to turn away from the door, walk downstairs and join Rosie in the lounge to watch *Buffy*.

'Are you sure you shouldn't just let her go out?' Rosie pointed towards the hallway and the sound of howling and battering that was issuing from up the stairs.

But Emma just reached for the remote and turned up the volume.

She knew she'd have to pay for it later. She knew that Phoebe would make a song and dance of it for months, that she'd undoubtedly be told off by her mum and probably her dad too. But she was at the end of her tether. For the last three nights, Phoebe had gone out after dinner and hadn't returned until it was light the next day. Emma had stayed up every night, worrying. Had driven around the village looking for her, and yesterday, had found her, semi-dressed and passed out in the village bus shelter. She'd had enough. And so, this evening, when Phoebe announced that she was going to get dressed to go out and 'meet a mate', something in Emma snapped, and she'd followed her up the stairs and locked her in her room. She knew it wasn't right, that it would only make her sister hate her more than she already seemed to, but tomorrow was her day. She wanted a good night's sleep. She wasn't nervous, as such, she was confident that the four A grades she needed to read Computer

Science and Philosophy at Oxford were a fait accompli, but still, she wanted to feel fresh, to have her make-up and hair done nicely in case the local papers wanted to take a photo of star students and, mostly, she wanted to have fun. Phoebe seemed to have nothing but fun; wasn't she allowed to have just one night?

They watched two episodes before Emma pressed mute and they both waited, listening. The house was silent.

'I'll make her some toast. A peace offering. You want some?'

Rosie nodded, then turned off the TV and rolled onto her back on the sofa. That's when they heard it. A strange cracking noise coming from outside, followed by a scream. A scream that they both recognised immediately as belonging to Phoebe.

Emma had run through the kitchen as if she were sprinting in a baton relay. In the conservatory, she'd had some idea that there was something on the roof, but when she'd struggled with the lock and pushed at the door, she'd been confused for a second by the tangle of branches and leaves that met her. She felt like the prince fighting his way into the castle to wake Sleeping Beauty as she tussled with the wisteria vines. They had been wrenched off the back wall of the house as Phoebe fell. But the young woman Emma was hacking through foliage to reach was not sleeping, but groaning and swearing at the top of her voice.

'Fuck! My leg, my leg! I've broken my leg!'

She hadn't broken her leg, though. Just the foot. She had broken her foot, and her arm.

'So that's the humerus.' Rosie had hovered over the nurse for the entire application of the plaster of Paris, evidently enjoying every moment of getting to see the procedure up close.

At least one of them was having a good time.

* * *

It was nearly ten in the morning by the time their granny arrived at the hospital.

'I'll have to push the front seat right back to fit you in, Phoebe. Emma, Rosie, I'll need you to help me lift her in and out.'

'I have to go straight to school, Granny. It's my results day.'

'Oh, yes. That.' Her granny had never once seemed impressed by any of her academic successes.

'We'll come with you! Then we can all drive back together and have a special breakfast. Or I can cook us dinner tonight.'

'That's sweet, Rosie. But I was planning to go into town with Sarah. We've booked an area.'

'Oh, Sarah this, Sarah that. Family first, Emmaline. Go and get your results and come home. I'll get your sister settled, and then you and I need to have a chat about what you've been getting up to these last few weeks.'

She was very aware of the state of her hair as she walked into the quiet assembly hall. Mr Reed was talking to Lena Wright and her mum, who was blushing and kept tucking her hair behind her ear, and Mrs Orford-Long was laughing with Simon Edmunds and Ollie Field, and so she entered the space without being noticed. There was a square of tables set around the perimeter of the room. Most of them were bare, but a few brown envelopes remained, the names of pupils yet to collect them visible through the little windows. She walked around the tables until she reached the letter R that had been drawn in felt-tip on a piece of A4 and Sellotaped to the table at an angle.

She had a fleeting thought about how odd it was that pivotal moments seem to occur in the most mundane environments, and then she pulled out the results from the envelope and saw them, the results that ran down the side of the page: A, B, B, A.

Dancing Queen, she thought.

She laughed, a little exhalation.

'*Huh.*'

And then she turned the paper over, looking for the real results, and saw the paper was blank, but for the watermark that went through it. It was then that she realised the paper in her hand was shaking violently and that the funny choking sound she could hear was coming from her, and oddly, she was struggling to breathe.

Twenty-five

Rosie steps down onto the patio and the baby shuffles on her bare shoulder at the jolt of the descent.

She pauses.

They still haven't noticed her, still deep in conversation. Danyal laughs at something Emma says, and a spike of jealousy runs through her.

She's been watching them for ages. She'd thought, hoped, that moving outside would have alerted them to her presence so they would stop their intimate little conversation naturally and she wouldn't have to barge in and break it up.

When she first saw them, from her vantage point inside the dark conservatory, she'd thought it was Phoebe. She had been trying to wrap her head around how Phoebe could have made it out to the garden before she did, when something about how the light fell from the tree changed, and she could see clearly that it was Emma.

Emma laughs now. Danyal refills his glass, leans back in his chair.

How odd it is that they haven't realised she's there.

Rosie always knows when someone's looking at her. She feels it. Her skin prickles, her ears warm, her throat itches. Danyal says it's not possible, that if there were a sixth sense it would have been covered at some point in their fourteen years of medical training, that claptrap like that is incompatible with the science of modern medicine. But he only says that because he can't feel it. He doesn't know that her awareness of it is so honed, that she can be walking on the street and feel the feeling and look up to a tall building, a tower block even, and her eyes will lock immediately with whoever it is who is watching her. She doesn't have to search them out. She just feels it, turns and finds them, she knows exactly where to look.

Emma throws her head back, really laughing now. She hasn't seen Emma laugh like that for years. She can't even remember when. She should feel proud that her sister finds him funny. And she does, but there is a proprietary bite too. She knew that bringing him here would mean sharing him. It's one of the reasons she's never brought any of her boyfriends back here since Anthony. She's seen it happen repeatedly, not just with Michael, but with Emma's other boyfriends, all of Phoebe's many partners over the years. The way they quickly become part of the family, the way they get swallowed, like an insect landing on a Venus flytrap, its leg protruding from the leafy jaws for a while, but then when the vegetal maw reopens it is gone, assimilated, part of the carnivorous plant.

Didn't the same happen to her, in a way?

Danyal is talking, emphasising with his hands. Emma laughs again and puts out a hand, touching Danyal on the forearm, as she drops her head down, her back shaking. What are they talking about?

'What's the big joke?' Rosie's voice reverberates around the garden.

The baby on her shoulder jumps at the noise. So do they. Emma quickly withdraws her hand, paints a smile on her face.

Rosie lowers her voice to an exaggerated whisper and picks her way across the patio towards them.

'I got left holding the baby. Phoebe broke a glass in the bathroom. She woke the kids up.'

Emma pulls a cigarette from the packet and lights it.

'She's trying to get Clara back to sleep. Have you seen Michael?'

They both shake their heads. The baby stirs, emits a little whimper.

'Want me to take over for a moment?'

The weight of the baby leaves her shoulder as Danyal lifts him away from her and cradles him against his chest. She can feel the coolness of the evening air where his absence is, keenly. Albie's big eyes are open. Searching.

'Oh, you're awake are you? It's a bit late for you to be awake, mate.'

If Rosie were to rank the things she loves about Danyal, a close second would be the way he talks to children of all ages as if they are his equal.

There is a lift in the breeze. It seems to catch the last of the day's heat and sweep it away. Rosie shivers, and reaches for her shawl. The noise of the tree above them is like the applause of a distant audience; a flutter of orange leaves fall around them.

Danyal, Emma and Rosie look up in unison. Their eyes searching for a further scatter of leaves. But the activity in the branches is fleeting and quickly all is still once more.

'Do you want kids, Dan?'

Emma's words are sharp, but they seem to become trapped in the air, a mosquito in amber. Lingering between them. Rosie had forgotten this. The way her sister's words seem so often designed to agitate.

'Em—' Rosie starts, but Danyal speaks too.

'That's a pretty intrusive question for someone I've known for –' he lifts his wrist, shuffling the baby to get a clear view of his watch '– less than twelve hours.'

He smiles at Rosie as he strokes the baby's back and her heart lurches from anger straight back to love. She feels light-headed with relief. He's dealing with her family so deftly; maybe, if she asks him, he'll give her some tips.

Rosie then looks at Emma. Where is the rapid and explosive reply? But, to her surprise, she sees she is smiling. And then Rosie is smiling too because she knows Emma has seen it, the thing that Rosie has fallen for: the steel beneath Danyal's softness. He reaches out then, with the hand that has been stroking the baby's back, and takes her hand. His palm is soft as it slides against hers, and she grips it, there, under the willow that she'd spent so many hours staring at when her heart was so torn that her pain was physical.

He'd done that on the day they'd first met. That day he'd discovered her in the supplies cupboard. He hadn't done what everyone else had done. He didn't smash the door open and see her all snotty on the floor next to the disposable aprons and hesitate momentarily before grabbing what he needed and smashing out of the room again. He'd just calmly crouched down beside her and waited for her to make eye contact, before offering her his hand and supporting her to stand. And though she could barely see his face through all the PPE, she felt the weight of the day lift a little.

'About time you had someone in your corner, Rosie. I like him.'

The song inside changes. The electric surge of something she vaguely recognises as prog-rock segues into a drum roll, the beat of a snare drum and a reverberating guitar riff. Rosie grips Danyal's hand, and he pulses it back.

'Can you hold him, Emma? I'd like to dance to this song with my girlfriend.'

'Go on then. Give it here.'

'Not "it" Em. Albie.'

'Albie. He. It. They. Whatever. Go on, you're missing your song.'

Twenty-six

Rosie knew that some jobs demanded it, but she'd never understand why people elected to live in London.

The walk from her dad's flat to the hospital was only around forty-five minutes, if she kept a good pace, but it could take almost as long on the tube, worse on the buses. It wasn't that Glasgow didn't have traffic issues or problems with public transport in general; it did, but she felt she breathed more freely when she was there. The streets were wider, there was more sky. It relaxed her to know that nature, vast landscapes, were just beyond the stretch of her fingertips. In London she felt hemmed in by concrete; in Glasgow – just on her walk from the flat to lectures – she went through the park, over the river, and in the early mornings she would barely see a soul until she reached the outskirts of campus. In London – even in the height of summer – there were people everywhere, no matter the time of day. People, people, hurrying in and out of the buildings that blocked out the sky. Some of the buildings were beautiful, she'd admit, but for every palace-like abode she passed on the walk from her dad's to Bloomsbury, there were ten of the ugliest pieces of architecture she'd ever seen.

Rosie shifted her backpack off her shoulder and spun it around so she could unzip the front pocket. She took out her phone. Still no message from Mo.

She shook her head. She needed to stop this.

She should have taken that young doctor up on his offer of a drink the night before.

Mo obviously wasn't thinking about her, so why was she thinking about him? She should be enjoying herself, as everyone kept telling her. She should be making the most of her youth, her freedom.

Still, with these thoughts at the very front of her mind, she found herself tapping out a text to him, asking what the weather was like, if he was having fun. She hated herself the second she pressed send.

It was a compulsion, trying to make him want her. She wasn't even sure that she really wanted him. What sort of future was there for them, really? He wanted a family. She fundamentally did not. He was on a lads' holiday, jetting off without a thought for the carbon he was putting out into the atmosphere. Did she really want to be in a relationship with a man who only seemed marginally interested in her, whose idea of a good time is a week in Magaluf, damaging both his brain and his body, and not giving a second thought to what impact his actions were having on the environment?

She inhaled and, with a quick look up to check she wasn't about to walk into anyone, she opened the address book on her phone, navigated to Mo's name and deleted his number.

Are you sure you want to delete this contact?

She pressed the button at the top right of the keypad and then snapped her phone shut decisively.

A rush of freedom flooded through her.

Life was too short to waste any more time on someone who didn't give her back what she gave them.

That's what Lizzie had said. Or something like that.

She felt the familiar feeling in her throat at the thought of Lizzie. A tightness, as if her soft palate was stretching. She flipped open her phone again and found her last text to Mary, ready to send a new one.

Morning! Walking to work and thinking of you. What are you going to do today? Thursday, so no work, right? You should get in the garden. Dad and I watched Gardeners' World last week. Monty Don said it was the last chance to sow runner beans. Please sow some runner beans! They'll be ready for when I come home before going back to Uni, won't they? Any news on Lizzie? Love you. R xxx

She pressed send and immediately thought of Emma: 'Your texts! Why send an email when a 3,000 word text will do?' It's true. She was used to her phone dividing up her texts into 1|2, 2|2, but none of her family seemed to check their emails. It was much harder for them to deny they hadn't read her texts since she'd installed message receipts.

She tapped out another message.

Oh and FYI watching GW with Dad is v funny because he is SO jealous of Monty. I'm going to frame a photo of him for you to put up in the downstairs loo to really wind him up! Xxxx

She smiled to herself as she turned off Horse Guards Road and onto The Mall.

Living with her dad had been eye-opening. The last time they had lived together for any extended period was those years at Mary's when he'd had his breakdown. Before that, before her mum died, they'd lived together too, but she'd been too young to be objective about his behaviour, to notice the quirks of his personality. He was her dad, he called her Petal, he worked long hours, and he was away every other weekend, seeing his other daughters. She secretly loved those weekends. Having her mum all to herself. They'd eat pizza and takeaways, and her mum would take her to galleries and to see Auntie Yas, and they'd stay up and watch films that her dad said were 'rubbish'.

So it was a surprise to discover her dad had developed something of a passion for trash TV. A couple of months ago, if someone had asked her what, if they were to live together, she and her dad would be likely to find themselves talking about of an evening, she would never have predicted that the backbone of their conversation would be based on not one, but two reality TV shows. It wasn't so surprising that he was into *Masterchef*, given that, if he wasn't working or sleeping, he was in the kitchen, but she still couldn't get her head around his obsession with *Big Brother*. And it was an obsession. He talked about the housemates as if they were members of the family. Every night, at about 8.30, he started to get a bit jumpy. If her shift ran over or she went to a class at Pineapple on her way back, he'd hurry along their meal, watching her as she ate, urging her on, and then as soon as she put down her fork, he'd whip away her plate, start loading the dishwasher, all while humming the theme tune.

'What are you going to do when this is all over, Dad? Your evenings will be a wasteland without Davina and the diary room.'

'Only a week or so before the regional auditions for this year's *X-Factor*, my little Rose Petal.'

Her dad, watching *X-Factor*? He was a weirdo in so many ways she'd never realised before, and it was such a treat to be discovering it.

That was another reason why she should be grateful for this opportunity at UCL. And she was grateful. She was grateful that she had been accepted, that her dad was paying her expenses, that she had somewhere to stay for free. But it would also have been nice to be at home, helping Mary in the garden, hanging out with Em and Phoebe, spending some time with Lizzie and Iain, after all if the surgery went to plan then they'd be in Australia at Christmas.

Everyone was going to be there this weekend for Phoebe's twenty-first. Or rather, the Suffolk leg of Phoebe's twenty-first, but Rosie had been signed up for a twelve-hour shift on Saturday. She wasn't sad that she would miss the hangover that everyone at Mouser Lane would undoubtedly be suffering from on Sunday, and she would have a chance to celebrate with Phoebe when she had her party in Brixton in a couple of weeks, but she was jealous that they would all be together without her. She was enjoying the internship, but she would prefer to be visiting Granny or sunbathing together under the willow or listening to Phoebe and Emma debating whatever it was they'd found to disagree on this time. Actually, she wasn't so bothered about missing out on that bit; if she closed her eyes she could almost hear the shouting before it had even begun, so familiar was she with the pattern of their arguments.

It was strange to think that there was a time when she'd only met her half-sisters a handful of times. Those awful forced-fun trips.

That time at the Science Museum when Phoebe had told her that she was 'a bastard, because a child born out of wedlock is called a bastard', and then proceeded to call her 'The Bastard' all day until Dad had literally spanked her bottom and Phoebe had screamed at him saying it was child abuse and then they realised that they'd lost Emma. Three hours later Mary received a call on reverse charges from Stowmarket station, by which point she and Phoebe had been given hot chocolate with little marshmallows for free in the museum cafe and were being looked after by a young woman called Helen who wore a lot of eyeliner, while their dad was with the police.

And then, they'd all lived together. The memory of those first months still made Rosie quite angry. She understood now it must have been quite an upheaval for Phoebe, having her and Dad in the house, but she still can't believe how mean she'd been to a girl who'd just lost her mum. It was jealousy, she could see that now – though she wouldn't dare say as much to Phoebe. Not for the same reason that she hadn't said things when they were younger. Then, her silence was about self-preservation. It took about a year of living with them before she'd found her voice. Phoebe had done something – she can't remember what now, but one of her stupid little tricks to rile her, like sitting in her place at the dinner table, or drinking her tea, or hiding her homework when she was in the loo – and rather than quietly accepting it and crying when she went back to her room, she fought back. She called Phoebe a spoiled brat, told her that she was the worst sister – half-sister – in the world. And after that, something shifted and she wasn't an onlooker any more, but a participant. She tried not to get involved when Mary was around, because she knew the constant bickering drove her up the wall, but she slowly realised that she was much, much happier because despite their quarrels and differences, she and her half-sisters had connected. For a while they seemed enmeshed in symbiosis, three limbs of the same organism. And then, Em had gone to Manchester, which was even further away than she'd planned, and then a couple of years later Phoebe went too, only to Cambridge, but it might as well have been Mars for all the contact she'd had. And then she'd gone up to Glasgow. This weekend would be the first time they would all be together since the Christmas before last. Because the year before, Phoebe had been in Thailand.

Christmas Day itself was lovely. In fact, it was the most harmonious Christmas she'd ever known at Mary's. That was down in part to Lizzie being on such good form and all of them wanting to make it a wonderful day for her, but, truthfully, the main reason was Phoebe's absence. The only fight had been a fleeting annoyance of her dad's when they didn't sit down at the breakfast table immediately he asked and he'd dramatically pronounced the scrambled eggs 'completely fucked'.

It was Boxing Day that had been awful.

She'd come down to the kitchen, feeling a bit gross from the overindulgence of the day before, and found Mary on the phone and her dad on the computer. Iain had his back to her, frying something at the hob, and Lizzie was at the table warming her hands on a cup of herbal tea, the neon pink of her turban making her face look particularly pale. When she saw Rosie standing there, she'd held out her hand to her.

'Now, don't panic, but something has happened in Thailand.'

She'd stood there for a moment after Lizzie had explained, listening to Mary talk to someone on the phone about where they thought Phoebe and Michael were staying.

'Get off the line, Mary! We need to leave it open in case she calls.'

She'd followed the sound of the TV into the lounge. Emma was sitting on the coffee table in her pyjamas. She remembered noticing her hands, her nails painted with the gold glitter nail varnish that had come out of one of the 'luxury' crackers at yesterday's dinner.

The picture on the screen was a map. India was at the centre of a big red bullseye, concentric circles radiating from the tip of

Sumatra out across the Indian Ocean. All the way across the coast of Thailand.

Emma turned to look at her, and Rosie was shocked to see her face glistening with tears.

'They showed a video from a bloke's phone. Everything was washed away. She's been banging on about a hut. A hut on the beach.' Rosie sat down next to Emma and tried to take her hand. 'Don't. Please.'

Rosie looked at Emma then, and saw that her face was rigid with concentration.

'Sorry.'

The whole of Boxing Day passed in what felt like slow motion. And then, some time in the late afternoon, just as it was getting dark, the phone had rung.

It was Phoebe.

Rosie turned on to Riding House Street and looked up at the buildings, trying to work out, as she did every day, which of them was the BBC where they recorded the radio. She always tried to be on the lookout when she passed. One morning, only a few days after she'd started the internship programme, she'd seen Jarvis Cocker and he'd smiled at her.

She checked her watch. Twenty to nine.

If she sped up a bit, she'd have time to get changed, stuff her things into a locker and down a coffee before her shift began. She was working on A&E that week. One of the best things about the programme was the opportunity to try different disciplines out for size, even before general training. When she'd first applied to Glasgow, she thought the part of medicine she was interested in was general practice. She had an image of living in the countryside, getting to know her patients, being a help to the community, keeping her life local; activism at a grassroots level. But then, just as she'd started her A level year, Lizzie started to deteriorate and the world seemed to be speeding up, and her perspective on how she might be of use had shifted. She was thinking about oncology or general surgery, though increasingly she felt the lure of anaesthetics. Because, essentially, wasn't that why she'd turned to medicine in the first place? Taking away pain.

She stood on her tiptoes on the edge of the pavement and looked down the length of Tottenham Court Road, checking it was safe to cross, then jogged over the road. She looked up at the sky. It seemed to be wedged between the square-edged buildings of the university. It was a clear blue, with only the slightest wisp of cloud.

Maybe it was worth the stress of travelling back to see them all this weekend, even if it was just on Sunday for the barbeque. If she didn't, she was in danger of missing the summer altogether. It was early July, that left what? Eight? Six weekends of summer. Though, with the way things were going, she would probably be able to sunbathe by the time she got back to Glasgow.

There it was. The plummet in her mood that came with even thinking about the state of the planet.

It weighed her down. The facts of it. The fact that everyone seemed so blind to it.

Emma buying a new car with every bonus. Phoebe, Michael, Mo, even Mary and Liz using planes like a bus service. And being in this city, everywhere she turned: the pollution, the fast food, the fast fashion, the consumption, the waste.

She inhaled and rolled her shoulders, trying to release them. Her mum's face flitted into her mind.

It happened all the time. Every time she recognised herself teetering on that edge of hopelessness, and somehow, it made her feel stronger, resolved not to give in to it. It made her more determined to try to do something worthwhile.

She turned into the hospital entrance and returned a smile to the paramedic who was leaning against the wall in his green uniform, smoking a cigarette next to the sign that said 'Strictly No Smoking.' As she swiped her ID card and opened the door, a flurry of sirens filled the air.

There was something about it that reminded Rosie of dancing.

She was at her locker when she was first aware of something happening.

The door to the changing room smashed against the wall as a young man with a shaved head barged into the room and ran past. He was moving so fast, he seemed to bring the air of the corridor with him; she could feel the temperature drop with it.

'Fuck, fuck, fuck.' He was fumbling with his keys, dropping them. She watched as he failed repeatedly to get the key into the lock and then successfully turned it and pulled at the door. A red hoodie dropped onto the floor and landed at his feet as he rifled through his belongings.

The buttons beeped as he dialled, his breath still staccato, fast. As he put the phone to his ear, she caught his eye.

'Are you okay?'

He just looked at her as if he didn't understand what she was saying, and then he hung up, swearing – not so quietly this time – and dialled another number. Rosie tried to catch his eye again, but his head was down and then he was shouting into his phone.

'Mum? Mum? Did Dad go to work? When did he leave?'

Rosie turned away and secured her locker. Someone else ran into the room. She seemed less panicked, more excited.

'Three. Two on the Circle, one on Piccadilly, near here.' The woman opened her locker, and rustled in her bag, retrieving a can of Red Bull. It hissed as she pulled the ring. Immediately Rosie could smell it through the changing room's scent of feet and sweat and deodorant spray. It reminded her of the smell of the pink amoxicillin she'd had as a kid.

'I'm supposed to be coming off.' The young woman took a long slurp of her energy drink. 'But it's going to be all hands on deck if it's as bad as they say.'

Rosie jumped at the slam of a locker behind her. The guy had finished his phone call. He rubbed his hands over his face.

'My dad goes through Liverpool Street to Aldgate every day, just before nine.'

The mention of the time prompted Rosie to look at her wrist. She was five minutes late.

There was a suspension to it, like the moment before the music starts, or the milliseconds you are fully airborne in a leap.

All but two of the bays had been emptied, the broken limbs and falls and pumped stomachs wheeled out to holding wards.

It was quiet.

The usual cacophony of machines, the mumble of voices, replaced with an eerie silence punctuated by the single electronic beep of a monitored heart in one of the only occupied beds.

Rosie followed orders.

She sanitised the beds. She checked the equipment, the stock at each station.

At the nurses' station, three people in grey scrubs crowded around the television.

Rosie surreptitiously pulled her phone from her pocket. Her message still hadn't sent. Her stomach fluttered. She knew her family were safe. She knew her dad walked to work, and for once she was relieved that Emma always drove to that obscene subterranean car park in Canary Wharf. She knew too that Phoebe and Michael were already with Mary in Suffolk, and Auntie Yas was as likely to cross the river as she was to get on public transport. But she just wanted to check, just wanted to know they were okay, to let them know she was. Her dad might be panicking, even though it was the wrong tube. In the top corner, instead of little bars, it just reads: NO SERVICE.

She put her phone in her pocket and pulled a pair of latex gloves over her hands, snapping them at the wrist. She closed her eyes for a second, acknowledging the smarting of her skin from the action, feeling the vibration of her heart in her chest, the clench of anticipation in her belly, and then a crash of metal and she opened her eyes as a gurney hit the doors.

There was a rhythm to it. A pattern. Like following choreography.

She did what she was told.

'Pressure.'

'Irrigate.'

'Intubate.'

'Clear.'

'Time of death?'

There was blood on her hands; the blue plastic of the latex stained red-black.

She changed her gloves.

She counted while pumping a BVM. She took over chest compressions. She tied a tourniquet.

She reassured a patient.

There was soot, black grime and dust on the paper that she'd helped lay on the beds, and as she looked down, as the doctor called a time of death, she saw that her legs – all the way down the length of them – her legs and her shoes were covered in blood.

She stopped. And it was as if the noise of the ward hit her like a wave.

Make me proud.

For a fraction of a second, she thought she was going to faint; her thoughts seemed to be distant and separate from her body.

And then she heard her name and she was back in the emergency department and she was following instructions and she was doing what she was told and she was giving everything to try to help.

Twenty-seven

Emma's posture had altered immediately when the baby was placed on her. He is much lighter than she'd anticipated, warmer too. His head lolls against her shoulder. How strange that he is relaxed enough to sleep while his body is bunched so tightly, like a fist.

She looks over to the conservatory to check they are alone and then rests the side of her face gently against his head. His hair is soft against her cheek; it reminds her of those big powder puffs that her mum used to have in her smelly talc. She and Phoebe used to look out for one another, while one dabbed the richly scented white powder along their arms and legs. She inhales. He smells of washing powder and milk and everything that is soft and warm and good. A yeasty smell too, under it all, like warm bread. Yes, he smells like a fresh loaf of bread, so hot that butter would melt on it immediately even if it was hard, direct from the fridge. And Phoebe, he smells of Phoebe, too, an aura of her perfume, that one in the little red bottle with the black lid.

Her heart is thumping as though she is running along the beach at full pelt.

It's too much; the scent of him is overwhelming. She can only—

She closes her eyes tightly, then takes a gulp of air, a full stop to that thought process.

Sitting down in the threadbare old armchair, she carefully shifts the baby into the crook of her arm so she can get a clear look at him. She focuses on the movement of his tiny chest as it expands and contracts with the rhythm of his breath. His face is twitching, his lips pursing, suckling. He's looking for milk, or dreaming of it.

She searches his face and sees so much that she recognises from years of staring at herself in mirrors. Of course Phoebe's children's features have reflections not just of their mother's but of their aunt's too. It is more evident in Clara, because she is older: her features have opened up, but even here in this brand new baby she can see the echoes of both Phoebe and Michael.

Her eyes are losing focus. She looks up, to try to stem the tears that are forming. The lights in the tree are diffusing into starburst shapes.

She has thought for so long now that it had receded, the sadness of it all. That all the tears that could be shed had been. Four years is a long time.

'Em?'

Michael is standing beside her. As they make eye contact, she can feel a treacherous tear snake its way down her cheek. She dabs it away with the heel of her hand.

'He's lovely, Michael.'

'Is he asleep?'

She nods at him, and tilts the sleeping baby towards him, showing him the baby's peaceful face. Then she pulls him back into her, lets him rest against her chest as she leans back in the chair. She closes her eyes, concentrates on her breathing, on the breath of the child against her chest.

The leaves on the tree above rustle, like someone scrunching newspaper to kindle a fire, and then another noise, a creak as Michael's weight is taken by one of the chairs. Even with her eyes closed she can tell it is one of the rattan things from the conservatory. She can picture him, leaning back into it, that infuriatingly blank look on his face as if he'd just witnessed a horrific car accident. She opens her eyes and looks at him, and there it is. She knows him so well, even after all that's changed.

The pain of acknowledging it makes her laugh. It rises from her belly and shakes her chest, causing little puffs of air to escape her nostrils, a small sound, the '*huh-huh*' caught in her throat.

He looks at her now. He looks hurt, almost.

'You're a natural.'

She didn't think it possible to dislike this man any more than she did, but that's one thing about Michael, he never seems to cease surprising her. And just like that, the fury is back, and every long run, and all those hours cross-legged on her yoga mat, all the words scraped into her diary, are rendered completely pointless because if she didn't have this baby in her arms she would be up and out of this chair and – what? Throttling him? No, nothing so violent. Throwing a glass of wine in his face? Maybe.

'Please go away. I've promised Mum that there won't be a fight.'

She says it as calmly as she can. But it still comes out as if she is speaking through gritted teeth. She hears it and opens her mouth wide, stretching her jaw muscles, like a snake about to swallow an egg. Something about the motion loosens more than the muscles, and she turns to him, fixes him with the softest stare she can.

He dips his eyes away from hers; she follows the direction of his gaze down to the baby on her lap.

'I thought it would be impossible to see him, to see Clara, and to love them. I wondered what sort of person that made me. What sort of aunt. To expect to hate a baby, to hate a three-year-old child.'

She can hear his exhale, like a deflating tyre, a slow long hiss. She doesn't look up at him, just stares down at the sleeping baby, but in the periphery of her vision she sees him sit back, slouched into the chair beside her.

'I shouldn't have come.'

And then, there is his hand against her cheek. His palm, cool on her skin. She closes her eyes, bites her bottom lip.

'Don't.'

Her eyes are still closed. She can smell Phoebe's perfume even more strongly than on the baby now. It must be on him too.

'Em.'

She opens her eyes, but she doesn't move. She is still, bunched, a coiled spring.

'Michael.'

'Earlier, seeing you here, under the tree—'

'Michael.'

'All day. All these things I'd—'

'Stop.'

She takes his hand by the wrist and removes it from her face.

He places it on his lap, staring down at it, as if his own hand were a separate entity and had touched her face of its own accord. He looks disappointed with it, angry.

'Sorry.' He speaks so quietly that she can barely hear it over the shuffle of the leaves above them, the soft breath of the baby, the background joy of the wedding party in the house.

He looks up at her. There is the distinct possibility that he is going to cry. She knows it, that concentration, she's seen it in action for years. It's one of his tells, and one of the reasons lots of people think he's a brilliant actor; that rare breed, a man who isn't scared for his emotions to sit close to the surface.

There it is: a tear, making its way down the side of his nose.

He raises his arm across his face, covering his eyes with the crook of his elbow. He inhales a shuddering breath. Then brings down his arm.

'It was my baby too, Emma.'

Twenty-eight

Emma put a hand on the lamp post to balance herself as she pulled her heel towards her buttock, stretching out her quads. She looked out to the ocean and inhaled as she continued her stretches.

It had been a good choice: moving to the sea.

Her mum had said as much when she was here.

'I'd always thought, after London, that I'd live near the sea.' They were standing on the balcony watching the sunset. 'But somehow, before I knew it, your father had me landlocked.'

Their conversations had been like that since her arrival. Reflective but anodyne. No mention of politics, or her job. No mention of Phoebe or Michael. Certainly nothing to do with pregnancy or babies or death.

'Lizzie loved the sea too. Always dragging me in, even when it was baltic. "Wild swimming." Or "swimming", as we used to call it.'

It was only after she'd left and the house returned to its quiet vacuum that Emma realised her mother had done the majority of the talking during her stay. Though there had been a little more input from her than there had been back in March.

The setting sun was starting to leak a coral colour that tinted the sky as she hit her stride.

It was cool enough to run now and the track at the top of the beach was busy, so at the next gap in the bollards she took a left and ran across the sand, down to the water's edge where the surface was more solid underfoot, and headed north again.

The movement in her body felt good.

The ban on exercise had been a particularly cruel directive. She had always turned to it, running in particular, to iron out any difficulties in her life, and without it she had felt as though she was closing in on herself, becoming harder and harder.

But now, she could feel the sea air in her lungs, the burn of the muscles in her legs as she pushed herself forward, and her thoughts came and went as swiftly as the waves crashed and receded on the sand. She increased her speed, pushing, racing no one but herself. The burn of it, the exertion that edged on pain, made her want to call out for joy.

Joy.

An emotion that had not made itself known to her for months.

Her mum had been with her at the appointment where her doctor warned her that any strenuous exercise could cause damage. Her mum had taken it to heart, outlawing any movement other than the most leisurely of walks on even surfaces. She'd been a bit of a zombie then still, and the pain of the surgery bothered her to such a degree that her mum made her up a bed on the sofa so she didn't have to tackle the stairs.

She wasn't sure what she would have done in those first few weeks without her mum.

It had been her mum that she'd called from the hospital.

Looking back, that was the decision that changed everything.

It would have been just as easy to call Michael. She was sure that most women in her situation would have called their husband. Most women would probably have called their husband the second they woke in the dark of the night bathed in sweat, with a searing pain across their abdomen, the sheets wet beneath them and their heart beating so hard it reverberated in their aching head like the thump of a bass drum. But she hadn't. She had called their private ambulance service, and then, in the hospital, when they told her that they were going to have to get the baby out and asked if there was anyone she wanted to contact, she'd called her mum.

The only person in the world that she had wanted was her mum.

Her breathing was laboured now. She'd pushed herself too hard, too soon into the distance she'd planned. She stopped and folded forward, her hands on her thighs and her face still facing ahead, dragging oxygen into her lungs, enjoying the rhythm of her blood pulsing in her ears.

He'd been so tiny. The baby.

He was cold by the time she could hold him. Tinged blue. But she was grateful to the staff for allowing it.

It had felt so unreal. She'd been sedated, she realised afterwards. Sedated and pumped to the gills with whatever they'd knocked her out with for the operation.

Everyone had been so kind to her.

They had washed him and dressed him and put a little hat on his head. She had held the bundle of the yellow blanket against her chest, as the lovely nurse took some photos on her phone, and she'd had a strangely lucid thought: at least nothing will ever hurt as much as this.

And when she next woke up, there was her mum, holding her hand.

*   *   *

They had let her keep the yellow blanket.

For the week she'd spent in that room, it had sat, folded on the table under the window, alongside the packets and packets of prescription medicines, some of which she was still taking twice a day.

When they got home, she'd let herself bury her face in it and inhale. But only once. Then she gave it to her mum and told her to put it somewhere safe. Somewhere safe that she wouldn't be able to find it.

It was her mum who had held her when the doctor told her that they'd had no choice but to perform an emergency hysterectomy.

It was her mum who'd phoned Michael.

He was on set in Romania.

They changed the schedule, moved the filming so that he could come and be with her, her mum told her. Unheard of.

But she didn't want to see him.

He'd come into the room once, barged in, past the doctor, past her pleading mum.

'She's my wife, Mary!'

But when he came and took her hand, she just started screaming. She'd screamed and screamed, and then they must have sedated her again.

She can still see the look of hurt on his face.

But she couldn't bear to have him and his grief and his love, his suffocating tenderness, anywhere near her.

He could still have children, he could be a father, but she would never, ever carry another child. Her baby had died. Everything she'd always wanted had been taken away from her, and her life sat before her, hollow and unfathomable. All she could cling to were her instincts, and her instincts were telling her that being with Michael, letting him hold her, love her, would make her heart shatter into so many pieces that she might never find a way to put herself back together again.

With her breath caught, she started to run again. At a slower pace now. One foot in front of the other. Heel toe, heel toe.

She'd had to name him, the baby.

An official cruelty that she hadn't foreseen.

And then the choice: burial or cremation?

Her mum had persuaded her to send half of the ashes to Michael, back in Romania by then.

She scattered the rest with her mum the day before she left.

Into the ocean.

Then a letter on blue airmail paper, the likes of which she hadn't seen since she was a child.

All those words she hadn't wanted to hear, there in his beautiful handwriting scored into tissue-thin paper that somehow smelled of him despite its transatlantic journey.

So many questions. But it was the statements that pierced her.

Maybe it wasn't meant to be.

We will find another way to have a family.

I love you.

She watched the waste disposal until every scrap of blue disappeared. Then she dialled Vivienne and told her that she wanted to engage her services for both her naturalisation as an American citizen and to represent her in pursuit of a divorce.

She reached the point that she knew was two and a half kilometres. The pale blue lifeguard's hut with its red windsock filled, then deflated as the breeze rose and fell.

She jogged on the spot briefly and then turned and started to run back to where she'd come from.

Over halfway, she thought, and pushed forward, focusing on the shrimp salad that she had waiting in the fridge at home, the cold bottle of Chardonnay in the door.

She didn't find it lonely, living in the house alone.

Every morning she spoke to her mum, at the weekend sometimes Rosie too. The odd call to her granny. Occasionally she was even surprised by a call from her dad.

'Just checking in, Bunny.'

Though their brief conversations quickly illuminated that it was his loneliness rather than her own that was the impetus for his calls.

She still had a little work to distract her if required, though her duties rarely stretched much further than signing off on things these days. Maybe she should reach out to old colleagues, get involved in something new. She'd consumed her twenties and thirties by submerging herself in work; maybe it would be wise to do that now too.

She kept herself busy though; she had more single, childless girlfriends out here than she'd realised, and most days there was a visitor or two. Maria came every day but Sunday to clean and make her evening meal, Marco came twice a week for strength, Lianne on alternate days for yoga.

It was the evenings that she had to watch.

It was then that she felt a tenderness settle over her.

It was then that she found herself missing Michael's laugh and wondering if, maybe, it would have been easier to navigate this together.

Could she possibly have got it wrong in the fury of her grief?

Might he have understood, if she had given him a chance?

Could he really have been happy in a relationship where it was just the two of them?

But how could she ask that of him when she was not even sure that it was something she could endure herself? When almost every evening she found herself opening a VPN so she could search, so she could scour the Internet for possibilities. Fostering, adoption, surrogacy.

Maybe it wasn't meant to be.

Wasn't meant to be.

Maybe it's for the best.

For the best.

Were there any phrases she hated more in the entire English language?

No, there would be no call to Michael.

There would be no call to Vivienne asking her to halt the proceedings of the divorce.

He'd be fine. He had his work. He had his team, his friends. Phoebe.

Phoebe would look after him. Maybe Phoebe would even let him look after her too.

The sky was streaking now to her left. The famous Malibu sunset, purple, orange and pink accompanying her as she neared the car. The air was cooling too, a breeze coming off the water whipping at her neck.

What would Michael have made of her cutting off all her hair? Of the dark colour that now stretched from her roots right to the tips of the blunt cut?

She hadn't recognised herself for the first few days.

* * *

One night, she caught her reflection in the balcony windows and thought, for a heart-stopping second, that Phoebe was there. That she'd come. That she was ready to apologise. To forgive. That she had come all that way to be there for her.

But, as she stepped forward, ready to take her sister in her arms, she'd realised it wasn't Phoebe but herself.

She'd got used to it now. And she liked it, this alteration in her appearance.

She looks like a different person.

And that made sense. Because that was exactly what she was.

Twenty-nine

Michael searches Emma's face for a reaction; there isn't the slightest hint of emotion about her features. But that doesn't mean it isn't there, beneath the mask. He's known her for too long for her to be able to pull this shit on him. Even in this low light he can recognise her game face.

'No.' Her voice is sharp, final.

His body takes on the word, it reverberates through his sinews. 'No' is right. No, she doesn't get to do this, to close it off. He deserves an explanation. She knows he does. He'll take it from all those that don't understand. He'll take the frostiness and the twist of dislike in a mouth as it greets him, or the raised eyebrows and silence on his entry into a room. He couldn't give a shit about all those that think him weak, that assume he is led by his dick – that he'd probably been cheating for years, by the time he got caught. He couldn't care less that that's what people think of him, as long as he can talk about it with those who really know what happened. And she is one of the few people who know what really happened, and he needs her to hear him.

'Why did you do it Em?'

She shakes her head. Closes her eyes.

'My baby died too, Emma. It was my baby too.'

He is going to cry again, he can feel it in the bridge of his nose.

When he's imagined them having this conversation, when he's pictured it, the hundreds, thousands of times that he has pictured it, he's never been crying. A folly, he realises now, to have thought for a second that, even after all this time, there won't be tears.

'He.' He wipes at his nose. 'He was my baby too.'

He inhales sharply, an attempt at a full stop to the emotion. He wipes his face on his shirt.

She is avoiding eye contact, looking down at his sleeping son, coiled on her lap.

'I was grieving too.'

'I know.'

Her voice is so quiet he wonders if he has imagined it. But then, there is the slightest nod of her head.

'I needed you, Em. It felt like you had died too.'

She looks up now and the eyes that meet his are glazed with tears.

'Why did you do it?'

She tilts her head and a tear rolls down the side of her left cheek; it glistens in the lights from the tree above.

'I think that, if I hadn't, then we might both have stayed sad for ever.'

A sob escapes his mouth.

What had he been expecting her to say?

Not this.

'And you are happy. I think.'

Her hand reaches out and takes his. Her long fingers around his own, and a wave of relief crashes over him. He closes his eyes, her hand warm around his.

Above them, the willow leaves rustle.

Whenever he hears that noise, in a pub garden or walking the kids in a park, he is straight back here, under this tree.

He is nineteen and clumsily drunk and full of food and laughing and in love. In love with this whole family. The olives and breadsticks before dinner, the wine with it. The conversations about books and politics and pop stars, and the arguments, the tears, and the laughter. God the laughter. Any memory he can recall where he is helpless with laughter involves Phoebe.

Phoebe.

The heat of shame washes over him to realise that his hand is still in Emma's.

Emma. Who broke his heart so completely.

The heart that Phoebe carefully pieced back together again.

He squeezes Emma's hand, two pulses, and then releases himself from her. She sighs and then shakes her head, laughing, a quick succession of snorting exhalations through her nose.

'Oh, Mike.'

A great cheering roar turns both of their heads towards the house. There are calls for champagne, for more glasses, for a toast.

Phoebe, breathless, appears at the door.

'Mike! Rosie's getting married too! Danyal just proposed! Isn't it great?'

'I thought marriage was an outdated bourgeois institution?' His voice cracks as he calls out across the garden.

'Oh it is. I hate it. But Rosie looks so happy! And even I think that proposals are romantic – don't you?'

'I do,' he says, 'I do.'

Thirty

Michael pulled down his cap and nuzzled into his scarf as he turned to walk down Fifth Avenue. It was cold. New York cold. Sunny and blue-skied, with a whip of ice on the wind that reached directly into the very marrow of your bones.

It was biting at the tops of his ears now, making him push his balled hands deep into the fleece-lined pockets of his coat. He needed to buy a deerhunter. A red one like Holden Caulfield.

He stopped at the end of the block and waited as the traffic zoomed past him.

A movement to his left drew his gaze: he was being watched. Two young women beside him were leaning into one another, mouths agape.

He suppressed a groan and turned his scowl into a smile, nodding his head.

'Happy Halloween, ladies.' He threw in a wink for good measure.

Michael hadn't really thought much of the phrase 'to go weak at the knees' until a few years ago. But now, he had cause to think several times a day about how on the nail it was. The girls sighed and then seemed to melt into each other: a trembling, puffa-jacket-clad creature.

'You too! We love your work!'

He nodded his thanks and smiled again, before taking the crosswalk and leaving them behind him in a peal of giggles.

The sidewalks were busy. He had to slow his speed to navigate the crowds; the usual tourists and natives, joined by hordes of those who journeyed to the island by bridge and tunnel. Everyone here to worship the gods of consumerism and pumpkin spice lattes. Later, they'd pull their spider deely boppers, green wigs and witches hats from their shopping bags to join the parties that would fill the streets downtown as soon as dusk began to settle over Manhattan.

He was an interloper himself. He would only be in the city for twenty-four hours, and then it'd be back to set with those idiots who refused to come out of their horrible characters because of The Method.

One of the only benefits of the job from hell was the proximity to New York.

That was the thing about this unbelievable life that he found himself living: even in the worst jobs where he felt like nothing but a flesh-puppet with a camera stuck in his face, there were always extraordinary privileges. On this occasion, other than the incredible fee, it was an understanding production manager and access to the fast train into New York. The train that whisked him away from that set full of divas and moaners, through the auburn-tinted upstate landscape into the very centre of the city – the Grand centre – with its arched windows and its streaming light and its golden symbols of the zodiac embellishing its turquoise vaulted roof.

Ever since Phoebe had lived in New York, they'd established the tradition of meeting there, in Grand Central. Rather than her picking him up from JFK or him ringing the buzzer to her fourth-floor walk-up, they'd agree a day and a time and find each other somewhere in the depths of the station. It was one of their things. Like each buying the other a Chelsea bun from Fitzbillies when they'd been dumped, or always sitting on the front row on opening night for any play either of them were in. A tradition he'd swapped for reading every single one of her columns since she started writing, and texting her about it straight away.

He had thought that telling her in Grand Central would be a moment. And it was. Just not the sort of moment he'd been expecting.

They'd agreed seven o'clock.

His train was scheduled to arrive twenty-five minutes earlier, and his plan was to be waiting with champagne and oysters when she arrived.

His train was right on time and so was he, other than a momentary hold-up under the herringbone tiles of the Whispering Corner as he joined the crowd watching what was probably the twentieth proposal that day. It all seemed to be unfurling just as he'd planned it. But, as he was perusing the little handwritten boards that hung behind the bar, trying to decide whether to go for one dozen huge oysters or two dozen small ones, he heard her voice calling out his surname.

From the bitten olive sitting at the bottom of the empty glass on the table next to her notebook and the fluidity of her movements as she embraced him, Michael deduced that Phoebe had already been in the bar for quite some time.

'Hey, Phoebs.'

'You look skinny, Regis.'

She kissed his cheek. He could smell the vodka on her breath.

Then, once they were seated and Michael had ordered them each a Martini and a platter of the waiter's choice of oysters, Phoebe raised an eyebrow.

'What does your girlfriend think of you buying cocktails and oysters for a woman of loose morals while she's on the other side of the country?'

And there it was, the cue he'd been waiting for.

'Well, Phoebs. It's actually Em that I want to talk to you about.'

He'd had an idea that there was a possibility she'd be a bit weirded out by it, that there was a chance she'd laugh at him, or be rude. But he hadn't anticipated how upset she'd be.

He'd assumed that, at some point, she must have considered the possibility. After all, he and Em had been dating for two years. He knew that the idea of 'settling down' was anathema to Phoebe, but surely she realised the time was nearing where it'd be natural that they considered what might be the next step for their relationship. After all they weren't kids; Emma would be thirty-three in just a few days. The idea of marriage, of children, of building a life together might seem normal, or boring, or – what did she call it? – 'Obvious!'. It might seem these things to Phoebe, with her hook-ups and her open relationships and her sneering at commitment. But she forgot that, if she fell, her family was there, waiting to catch her like one of those big trampolines that he'd got to use in that fire-fighter show. He wanted a family too. He wanted all the 'boring stuff'. The dirty nappies. The nights on the sofa. The early mornings. The broken sleep. He wanted a house that smelled of last night's dinner and the breath of people he loved. He wanted a kitchen with a long wooden table, dented by forks and crayons, stained by red wine and candle wax. He wanted to grow old surrounded by laughter and raised voices and tears and hugs. And Emma, as far as he could tell, wanted to build that family with him.

His stomach flipped.

Well, he'd know the answer to that question soon enough.

He looked at his watch. There were only ten minutes till his appointment.

When he'd booked it, he'd had an idea that he'd turn up early, after a night out with Phoebe. He'd anticipated rocking up, with his sunglasses on – slightly the worse for wear from his farewell to bachelorhood with his best friend – eating a croissant and sipping a coffee while looking in the windows like a six-foot-three Holly Golightly.

The only part of that little fantasy he'd achieved was the hangover.

He was still reeling from Phoebe's unexpected response. He'd thought she would roll her eyes, or give him a lecture on the narrow possibilities of a heteronormative lifestyle, how monogamy was a capitalist invention, but he hadn't expected the complete shutdown.

It was as if he'd told her that someone had died.

It was as if he was breaking up with her.

There had been a long time when he'd thought that it would be Phoebe that he would be buying a ring for.

He'd fancied her on sight. She'd shaken his hand when they'd met. Her hand was hot in his, her fingers weirdly long and bony. And then, she'd flicked her hair and laughed and said, 'Sorry! I don't know what that was! I was trying to be posh, I think. Do poshos even shake hands? I'm nervous – you know – that everyone is going to think I'm a pleb.'

And they did think that. A lot of them. That's what threw them together, really.

She was posher than him; she went on European holidays with her family and thought cooking was a hobby. But none of those differences between them were noticeable to all those other first years who asked where you went to school.

'They're not interested unless your school uniform involved a boater or a pleated plaid skirt. Disgusting, inbred snobs,'

Phoebe had said, when they both had to settle for different parts from the ones they were after in *Hamlet*.

It was during that production though, over the course of the evening and weekend rehearsals, that he'd realised he was falling head over heels for Phoebe Roberts.

'Rosencrantz and Guildenstern are dead . . . cool!' She had whispered it to him each night when they'd high-fived in the wings before their entrance in Act 2, Scene 2.

He'd never told her though, how he felt.

And neither had she, him. If she felt it at all.

There was that night.

The one in Bangkok in the hotel airport. Both of them dazed and quiet, waiting for their flight home. He'd opened the door with the key card they'd been given, and his heart had sunk. One bed.

He'd let Phoebe shower first, and resigned himself to a night in the horribly uncomfortable-looking armchair.

He'd expected that she'd be asleep when he emerged from the bathroom. But she wasn't. She was awake, sitting on the bed with her legs pulled into her chest, crying as she watched the news.

He sat down on the edge of the bed and tentatively put a hand on her back.

They'd fallen asleep with their arms around each other that night. And as he was falling asleep he felt her fingers stroking the inside of his forearm.

But then, in the morning, it had been action stations. Another long day of waiting in queues, and then finally, thankfully, they had buckled their seat belts on that 747. And other than a brief hold of each other's hands at take-off, the respectful distance of their physical proximity had been resumed.

He'd started dating soon after that.

It hadn't been hard to do at that point. He went to see friends from his MA in their shows and got them to introduce him to anyone who had caught his eye on the stage in the bar afterwards. And then, with those first few jobs, the thrill of not only a pay cheque for practising his craft, but the intensity of the connections that he'd form with his cast mates: friendships and passionate affairs that would consume him for the run of the show, and then, after the last-night party, would dissolve just as that 'illusory pageant' had. Some had lasted a few months. There was Zosia. He'd thought that might be love. He'd really fallen out with Phoebe about that, hadn't answered her calls for a few days after she called Zosia his 'most recent showmance'. But she was right. He'd lost interest in poor Zosh the moment the plane's wheels had screeched on the tarmac in LA for his first pilot season.

He looked up as he crossed West 50th. The Rockefeller building was glinting in the morning sun. It wasn't long now until Christmas.

Christmas.

Would he get to spend it in Suffolk, if Emma said yes?

He'd always nursed a secret desire to spend Christmas at the Roberts'. To be a part of one of the screaming rows that Phoebe had reported back to him for the last decade. To have six, eight, ten presents to buy rather than just making a bank transfer to his sister and slipping a £50 note into a card to his nephew and receiving only a curt text in return. They'd long given up on the pretence of a family Christmas. Nan had forced it when they were kids, got a tree and a turkey, put up a bit of tinsel, dressed them up smartly and marched them out to church. Then there had been an odd few years when Nan fell out with the church lot and Simone got pregnant, and then for almost a decade

– other than the Thailand trip – it had just been him and Nan with a roast on their laps in front of the telly. But for the last few years of his nan's life, he'd had money. He had flown her out to Barbados and they'd celebrated by doing very little in a sun-drenched five-star hotel.

He'd quite fancy somewhere hot again this year, if Suffolk wasn't an option. But maybe Emma would want to start building their own traditions. In their own home. This year just the two of them, but next year, maybe – hopefully – they'd be three.

Where would their home be?

For him, it could be anywhere really. Though he'd always imagined home would be somewhere in the UK. But for Emma, it would have to be in the US, he guessed. At least until the election.

That had been the only thing Phoebe had said last night.

'You do know what she's doing, don't you? You do know how she earns all that money?'

If it wasn't so fucking weird, he'd have laughed. He told his best friend that he was going to ask her sister to marry him and she asked him if he'd considered the ethics of her job.

'You've got to get over it, Roberts. You love each other. It's madness to fall out over a bit of data analysis. Anyway, you can put away the fucking tinfoil, you love social media!'

'Fuck, Regis. How can someone so clever be so fucking stupid. It's not just "data analysis".'

The people at the next table had raised their eyebrows at them.

'If it's so benign: why isn't she on social media herself? She might not be the actual bad guy, but she's helping them. Doesn't it bother you, at all?' He'd motioned then, for Phoebe to keep her voice down.

'Don't you dare tell me to shut up! You know I fucking hate that.' She'd made a funny noise, an animal noise, like a growl, and rubbed her hands across her face. Then she'd raised her head and shaken it, looking at him, her eyes hard.

'What a disappointment.'

She'd downed the last of her Martini and stormed out. By the time he'd paid the bill, apologised to the table next to them and signed them an autograph for their granddaughter, she'd long gone.

She hadn't answered her phone to him since.

He pulled his phone out of his pocket. Opened his texts – double-checking he hadn't missed a message from Phoebe – then on autopilot opened his Instagram. The flood of notifications made his hangover infinitely more present. He had an urge to call Em. But he couldn't, not till the evening when he'd be back at his accommodation. It'd be a dead giveaway that he was up to something if she heard the sounds of the city, and he didn't want her to suspect a thing. He wanted it to be a proper surprise.

He wanted it to be romantic, like a moment from a film.

A trip away for her birthday, the surprise of a private dining room at the restaurant in Mexico City that she'd been talking about for months. Candlelight, music, perfect food, and then he'd drop a fork and he'd be on one knee and he'd look up at her and . . . his heart beat faster at the very thought of it.

Maybe it was a good thing that Phoebe had stormed off before he'd had the chance to tell her of his plan, he could just imagine the gagging noises he'd have got in response.

But he knew that Emma would love it.

He knew that Emma would be delighted.

He knew, without a shadow of a doubt, that Emma would say yes.

There was still a part of Michael that was surprised by the strength of his feelings for Emma.

When they'd first started hanging out in LA, he was just being polite. And, if he was honest, there was something about spending time with her that eased his homesickness. It was nice to have a friend out there who knew him, or rather, knew the him he was before his 'success'.

Then there'd been that night – a Tuesday, he remembered, because they were in Pink Taco for the deal – and he'd found that he was laughing. Really laughing. And it was familiar, the people they talked about, what they talked about – the things that they missed about home, found bizarre about California – but also, her voice. She had the same voice as Phoebe.

Then they'd started sleeping together, and things had shifted. The sex was incredible. When he was in bed with her, in the shower with her, on the kitchen floor with her, he lost all sense of time, he was overcome with a desire so strong it felt like a sort of madness. And then, afterwards, there'd be a softness to her, her face open like a new page in a notebook. Gradually, she was shedding her shell, exposing her tenderness. He'd known her for a decade, but there was so much more to her than he'd realised. She wasn't just Phoebe's quiet, contained older sister who seemed to love a good argument. She was complex. She found her family suffocating, but she loved them fiercely. She loved running, and she meditated every morning. She loved animals, the smaller and fluffier the better; if she couldn't sleep she'd watch animal videos on YouTube until she did.

It was getting to know these surprising details about her that had scared him. That, and the fact it wasn't just their voices that made them similar. Their movements. The way they both wore that little gold letter around their necks. Their faces too, if you ignored the colour of the hair that framed them, were remarkably alike.

He'd woken up one morning in Emma's bed, rolled over to check his phone, and on seeing Phoebe's name on the screen, his heart had leapt.

It was so confusing.

Was he sleeping with Emma because he wished she was Phoebe? Or was he falling in love with her because she absolutely wasn't?

He'd called it off then. Said that he was too busy on set. Answered her texts with one or two words: 'Cool', 'Nice', 'Sounds Good' or – the worst – 'Have fun'.

I was thinking of a drive out to Malibu at the weekend.

Have fun.

Taco Tuesday seems to have come 'round again . . .

Have fun.

He was a shit.

So he was lucky, really, that she'd even deigned to talk to him when he'd seen her in Trader Joe's on that Sunday morning.

'Mike!'

His stomach had turned a somersault at the sound of her voice saying his name. He turned and she'd placed a hand on his forearm.

'Oh, thank God. It *is* you!'

He'd laughed and nodded.

'It's me!'

'It's you.' And then she'd tilted her head and looked serious and squeezed her hand on his arm. 'I've missed you.'

'I've missed you too.' It was an impulse reply but as soon as the words had left his mouth, he knew they were true.

He arrived outside Tiffany and looked up. There was the carved man holding a clock on his shoulders, the weight of time bending his green neck that once would have sparkled in polished copper. Michael had four minutes to get inside and locate the 'Diamond Expert' with whom he had the appointment.

There had been a part of him – admittedly the more idealistic part – that had hoped that Phoebe would be with him today. He'd somehow thought, after he'd told her, that she'd be happy for him, and they'd toast his engagement, and he'd ask her to be his 'Best Person' and then this morning she'd be here, beside him, helping him to choose the ring. She probably had the same size finger as Emma, even if they didn't have the same taste.

Though he could just imagine the awkwardness of Phoebe quizzing the salesperson about the provenance of the diamond.

He could feel his face warming at just the thought of it.

It was for the best that he had come alone.

He would be able to tell Emma that too. *She would be pleased*, he thought. That he'd made the decision all on his own.

Thirty-one

Phoebe bounds over to Michael and wraps her arms around his neck. He feels stiff and cold compared to the sweaty, dancing people she's been hugging inside.

'What are you doing out here all alone? You missed Bloc Party!'

He places his hands on her hips, staring at her pointedly. His eyes are glistening in the light and, she notices, they look slightly bloodshot.

'What?'

He tips his head behind him. Oh, he's suggesting they slink off? She could actually go for that: a quickie down the path, under the light of the silvery moon. She smiles at him and takes hold of his hands, sliding them up her body across the sequins of her playsuit, to bring them to her breasts.

'You'll have to descale me first. I feel like a big silvery fish!' She laughs.

'Stop shouting, you'll wake the baby.'

Phoebe starts at the voice, but she knows immediately that it's Emma. Just a few yards away from them, sitting in Granny's armchair. Emma, her older sister who hasn't spoken to her in five years, who has ignored every letter she's sent, is holding her son. Rocking Albie in her arms.

Phoebe jumps away from Michael, as if removing her hands from around his neck could cancel the intimacy between them moments before.

She looks towards Michael. He appears to be very interested in his shoes.

She looks back at Emma. Her face is blank, set like stone. Just as it has been ever since she arrived.

Her stomach plummets.

She interrupted something. Something between Michael and Emma.

She gathers herself. So they are talking. She should let them talk. She has nothing to worry about. She must not panic. She will take the baby from her sister, and leave them to it. She's known ever since she picked that invitation up from her doormat that this conversation was bound to happen. She will leave them to it, leave now. She will give Emma her space, she won't force herself on her, she will let Emma choose who she is comfortable with speaking to, who she is willing to forgive. It's a strategy that she has planned and has been employing successfully since Emma's arrival this afternoon. Even though, from the second she saw her standing at the back gate, all she has wanted to do is throw herself into her arms and beg her forgiveness, she knows that if a dialogue is ever to be re-established, she has to wait for Emma to come to her.

But looking down at Emma now, and seeing her eyes glistening, the streak of tears sliding through the mask of make-up on her cheek, she is wrong-footed. She doesn't reach down for the child that is so peaceful in her sister's arms, but stands still, looking directly into those eyes that mirror her own.

'You're crying.'

An obvious statement, that spilled out before she'd even recognised she was speaking.

Emma drops her gaze and paws at her face. Then lifts the baby away from her chest.

'Here.' She holds Albie up towards Phoebe, without making eye contact. 'I should go in.'

Phoebe lifts her sleeping son from her sister's arms and the second she is released from the baby, Emma pushes up on the armrests of the chair to stand. She looks between them, her and Michael, and nods. Then she picks up a champagne flute full of red wine from the table and walks back to the house.

'Michael?'

Michael turns from where he was watching Emma's departure and looks at her square.

She can feel her heart pounding.

He moves towards her, and places his hand around the baby's head, then leans over and kisses her, resting his forehead against hers. For a moment she feels safe, secure, known. But then the heat of jealousy rips through her.

'Why was she talking to you? She can't meet my eye for longer than a split second.'

He exhales, the long hiss of a tyre deflating, he moves away from her and rubs his hands across his face and shrugs.

'Phoebs—' He raises his palms to the sky, shrugging.

She looks away from him, but he gently takes her chin and draws her eyes back to his face.

'Talk to her.'

He leans in and takes the baby from her arms.

'Come on, little man.'

She shivers as the heat of her son is removed from her arms.

'Tea?'

'I was trying to find the kettle in the kitchen. It's been moved from where it's been for my entire life.'

'I'll make you some tea. Camomile.'

He winks at her.

She watches as he disappears into the flashing lights of the kitchen, beyond the conservatory, and immediately her attention is pulled upwards, by a light coming on in the far bedroom window. Emma is illuminated within, a mannequin in one of those creepy Victorian doll's houses. Phoebe watches as her sister pulls her hands through her hair, then places her palms to her face. She is still crying?

A tug of compassion as she realises, for all the times she has imagined Emma, she has only envisaged her fury. In all her fantasies about flying all the way out to California, of hurdling her security fences, or wedging her foot in an accidentally answered door and barging in, making her sister listen to her side of the story, she has never pictured her with the glisten of tears on her cheeks, but always pristine and manicured and incandescent with rage, just as she seemed when she arrived this afternoon. Has she misread her?

In the bedroom, Emma, lit by the LED glare of the light above her, pulls her hands away from her face, pawing at the tear streaks to wipe them away. She bends out of view momentarily, then rises again, with her holdall slung over her shoulder. She walks away from the window, across the room to the door and then turns back with her hand on the light switch, looking around the room. Time lapses, thirty seconds, a minute. It is as if she is memorising every nook, every cranny. Then the light flicks off and Phoebe recognises the surge of adrenaline.

She hadn't even considered that Emma might leave before they'd found a chance to talk. Surely Emma wouldn't come all this way without at least giving her a single hug.

She's running out of time. She thought she had tomorrow, the weekend, possibly even into next week as they packed boxes and sorted through bookshelves, arguing over who got to keep which of the books they'd cherished as children.

She thought that she'd have to wait for Emma to come to her, that she couldn't charge straight at her and beg for her forgiveness. She knew she mustn't ruin Mum's wedding trying to make it happen, but she thought that surely it would happen, that surely there would be a moment – perhaps the two of them in Mum's car, the back seat loaded with boxes and bags stuffed with clothes and crockery to offload at Cancer Research – where she would have the opportunity to tell her sister how intensely she misses her.

Despite everything, there is a part of her that truly believes that if she says the right thing, at the right moment, they will slip back into each other's lives and everything will be fixed, the way it used to happen. But now – if Emma leaves now – then they will never do that.

I'll head her off, she thinks, and strides to stand guard by the back gate. She'll confiscate her car keys. She can't drive when she's drunk so much. Phoebe pauses, baulks at the irony of the very idea: her chasing Emma down for the car keys because *she's* drunk too much. Life really is just patterns repeating in different configurations.

But then, a panicked thought: *What if Emma sneaks out the front?*

That would be too obvious, it would mean going through the lounge. If their mum, if any of them, saw Emma's bag, it'd be yanked off her shoulder, another glass of champagne pressed into her hand. Rosie would wrap herself around her neck and hang there for days, rather than let her leave.

Then, in the gloom along the side of the house, Phoebe sees Emma's silhouette, the cream of her trouser suit glowing against the dark wall of shrubbery. She sticks to the side of the garden. An old trick that Phoebe knows well – the light from the house doesn't stretch that far, and escape to the back field would be just as possible as it had always been if it wasn't for the vast pool of light shining out from the bulbs dancing in the branches above.

'Em?'

Emma looks up, a rabbit caught in the headlights. Her make-up is running, two black rivulets from lash to jaw.

A flash of a memory, so strong she can taste it.

Emma's face above hers, her make-up smudged. Emma's voice. It rasped, rattled, as if she smoked forty a day. 'Phoebe? Phoebe!' Her sister's warm hand on the side of her wet, cold face, an awareness of the enamel of the bath, hard against the small of her back. The taste of acid at the back of her throat, and a memory of the phone call earlier that night, the computerised voice: *please leave a message after the beep*. Saying, 'Goodbye.'

The guilt engulfs her, and Phoebe wants to grab the keys from Emma's hand and run to the car herself. But she doesn't. Instead, she lets the guilt sit on her, work through her and, rather than running, she looks at her sister and speaks.

'Please don't go, Em.'

'We made a promise.'

'I'm just asking that you put down that bag and sit down with me.'

She can feel her breath coming short and fast. She tries to control it, to lengthen the breaths, to make the noise of her panic less audible.

A whip of breeze jangles the lights in the tree and a piece of paper takes flight. It whips up from the table and dances into the dark, a dove escaping from a magician's hat.

Emma slides the bag from her shoulder and stoops to place it on the grass, then sits down on the piano stool. Phoebe exhales and sits on one of the dining chairs on the other side of the table, shifting it as she sits so that she is facing Emma.

There is a silence between them.

Above them the breeze rustles the leaves.

'Is it still hot in LA too?'

'It's not on fire like it was this time last year. But, yeah. It's hot.'

'We tried to contact you, you know. During the fires. Mike said they were really close to your—to where you live.'

Emma nods but still doesn't meet her eye.

Phoebe looks at the table. It is littered with bottles, all with remnants of wine. She has an urge to grab one and pour it directly into her mouth. She imagines herself emptying every bottle at the table, drinking the dregs from every glass.

She inhales and looks up from the table, back to her sister.

'I'm so sorry, Em—'

Emma holds up her hand. All at once everything around them seems very still.

'I read your book.'

Phoebe is suddenly acutely aware of the pulse at the base of her throat.

'You're a much better writer than you were an actor.'

Phoebe attempts to moisten her mouth by swallowing. This isn't the conversation she was expecting. She hasn't prepared for this.

'What did Mum make of it?'

Phoebe rolls her lips into each other.

Emma makes a small noise – a laugh? Or maybe she's just clearing her throat.

'Rosie told me you broke a glass.'

'I put it by the taps while I was peeing. It fell into the sink.'

There is eye contact then. Steady, searching eye contact.

'I'm sober. Honestly.'

'You have a beautiful family, Phoebe.'

She closes her eyes. An attempt to stem the tears. But it is too late. She can feel her cheeks are wet.

'I'm so sorry.'

'Don't fuck it up.'

'I'm—'

'Phoebe, stop. It's too late.'

A pain in her chest.

She knew that it was possible that the silence, the ghosting, would continue even if they were face-to-face. But it is still surprising. The enormity of this grief. The horrible understanding that this person whom she loves so profoundly, who is just within the reach of her fingers, is so completely lost to her.

'There you are!' Rosie is crossing the patio. She is carrying a tray laden with glasses and mugs and a bottle of Scotch. 'I haven't had a chance to show either of you the ring!'

She reaches the end of the table. The glasses clink as she places the tray down. She looks between them.

'Oh God. What's going on here? Please tell me you aren't *talking*. Not tonight.'

Phoebe runs her hand through the front of her hair. She looks up to see Emma, mirroring her movement.

'Oh for fuck's sake. You two! How is it possible, even after – what is it? Four, five years – you immediately fall back into the same shit. You just can't let anything not revolve around you, can you?'

'Rosie.' Phoebe reaches out her hand.

'No, Phoebe. Stop. It's Mary's wedding day. I've just got fucking engaged. Let it be about other people for just one second. You know, don't you, that from the outside, both of your lives look pretty damn perfect? I know, I know. You've both got your shit. You're an alcoholic. Which is undoubtedly really awful for you. And you – poor you, Em – you lost your baby, your lovely little baby, and that is so, so sad. So sad. I am so, so sad for you. We all are. And yeah, Michael. I get it, it sucks – you both fell in love with the same person. Awkward. Horrible. Heartbreaking. But . . . none of it matters. The world is burning! All of the people we know will one day be dead! There's war in Europe. People can't afford to eat. To keep their children warm. Bad things happen to us all, I know – a lot of very bad shit has happened to me. Or to other people around me. And – oh mate – the last few years have been – fucking gruelling. But, I'm in therapy – which by the way, you should both look into – and I'm putting one foot in front of the other. And doing my job. Trying to help. And Danyal wants—' She holds up her left hand in front of her face and squints to look at it. Phoebe notices that she is swaying. 'Though – a man isn't the answer. I don't need to tell you that. You've got to take responsibility for your own life. And—' She places her palms to her face briefly before pulling them away. 'I've actually forgotten what I was saying. But headline is: sort your shit out sisters.' She sits down, and starts unscrewing the lid of the Scotch. 'But not today. Today is Mary's day. And mine. It's our day.'

Phoebe looks across the table to Emma and they catch each other's eye. She can feel a smile tugging at her lips, just as she can see it is at Emma's. Her shoulders are starting to shake, her stomach muscles rhythmically contracting, her breath short and sharp through her nose, and then the noise swiftly follows. Her squawking laughter echoes through the garden, up through the branches of the willow and quickly it is joined by another laugh. A laugh she's been trying to summon in her memory for years but has been unable to. Yet, to hear it now is like a song you've forgotten you love being played on the radio and immediately remembering every single one of the lyrics.

'Yeah, yeah. I'm drunk. Laugh it up. But you know I'm right. Name me one occasion that I haven't been.' Rosie raises her glass to them both, a huge grin across her candlelit face.

Inside, the soft snare and surge of a Beatles song seeps into the spaces between the three of them.

Thirty-two

Phoebe flinched as she put a foot into the water. It was uncomfortably hot, scalding, and almost painful. Just how she liked it. She lowered herself into the bath, feeling the water tightening the skin of her legs, her hips, her buttocks, and then the expanse of her belly where it bit at the scar tissue beneath the mound of it. Her Caesarean scar, her two Caesarean scars, one on top of the other.

Was Emma's scar as purple and silvery? Did her belly hang over it like a flap of flesh?

She shook her head, and focused back on the heat of the water that was searing up her spine. Then she relaxed and the burn of it lapped over her ribcage, the sides of her breasts, her shoulders.

They'd had a deep bath installed after Clara was born. A surprise – one of Michael's gifts – and, as it turned out, her favourite gift ever. He'd had it shipped over from Japan as a surprise when she'd complained that the water in the existing bath, though enamel and pretty with its gilt claw feet, barely covered her hips; she couldn't relax lying in a teaspoon of water. And the new bath was incredible. Deep, and wide enough to cover nearly her entire body; there wasn't a bath in the world that was big enough to cover her breasts. They floated above the surface of the water like islands, her nipples two volcanoes erupting out of the lava-hot bath.

She heard the cry of her son and held her breath, listening for Michael's response. A few moments later, she heard the tread of his feet on the stairs, and then, in the baby's room on the next landing, the rumble of his voice as he spoke to their son. She closed her eyes, inhaled, and slid down into the water until her head was completely submerged.

And – silence.

She'd given up so many of the things that could quiet her thoughts but, thankfully, no one was going to make her give up water. Her hot baths and the cold, cold sea were her refuges. Well, them, and finally giving in to the knowledge that so much of life was out of her control. Both things that her mum had been trying to encourage her to recognise for years.

'Why don't you come with me to church, Phoebe? You might find it helps.'

The number of times she'd heard that through the duvet she'd pulled over her aching head in her teens.

'Come in and join us. It'll do you the world of good!' She can still remember her mum and Lizzie hooting, as she watched them ungraciously make their way into the grey waves while she sat on the beach with a blanket wrapped around her shoulders.

Now, every time she made her way into the water and felt the urge to squeal, the sudden rush of endorphins, she thinks of them: her mum and her best friend's hands clasped, held high above the water, screaming with laughter, chest deep in the North Sea.

Phoebe pushed her head back above the water, rubbing her hands up and over her face and then over her head, running her fingers through the lengths of her wet hair. She opened her eyes. The water was stained with opaque streaks of white. Her tits were leaking.

That's going in the column.

Since she had returned to journalism, she'd become aware that motherhood had infested her weekly five hundred words like a fungus. It was slowly taking the words over, controlling their form, their movement, and she wasn't entirely sure how she felt about it.

She knew, certainly, what the Phoebe of five – even four – years ago would have made of it.

There's nothing special about pushing a baby out of your vagina, she'd once written, *it's simply a biological function, like digestion.*

Her mum had called her about that one. Asked her how she thought her sister, her sisters, indeed many of the women who happened to read her work, might feel if they read it.

'Mum, Emma one hundred per cent isn't reading my column. She'd probably burst into flames if she even touched the paper. And Rosie doesn't want kids, like me.'

She'd really believed that. She hadn't wanted children.

And it had been true, hadn't it?

Recently, she hadn't been so sure. There was something about the web of connections that has revealed itself to her during the long journey of self-examination that is sobriety, that had made her think that there might be a link between all the mess – the booze and the anger and the sex with random and inappropriate people – and a deep-seated desire that she wasn't even aware of.

She'd meant it though, when she wrote it. She'd honestly thought that wanting to be a parent was a bit naff. Everyone was doing it, and she'd never liked to do what everyone else was doing. Like Rosie, she thought it didn't make sense to bring any more people into a world that was burning. And it was all so . . . heteronormative. So *normal,* full stop. It was something the Boomers had done without thought – like buying all the houses and getting university grants. Something that Granny's generation had done out of duty to sustain the Empire, to replace all the fallen of the two wars. Frankly, she'd thought that having children was something that she was somehow above.

That's something the self-examination has highlighted too; her exceptionalism. Laughable, but she'd really thought that she was too special, too unusual, to have the same basic desires as the majority of humankind. That the fundamental programming of every species on earth had somehow bypassed her. That she was above biology! She cringes to think that those thoughts made it into print in an international newspaper, where her sister and so many friends, so many women, men, people, who were desperately struggling to create new life, could read it. And then there were all of those people who had tried, who had faced repeated losses and heartbreak, and still emerged with empty arms.

Like Emma.

Like Michael.

She plunged her head under the water again. It was still hot enough to puncture her thoughts.

She popped up and inhaled deeply.

'I don't hate myself, I hate the actions of my addiction.'

She pulled a face. She still hated the affirmations. Even when she was alone it made her feel like an absolute knob to talk aloud to herself. As if repeating a few words in the mirror could relieve the guilt of two decades of wreaking havoc.

She sighed.

'I don't hate myself, I hate the actions of my addiction.'

She shook her head and reached out for the bottle of ridiculously expensive shampoo.

She hadn't thought she'd succumb to it, the money. But slowly, with a creeping sense of disgust, she'd realised she was enjoying it. She liked the glossy hair that stupidly expensive shampoo gave her, the way that cashmere kept her so much warmer than synthetic stuff. She liked that she didn't even give a thought to buying organic, or putting bronze cut pasta or sourdough or Clarence Court Eggs in their supermarket delivery. And, after years of having plenty to say about Emma having 'staff', she couldn't have got through that first lockdown if Elise hadn't been live-in. She needed to be able to work. It kept her tethered, on an even keel. It allowed her to give her family as much of herself as possible.

It was confusing though. Because it wasn't just money, it was wealth. If she – they – were wealthy, then what did that mean in terms of class? Michael was still often referred to as 'working class' in profile pieces. But she had never thought she was that. Her parents both banged on about how they were working class for most of her childhood, but when she'd been bullied at school for a good six months after letting slip that she'd spent two weeks of the summer holiday in France, her mum had sat her down and talked her through the concept of social mobility. But it was only when she'd arrived at Cambridge that she really started to understand it.

Nineteen-year-old Phoebe would be pretty disgusted by the comforts that her life with Michael afforded. She had flat-out refused a stupid mansion though, or any property that included the word 'gated' in its description.

'Where do you want to live?' he'd asked her, when they finally admitted to each other that they wanted to keep the baby. 'The world is our oyster.'

'Somewhere normal.'

She'd never been to the Malibu mansion, she'd never been invited. But she'd heard. Her mum and Rosie had told her about the glass-surrounded verandahs, the infinity pool, the security gates that kept the hoi polloi out and let the cleaner and trainer and gardener and cook and pool boy in. She didn't want all that.

'I want the sea. I want real life and art and food and friends and sky and water.'

And she loved Brighton. Well, Hove, she loved Hove.

They couldn't have chosen a worse time to move as far as making friends was concerned. Thankfully she'd found a meeting and a sponsor before everything closed down, but it had been slow going connecting with anyone who wasn't in recovery.

Recently, though, she had started to meet a few people. She'd got chatting to a nice woman at the playground, exchanged numbers and discovered her and her husband to be very funny. And though her pregnancy yoga had been online, they'd had a meet-up when the babies were born and she felt sure at least a few of them would stick to their promise of making it a regular thing. Making new friends these days not only involved navigating the no drinking thing, but there was always that moment when she introduced Michael. Often, they would greet him heartily, thinking they recognised him from the supermarket or five-aside, or they'd say, 'Blimey, you look just like that actor.' Then there was the mortifying moment when they realised that they didn't actually know him, and that he was, in fact, *that actor*. Occasionally, she'd overhear people saying – 'all over Twitter', 'photos of them holding hands in Borough Market', 'yeah, her sister!'. She was trying to make her peace with that stuff. After all, she'd known that was part of the bargain – one of the things she'd have to accept – when they made that decision in the car park of the Marie Stopes clinic. For now, Clara was too young to notice the people staring as he pushed her down the street. But she did worry how Michael's fame was going to impact the children as they grew up. People were generally polite and respectful of their space though, and it was rare that anyone asked him for a selfie, particularly since Covid filming insurance meant he was almost always masked in public when he was working. On those rare occasions they were approached, she tried not to be too spiky. It is exciting to see famous people in real life, isn't it? She couldn't say she exactly behaved herself that time she'd realised she was behind Nick Cave in the coffee queue. If she was going to enjoy the advantages of fame or, indeed, share a life with someone who was famous, then it was something she needed to get used to.

Sometimes people recognised her, too. It was a much rarer occurrence for her than it was for Michael, but there was a significant readership in the area. And she'd even had a couple of people approach her with her memoir, asking her if she'd sign it for them, or dedicate it to a friend who's going through the mill.

The book.

In retrospect, writing it with a bit more distance, a bit further down the road into recovery would have been preferable. But having spoken to other authors, that's not just a timing thing; there was never a perfect time to write about the most mortifying moments of your life. You had just got to hope that by doing so, you were helping others.

Anyway, she didn't really care what people thought about her past behaviour. She wasn't writing for approval.

She did wish her mum had liked it though.

She did wish that her mum understood why she had written it. That she hadn't meant for it to embarrass her. That, if anything, the writing of it, the whole book, was a love letter to her.

But her mother hadn't seen that. Or she didn't want to.

It couldn't have helped that she read it just as the world was closing down, or that, the week afterwards, Iain was rushed into hospital and put on a ventilator.

She could only hope that when she calmed down, when they were able to talk face-to-face, properly – not through a bloody screen – that she'd be able to explain to her that a memoir isn't fact, it's a point of view. A story told from one perspective is only a part of the story.

She knew her mum knew that really.

That was the surprise: that her mum, her journalist mum, couldn't seem to understand why she'd written what she had. But, just as she'd said in the book that seems to have hurt her so much, Mary hadn't really been a journalist for a long time. Her agony aunt column might be read and adored all over East Anglia, and she might be considered as something of a local celebrity, but it was a compromise. It was all compromise.

Yes, Phoebe had written about how unhappy she'd been, her sisters were, her generation were. She'd written about how she'd been so unhappy that she'd tried to destroy herself, despite the compromises her mum had made, the sacrifice she and so many women had had to make to have families, for their families. But she never meant to lay any of that self-loathing, that worthlessness at her mum's door. Anything that was good in her, in her life, was all because of her mum.

She wrote about it because she was grateful.

She thought she was saying thank you.

She could have written about her dad and his meteoric rise from dry cleaner's son to household name, and how that had left her flailing around for her place in the world too. But plenty of other people spoke about that. There were enough stories about the 'boy done good'. What about the girl done compromise? What about the girl who flattened herself at the expense of her cheating husband, for the elevation of her privileged, entitled daughters?

'I'm not a victim you know, Phoebe. I've had a full, happy – no joyful – life and career.' Her mum's voice had been shaking as she'd said it. 'I made a choice. I had agency. It might not have been what I'd imagined. But I'm not finished quite yet, thank you very much.'

That's it! She'd wanted to shout. *That's exactly what I was trying to say!* But she didn't say it. She'd been so shocked by the anger in her mother's voice, that she hadn't said much at all.

'You claim to be writing about your own life, Phoebe. But for all I can see, you're just giving your opinion on everyone else's.'

She heard the twangs of the *Newsnight* theme tune echo through the hall and up the stairs, and felt her shoulders relax further, the length of her neck increasing, knowing that Michael must have got the baby back to sleep. There was the sound of his gentle run on the stairs and then a tap, two knuckle raps on the door. It opened and his face appeared. His beautiful smiling face.

'Oooh! Booboo booboo!' His eyes were wide, using the term their daughter had coined for her breasts.

She covered her chest with a sud-spotted arm.

'Mummy's having quiet time.'

'Sorry.' He covered his eyes with a hand. 'Just wanted to let you know that your dad's going to be on. He's on Zoom, beaming into the studio from Mary's spare room.'

'So weird.'

'You're weird,' he said, peeking through his open fingers.

'I am. I'll just rinse my hair.'

'Kettle's on. Camomile?'

'Please.'

He blew her a kiss and the door clicked shut, followed by the pad of his steps down the sisal runner on the stairs.

She kept her arm where it was, over her body, and pulled it in close, then wrapped her other arm over it and gave herself a hug. She squeezed herself. She squeezed her beautiful, healthy body that, despite all the damage she'd inflicted on it, had made two beautiful, perfect children.

How did this happen?

How did she get so lucky, that this was her life?

She tried to recognise it, to savour it, every time this feeling came over her. Every time she noticed that she – with her children sleeping upstairs, and the love of her life, her best friend, downstairs making her a cup of herbal tea in their beautiful Regency home, where she can see the sea from almost every room – is the luckiest woman alive. She tried to be grateful, to give thanks to whatever it is out there – God, the universe, science – that had given her this second chance to live, to love.

To acknowledge this feeling though, is to recognise its shadow.

To remember that her joy has come at others' expense. To recognise that she still isn't entirely convinced that she deserves it. This happiness.

For a long time she absolutely didn't believe she deserved Michael.

She's often wondered how things might have been different if she had dared to believe that she did. If she had just spoken at that moment, when she first knew that she loved him.

* * *

It was because of her that they'd missed their flight to Phuket. Michael had suggested that they should just get something to eat and an early night, but she'd insisted they hit the Khao San road. She was the last to leave their room, and couldn't have padlocked the door properly because, when they returned to the hostel, in the early hours, their backpacks were gone.

If she had locked the door, they would have caught their flight. They would have been on that beach.

In the airport hotel that her dad had booked for them, as he had their flights home, she'd sat watching CNN as the news rolled. She remembered Michael coming out of the bathroom and sitting on the bed beside her. He placed a hand on her back. It was still damp from the shower. And then – she'd let him hold her. Something she'd never done before, despite the countless times they'd shared a bed. It was uncomfortable at first; she was aware of his flat torso against her own curvy one, the oddly damp scent of his body. And then she had relaxed. She could still remember the sensation.

She'd let her fingers trail up the soft skin of his inner arm. She felt her stomach contract. She looked up at his face; his features softening into sleep, and she opened her mouth to speak. But then he had inhaled. A jagged, controlled noise. He was still awake.

If she hadn't frozen. If she had spoken rather than waiting, watching as he fell asleep. If she had just had the guts to tell him how she felt. Would the last two decades have been less painful? Would they have been more? Would they still be together now? Would he still have married Emma?

Emma.

Unwise to think of her. Picking at a scab. Worrying a wound.

But she couldn't help it. She thought of her often. What was she doing? How was she feeling? She wondered what had happened to all of the letters she'd written. Had Emma read them? Or were they all in a pile in a cupboard, the unopened envelopes stacked one upon the other? Were they simply chucked in the bin?

Phoebe slid the little golden letter back and forth along the chain around her neck, then brought her hand down her body and let her fingers reach beneath her belly, to the silvery purple scar above her pubic hair.

Her heart ached for her sister.

Her heart ached for herself.

Ached with shame.

'Maybe it's for the best.'

A fucking stupid thing to say to anyone. But to her sister? Her sister who had been trying and trying and trying to have a baby.

She'd been drunk. Hollowed out by a day of pretending to be okay. Pretending that they were all okay, that having a party on a beach somehow lessened the ache of losing their Lizzie, and so she'd drunk. She'd drunk until she was sick, and she couldn't remember much of what happened, how the argument started, or much of the argument itself, but she did remember that. Saying that.

'Maybe it's for the best that you keep losing them. You'd be an awful mother, anyway.'

She remembered Rosie gripping the top of her arms then. Pushing her into the kitchen. And Iain – Iain, who had just lost his wife – telling her that it was time she called it a night. She remembered Emma's face, not angry, but blank, closed.

A face that hadn't opened to her since. And now probably never would.

'I don't hate myself, I hate the actions of my addiction.'

When Mum and Iain announced that they were getting married, she'd been so excited. For her mum, of course. But for herself too, because she knew that it was one occasion Emma couldn't avoid. That she wouldn't miss their mum's wedding, even if it meant having to be in the same room as her and Michael. As Clara. And then maybe, if Emma heard her say it, if she let her say, 'I'm sorry', she might forgive her. And she thought, hoped, Clara might help to change her mind too. But then Granny had fallen, and the pandemic happened and Iain got ill and the wedding was postponed. And whilst she knew they were hoping for this September, before the move up to Scotland, all it would take was another wave to scupper it.

She needed to find another way.

She thought of the letter she'd seen from Emma's solicitor. She thought of those embryos, those cells of her sister's and Michael's suspended in stasis. Those bundles of potential stored in a Californian deep freeze, just a few miles from where her sister lay on her yoga mat, seething her way through Savasana.

Phoebe dunked her head under the water one last time and then yanked at the plug. The soapy water drained away around her and she lay for a moment, her warm naked flesh quickly puckering to goose pimples.

She'd try again.

She groaned slightly as she struggled to heave herself out of the bath.

She'd send a card this time. A card with a clipping of last week's column.

Maybe Emma had read her words, in the paper, or even the book, as her mum had suggested. But she couldn't believe she had. Because if Emma had, then how could she keep this distance? How could she know how much she loves her and still not forgive her?

Yes, she thought, wrapping a towel around her hair.

She'd send the card tomorrow.

Because this perfect life of hers wouldn't truly be perfect until she had her sister back in it.

Thirty-three

Mary steps out of the conservatory down onto the patio; she wobbles slightly and giggles as she tries to restore her equilibrium. Her feet are bare now, her shoes discarded as the burn of the day and the dancing has worked its way into the balls of her feet.

She stops and peers through the darkness, trying to make out who it is sitting at the table, then places her hand on her chest. Emma, Phoebe and Rosie sitting together at the end of the garden.

Now. Now she'll say it.

'What a perfect day!'

The three girls all turn towards her raised voice.

'Coming through.'

Mary turns back to see Irene wheeling her rollator through the conservatory, following her, and she silently groans to herself. She wants just a moment of peace with her daughters in the garden. But here she is: her constant companion of the last forty years. She is wearing the sunflower hairband that Rosie had been wearing during the ceremony earlier, the colour in her cheeks is high, and the frilled collar of her dress undone at her neck. At the step she pauses momentarily before lifting the walker, with seeming ease, and stepping out onto the patio.

'Are you okay, Granny?'

Rosie shouts out as she jumps up and runs across the garden to Irene, and hovers solicitously, but slightly unsteadily, behind her.

'I'm not an invalid.'

'Ach, she's fine.' Mary meanders her way down the garden to where her daughters sit at the table, beneath the tree. She gestures back to Irene and Rosie's slow procession across the patio. 'Your grandmother never moves so well as when she's had a drop or two. Forgets her limp act.'

She giggles and takes a seat and claps her hands before her like a small child thrilled at the appearance of a cake.

'Mum thinks Gran is somewhat overstating her reliance on the walker.'

Emma says nothing in response to Phoebe, but raises her eyebrows. Mary brings her hands to her mouth. Oh it fills her heart to see it. How she's missed these two talking about her as if she weren't there.

Irene and Rosie arrive beside her. She watches as Irene heaves herself into the chair with a groan and then pats the arm rest. 'One of the only things left, you know. I had this armchair when your grandad was still alive. It was a lovely three-piece suite. And now I've only got this.'

'Here, Mary.' Rosie hands her a rather generous pour of Scotch. 'Maybe this'll bring you down off the ceiling.'

'Whisky, Granny?'

'Just a small one.'

'Told you. She's always liked a drop. It's probably where Phoebe got it from.'

'Mary!'

'Sorry, sorry! Just a joke. You love a joke, don't you, Phoebe?'

'I do, Mum.' Phoebe sips her tea.

A wave of guilt. Mary stands, wraps her arms around Phoebe's shoulders and places a kiss on her head.

It is almost cold now, and Mary is suddenly aware of the expanse of her bare skin. She rubs her upper arms to warm them.

'Autumn's on its way.'

'Autumn should already be here, Mary.'

'Aye, well I'm happy for it to hold off for as long as possible if it's going to be as bleak a winter as we're being promised.'

'We'll all be burning the returns of my book to keep warm.'

Rosie and Mary chuckle, but Emma tuts at her sister's self-deprecating remark, and even in the low light Mary can see Phoebe's cheeks colour slightly.

'Well, hopefully there'll be an uprising before it comes to that.'

'Planning to take down the government from your ten-bedroom house with sea views, Phoebs?'

'Hush.' Mary raises both her hands, palms out. 'Let me have my day. Climate change and viruses and the cost of living and this bloody government will all still be there tomorrow.'

'Well, actually Mary, it's seven minutes past midnight, so it *is* tomorrow. And I'm afraid your contract is null and void.'

'5–4–3–2–1 . . . Fight!'

And they laugh. Her girls and her mother-in-law, all laughing together.

'Aye, yes, yes. You laugh, the lot of you. But I am grateful you know. I am so grateful that you are all here and laughing. I didn't dare to dream that I might get what I wanted.'

'Have you, Mum?'

Phoebe.

Watching her today, with Michael, with the children, there is a partnership there, a maturity, a sobriety – and not just because she is sober. And just now – talking to Emma, to Rosie – she might have been a little hard on her younger daughter. To consider the path of her own life, you'd think that the act of absolution is as easy an act as breathing. But she's discovered that forgiveness is a harder task when the happiness of one child is pitted against that of another. Emma had told her, again and again, that Phoebe and Michael weren't the issue. That, in a way, she was pleased Phoebe was sorting herself out at last but, still, Mary had been angry, hadn't been quite able to align the dates, and it felt, despite what everyone told her, that Michael had just done a straight swap of one daughter for another, and that, once again, Phoebe had somehow got lucky at her sister's expense. And then, the baby. It was just so unfair. She was angry. At Phoebe. At life.

But that was before Iain took her hand on that terrace in Puglia.

Life.

It is unfair. It's complicated and messy and no one can judge what happens behind closed doors. No one knows what goes on between two people, or, in both of these cases, three people.

For years she thought it was Phoebe's fault, the rift between her and Emma. The fights and the screaming and the heart-break, and undoubtedly part of it was. But some of the blame could also be found at the bottom of a bottle. And whose fault was it that Phoebe had needed to drink in the way that she had? Just look at them all now: Phoebe's the only sober one among them. And there have been plenty of occasions over the years when all of them have taken the fun a little bit too far. The thing is, she's always been able to take it or leave it. So has everyone else she knows. That's why it's been so difficult to understand that Phoebe wasn't just pushing the boundaries, as she always had, ever since she was wee. She is ill. How many times has she been told that? How many times has she told herself? It's a disease. And she knows all too well that trying to apportion blame for disease is pointless.

She shakes her head.

It's always been there, this desire of hers to have someone, something to blame. It's something she's prayed about. And maybe it's that that's helped. Or maybe it's just getting older. But she's come to realise that, as for so many things in life, when you untangle it all, every moment, every decision, it becomes harder and harder to apportion any blame at all.

Things happen and it isn't always fair.

'Mum? Mum!'

Mary laughs and looks up, to try to stem the tears that are threatening. Above her the lights in the tree are smeared like daubs of paint in a Van Gogh; the brine is brimming in her eyes, distorting them and giving them texture.

'I'm happy right now, here under this tree with you girls. But have I got what I wanted? Am I happy? Who knows! There could be great things coming for you just around the corner, or there could not. It could all be about to get worse. Life is jumbled up, out of order, random. The loose threads don't get tied up in a bow.'

'But today they have, haven't they? You and Iain, it's a perfect bow.'

'Aye, today yes. But then, tomorrow, there'll be some other shit to worry about.' She groans and spreads her arms wide to the garden. 'We'll have to tidy up all of this, and then there's all the shit in there to sort out, never mind all of your shit!'

'Mum!'

'Shit?'

'Mary!'

'Honestly.'

'I can say shit if I want to. Shit! Shit! Shit! Shit!'

They laugh, the five of them. And for a moment, it is as if it is the middle of the day again, the garden alive with birdsong.

'It's going to be so weird, this place belonging to some other family.'

Rosie, standing behind her, places her hand on her shoulder. It is warm against her cold skin.

They all look back at the house.

It is lit up from within, like a lantern. The music is at a slightly lower volume now, likely Iain or Michael turned it down, noting that they were past midnight, thinking of that bastard at number six. She can hear the voices and chatter of their guests still, though. They'll be leaving soon. She'll have to say her goodbyes. For some of them – most of them – it'll be the last time she sees them before she leaves.

She feels her throat tighten. She looks at Irene and then at her girls. These women. Emma and Phoebe, smiling at her, nodding, and then up at Rosie, her face wet as she feels hers is now. And then she's laughing.

'Oh, I'm a silly woman! Greeting over a pile of bricks.' She wheezes it almost, wiping at her eyes, dislodging the tears that she can no longer tell are of joy or loss.

She leans in to Rosie's warmth. Her stepdaughter is standing behind her now, reaching down to wrap her arms around her. Mary rests her head back onto her shoulder and looks up into the branches of the tree.

'It was the tree, you know, that made me choose this house. You were just a few weeks old when we saw it, Emma. Maybe a month or two. Your father wasn't interested. More worried about the paintwork on his bloody car.'

'Dad and his cars.'

'The house was too big, he said. And the village didn't even have a pub then, but I wanted to move here to be near to Lizzie – Iain and Lizzie. Richard was worried that we were too far from the town if one of you were to get sick. He was petrified that one of you would fall in the pond and the ambulance would take too long. Or there'd be a fire and it'd all burn down to the ground before a fire engine would be able to get to us. But our time in this house has been pretty catastrophe free. I've spent the last forty years tripping over those bloody fire extinguishers, for nothing.'

'They probably haven't worked for about twenty years.'

'I didn't much like the house itself then, either. It was a lot to manage. Especially when your father left.'

Irene clears her throat.

'Yes, Irene, I wouldn't have coped without you. Or Lizzie—' She stops then and raises her glass. 'Lizzie, oh we miss you.'

'We love you, Lizzie.'

'To Liz.'

'Miss you, Lizzie.'

'Dear Elizabeth.'

There is a moment of silence as they drink, the shuffle of the tree above them, a momentary sweep of breeze that makes them all raise their shoulders against the chill.

Mary snaps her fingers.

'Each day feels like an eternity and then, *poof*, you're on to your second marriage, half cut in a rather revealing tartan wedding dress, giving your daughters a lecture about the brevity of life.'

She tips the last of the whisky into her mouth.

'Hold on to each other girls. You don't know how long you'll have the chance to.'

Thirty-four

Mary closed her eyes, pressed the lid of the aerosol down, sprayed a halo of Elnett around her head, then stepped back and took in her reflection. The dress didn't quite suit her, but it fulfilled requirements. A vivid turquoise with a yellow and red flower print. It was bright, it was bold. A dress for a day at the coast. A dress for a celebration. A dress that absolutely, one hundred per cent didn't say funeral.

She rifled through the disorder of toiletries on her dressing table, seeking out the little vial of expensive Italian perfume that Richard had given her last Christmas.

She opened the little stoppered bottle, pressed it to the pulse points on her wrists and automatically brought it to her nose to inhale. A mistake. Immediately she was in the garden, on that last day, holding that soft, cool hand that she would never hold again.

It had been just three weeks since they'd sat on the patio. Lizzie had been in her wheelchair with a blanket over her knees, the evening chorus of birds backed by the constant hiss of the oxygen tank that stood on the patio beside them. They'd drunk a bottle of very expensive wine, evident by the dark red stain in the corners of Lizzie's mouth.

'Wear that perfume, won't you? I love it.'

She'd got used to it, by then, the constant discussion of funeral arrangements. The casual references to it, as though they were planning a party they both looked forward to attending.

'I only wear that for special events.'

Lizzie had smiled and shakily brought her glass to her lips, and then held out her hand to Mary.

'Mum?'

Emma's voice calling up the stairs.

'We need to get going. Are you ready?'

Was she ready? Would she ever be ready?

'Coming, love. You all start getting in the cars.'

She could hear them, the quiet ruffle of the exodus, everyone whispering to each other. The last time anyone had whispered in this house was when Phoebe was a baby and Mary had instigated a game with Emma in the vain hope of not waking her during nap times. Or maybe it was more recent, when the girls had all gone off to university and she'd gone with Lizzie to see Depeche Mode in Thetford Forest and they'd got absolutely rat-arsed and spent the next day conversing in whispers and trying to keep down cups of weak Earl Grey.

Mary realised she was welling up again. She hadn't even made it out of her bedroom and she'd had to redo her eye make-up four times. What chance did she stand of making it through the day without collapsing entirely?

She sat on the bed for a second to gather herself, and looked around the room.

Her funny pink bedroom.

She'd been insistent that Richard paint it before they moved in. She remembered having an instinct that if they didn't do it then they never would, and she had been right. There just had never been enough time or, if she was honest, desire, to make her bedroom's paintwork a priority. Thirty-odd years later she still had pink skirting boards. Maybe she would until she died now.

It was unsurprising really, that over the last few weeks, her thoughts had increasingly turned towards her own mortality.

When Lizzie first got her diagnosis, and time had seemed so very short, the emphasis had been all about living. She had found her friend's attitude of throwing caution to the wind and grabbing greedily at experience intoxicating and, though there had been periods of ill health, pain, in many ways the urgency with which Lizzie had faced her diagnosis had almost made Mary forget why they were living with such force.

So, recently, when it became obvious that the end of Liz's life was approaching, it had been strange to remember that much of the fun, many of the adventures they'd had, had been born out of Lizzie's illness. And for the first time in a long time, her thoughts had turned towards her own finite time in this life. There had been numerous occasions, when Lizzie was discussing some practical or philosophical question that her imminent death raised, that Mary had realised with a flush of guilt that, though she was listening to her friend, she was also thinking about herself.

What would happen to her?

Would she just live in this huge old house that she had never particularly liked, in this part of the country that had never really felt like home, until she was too old to do anything about it?

And what about companionship?

What about love?

She had watched Lizzie and Iain growing increasingly close as the end neared, and the idea of finding a partner – an idea that had somehow become sidelined, or hadn't seemed important, over the past fifteen years – had raised its head once again. Odd to be considering her romantic future on the day of her best friend's funeral, but there you go. Death and love, an eternal partnership.

*   *   *

'Mum?'

Phoebe calling her now.

Mary's stomach twisted. She sent up a private little prayer. *Please, please let her behave herself.*

'Just coming, Phoebe. Get in the car, I won't be a tick.'

'Okay.'

They had all been behaving themselves. An *entente cordiale.*

It wouldn't last, of course. She'd braced herself for it. She'd even talked about it with Lizzie.

'It might be the chance.' Lizzie was sitting in the peacock chair in the conservatory as Mary handed her a mince pie. 'So, they won't bury the hatchet for Christmas, but surely they'll do it when I'm cold in my casket. I've been like an auntie to them.'

Mary didn't hold out much hope for any hatchet being interred. But for now, they were all here, dressed in vibrant colours – even Phoebe was wearing purple – and no one was drunk or screaming, so she would take the breaks where she could get them.

She sighed and reached down to put her shoes on.

Another memory. Lizzie and her, drenched, screaming with laughter after the sole of her sandal had torn off when they'd run through the rain back to the hotel on that weekend to Leeds. She'd bought these shoes to replace them.

So much of her life was embroidered by the length and breadth of her friendship with Lizzie. Just looking around the room she could see it in the shawl over the back of the chair, the photo of them standing in front of the Sagrada Familia on her bedside table. All of the trips, all of the adventures. She'd loved them all. But it was those afternoons chatting in the conservatory with a pot of tea, or the Saturdays when they'd continued setting the world to rights long after Iain had fallen asleep. And the phone calls, those times when she'd just needed someone to listen, those times that she'd listened to Liz. Those were the moments she was really going to miss.

She stood and wiped her cheeks, making her way back to the dressing table to add another coat of mascara. She needed to stop. She'd made a promise that there would be no tears today. That today would be a celebration.

The vehicle the concierge service had arranged for Michael was ostensibly big enough to take them all, but Phoebe and Rosie opted to go with Richard to pick up Irene in the Jag, so Mary had the entire back of the Range Rover to herself.

She was aware that being here, for both Michael and Emma, must have been logistically difficult. Phoebe too, had flown in from New York, but for Michael and Emma to be there meant not only Emma coming from LA and Michael from Malta, but – and she'd done her best not to pry about this – she knew that juggling timing for their fertility treatment must've been hard enough with Michael's schedule without making last-minute trips back to the UK.

The blacked-out windows gave the journey an even more surreal quality than she'd anticipated and she itched to start a conversation, but, unusually she found herself tongue-tied, unable to think of any subject matter other than those she knew would be inflammatory, and so, she just looked out of the window, watching the picturesque little villages slide by as they made their way to the coast.

'I don't want you all crowding into a bloody crematorium. I want you to think of me outside, in the open air, on the beach.'

It was Saturday night and they were enjoying their usual takeaway. It used to be the high point of Mary's week. The routine of putting the plates in the oven to warm, the wine into the fridge to cool come 6 p.m. Iain and Lizzie turning up an hour or so later with a fragrant carrier bag full of hot food and a CD or DVD to play after dinner. But recently, the conversations that used to turn into hatching plans for trips away, or celebrations, had turned into discussions about what was going to happen after Lizzie's death.

'I don't know, we spend a decade living out your Bucket List, and now we discover we're also going to have to continue to bow to your every command even after you've left us.' Iain raised her hand to kiss the back of it.

'I just can't bear it. The idea of you all being sad sacks when, really, I got so much more time than I'd ever expected.'

'But it's not enough, Lizzie. We want more time, and you have to let us be a bit sad about that. A bit angry.'

Lizzie had smiled, tipped her head towards Mary.

'It'd never be enough for us, would it? And I think that deserves celebrating.'

Even from where they'd parked, Mary could see the vivid cluster of people on the shingle that curved down to the waves.

She'd only been to this particular beach with Lizzie a few times, but she knew she and Iain liked to walk this stretch.

'You know, I'd like to think that you two will still be friends when I'm not here any more. I can't stand it, the image of the two of you, less than a mile apart, eating your microwave meals for one.'

'This again! I'm not a complete disaster in the kitchen you know. I might not be Richard Roberts, whizzing up your foams and whatnot, like he's East Anglia's answer to Heston Blumenthal, but I'll not be surviving on boiled eggs and soldiers.'

'You know what I mean. I want you to—' Lizzie broke off and reached out to the bottle of wine, refilling each of their glasses. 'Look after each other, that's all.'

Mary looked across the pebbles now, to where Iain was in conversation with his brother.

He looked tired, but relaxed. It was the end of June, and the summer holidays were beckoning. Lizzie had worried about that too, that the timing of her death would disrupt his six weeks off, that if she died in the school summer holidays or too close to them, he wouldn't be able to go on the annual holiday that had been one of the reasons for him transitioning in to teaching in the first place.

'I'm leaving you in charge Mary. You've to make sure he goes. I'll allow him Iceland this year, if he really does want to get all maudlin about his dead wife by looking at waterfalls and listening to Sigur Rós, but next year: sun! The pair of you. Get off to somewhere gorgeous and sunny, with beautiful food.'

Another selfish moment for Mary, another wobble of guilt, when she had realised that, when Lizzie died, she wouldn't have anyone to go on holiday with. She'd felt a pang of pity for herself. It was like getting divorced all over again, but this time she didn't have the house full of kids to distract her. She could visit the girls, but she wasn't really a fan of New York, and Los Angeles was so far away. Rosie had offered to get the Eurostar to Paris with her for a few days, with her typical sensitive foresight. But she was actually just going to stay put for a change, enjoy her garden in the height of summer. She was scared that it would be lonely, that the house would seem even bigger than it had since Rosie left.

Why hadn't she spent more time making friends? Why had she put all her eggs in one basket?

The fact was, other than her immediate family, she just hadn't been that interested in spending her time with anyone but Lizzie and Iain. Like the dating, making friends had felt on the back burner when the girls were little, and then, Richard had lost Dee and she'd been given the agony aunt gig at the paper, and there'd been so much going on with the girls and then Lizzie's diagnosis, and somehow, she just hadn't had time to make time for it. And now, with Lizzie gone, that was all she could see, an arid stretch of unpeopled time ahead of her. Particularly as, in just a couple of years, she wouldn't have work to busy herself with either.

She was turning into Irene!

No. There were a few stark differences. She didn't have a daughter-in-law fifteen minutes down the road that she could drop in on when she got lonely, nor did she have any grand-children to fill her weekends, and she certainly wasn't going to be attending parish council meetings in the hope of attracting an admirer.

She had hoped that by now there'd be a few grand-kiddies running about the place, but Emma and Michael hadn't been lucky in that department yet, and neither Rosie nor Phoebe wanted them. Though it was only Phoebe who had felt the need to put it in print.

'See! Do you see?'

Lizzie had leaned her head back against the pillow and let the iPad in her hands relax against the bedcovers.

'I'll admit, it is quite an angry piece.'

Mary had subscribed to the paper the day Phoebe got the job. She'd been excited. America had never been in her sights, but still, when she downloaded the app and navigated to *An Englishwoman in New York* under the *NEW FEATURES* title, seeing her daughter's name, her picture alongside Pulitzer Prize-winning journalists, had made her feel both immeasurably proud and surprisingly jealous.

She read it religiously each Saturday morning when she had her coffee in the conservatory, though occasionally Richard beat her to it and told her that it might be an idea to pour herself a measure of brandy to go with it. That day had been one such morning.

She had called Emma immediately.

'Honestly Mum, I'm not going to read it. I never read it. So don't sweat it. You shouldn't read it either, if it upsets you. As I've been trying to tell you for a long time, Phoebe won't stop hurting us until Phoebe stops hurting herself, and while she's prancing around New York pretending to be Carrie Bradshaw, that isn't going to happen.'

Then she called Rosie, but, as usual, it was her answerphone. So she sent her a text.

Don't read Phoebe's column this week. Very silly, about having babies. Might upset you. Xx.

And then, just as she was getting out of the car, as she arrived at the hospital for visiting hours.

I read it. Classic Phoebs. Not upset though. Is Em? Will call later R xxx

Lizzie had smiled at Mary and taken off her reading glasses.

'What is it about this article in particular that has upset you so much, Mary?'

'I, well, she's, saying that I— She's saying that—' Mary paused, gathered her thoughts with a deep inhale. 'Well, it makes me feel silly, old-fashioned for having children. It misunderstands that it wasn't a choice, not entirely, it was just what you did, if you were married and you got pregnant.' Mary paused, felt the heat go to her face. 'I mean, if you were lucky enough to.'

'Are you worrying about me?'

Mary had felt hot. For all their many long conversations, for the times they'd both let themselves be truly vulnerable in each other's presence, they'd never discussed this. Never talked about the fact that Lizzie and Iain hadn't had kids.

'You and every other woman – every couple – who didn't have a family.'

'Oh Mary.' Liz had reached out to take her hand. 'We have a family.'

Any heat that had been coming from the sun was fading by the time Mary had the chance to talk to Iain.

She was saying goodbye to some of Lizzie's colleagues from the research centre that she'd met a few times at parties over the years. She noticed Iain alone, for the first time that day, standing close to the water's edge, peeling the label off a bottle of beer.

'Hello.'

He pulled himself away from looking at the sea, towards the sound of her voice behind him.

'Hello yourself. I've barely seen you all day.'

'How are you doing?'

'Okay. You?'

'Better than expected. Mascara still intact.'

He briefly looked at her face. The sides of his eyes crinkled as he smiled at her.

'You going for a swim?'

'It was always Lizzie that dragged me in. It doesn't hold the same attraction without her.'

Behind them, the distinctive tenor of Richard's voice rose above the sound of the surf, and then, a peal of laughter.

'I've heard him call Lizzie "his oldest friend" more times than I care to mention.'

'It's never a complete lie, with Richard, is it? There's always a grain of truth.'

She smiled at him.

Iain turned towards the people gathered around the bonfire on the beach behind them, and so she did too. It was just them really now. Richard, Irene, Emma, Michael and Rosie sitting on the deckchairs around the fire, blankets on their knees, their faces caught in the orange glow of the flames. Then, a little further away, Phoebe stood, with Iain's family, down from Scotland. She was nodding as a young man with deep auburn hair talked to her. Mary's stomach plummeted to notice a beer bottle in her hand.

'She would be pleased. That they all made it.'

'I wasn't sure they would.'

'And no brawls.'

'Yet.'

Iain nodded.

'Aye, yet.'

They stood for a moment, the two of them, looking out towards the horizon. The sky was turning a deep shade of purple, the ink of dusk spreading rapidly, reflected in the water below it.

It was the first time, she realised, that it had been just the two of them since the day when she'd sat in their kitchen, waiting, and he'd entered the room, his face heavy. He'd nodded, letting her know that it'd happened, Lizzie had gone.

'Oh!' Iain was patting the top of his suit and reaching inside. 'A letter. For you.' He pulled out a yellow envelope from the inside pocket of his jacket and handed it to her.

She recognised Lizzie's hand immediately. *For Mary.*

'Oh no.' She put her hand to her throat. 'I was doing so well.'

'Ah, hen. I know.' A hand on her back, between her shoulder blades.

There was a minute, maybe two, where she closed her eyes tightly and concentrated on steadying her breath, and then, she wiped the side of her eyes, nodded and held out her hand for the envelope.

Iain placed it in her hand, and the weight of it surprised her.

'I'll give you a moment. Tell this rabble to start packing up.' He looked at his watch. 'We should hurry if we're going to get to the chippy on the way back.'

She gazed out at the sea, holding the envelope in her hand, listening to the sound of Iain's feet retreating on the shale, the call of his voice to her family and his, the collective groan at the order to pack up, the cheer at the mention of fried fish before they departed.

She looked down at the envelope. The light was fading fast now, casting a blue tinge on the paper.

She inhaled and slid her finger into the top corner, where the seal was spare, and tore the paper with one, two, three rips. There was no letter inside, and for a second, her heart plummeted, but then she understood.

She lifted the envelope and tipped the contents into the palm of her hand. She closed her fingers around the sunflower seeds as her vision blurred with tears.

Thirty-five

Clara wakes to a room full of silvery blue light.

There are patterns on the ceiling. Shifting shapes of light that make her feel like she's under water. There is noise too. A pulsing beat, like the noise she hears when she presses her ear against Mummy's chest. And talking, below her, downstairs and outside too, coming in through the open window. A laugh. Her mummy's laugh.

Clara sits up in the bed and it moves beneath her, a swish of air that makes her think she is going to fall. And then she remembers: she is in Nana's house, sleeping on the blow-up bed that Daddy and Grampy inflated with a foot pump before they did her balloon.

Her stomach drops.

Her balloon! Where is it?

She pushes back the covers and feels around her legs but finds nothing. It is hard to see in the dark but she tries to look around the room; at the rug, the floorboards beyond it, and beneath the bed that her parents will sleep in tonight. Still nothing.

She climbs off the squishy mattress and stands, then peers over the top of the travel cot next to her. No balloon, no Albie.

Clara can feel an aching in her chest, a pricking at her eyes, and she is just about to cry when she turns, and sees it: her balloon! The yellow ball of it on the dressing table, swaying slightly in the breeze coming through the curtains.

She stands on her tiptoes and reaches out for it. It is softer now than it was yesterday. When she holds it, her fingers press into the shape. The skin is wrinkled in places, like under her grampy's arms when he was wearing that T-shirt earlier.

She holds the balloon against her chest and looks again at the empty travel cot.

Mummy told her that the party was only for grown-ups.

'Drive safely! Yes, I'll be sure to let her know. Yes, I will!' Grandad Iain's voice is shouting downstairs. Not angry shouting. He's laughing too.

Another voice now.

'My pleasure, my-absolute-pleasure!'

Grampy! And then laughter. Daddy!

It isn't easy to walk down the stairs and hold the balloon at the same time. She squashes it to her chest with one arm, and holds on to the bannister with the other, slowly descending as her mummy has taught her.

One step.

One step.

At the bottom of the stairs it is much noisier. The music is very loud and it smells funny, like a mixture of perfume and burning and the inside of the car when it's too hot outside.

There are people huddled in the lounge, talking and laughing. The little table that Nana gave her some lunch on this morning is covered in glasses, most of them empty, but some with different coloured water in them.

She tries to pass a lady to see if she can see her daddy, but accidentally touches the lady's leg and she jumps.

'Oh, sweetheart! I thought you were a dog!' She laughs. It is a horrible laugh, like a witch. She makes her mouth really wide, and Clara can see her big pink and white tongue and black bits in her teeth at the back.

'My grampy. My daddy.'

That feeling again: the stinging in her eyes, her lips moving although she doesn't want them to.

'Oh dear.' The lady bends down with her hands on her knees. 'Don't cry. Shall we go and find your daddy?'

She breathes into Clara's face and it makes her crinkle up her nose. The lady's breath doesn't smell good; it's sweet and hard and makes her think of the time she ate too much chocolate and was sick all over her purple tights.

The lady reaches out her hand; she has shiny red nails that are pointed at the tips, like a bird's claws.

Clara shakes her head and pulls her balloon closer. Nails like that would definitely puncture it.

The lady laughs again and her big earrings shake, making a tinkling noise like little bells.

'Okay, wait here, sweetheart, and I'll bring him to you.'

She doesn't wait there though, she follows the lady in her wide floaty grey trousers and golden sandals through the people standing in the dining room and talking so loudly that it's even hard to hear the music. She follows her through to the kitchen, where it is dark and lights flash, turning everything blue, then pink, then yellow, then blue again. Clara notices that her feet are sticking to the floor with each step, as if someone has painted the brown tiles with glue. But then there are hands around her waist and she is whipped up into the air, so high that she could touch the ceiling if she weren't hanging on to her balloon so tightly.

'My li'l' Clara Belle!'

Grampy turns her around then squashes her to his chest.

'My balloon! Grampy! My balloon!'

'What, my princess?'

He has moved her onto his hip now, angling his ear towards her. There are grey hairs sprouting from inside the shell of his ear.

'My balloon, Grampy. You squashed it!'

'Did I! Oh goodnussme, thad wondo.'

There is something strange about the way he says it: the words are all joined up and running into each other. And that smell is on him too, like the one coming from the lady. He kisses her cheek and it leaves a wetness on her face that she wipes away with hand. She turns away from Grampy's breath that is tart and strong and smoky like a fire.

'Caamon,' he says, and he pushes through some people who are dancing in the flashing lights and takes her into the fresh air of the conservatory.

She can hear Mummy laughing again, and there, standing in the door, looking out into the garden, is Daddy.

'Ah, the shoe thief!' Grampy says, slapping her daddy on the back. 'Whaddareya doing?'

'Just watching them, those three generations of women, shouting at each other and laughing and crying. I wish I had a camera.'

'Four,' says Grampy.

Her daddy turns and his face opens up with surprise.

'Clara! I thought you were fast asleep!'

'Well, ashe's not, let's get them together an' you cun take y'ur picture.'

Then her grampy steps past her daddy and looks out towards the group of people at the end of the garden under the tree.

'Mary?' her grampy calls out suddenly. 'Mary? We neejyou! Mary?'

Clara can see her nana, then, standing up in her checked party dress and walking towards them.

'Here! Here Richard! I'm out here! What's the matter?'

'Ah ha! There shis!'

And he steps out of the conservatory down onto the patio.

'Whoopsie daisy!'

He wobbles and Clara giggles as he jiggles her, trying to regain his balance.

'What is it?' Nana, breathless, meets them halfway across the patio. 'Is it Iain? Has something happened? What's happened?'

'Woah, woah, woah!' Grampy holds up the hand that isn't holding her. 'Don't panic. We juswan' to gedda family photo, don' we Michael?'

Nana swipes at Grampy then, her hand landing with a loud smack on the top of his arm.

'Oh Richard! You scared me half to death!'

'What?!' His voice is high-pitched and he is wrinkling up his forehead, rubbing at his arm where Nana hit him.

'Come here, Clara darling. You've drunk too much to be holding the babies, Richard.'

'We're havin' fun, aren't we Clara-Belle?'

'Nana's more fun than Grampy, isn't she Cla-Cla?' And suddenly her nana has lifted her up and she is turning, spinning, around and around!

'Nana! Nana!' she cries as the lights in the tree smudge and become trails going around and around and turning into long lines of light in the dark of the garden.

'Mum! She'll be sick!'

'You won't be sick, will you Clara?' Nana giggles, wobbling a little as she stops spinning.

'Easy Mary, let me take her.' Auntie Rosie is walking towards them and she is quickly scooped out of her nana's arms. Auntie Rosie smells of flowers and vanilla cakes.

'Did you see that? Your mother hit me!'

'You did sound a bit panicked, Dad.'

'What have you got there?' Auntie Rosie presses her fingers into her balloon.

'It's my balloon.'

Why do all the grown-ups keep asking her what she's holding? Surely they all know what a balloon is? *Is this the only party they've ever been to?*

'I thought all the ratbags had gone to bed?'

'Mummy!'

Her mummy is sitting under the tree. She looks like a mermaid with her hair all curly at the front like that, and the way her top shows off the round mounds of her boo-boos. Her legs, too, are like a big tail, the way she has them curved around the side of the chair, the way the lights from the tree shine down on her legs making them sparkle.

She reaches out her arms towards her and Auntie Rosie lifts her down so she can sit on her mummy's lap. Clara strokes the sequins that shimmer on her mother's shoulder.

'It's like a fish, Mummy.'

'It is darling, but you should be in bed.'

'Albie isn't in bed.' She points at her brother, his face squashed against the shoulder of her new auntie from America who doesn't say very much.

'Let's all stay up to watch the sunrise!'

Her nana makes a noise then, a *cock-a-doodle-doo*, like a cockerel does in the morning, moving her arms like they are wings.

'Mum!'

'Mary!'

'Goodness gracious, what a display!'

'How much have you had, Mum?'

Everyone is laughing then, good laughter, like the joke is really, really funny. Her mummy squeezes her against her soft tummy and she feels warm and safe.

'Nana's just like you when you've had too much sugar, isn't she Clara?'

Clara squeals as her mummy kisses her once, twice, three times in the crease of her neck.

'Right.' Her grampy is holding up his phone. 'Whaddabout this photo, all together in the garden, one last time.' He is swaying as he looks at the phone, as if he is dancing. He is pressing at it with his fingers, one of his eyes closed.

'Let's all sit around Granny.'

Her mummy is standing up then, and Auntie Rosie is sitting on the arm of Granny Reenie's armchair, Nana putting her arm around her American auntie, who is holding Albie, guiding her towards them.

'Where's the shoe thief?'

'Here.' Daddy is crossing the patio with Grandad Iain, letting him hold his arm to help him walk.

Everyone is moving around her, and for a moment, she wonders if she is really awake. It is strange to be awake like this, in the middle of the night when everyone is laughing and shouting and their faces have streaks of make-up on them, and the lights above them are making the shadows long and strange and her feet are cold, because she isn't wearing any socks, because she doesn't wear socks when she wears pyjamas. And there, where all the food was, next to the pond that is alight with stars, there is the horrible pig that Grampy burned in a fire.

She turns her head away, closes her eyes and pushes her face into her mummy's chest.

There is an argument then. Not an angry one, because there is still laughing, but shouting voices and people saying who should stand where and everyone is talking at once and no one is listening to anyone else.

'No, no, Iain should be in it and, and you Michael.'

'Getthe Doc! Hesh not familyet. He cantakeit!'

'Honestly Dad, you're such a dick!'

'You need to start watching your mouth around the little ones, Phoebe, they're like sponges, you know.'

'No, let's have the three girls behind Granny, flanked by the boys.'

'Whereshudistand?'

And then Auntie Rosie's boyfriend is outside too and he is nodding and smiling as her daddy shows him the phone, and then Daddy is lifting her from Mummy's arms, and then, the wind moves the lights in the tree so they all jangle, and her mummy says, '*Brr*, hurry up! It's getting cold out here now.'

The gust of air comes just as she moves into Daddy's arms and she can't have been holding onto her balloon tightly enough because the wind grabs it, pulls it from her cold fingers, and suddenly it is flying, up, up, up and away from the hand she is stretching over Daddy's shoulder. It is blowing it up and into the branches of the tree, so that for a second she thinks it will pop on one of the lights, but it doesn't because then, it is falling. It is tumbling down, down, down. And then it lands on the mirrored surface of the pond and it looks as if it is floating among a sky of stars.

She inhales.

She draws in so much air that her chest feels as if it might split at the seams and then, through the yatter and chatter of her family's voices, she screams.

'MY BALLOON!'

Her face is wet then. The tears are making everyone around her blurry and Daddy is bouncing her up and down, like he does when he's trying to get Albie to sleep.

'Let's leave the photograph.'

'It's getting cold.'

Albie is crying now too, her mummy is lifting him from her auntie's shoulder.

'We should say goodbye. People are leaving, Mary, love.'

'Yes, let's do the photo in the morning before you all go. It'll be better in the sunshine.'

'Are all the candles out?'

'Much better.'

'I think I felt a few drops.'

'Everything will get drenched.'

'Oh leave it, there'll be less to pack!'

And then Grampy is wiping her eyes with the corner of his handkerchief and he is winking at her.

She is struggling to stop her breathing being so jumpy and she is sniffing to stop her nose running, but then she presses her face into the soft material of her daddy's shirt and moves her face from side to side to dry it.

Her daddy pauses, to let her nana and Grandad Iain pass them onto the patio back into the house, and then her mummy and Albie, who is screaming.

'Mike, take him while I pee, would you? It'll take me about twenty minutes to get out of this bloody jumpsuit.'

Her daddy is putting her down and the conservatory tiles are cold beneath her bare feet. And then he is holding Albie and whispering to him.

'Come on Cla-cla, everyone is saying bye-bye now.'

And he's walking through the conservatory, away from her, and carrying Albie into the music and laughing in the kitchen and further into the house. Then suddenly, the music stops, but the voices that were shouting remain, a tangle of noise through which she can still identify her brother's cries.

She turns then, holding on to the door frame, looking back out to the garden. She rubs the back of her hand over her cheek, removing the last traces of her tears, and sets her jaw.

The patio stones are rough under her bare feet as she runs, but quickly she is in the cool of the grass. She looks over her shoulder towards the house. No one is watching. If she's quick, no one will ever know that she's broken the rules.

She reaches the fence. It is too high for her to climb over so she walks around it, to the little gap by the tree trunk. It looks too small for her to squeeze through, but, if she does one leg first and then sucks in her tummy and stands on her tiptoes . . . she's through! She's standing on the dry mud at the base of the tree, and there, floating between the tangled roots that poke out above the water's surface, is her yellow balloon.

Clara puts one foot out, stepping closer to the water's edge.

She bends her knees, reaches her hand towards the balloon. But she can't reach it.

She thinks of the boating pond that her daddy sometimes takes her to, near their house. How once their miniature ship went too far away and they had to use a stick to get it back. She looks around her feet, searching for something to use. She turns, and looks at the ground behind her by the trunk of the tree. Her foot is cold, the sole of it feels wet. She lifts it, looking down to find a dry spot to put it in, but then, something shifts. Everything tilts and her other foot slips. And then cold.

So cold it takes her breath away.

It burns almost, the cold of it.

She is reaching, pushing out her hands, her legs, trying to find a grip, something to hold on to, somewhere to put her foot. And she does, her foot is touching something, but it is soft and her foot is sinking in it. And it is then that she realises her mouth is full of water. She can feel it pressing in her chest as she tries to do what is so normal, so natural.

She cannot breathe in.

She cannot breathe because of this hard pain in her nose, this fist in her throat.

She is aware of noise; a distant noise of water rushing, moving.

So this is why she's been told so many times that she mustn't go near the pond. This is why she wasn't allowed to go near the little white fence, and she feels sorry. She feels so sorry. Sorry for how disappointed her parents will be when they know what she has done. Sorry that they won't think she's a good girl any more. She likes to make her parents proud more than anything.

But then, she doesn't just feel sorry, she also feels sad. Because she wonders where they are, her mummy and her daddy. Because she was sure. She was so sure that they wouldn't let anything bad happen to her, like they've always said. That they'd look after her. But this is bad, she can tell, by the pain in her chest, by the weight that seems to be pushing on her skin, by the deep, deep need to close her eyes and go to sleep. And, she thinks, where is Grampy? Where is Nana, Auntie Rosie, her auntie from America, with the shiny hair and the face so like her mummy's?

They are the grown-ups. They are the ones who make sure she is okay.

Where are they all?

She wonders how long she's been under the water. Did she *just* fall in? Or has she been here for a long, long time?

But then none of it matters. Because there is softness closing in on her. A fuzziness that is blocking out the cold, that is slowing down her thoughts. And just before it all goes quiet, she is absolutely sure that everything is exactly as it should be.

Everything is going to be all right.

Epilogue

Clara had always claimed that it was her first memory.

'You are so full of it.'

'You were only three, Clara. I'm just not sure it's possible.'

It did seem strange. Her earliest memory after that wasn't until she was school age. But could she have made up a memory when she can recall the sensations so clearly?

Had she pieced it together from the stories? A composite memory fed by all those collected recollections over a lifetime of carved turkeys and wedding breakfasts and drinks to wet the new baby's head? The lore that was scattered alongside the laughter, the confetti, the ashes, each time this family was gathered. Is it possible that her imagination built those pictures that are so clear in her mind's eye?

She can see it vividly: the branches above her. Moving like the tentacles of some great monster, a titan waving silvery baubles. It haunted her dreams for her entire childhood, that monster.

She remembers the cold. The pain in her throat, her chest. And the tenderness for the weeks after too. The bruises on her legs, her arms, across her ribcage.

The warmth of the body that lifted her. That carried her. The voice calling out: 'Phoebe! Phoebe! Phoebe!' The shaking as her aunt ran with her in her arms.

A flash of blue lights. That is clear too.

The reflection of the lights on the faces around her like the blue-tinted flash of a camera, capturing their images. Her Aunt Em, a silver blanket around her shoulders, answering the paramedics' questions. Mum with her mouth open; the bundle of her brother on her shoulder; her dad, his brow furrowed, his bottom lip tucked into his upper teeth. Nana, the light particularly highlighting the streaks of tears down her cheeks. She's sure she remembers both her grandads' faces too, Iain and Grampy, lit blue, then plunged into the dark and then blue again. But maybe she's misremembering that part. She must have made up the detail of their faces from photos.

She doesn't remember anything of being in the ambulance, even though it is the only time she'd been in one. But there are flashes of the hospital. The bright lights. The orange curtain around the bed. Her mum shouting at a doctor. It's blurry. Snatched images. From what her parents have told her, they weren't there very long. They'd left as soon as it was ascertained that none of her ribs had been broken by the CPR.

'We were so lucky. We *are* so lucky.'

The mantra of her mother's – constantly echoed throughout her childhood – repeated even more frequently whenever that day was discussed.

It's her memories of the morning after that provoke the most raised eyebrows. From her brother, of course, but from her cousins too.

'Full. Of. It.'

'You were three, Clara! How's that possible?'

'You remember what she *said*? I can't even remember what I had for breakfast!'

But she remembers it clearly, how, still in their clothes from the night before, Aunt Rosie and Uncle Danyal were out in the garden packing up crates of glasses. Grampy was busy in the kitchen, making everyone breakfast – fried egg sandwiches in soft white bread that they all ate standing up in the kitchen. She remembers her bare feet sticking to the floor. She was turning in circles, enjoying the noise it made each time she peeled a foot away, when Nana, in a dressing gown covered in sunflowers, her eyes puffy and red, had grabbed her up and hugged her so tightly it hurt her bruises. And she told her that she had to put shoes on, even though they were inside, because she might stand on some glass and she 'simply couldn't take another thing'.

And then – and she's sure of this – it rained.

It came down in sheets.

Again, maybe her memory is editing itself – inserting the rains of the floods into the wrong time period. But she's sure she can remember the sound of it. The rattle of it on the conservatory roof. Rosie and Danyal running into the house shrieking with laughter and her grandad saying: 'It doesn't rain, but it pours!' Everyone laughing.

There are lots of other shards of memory from that day and the few days after – when everyone was together, packing up the house. It is these memories that make her doubt herself. Some just don't make sense, or don't happen in that big long kitchen emptied of all its furniture, but are jumbled-up images of other kitchens on other after-party mornings over the last twenty years.

But there is one memory that she's sure is real. An image that has been with her all her life, but for some reason she's never shared. Maybe because she knows it would upset her mum. Or maybe it's because she wants to keep it for herself, because she so wishes she could see it again.

If the other memories of those few days are sensations, or snapshots, this is a film clip. The memory features her father, and is just as clear as all the films she's seen him in.

She remembers him, standing at the back door of the conservatory, looking out into the rain. She walked to him and leaned into his leg, trying to see what he was looking at. She remembers squinting, trying to look beyond the sheet of rain and the splatter of it as it bounced off the patio. And then she saw it, two figures: her mother and her sister, Auntie Emma – the same dark hair wet, plastered against their heads, their clothes soaked through and sticking to their bodies.

Arms wrapped around each other in an embrace.

Together.

Acknowledgements

I want to thank . . .

My agent Claire Wilson, who read this manuscript more times than many agents would, who always has my corner and kept me writing by lifting me up and talking me down at exactly the right moments. I'm in awe.

Safae El-Ouhabi, Katherina Volckmer and all the team at RCW.

My editors Melissa Cox, Hannah Black and Erika Koljonen who all worked so hard at different times in the process, giving me confidence in my words, promising me that 'David was there in the marble' and allowing me the space and support to find the truest expression of this story. I am so grateful to you all.

The rest of the Coronet team who perform the magic that turns the manuscript in my laptop into a book and do everything they can to get it into readers' hands, particularly Tom Atkins. Alara Delfosse, Alice Morley, Vero Norton and Ollie Martin for their constant creative support in publicity and marketing. Alasdair Oliver, Kate Brunt, Libby Earland and Anna Woodbine for the cover. Charlotte Webb for copyediting and Sadie Robinson for proofreading. Matt Everett and Inayah Sheikh Thomas for production, and Drew Hunt and Sarah Clay for sales.

Mrs Porter, one of my teachers at Westley Middle School, Bury St Edmunds, for once telling my Year 6 class a story about two punks in the market and my nana, Dolly, for her story about the escaped pig. You both unwittingly inspired the characters who are the glue of this novel, written thirty years later.

All the booksellers and bloggers who got behind *The Stranding* and *This Family*, I am so grateful to you for welcoming me into your shops, inviting me to events and pressing my books into readers' hands.

My fellow 2021 debuts and all the authors who have supported me and my work, been great friends, both online and in real life, and given their time to appear on my podcast, *Novel Experience*. I'd always hoped that writing would bring new people into my life, but knowing that writing largely happens in a room alone, I hadn't anticipated gaining so many colleagues and it's turned out to be one of the best things about this whole journey.

Julia and all the team and audience of the Bury St Edmunds Literature Festival.

My friends: Claire, Ali, Jo, Matt, Clare, Jess, Matt, Chris, Shelley, Rach, Anna-Maria, Morgan, Rosanna, Emma and Zoe, for listening to me talk about these characters as if they were real people, for their unwavering support and for turning my book face-out in shops. James Ronan and Suzanne Goldberg, who both read the earliest sketch of these characters back when I was trying to work out what I was writing and gave me their valuable feedback. Afua Hirsch for listening to me talk about it for the last year. And Ros, who left us twenty years ago now and yet is always with me.

My family: Zo, Lexi, Greg, Simon, Jack, Sacha, Etta and my dad, Graham, for their constant support and love. Pete, Siobhan, Inger, Don and all the Danish cousins and second cousins. Dolly and Frank, who brought us all to East Anglia in the first place. My mum, Valerie, to whom this book is dedicated, who reads and considers and discusses my work with me. Who held the baby as I wrote the first draft and read to the toddler as I polished the last, and who gave me my love of words and stories and people that fuels my drive to write. And Ruby, my daughter. I love you.